Brendan DuBois is the author of the Lewis Cole mysteries and numerous short stories, which have earned him a Shamus Award and three Edgar Award nominations. He lives in Exeter, New Hampshire.

RESURRECTION DAY

BRENDAN DuBOIS

WARNER BOOKS

A *Warner* Book

First published in the United States in 1999
by G. P. Putnam's Sons

First published in Great Britain in 1999
by Little, Brown and Company

This edition published by Warner Books in 2000

Copyright © 1999 by Brendan DuBois

A CIP catalogue record for this book
is available from the British Library.

ISBN 0 7515 2549 9

Typeset by Palimpsest Book Production Limited
Polmont, Stirlingshire
Printed and bound in Great Britain by
Clays Ltd, St Ives plc

Warner Books
A Division of
Little, Brown and Company (UK)
Brettenham House
Lancaster Place
London WC2E 7EN

THIS IS FOR MY WIFE,

MONA.

The author expresses his deep gratitude and appreciation to the following individuals and institutions for their assistance with this novel: Joe Encarnacao, Bruce Seymour, Ron Thurlow, Brad Jacobson, Todd Mills, Andrew Thornton, and Erich Weinfurter, as well as the staffs of the Exeter Public Library, Exeter, New Hampshire; the Dimond Library at the University of New Hampshire in Durham; and the Phillips Exeter Academy Library in Exeter.

Thanks to Liza Dawson for enthusiastically starting this process, and to David Highfill at Putnam for expertly completing it. Hilary Hale provided wonderful suggestions from her side of the pond. My agent, Jed Mattes, and his associate, Fred Morris, provided their usual marvelous support.

Finally, thanks to those military veterans who provided advice and suggestions, and who requested anonymity. You helped more than you realized. I am thankful also that in October 1962 you and your comrades were never called on to perform the actions described in this book.

History will record the fact that this bitter struggle reached its climax in the late 1950s and the early 1960s. Let me then make clear as the President of the United States that I am determined upon our system's survival and success, regardless of the cost and regardless of the peril.
                                                        —President John F. Kennedy
                                                        April 20, 1961

I want peace, but if you want war, that is your problem.
                                                        —Premier Nikita Khrushchev
                                                        June 4, 1961

We will use nuclear weapons whenever we feel it necessary to protect our vital interests.
                                                        —Secretary of Defense Robert S. McNamara
                                                        September 25, 1961

PROLOGUE

THE BOAC JET AIRCRAFT BANKED as it approached
Boston. He was glad he had a window seat, because he
wanted to get a good look at the city. As the aircraft closed in
on the buildings and spires, he felt an illicit thrill.

Ten years, he thought.

A decade since he had last set foot in this country. If it
hadn't been for that opportune visit out to that American
SAC airfield that October, he would have remained in this
country. Forever. Cooked, crisped, the fused remains of his
atoms mixing in eternally with the Washington embassy
building and the dozens of people on that doomed staff. He
shivered and looked again at the old brick buildings and the
narrow streets of Boston below him. Almost two hundred
years ago a revolution began here, and his ancestors no doubt
had a hand in it. Ironic, he thought.

The aircraft made a smooth enough landing. As he
grabbed his overnight grip from the overhead compartment
he was embarrassed at the quickening of his heart. He knew
everything would be fine. The chaps back home were the best
in the world, and besides, the passport he was carrying was

accurate enough. It said JOHN SHEFFIELD, which was true. If it didn't say GENERAL SIR JOHN SHEFFIELD (Ret.), OBE, CB, well, then, whose bloody business was it anyway?

He stood in queue for Customs. The room was crowded, the tile floor scuffed and dirty. Only a handful of passengers moved over to the line for American citizens reentering the country. Few could afford to go overseas and there were even fewer countries where Americans felt welcome. The queue was moving now.

He handed his passport over to a paunchy-looking fellow wearing the U.S. Customs uniform of black trousers, white shirt, necktie, and billed cap. As the Customs man gazed over his passport he felt, again, that quickening of the heart. It would be all right, he knew. It would be fine.

He wished he could forget that last conversation with that disturbing man in the Foreign Office. His contact seemed innocuous at first, gently puffing on a Dunhill: 'You do realize, General, that if anything goes bollocks up, we can't possibly assist you? I do hate to say this, but you're on your own. We're eternally grateful for your assistance, of course, but we can't be linked to your mission. Either officially or unofficially.'

It had been a jolt, of course. No backup, even for a general. The Foreign Office man had smiled slightly, patronizingly, looking like a sad hound with his thick eyebrows and sagging cheeks.

'Fair enough,' he had said, speaking quickly, before he changed his mind about going back to that awful place.

The Customs agent was eyeing him. The agent's beard was a day old and his stubby fingers were ink-stained. His hat looked to be about one size too large.

'Purpose of your trip?'

'Business,' he said. He had practiced saying the word in front of a mirror.

'What kind of business?'

'Textiles.' The lie came easily to his lips. 'I'm here to visit your mill towns in the north. Lowell and Lawrence. I represent a concern that's interested in purchasing some textile mills, put them back into business.'

The Customs agent glared at him as he stamped the passport. Sheffield knew the look. Ambivalence, that was it. The Yanks had two attitudes about their cousins across the ocean: gratitude for the help and aid they had received this past decade, from food to medicines to seeds, and hatred for everything attached to that aid – the scholarships, raiding the American schools for their very best students and sending them to Britain; the medical programs, helping just a fortunate few each year for the best in burn and cancer treatments back home; and the businessmen, like the one he was trying to portray. Coming in, year after year, to buy up the shattered industries and fallow earth of this wide and wounded nation, to make a tidy profit, of course, but also slowly to bind this former colony back to its former mother country.

The passport slid back across the greasy metal counter. 'Welcome to the United States.' The agent's voice was as cheerful as a gravedigger's. Sheffield picked up the passport, noticed that the man's uniform shirt was mended in three places.

'Thanks, awfully,' he said.

After being cooped up in the tiny aircraft seat, the brief walk through the crowded terminal was a pleasure. Outside the air was smoky with car and bus exhaust. He was fortunate, only having to wait two minutes or so for a white and orange taxi cab at one of the stands outside of the terminal. He carried his hand luggage into the rear seat and said, 'The Sheraton,' and the taxi driver – a black man about his own age – grunted and off they went.

The driver said nothing as they joined the other cars leaving the airport and then went through a tunnel into Boston. That suited him fine. When they emerged from the tunnel he looked out the grimy windows of the cab as the driver maneuvered along the narrow and twisting streets. He had expected the place to look old and tired, like Manchester back home, but what surprised him was the dreariness of it all, like everyone had just given up. Most of the cars were old and rusted out, the buses belched great clouds of diesel smoke, and many buildings looked like they had gone for years without paint or repairs.

Fifteen minutes after arriving at the Sheraton he was in his room, lying down on the bed with his clothes still on and his shoes off, fighting exhaustion and jet lag. He got up and went into the washroom, putting a cold compress at the back of his neck. He looked in the mirror, seeing the tired blue eyes, the collection of wrinkles from squinting into the sun for years and years while in the Army, the freckled and sunburned top of his head, fringed by a faint crown of short white hair. He knew he looked his age but he was also proud that he was only a half stone over his enlistment weight, when he was just seventeen years old and entered the service of the King.

And such years of service, from the muddy fields of France to occupation duty in Germany, and then climbing up the long ladder, becoming more and more involved with the diplomatic side of things. Now, he was in service to a Queen, meeting an American he had not seen in a decade, an American who claimed to have something vital, something important for both nations' future.

He washed out the compress, went back into the room, stood near the bed. Of course, the poor bastard was probably as crazy as a loon. He sat down on the faded bedspread for a moment, looking at the phone. Wendy. He could pick up the phone and get an overseas line, and in a matter of minutes, he could be talking to Wendy. The time difference was six hours. She'd be in bed – no doubt with the telly in the corner droning on as she dozed – but he knew his girl. She'd be happy to hear from him, despite her anger at his being in Boston.

He reached to the phone, but stopped. No, it wouldn't be smart. He had no idea who might be listening in from the hotel's switchboard. He got up and put his coat back on. He'd get a quick meal in the hotel dining room before going to sleep. Besides, he had to concentrate on what was ahead of him. He couldn't afford to be distracted by Wendy, as much as he dearly wanted to hear that voice.

The last time . . . they had been in the sunroom of their pleasant home in Harpenden when he had told her he was going overseas. She had to put her teacup down, her hand was shaking so hard. She had glared at him, her face a mixture of fear and dismay. 'Tell me you're joking, John. Please.'

'I'm afraid not, love,' he said, sitting down in the cushioned wicker chair. 'I'm told that it's something quite important, something that only I can do.'

'You haven't been on the active list for three years! Surely they can send someone else.'

He spoke firmly. He hadn't used this steely tone since his retirement. 'They can't. There's . . . an American. Someone I knew when we were stationed in Washington. He will only talk to me, and me alone. That's why I'm going.'

Tears were slowly trembling down her cheeks. Her voice was begging now. 'I've been with you many a year, John Sheffield, with nary a complaint. You've been to Malaya and Cyprus and Aden. I've been with you in Germany and Belgium and Washington and Melbourne. Not once have I ever said a word.'

'I know, Wendy. It's meant everything to me.' But he wouldn't back down.

'And you're a silly old man, riding off again for Queen and Country,' she said, raising her voice. 'You've done your duty, more than any man I know! And now they want to send you, a man on pension who has to go to the loo three times a night. They're sending you on some silly James Bond mission to a country where they shoot students and people still starve in the countryside. I forbid it.'

'Wendy, I've already told them that I'll go.'

She folded her arms, stared out at her garden, her most favorite place in the world, and whispered the words again. 'I forbid it.'

But in the morning she silently packed his overnight bag. The car to pick him up had been late and he went out to the garden, to her bent-over form digging at something with a spade in the soil. He wanted to say so much but didn't know where to begin. So he had gone without a word.

Now he gave one last glance at the silent phone and left his room.

An hour later, he knew he had made a terrible mistake. He had a solitary and quite awful meal in the hotel's dining room, some baked cod dish that was dried and tasteless and an American beer that was flat and without any body. He remembered a joke he had heard once, from a subaltern. 'What do American beer and making love in a canoe have in common? They're both frigging close to water!'

A good joke, but he wasn't in a joking mood. After dinner he decided to take a quick walk outside to clear his head. He stepped out onto Boylston Street and joined the night crowd. There seemed to be a Boston copper or an Army MP on almost every street corner, and he tried to blend in, though he knew it wouldn't work, based on the way he was dressed. Most of the men and women looked like they were wearing clothes from the last decade, worn from being mended, washed, and re-mended.

At Exeter and Newbury Street, he turned left and stopped. A group of Boston police officers and Army MPs were swarming out of a storefront door that had a FOR LEASE sign posted in its window. They had clipboards and wooden sawhorse barriers in their hands. He wasn't sure what was going on, but he had seen enough. It was time to get back to his room. He turned and saw a man with a tired face, in a suit better cut than others he had seen, who had his palm up, holding a police badge. He glanced around and saw other men in suits, doing the same thing to about a half dozen people who were walking away from the quickly erected barriers.

'Not so fast, mister,' the policeman said. 'You got someplace you gotta go so quickly?'

'Yes,' he said. 'I'm going back to my hotel.'

The man cocked his head. 'You're a Brit, ain't you?'

'I most certainly am,' he said, reaching into his coat pocket. 'Here's my passport.'

The policeman quickly glanced through the small book

and handed it back. 'So it is. Go right ahead to your hotel.'

He put the passport back and said, 'What on earth is going on?'

The tired man shrugged. 'Residency check, that's all. Make sure these citizens have permission to live here. You need permission to live and work in Boston and every other city in this country. If you don't, it's back to the suburbs and countryside for you.'

'But they're just trying to survive, aren't they?'

'Yeah, but if everyone moved into a city, who'd be out there to grow crops and raise cattle and – hey! You there! Hold on!'

The policeman started running after a scared young man who was racing down an alleyway. Sheffield quickly made his way back to the Sheraton. He should have stayed home. This was an awful place. The only work here was for the young and fearless, and he was neither.

He leaned against the wall of the hotel's lift, exhausted. Just twelve more hours, that's all, he thought. Twelve more hours. A good night's sleep and a bracing shower in the morning. Then there would be a quick meeting at some little pub in this city with that bloody American. After a quick pop over to the consulate, he'd be on an afternoon flight back home. If some young guttersnipe from the Foreign Office ever darkened his door again, he'd toss the bloke out on his arse.

He used the key, opened the door. Wait. Could this be his room? He stood there blinking in confusion as he went in. What the hell! There, in his bed, blanket and sheets just above her breasts, was an attractive young woman.

'Johnny,' she said. 'It's about time you got back.'

He went forward. He'd have this straightened out in a few minutes and then he'd get some sleep. It wasn't a woman at all, but a young girl. Barely eighteen. Her hair was blond and pulled back.

'I'm sorry, young lady, but you have the wrong room.'

She shook her head. 'Nope. You're Johnny Sheffield, and you bought me for the night.'

There was a noise behind him and he turned. Three men stepped out from the bathroom, wearing dark suits, white shirts, and black ties, their faces utterly expressionless. He took a deep shuddering breath, felt his hands relax. So. This was where it was going to end. He looked back down at the girl, saw that her hands holding the blankets were trembling. Sitting gently down on the bed, he grasped one of her hands and said, 'M'dear, would you care to join me in a prayer?'

She nodded frantically, and as he looked up at the three approaching men, he noted the phone by the bedside.

Damn it, he wished he had made that call.

ONE

THE DEAD MAN LAY ON HIS FACE in his bed, the
sheets and blankets pooled around his feet. The back of his
head was a bloody mush. He had on a pair of baggy white
shorts and his skinny legs were quite hairy. The apartment
smelled of old clothes and dusty air and something else. Carl
Landry recognized that third smell. It was the odor of a body,
brutally violated, giving up its life. It was a smell that had
intrigued him once. Then it had saddened him. Now, it was
just something he was used to. Just part of the job.

Carl was a reporter with the *Boston Globe* and he stood at
the dead man's bedroom door, notebook in hand, carefully
recording everything he could see, writing in a cramped style
that had seen him through high school and the Army and
four years of newspaper work.

Detective Paul Malone caught his eye and separated himself from the chattering group of cops. He and Carl were
friends, sort of. As much as a cop and reporter can be. Malone
was in his late forties, overweight, and wore a tan coat that
flapped about his shins. There was a faint patch of gray stubble on his chin where he had missed shaving that morning,

and his thick gray-black hair was combed to one side with some wet-looking goop.

'C'mon, Carl, get out, will ya?' he said, shooing him backward. 'I let you see the stiff and that's fine. Any more and when the *Herald* shows up, they'll expect the same treatment, and we can't have none of that. Turn this freakin' place into a freakin' circus, you will.'

Carl smiled his best buddy smile and said, 'Come along, Paul. Chat with me for a second or two, will you? Deadline's coming up and I want to phone this in. Make the morning edition.'

'And beat the pants off the *Herald*, right?'

'You got it.'

Two steps and they were in the kitchen. A younger detective was dusting the countertops for fingerprints. There was a flash of light from the police photographer in the bedroom.

The apartment was small and cluttered and to Carl's practiced eyes it had been tossed. Drawers were open, closet doors were ajar, and clothes and dishes were scattered across the floors and on top of the furniture. The kitchen floor was linoleum and an empty metal bowl was on the floor, jammed up in the corner. The breakfast dishes were still in the sink. One cereal bowl, one coffee cup.

A tiny prewar TV set and a bunch of newspapers and magazines were in the living room. A jet screamed overhead, going toward the landing strips at Logan Airport. The carpet was light brown and threadbare along the edges, with a faint pattern of flowers that had been trampled away by years of foot traffic.

The door had three locks, a sensible precaution, especially during the winter, when supermarket shelves emptied by ten every morning and the prostitutes in the Combat Zone bartered their wares for cans of beef stew. But none of the locks appeared broken.

During the past couple of years at the *Globe*, Carl had run into Paul Malone on a fairly routine basis. Carl's job was general assignment reporter. Because of his military experience, his editors thought he'd be used to seeing dead bodies, so more often than not, he was sent out on crime stories. He and the older detective had a cautious but respectful relationship. Malone was relatively straight when it came to news, and Carl was equally polite when it came to asking the questions.

'What we have here is one Merl Sawson. Age sixty. Apparent gunshot wounds to the back of the head.' Malone's accent was pure Boston.

Carl scribbled away. 'Looks pretty apparent to me.'

'Sure it does, young fella, but I ain't putting my name to it until he's at the morgue. Would look pretty funny if we turned him over and found a knife to his heart, now, wouldn't it?'

'Yeah. A laugh and a half. You wondering who might have done the shooting?'

Malone grunted with what might have been amusement. 'Now, there's somethin' they must've forgot to teach us in detective school. Wondering who done the shooting and all.'

'You know what I mean. This poor guy was shot. Who's got guns and ammunition nowadays? Only the Army and the mob. Not civilians. So what do you think?'

'I think you're crossing the line from being a reporter to being a pain in the ass, and that's a mighty short line.'

'Thanks for the geography lesson,' Carl said. 'How did the call come in?'

'He's got a pal downstairs. He heard some shouts last night. Thought it might have been the television. Then Merl didn't show up for their usual lunch. When nobody answered the door, he called us.'

'Suspects?'

The detective looked pained. 'C'mon, we've been here all of a half hour.'

'Burglary, though, that's what it looks like.'

'Look, Carl, get the hell out, will ya? I got work to do.'

'Just a sec.' He looked around the room. No pictures. That was funny. You'd think a guy this old would have pictures of family and people on the walls. But no. Nothing. He looked at the magazines on the floor. *Time*, with a picture of Nelson Rockefeller on the cover; *American Legion*, with a picture of Nelson Rockefeller on the cover, and *Sports Illustrated*, with a picture of Joe Namath and Nelson Rockefeller on the cover. A veteran and a sports fan.

'Carl . . .'

'I'm outta here.'

By the door, he finally figured out what was bothering him.

It was the boots. Old work boots, their soles held together by gray duct tape. They stood neatly by the door on sheets of newspaper. Just like . . . Carl glanced back into the open bedroom door, seeing the legs of the dead man. Sweet Jesus. Sure was the right size. And the guy had claimed to have been a veteran. And he remembered.

It had happened a month before, the first really cold day of September. A truly awful day. For six hours he'd been standing on a pier by Boston Harbor, waiting for the police to dredge up a stolen car. A couple of Roxbury kids had driven straight off the pier during a police chase the night before. Their stunned parents were huddled by the end of the pier, ready to claim the drowned remains. When his relief came before the car was recovered, he almost cheered. Thank God he wouldn't have to talk to the families and get the usual 'How do you feel?' crap for the next day's story. Now, he could go home and have a beer or three and try to forget the drawn faces of these people waiting for their dead children.

Then he felt a touch at his elbow, and heard the old man's voice. 'Excuse me, are you a reporter?'

Carl turned around. The man stood on the cracked sidewalk, dead leaves and discarded newspapers swirling about his feet from the harbor wind. A few people walked by and looked at Carl sympathetically, silently saying *Sorry he grabbed you, fella, but better you than me.* The man was tall, wearing a long Army overcoat devoid of insignia or even buttons. His work boots were scuffed and cracked, held together by gray, grimy duct tape. His hands were quivering, and when he saw Carl notice them, he quickly shoved them into the coat's pockets. His face was red and pockmarked, his nose dripping, and there were dark bags under his eyes, like he had gotten one night's sleep a week for the past decade. His thin gray hair was tangled and unwashed.

'Yes, I am, and I'm sorry, but I've got an appointment and . . .'

'You're a vet, right? See you're wearing the old field jacket.'

Carl nodded wearily. 'Yep, U.S. Army. Just like you, right?' He reached into his pocket for a quarter.

The old man shook his head violently. 'No, no, put your money away. That's not what this is about. I'm a veteran, too, but I've never begged. Not once.'

'Oh. All right then, what can I do for you?'

He looked around and stepped forward, his breath

smelling of beer. 'Got something for you. A hell of a story. But only if you have the balls to print it.'

'That's for my editor to decide. What's it about?'

The old man lowered his voice. 'Something awful. But something you'll want to know about. It's just about the biggest story *ever*, just you see. You know, even ten years later, some people still enjoy killin', and that's gotta be stopped.'

Carl nodded seriously. That word *ever* sounded like it was said by a nine-year-old boy. But there was a faded look in the old man's eyes, and his thin shoulders shivered pathetically under the coat. Damn it, the man was a veteran. Just like him. He deserved better. Hell, they all deserved better.

'I tell you what, Mr. . . .'

He shook his head again. 'Oh no, no names, not yet. But tell me, will you do the story?'

'No promises, but I'll look at what you've got.' Carl said it seriously, respectfully. The old man was owed that.

He smiled in relief, showing brown and misshapen teeth. 'Good, that'll be good. Look, I've got some important documents, something important to show you. Here's just a taste.' He handed Carl a much-folded piece of lined notebook paper.

'Right there, that's where the story should start. In that piece of paper. I'll be here tomorrow afternoon, right at this spot. We'll go over the other papers together. Okay? But I won't come if I don't think I can trust you. I'll go somewhere else. These are bad times, you know.'

Carl knew what he was in store for. He had seen it before, with other reporters and other 'sources' that had latched on to them. But despite that, tomorrow he'd take the old guy to a nice diner, buy him probably the best meal he'd had in ages, and listen to his tales of dark conspiracies involving no doubt the Rockefellers, space aliens, the Romanovs, and whatever.

Carl would nod politely in all the right places, slip him five bucks, and then go home and get drunk at all the old memories the man had disturbed. So be it.

'Fine,' Carl said. 'Tomorrow, right here.'

'Good.' He looked like he was about to say something, but then he swung around and walked away, his step more confident. That was the last Carl had seen of him. The fellow veteran had not come back the next day, or the next. After a week, Carl had given up on him.

The piece of paper had a list of five names on it, and Carl had spent a few minutes looking them in up a phone book and city directory. When not a name was found, he put the paper aside.

Now, Carl stood outside Merl Sawson's apartment, breathing deeply, glad to get out of the stuffy rooms. Focus, he thought. Focus on the story. He looked at his watch. An hour to deadline. He shook off his promise to Detective Malone and took the creaking stairs up to the next landing and knocked on the door. No answer. Well, let's try his downstairs lunch pal. He went back down and stopped at the first-floor apartment. An older man answered the door, his face flushed and his eyes wide with concern and questions, a plaid bathrobe about his skinny body.

'Yes?'

'Carl Landry from the *Globe*,' he said. 'And you are . . . ?'

'Andrew Townes.'

'You rent here?'

'I own this place,' he said, one gnarled hand holding his bathrobe closed. 'My parents left it to me.'

'So you knew Mr. Sawson?'

Eyes still wide, he nodded. 'He's rented from me near on four years.'

'And what did he do for work?'

'Retired, I suppose.'

'He was a veteran, wasn't he? I saw he had a couple of issues of *American Legion*.'

Townes paused for about a second too long. 'I really don't know. We didn't talk much about that. You see, he—'

'Landry!' came the detective's voice from upstairs. Malone leaning over the railing, snarling at him. 'Damn it, man, when I said leave, I meant leave the building! Stop getting in our way, will ya?'

Carl waved a hand up, resisting an urge to use one finger, and rummaged in an inside pocket of his coat, the same U.S. Army field jacket the old man had noted the previous month. Jesus, he thought. It must have been him. Had to be. He pulled out a creased and slightly soiled business card, which he passed over.

'Call me, will you? I'm doing a story about Mr. Sawson and I'd like to give a good accounting of his life for the paper. Hate to just run a brief story. I'm sure he's worth more than that.'

Townes took the card and retreated into the apartment, 'This is all so awful,' he muttered as he closed the door, and Carl went out to the porch. The crisp October air felt good after being inside the apartment house.

Poor Merl Sawson. Probably just a crazy dead vet. Their meeting last month? Just coincidence, that's all. Still . . . it wouldn't hurt to look at that list of names again. The old wooden apartment building was three stories, painted white, each floor an apartment with an outside porch facing the street. In this Hibernian town they were affectionately known as Irish battleships. He looked at the three mailboxes on the porch. Townes, Sawson, and Clemmons. He wrote down the names and stepped off the front porch, past two uniformed Boston cops. The older cop said, 'They get anybody yet?'

'Not that I know of.'

The younger cop tried to make a joke. 'Chances are, the perp's out of state. He'll be as hard to find as a Kennedy 'fore the night's out.'

The younger cop laughed, but the older one frowned and stuck his hands in his uniform coat pocket and turned away. The cop's name tag said 'Mooney.' Maybe he was one of the true Irish believers, still pining for that lost promise. Could be. This was Boston, after all, and even Carl sometimes still felt the faint stirrings of that old promise, an old promise he often tried to forget.

A man in a tweed jacket and jeans stood on the sidewalk, a camera bag over his shoulder and a 35mm camera in his hands. It was Mark Beasley, a photographer for the *Globe* who wore a beard that reached the middle of his chest and was nicknamed the Beast.

'What have you got, Carl?'

'I don't have much, but the cops have a dead man up in the second-floor apartment.'

'You want me to wait around?'

Most reporters simply tolerated the Beast, but Carl found he liked the guy. He might have the charm of a bull sniffing around the entrance to a china closet, but he did get the job done and didn't treat his work as an impediment to a 'serious' career as an artist.

Carl checked his watch. 'Yeah, if you can. If there's a hole in the metro section, they might be able to use a picture of the cops dragging this guy's body down the stairs.'

Another jet flew by overhead. Beasley looked up, camera

in his hands. 'Jesus, what a place to live in. Freakin' noise would drive me crazy.'

'What noise?' Carl asked, oblivious.

'Typical reporter,' the Beast said, grinning. 'Wouldn't notice a naked woman in front of him unless it had something to do with his story.'

Carl smiled back. 'Typical photographer. Wouldn't notice a naked woman in front of him unless he had film in his camera.'

He walked away quickly, past a faded MCGOVERN FOR PRESIDENT sign flapping from a telephone pole. No neighbors were standing around, and he didn't have time for a door-to-door to get local color. If he was lucky he could make it to the *Globe* in fifteen minutes – if there were no checkpoints set up along the way – and have almost thirty to do the piece. Already, as he unlocked the car door and got inside, he was writing the story in his mind. It shouldn't be too hard.

The inside of his '69 Coronet was cluttered with old *Globes*, notebooks, and maps. The outside was light blue and freckled with rust. It was sloppy but comfortable and, most days, reliable. Today it started up after three tries. At the first stop sign, he saw some faded graffiti on the side of a liquor store. HE LIVES, it said.

Jesus, he thought. Maybe there were true believers everywhere.

Walking into the newsroom of the *Globe* was always a jolt to the system, even after four years. The noise was a constant hum of conversations, ringing phones, chattering teletype machines, and the slapping of typewriter keys. The closer it came to deadline, the louder the noise, and right now it was almost deafening. But even after deadline, it never got quiet. Before one newspaper rolled out and hit the streets, it was time to work on another. As his editor once said, the news never stops and never do the goddamn newspapers.

There were a couple of dozen desks, arranged haphazardly over the dirty tile. Floor-to-ceiling pillars broke up the space, and also served as a convenient hanging place for calendars, notices, and framed front pages of *Globes* past. At the far end of the room was a large horseshoe of desks belonging to the foreign, national, metro, editorial, features, and sports editors. Carl aimed for a heavyset man behind one of the metro desks, his boss, George Dooley.

At the very end of the room were the glass-enclosed offices of the managing editors and the executive editor. Off to one side by itself, as if he didn't really belong, was the office for the oversight editor. The curtains to the glass windows of this office were closed. They were always closed. Like most reporters, Carl had never been in that office and that suited him just fine.

He passed one pillar. The framed front page was from August 14, 1945: JAPS SURRENDER. Another one was from June 28, 1950: AMERICAN PLANES BOMB FLEEING REDS IN KOREA. Carl dodged a copy boy, racing out to Composing with a fistful of papers in his hand. Another pillar, another front page. This one was January 21, 1961: KENNEDY OFFERS WORLD NEW START FOR PEACE. It was hanging crookedly, and the broken glass had been poorly repaired with masking tape.

George had a phone to his ear but glanced up as Carl approached. As always, he gave Carl a look of skepticism, a look Carl had gotten used to these past four years. Dooley's desk was covered with paper, pencils, half-empty Styrofoam coffee cups, and damp photographs, fresh from the darkroom. His thin brown hair was plastered to a freckled scalp, and he wore black-rimmed glasses that were always sliding down his large nose. He had on a wrinkled white shirt with the sleeves rolled up massive forearms, a black necktie tugged open, and black slacks. He called it his uniform and claimed it saved him from wasting time in the morning, choosing clothes while fighting his daily hangover.

'Yeah, yeah,' George growled into the phone. 'Hold on for a moment, will ya?' He turned to Carl. 'Whaddya got?'

He stood before his editor, flipped through his notebook. 'A homicide from East Boston.'

'Yeah, I know. Male or female?'

'Male, old guy. Looks like a vet. Shot in the back of head.' He thought about telling George about his earlier meeting with the man, and decided not to. There was a pecking order in the newsroom, depending on how many stories saw print, and he didn't want George delaying this story because of some odd meeting last month.

George picked up a pencil, scratched a few notes. 'Too bad it wasn't a college girl. Could use something to spright up the front page. All right, get me something in ten, page and a half.'

'George, come on, you know I've got twenty minutes. And besides, the guy was a vet. That should be worth something.'

'Don't be offended, Carl, but I'd rather have a dead coed than a dead vet,' George said. 'And you still get just ten minutes. Oversight took a long lunch and he's running late.'

He knew better than to raise a fuss. 'All right, ten it is. Did the Beast call? He was trying for some pictures of them taking the body out.'

'Yep, he called and nope, there's no pics. They took the body out the rear, to avoid all the attention.'

Something seemed to tickle the back of his hands. 'That sounds strange, George.'

'Strange? Yeah, the whole world is strange. And now you've got nine minutes, Landry.'

'On my way,' he said, looking up again, as he always did, to the framed *Globe* front page from October 31, 1962, that hung on the pillar just behind George's chair. REDS BOMB DC, NYC; MILLIONS FEARED DEAD. A smaller subhead read: 'Kennedy, First Family Perishes.' And the first paragraph of the story: 'The horrors of this past weekend's invasion of Cuba to attack Soviet missile sites struck home with an apocalyptic vengeance yesterday, with news that atomic bombs had struck Washington, D.C., and the outskirts of New York City, killing millions of Americans and destroying the upper reaches of the federal government. Military sources confirm that President John F. Kennedy and Vice President Lyndon Johnson perished in the attack. The whereabouts of Speaker of the House John McCormack – the next in line to the presidency – are not known at this time.'

After his first six months here, shuddering every time he'd passed it, he eventually asked George why that particular front page was in such a prominent place. George had replied in that gravelly voice of his, 'Why the hell not? It's news, ain't it?'

Carl turned and headed to his desk.

TWO

CARL HUNG HIS COAT on the back of his chair and made some room on the cluttered desktop. Somewhere in that mess was the piece of paper with the list of names that the old vet – Merl – had passed on to him. He'd look for it, soon enough, but for now he had a deadline to meet, and quick. He propped his notebook on his telephone and rolled a book into the Olympia typewriter. The book was three sheets of 8½-by-11-inch paper with carbon between each sheet. He looked at his notebook, and then started typing:

LANDRY/EAST BOSTON HOMICIDE

Boston police are investigating the apparent murder of Merl Sawson, 60, of Winthrop Street in East Boston. Sawson, a retired serviceman, was found in his bed, with a gunshot wound to the back of the head.

Police said neighbors heard noise in the apartment early Wednesday morning, and one neighbor called police when Sawson did not show up for an expected lunch meeting.

Carl paused. It was pretty thin, but that's what happens when you're just a few minutes before deadline. Again, he started tapping at the dirty keys of his typewriter.

While no suspects have been identified, police are investigating whether Sawson was murdered during the course of a burglary. The apartment was in disarray and police are checking to see what may have been stolen.

A few more seconds of paper shuffling on his desk, and Carl typed some more.

The death of Sawson marks the seventy-third homicide this year in Boston, four homicides ahead of 1971's record year.

He rolled the papers out from his typewriter and walked over to the metro desk.

'Here you are, George,' he said. 'Ninety seconds ahead of schedule.'

'Well, there you go,' George said. 'You want a candy bar or somethin'?'

'How about a raise?'

'How about leaving me alone?'

After some digging he found the notebook page with Merl's list of names and he slid that into the top drawer of his desk.

He was tired and it was late, and he knew he couldn't do much about the names right now. Tomorrow, first thing, he'd take another look at it. They had to have meant something to Merl Sawson, since he had passed it over to Carl. But then again, they could have just been names lifted from magazines or books for no good reason. Lots of things happened in this city and country for no good reason.

On this afternoon George didn't yell over at him with questions about the Sawson story, so it looked like it was going in golden. A few minutes after he had passed in the story, the door to the oversight editor's office opened up and a slim man walked out wearing gray dress pants and a matching vest. Cullen Devane, the current oversight editor and a major in the U.S. Army Signal Corps. He stopped at each of the editorial desks, picked up copy for tomorrow's newspaper and then, with a chilly smile, he went back to his office.

Carl looked around. Everybody was studiously ignoring Major Devane's appearance, and there was a general sigh of relief in the newsroom when he went back to his office. Usually Devane only came out to talk to the editors about the next day's stories, but on very rare occasions, he chatted with a reporter. On extremely rare occasions, he would invite a reporter back to his office and close the door. That experience was known in the newsroom as the Killer C; shorthand for killing one's career, and also for being sent someplace where an eventual death from cancer was fairly likely, since Devane had the power to have someone detained or re-upped into the service.

Two months ago a features writer – Laura Dobson, if Carl remembered correctly – had emerged from Major Devane's office in tears, hands trembling, and later that day she was gone. Despite earlier warnings, she had continued to submit stories about the antidraft movement to her editors. A month after her departure, the newsroom had received a postcard from her from a decontamination work camp outside of Miami. And that had been that.

After Devane's door shut the noise level in the newsroom rose and there were looks cast Carl's way. Even though he had been out of the Army for four years, some people still thought he and Cullen Devane worked together, though he had shared maybe a fistful of words with the major during his time at the *Globe*. Irrational, he knew, but it still made for a lot of solitary lunches, muttered greetings in the morning, and break-room conversations that dribbled off whenever he went in to get a cup of coffee.

He looked over at the clock. Past 5 P.M. His stomach grumbled and he was in the middle of wondering where in hell he was going to eat dinner when Jack Burns came over to his desk, pulling a leather coat over his thin shoulders. Jack was a few years younger than Carl; wore loud shirts with wide-bottomed pants, and was a music critic for the *Globe*. His wavy brown hair touched the rear of his shirt collar and his sideburns were the style still popular with Elvis Presley – who was on tour this fall for refugee relief. Carl thought it was incredibly funny that someone could write for the *Globe* and get paid for writing about music, but he kept that thought to himself. Jack was a good sort and one of the few people in the newsroom who treated him nicely.

'Some of us are going over to the Old Sod for a newsroom meeting,' Jack said, buttoning his coat. 'Want to join us?'

'Newsroom meeting? Isn't that just another excuse for getting drunk?'

Jack smiled. 'Who needs an excuse? Besides, it gives you a chance to see your colleagues drooling and slobbering over each other. Makes for a good week of wicked gossip. So that's the kind of meeting we're having. Are you in?'

Going home, which was an apartment, meant dinner from a can or an old field ration from his Army reserve days. The alternative was an overpriced beer, cheeseburgers, and smoky conversation at the Old Sod.

'In,' Carl said. 'I'm very in.'

Jack smiled again. 'Of course you are, but I'm not telling.'

A cheeseburger and fries later, Carl was working on his second beer of the evening and doing fine. He had a corner stool at the bar and could keep an eye on most everything in the pub, which gave him a bit of a warm feeling. Something from his Army days, he realized, about assessing the territory and keeping your options open. The fries had been tasty and the burger was a good sign of how well recovery was going. Even just a few years ago, hamburgers were stretched with all kinds of filler – and the wise consumer never asked too many questions – but tonight's had tasted like 100 percent beef.

Someone with a taste for old Irish music kept pumping quarters into the jukebox, and he had shared his mealtime with Jack Burns. Jack talked about rumors of an upcoming Led Zeppelin tour of the United States and Carl talked about that afternoon's murder. After a while Jack shook his head at him. 'My dear Carl, I want to talk about the wonders of rock and roll, and all you want to talk about is some poor old man, murdered in his bed.'

'Because it's news,' he said.

'Bah,' Jack said, raising up a glass. 'My stories, that's the news people care about. Whether they'll have some entertainment in their gray lives over the next few months, get their minds off this awful election. Not another story about a corpse. Hell, that dead British general, the Sheffield guy who was found dead in bed with a hooker a couple of weeks ago, even that only made a few paragraphs in the metro. Who cares about another dead old man?'

'I do,' Carl said, remembering the earnest look on the lined and nervous face, and those old boots, carefully kept together with duct tape. 'And so should you.'

Jack laughed. 'You should bottle some of that excess idealism you have, sell it on the street corners. I hear it's still quite rare.'

Carl kicked him and Jack laughed again and wandered off.

The Old Sod was near the *Globe* and filled mostly with people from the paper. Jack was now with some of his friends from the living page. Even here, in a bar, the people from the newspaper automatically segregated themselves into groups. Some of the ad reps were over in a corner, overdressed and laughing hard, and some of the print shop boys, with their ink-stained hands and their blue work clothes, were at the other end of the bar.

Nearby a couple of sports reporters were talking about the World Series between the Cincinnati Reds and the Detroit Tigers, and Carl tuned them out. Unless the Red Sox were in it, he wasn't interested, and the Sox hadn't been in anything since the '48 series, a lifetime ago.

At the far end of the bar, a few reporters were laughing, talking about State House and city council shenanigans. There was Kathy Proulx, a State House reporter, and Jeremiah King, who knew the city council in and out, and Bobby Munson, a general-assignment reporter like Carl who worked the court system. Every ten minutes or so, Jeremiah would shout, 'Beer trivia!' and bet a drink he could outsmart anyone at the bar, and for the most part he did, with Kathy and Bobby groaning and forking over money.

For a while Carl just quietly observed, letting the second beer wash away the taste of the burger and fries. Except for Jack, he never really connected with anyone else in the newsroom, but he understood why. He'd gotten his job through his veteran's benefits. Day one on the job, someone had put a toy soldier on his desk, with a little handmade sign that said 'student killer.' He'd kept his mouth shut and tossed the toy soldier away – he knew some in the newsroom were hoping for an outburst, to reaffirm the stories of the crazy 1960s vet – but he hadn't given them that satisfaction. He had done his job and had remained quiet, just like tonight.

Office politics – who was in, who was out, who was backstabbing whom – bored him. He liked talking about things that mattered. Like the residency laws in the cities and how long they would last. Or stories about the outlying towns in western Massachusetts. Were there really pockets of hunger out there, ten years after the war? And the rumors about the British. Now that would be a story to report. Last week he had listened to two pressmen talking in line in the cafeteria, guys who were in the Air Force Reserve. They had come back from a tour of duty up North, near Minnesota, and the radar stations there had seen a lot of transport traffic flying into Canadian bases. 'I tell ya, it's like a regular train schedule up North, all these Brit planes coming in. Makes you wonder what they're up to.' And the other pressman had said, 'Maybe it's just kippers and beans, more relief food,' and the other had snorted. 'Not hardly. Them transports were carrying Brit troops, that's what, and the officers I talked to, they don't think all those Brits are up there for a training exercise.' But these stories would never get reported.

He had about a swallow left of his beer and then Jeremiah raised a hand and again challenged, 'Beer trivia!' Kathy raised her hands mockingly to her face and said, 'Enough, already,' and Bobby said, 'Jesus, I thought you'd be done by now.'

Jeremiah waved his hand. His brown hair was combed back and even when he smiled, his sharp face looked unpleasant, like he was a guy who enjoyed being a reporter because it gave him an excuse to be a nosy bastard and get paid for it.

'C'mon, one more, and a special one,' he announced. 'Winner of this one gets a free drink from me each night for a week. All right? Ready?'

Some moans and groans, and Jeremiah plowed ahead. 'All right, here we go. Last beer trivia question of the night. All you have to do is name the last American in space. Pretty simple, eh?'

Bobby just shook his head and made a motion of going through his wallet to pay for another beer, while Kathy rolled her eyes. Jeremiah was laughing, looking so confident and cocky and full of himself, and Carl couldn't stand it.

'Schirra,' he said.

Bobby and Kathy looked over at him, and Jeremiah said, 'What did you say?'

'Schirra,' he repeated, feeling a grin spread over his face. 'Wally Schirra, flew a Mercury capsule he called Sigma Seven. Back in October '62. Just before the war.'

A few shouts and laughs from people who had been watching, and Kathy eyed him and Bobby sort of nodded in a 'good for you' look. But then Jeremiah shut it down.

'Forget it, Landry,' he said. 'This was private, among us. Your answer doesn't count.'

Their part of the bar got quiet. He guessed he shouldn't have had the second beer. He leaned a bit toward Jeremiah.

'Sure it counts. It's correct, and you don't like losing. Right?'

Kathy and Bobby were staring into their drinks. Jeremiah picked up his beer, face red, and started to turn to Bobby, muttering something that only a few people, Carl included, could hear.

'Goddam quota baby.'

Carl started to get up from the bar, to head over and talk to Jeremiah face-to-face, when one of the copy boys came in with a fistful of the next day's *Globe*s. 'Still warm, still warm, still warm,' he chanted. Carl grabbed a copy of tomorrow's paper and decided to go home. Why not? He threw a dollar bill on the bar and pushed through the crowd of newspaper people. No one asked him to stay, no one asked him how he was doing. He stood outside in the cold night, letting the air clear his head, knowing he'd soon be sober but that the bad taste in his mouth would be there for a long while.

After four years, he was still an outsider.

Home was a second-floor apartment in a brownstone on Commonwealth Avenue, which everyone in Boston called Comm Ave. The neighborhood had become pricey over the years, and fancy shops had opened up on nearby Newbury Street. A lot of people coming into wealth – mostly bankers and shippers working for the increasingly busy port – but his veteran's benefits kept the place rent-controlled and he was comfortable. As he walked around from the rear alley he looked for Two-Tone, the neighborhood homeless guy, who kept an eye on the cars at night, but Carl didn't see him. It wasn't that unusual though, since Two-Tone always kept his own hours.

On the floor of the apartment was the day's mail, which

consisted of a bill from New England Bell and an envelope with an American Red Cross return address. The envelope was thin, which meant it wasn't good news. He opened it and quickly scanned the form letter. Handwritten notes filled the blank spots:

Dear *Carl Landry*

We regret to inform you there is no news regarding the whereabouts of
your sister, Sarah Landry,
Newburyport, Massachusetts

whose last known address in 1962 was
the University of Nebraska, Omaha, Nebraska.

We will next contact you in
six months

Please use the reverse of this form to report any additional information that will assist us in locating the above-referenced individual. A self-addressed envelope is enclosed for your convenience.
Sincerely,
J. J. McCain
Bureau of Missing Persons
American Red Cross

Sorry, sis, he thought, putting the envelope and letter down on the counter. He thought about throwing the letter away but didn't. In the morning, he'd put it in the thick file that had similar letters and postcards from the Red Cross and the Salvation Army and Searchers, Inc. and Catholic Charities. He knew that she was probably dead, killed in one of a half dozen ways in the awful chaos after the war, but still . . . there was always that one chance. Just the other day, the *Herald* had run a heartwarming story of some young man being reunited with his family after spending ten years walking home from a Peace Corps posting in Bolivia.

He closed his eyes, just for a moment, seeing her pug nose and bright blue eyes and the dark brown hair that she kept long and unpermed, much to their mother's dismay. She had listened to strange records, stuff she called folk music, and she had even stranger opinions. When he had announced that he was joining the Army, she could not believe him.

'Big bro, why not wait for the draft? Why join up?' When he had said that he was just doing his duty, that he looked forward to serving under a president like JFK, she shook her head and said, 'Duty to a military-industrial complex, that's all.' Later, when he was stationed overseas and she won a scholarship to the University of Nebraska in Omaha, she had sent him just a few letters. The last one had come in the summer of '62, after she had been at some sort of student conference in Michigan. The group was called Students for a Democratic Society, and they were going to change the world. Sarah had enclosed a manifesto about the group's plans, and Carl had read the papers and tossed them. It was a mishmash of pie-in-the-sky dreaming, but one phrase had stuck in his mind: 'We would replace power rooted in possession, privilege, or circumstances by power rooted in love, reflectiveness, reason, and creativity.'

Well, a few months after Sarah's letter, the whole world

saw that real power came from the splitting of atoms. Carl never heard from his sister again. That had caused many a late night, staring up at the ceiling, wondering how he – in the military – had survived the war and how his parents and his sister – a college student! – hadn't.

He made himself a cup of instant coffee and tried to put Sarah and the damn letter out of his mind, the whole damn day out of his mind. His left leg was aching, which it usually did after a long day. It was well past midnight and nothing would be on television. He sat down in one of the two couches and put his feet up on the cluttered coffee table. From where he sat he could make out the open door that led to his office, which was almost a twin to his desk at the *Globe* in terms of its collection of papers and files. It was where he half worked on the book that all newspaper reporters say they're writing. The other open door led to his bedroom and nearby bathroom. Large windows in the living room overlooked the sidewalk and streets and narrow park in this part of Comm Ave.

The walls were bare, except for a framed print of some skiers on a mountain in France that was left over from the previous tenant. In a cardboard box in a back closet were a small collection of framed photos, pictures of himself and his family, taken back when he lived in Newburyport. He had packed them with his Army gear. One of these days, he'd put those pictures up. But not tonight. And not tomorrow.

He thought about his gear. Uniforms and fatigues and an idealism he once had, back when the President issued a challenge for his generation and he had answered with enthusiasm. Now, all that was packed up as well, with the memories of a dead family.

At his elbow was his shortwave radio, and he switched it

on, hoping to catch a BBC news broadcast, but all he got was static. Jamming again, and although the British complained often to Philadelphia, there was no proof that it was official jamming. Maybe it was the Zed Force. They were blamed for a lot of things. He moved the dial around until he got another frequency, then sat back, letting the coffee warm him up and trying to forget what had happened back at the Old Sod. As he listened to the proper-sounding announcer describe the latest crisis in Uganda, that nut Idi Amin exiling thousands of Asian residents, he felt sleepy and knew that if he didn't move quickly, he'd end up spending the night on the couch.

He sat up and switched off the radio, finished the coffee and looked down at the next day's *Globe*. Well, actually, it was now today's *Globe*, and he started flipping the pages, yawning and scanning the stories and the headlines. McGovern makes a speech. Rockefeller makes a speech. Polls still show a Republican trouncing in a few weeks. Robbery in Dorchester. Secretary of Relief and Recovery makes a speech. Franco-German spy ring allegedly broken up in Seattle. Progress made in releasing interned B-52 crews from Mongolia.

After a few minutes, he wasn't yawning anymore.

His story on the East Boston murder wasn't there.

THREE

THE NEXT DAY CARL WAS AT HIS DESK for ten minutes before going up to metro to talk to George Dooley. It was ten in the morning and his head ached from the late-night coffee following the beer, and too much thinking. George was looking through the *Globe*'s competition – the *Herald* – and muttering to himself as he saw what the tabloid was covering. There had been a bad traffic accident on the Southeast Expressway and the photo showed a bleeding woman trapped behind a steering wheel, being scissored out by Boston fire-fighters.

George looked up and said, 'There you go, young fella. If it bleeds, it leads.'

Carl pulled up a spare chair and sat before the desk. 'If it's written, does it appear?'

'Hunh?' George put the *Herald* down on his desk.

'My story about the East Boston murder. Sawson, the vet. Why did it get spiked?'

'Lack of room, Carl, lack of room.'

'You said there was room in the metro section when I got in. You're telling me the news hole got filled by something else in ten minutes?'

Dooley looked straight at him. 'That's exactly what I'm saying.'

'And what replaced it?'

'I can't remember.'

'You *can't* remember?'

'All right, I *won't* remember,' Dooley said. 'You see, I got some real work to do. For tomorrow's paper. I don't got time to worry about one that's already done.'

Carl thought about last night at the Old Sod. Quota baby. 'The story was okay, though, right?'

George picked up a pencil, started scribbling. 'Sure. It was great. Here. Go down to the Parker House. There's an announcement at one today about some new anti-orfie gang measures being proposed by the mayor. Get the story and get it on my desk by three.'

He glanced down at the piece of paper. 'I was thinking about doing a second-day on the homicide, since the story didn't make it in today's paper.'

George didn't look up. 'Forget it. If there's time, I'll make it a news brief for tomorrow. I want the anti-gang story. Got it?'

He rose up from the chair. 'Got it.'

Back at his desk he looked across the room at George. As bosses went, he was all right, though he had the healthy ration of gruffness that all newspaper editors seem to share. From the first day, George had acted like Carl was just another reporter, which Carl was grateful for. George talked only about newspapers and his niece, Tracy, who lived in Rhode Island. A couple of years ago Tracy had developed childhood cancer and she had been lucky enough to be taken overseas for treatment, and she had done well. The first and

only time Carl had seen George get weepy was the day a letter arrived from London, a note from his niece saying that she
was feeling better. So Carl knew that more than just printer's
ink ran through that man's veins, but something was going on
this morning with George and the old vet story.

But he didn't want to push it with George, not yet. He had
other things to do. He opened up the top desk drawer and took
out the folded piece of notepaper. Five names in a column:

Q. Dooley
T. Isaacson
C. Porter
N. DiNitale
F. X. Tilley

The handwriting looked shaky, and the name at the top –
Q. Dooley – was more faded than the last name, F. X. Tilley.
When Merl had first given him the list, an afternoon of
research hadn't turned up anything. Carl held the paper up to
the light. Faint indentations were present next to each name.
He laid the notepaper down on his desk and gently rubbed a
pencil tip across the markings. Numbers appeared, next to
each name:

Q. Dooley   65
T. Isaacson   65
C. Porter   68
N. DiNitale   71
F. X. Tilley   72

So. It looked like Merl had turned to another notebook
page before copying the names, and the numbers written on

the previous page had made the indentations. Numbers. Ages? Maybe, but the way the names were ordered . . . years. That's what. Something happened with Q. Dooley in 1965, and something happened to F. X. Tilley in 1972.

'All right, Sherlock,' he whispered to himself. 'What next?'

Something cool and uncomfortable seemed to settle into the back of his throat. He knew what he should do, what would make sense in these times when the unemployment rate was still considered a military secret, and he had as good a job as could be got these days. What made sense was to throw away the list and go to the Parker House at 1 P.M., as ordered by his editor, and then do the next day's story and the story after that. Never lift your head. Never think for yourself. Just do your job. That's all he had been doing these past four years, ever since leaving the Army. It was hard to remember that there was once a time when that would have never happened.

Carl looked down at the trembling writing from a fellow vet. What to do? Be a good little boy and follow orders, or do something for the poor old man with the taped-up shoes who once wore the uniform of this country? It was almost eleven. He saw Jeremiah King – self-proclaimed beer-trivia god – ooze in from the other side of the newsroom. Jeremiah looked over at Carl, smirked, and gave him a sloppy salute. That decided it for him. He typed the names and the dates on a piece of paper and left the newsroom. Time to get to work.

In a dark and dusty part of the *Globe* building, he sought out Grace. Behind the counter of the claustrophobic, overstuffed office were rows of shelves and filing cabinets, and to the left was a desk, piled high with phone books, almanacs, calendars, and file folders. A large woman stood up from behind the desk and came to the counter, moving quietly, a pencil in her hand. She wore black slacks and a dark red pullover sweater, and her gray-blue hair was done up in curls. Eyeglasses hung from a thin chain around her neck. On the counter was a nameplate that said 'GRACE HANRATTY, Librarian.' She cocked her head and said, 'What do you need?'

'Something chased down,' Carl said, sliding the typewritten sheet of paper across. 'Names and dates. I need to know what happened to these guys during these years.'

She picked up the piece of paper and frowned, as if it were a report card from her son, covered with D's and F's. 'What's this, you don't even have first names?'

'Nope.'

'Or residence? Or place of business?'

'Grace, I know it's a lot of work—'

'Jeez,' she said, heading back to her desk. 'Let me tell you, they ought to give me part of your salary, the work I do to make your lives easier.' She sat down at her desk, made a dismissive motion with her hand. 'I'll let you know in a few days, if I find anything. But don't hold your breath.'

He caught up with Detective Paul Malone in the Lane Street Division's parking lot. The detective didn't look happy to see him, but Carl matched him, stride for stride, as he walked around the rear of the brick police station to get to his car. It was cold and the wind was blowing dead leaves around the worn tires of the police cruisers. The lot was fenced in and the windows of the station were covered with chicken wire, the better to deflect tossed rocks or Molotov cocktails.

'Sawson?' the detective said. 'The old vet? Nothing new there.'

'Any usable prints from the apartment?'

Malone grinned. 'No comment.'

'Well, how about motive. Burglary, right?'

He shook his head. 'That's you talkin', not me.'

'Come on, Paul, you saw what the place looked like. Somebody had tossed it.'

They reached a dented dark blue Chrysler with one fender almost rusted through. Malone put his cardboard cup of coffee on the car's roof and fumbled in his coat pocket for the keys. 'Again, that's you talkin', not me. Maybe the old guy was just a slob. It happens.'

'Was the apartment broken into?'

'No comment.'

Malone sighed as he unlocked the door and got in. 'Shit,' he said. 'Hey, Carl, hand me my coffee, will ya?'

Carl picked up the cup and held it close to his chest. 'Come on. Coffee for one answer. Was the place broken into?'

'Oh, you're being such a shit today.'

'Doing my job.'

'All right, no signs of forced entry. Okay? So hand it over.'

Carl gave him the coffee, not feeling particularly triumphant. 'So. What do you think? What's your theory?'

The detective turned the key a few times as the engine ground with no success. 'Goddam piece of shit. My theory? I'll tell you my theory. He's an old guy, living alone, no wife or girlfriend that we know of. What does that tell you?'

'Tells me he's an old guy, living alone, no wife or girlfriend.'

Another turn of the key, another grinding of the engine. 'Blessed mother, I can't be late for this flippin' court appearance . . . Carl, you'll never be a cop. Your mind's not devious enough. What I see there is the stuff I see all the time. Old guy living alone, likes to spend time with young boys. Sometimes it takes some money, and sometimes the young boys, they want a little more. The old man gets mad, the young boy-o gets mad, and bang-bang, that's all she wrote. Probably one of those college boys across the river starvin' for some extra green. Probably had an arrangement with our Merl Sawson and then it went sour. You'll see. A couple of days, we'll have it all tied up with some Hah-vad boy. Ah, Jesus, there you go!'

The engine finally caught with a burping roar and then gurgled down as exhaust rolled out the tailpipe. 'There,' Malone said. 'Now, if you'll excuse me . . .'

'One more thing.' Carl had his hand on the car door. 'How much work you folks putting into this?'

The engine died. Malone pounded at the steering wheel with his fist and said, 'Look, you know the drill. We're having another bang-up year for murders in this fair city, and look at the crap I get to drive. We can only work the cases where someone's connected, or someone's raising a stink. Ain't no one raising a stink for this old guy, and he ain't connected. Money, Carl, money is what keeps us going.'

There was a rumbling noise from the other side of the parking lot, as three olive-drab deuce-and-a-half Army trucks drove in. The trucks looked new and recently washed. They parked and the rear canvas flaps were undone and soldiers jumped out, laughing and talking. They formed a line and moved toward the police station, heading into the basement entrance. All of them carried M-14s slung over their shoulders as well as small knapsacks, and a sergeant good-naturedly moved them along.

The detective spoke again as he restarted the engine. 'You

see where the money goes, Carl. It's not this police division. Take it up with General Curtis, next time you see him.'

'Is there a raid on for tonight?'

'Even if I knew, I wouldn't tell you. Now, please leave me alone, all right?'

Malone slammed the door and backed the unmarked cruiser out of the lot. Carl stuck his fists in his jacket, and stared at the empty trucks, wondering how many deserters or draft dodgers would be crowded in there tonight. Not his problem, not his story, but the sight of those trucks made him feel slightly nauseated.

Andrew Townes either wasn't home or wasn't answering the door, and there was a Boston Police Department evidence seal on the door to Merl Sawson's place. It was time to try the third-floor apartment, and after a couple of knocks the door opened just a crack. Carl made out a scraggly bearded face, brown eyes, a door chain, and an attitude.

'Yeah?'

'Mr. Clemmons?'

'Who's looking for him?'

He slipped his business card through the barely open door. 'Carl Landry, *Boston Globe*. I'm doing a story about the murder of your neighbor downstairs, Merl Sawson.'

'Some neighbor.' The card came back and the door opened wider. The man looked to be in his early twenties, with patched jeans and a tie-dyed T-shirt. 'How do I know you're from the *Globe*? Could be a cop or Army. Hell, you're wearing an Army coat.'

'You can call the *Globe*, verify who I am,' Carl said, hoping he wouldn't. 'I'm wearing the coat because it keeps me warm.

That's all.'

The door slammed shut, and then with a rattling noise the door opened and the man motioned him in. 'I'm Troy Clemmons, and I'll give you a couple of minutes. That's all.'

'Thanks.'

'Oh, it's more for kicks than anything else. Never talked to a real reporter before.'

The apartment was warm. It was a twin to its neighbor below, with the same kitchen, a small living room that connected to a porch that overlooked Winthrop Street, and a bedroom off to the side. But while Merl Sawson's place was the cluttered home of a retired man, this place was . . . well, it was a mess. Dishes were piled high in the sink and along the counter. Pillows and blankets were strewn across the living room floor, along with old newspapers and textbooks. Tapestries and posters covered the walls. One was for a Grateful Dead concert this past summer at the Boston Garden, showing stylized pictures of the band members as skeletons. Next to it was a popular antidraft poster that had come out last year: it showed a flight of B-52s over Soviet Russia. Below the B-52s was a blasted landscape of red and black, showing cities burning, children crying, and parents covering their heads in fear. One of the B-52s had a caricature of a pilot that looked like General Ramsey Curtis, cigar in mouth, smiling and saying, 'Sorry 'bout that!'

In smaller type at the bottom it said BOSTON AREA ANTI-DRAFT COALITION 1971.

Another, smaller poster was a simple black-and-white photo showing two Army soldiers in decon gear taking a break somewhere. It was just dust and dirt. No grass, no trees, no plants. Their protective hoods were thrown back and they were drinking from canteens, laughing as if sharing a joke. By their feet were the fused and melted remnants of what looked like a child's tricycle. The caption was to the point: 'Get Drafted and See the World . . . What's Left of It.'

Carl moved a couple of textbooks from the couch and sat down. Clemmons sat on the floor before him, leaning against a pillow propped up by a coffee table. He was barefoot and lit a cigarette. Incense was burning at the table's center, and Carl was sure it was there to mask the odor of something else. He glanced over at the bedroom, where a pair of slender bare legs were moving among blankets and sheets.

'So, you're ex-Army, right?'

'That's right,' Carl said. 'Now, about your neighbor—'

'Hold on,' Clemmons said, smiling but not looking too friendly. 'Here's the deal. I'll answer some of your questions, but first I gotta couple of my own. You see, I don't get to talk to too many ex-killers.'

Carl stared right back at him. 'I can't see why, since you're so bright and charming.'

'Hah hah, very good,' he snorted. 'You're right, I'm not bright and charming, and there's a reason. I'm going to school over at MIT to keep dear old Dad happy and to keep my butt away from my local draft board. But to tell you the truth, I'm more concerned about my butt than my dad. There's something wrong when a guy can't go to school and concentrate on getting ahead, instead of worrying about getting drafted and being sent to DC or San Diego or Omaha, and eight weeks later, start puking and seeing his hair fall out.'

Carl said carefully, 'It's been said that every precaution's taken.'

'Yeah, I'm sure. So tell me, when were you drafted?'

'Listen, Troy, this is all very interesting—'

He held up his cigarette. 'C'mon, newspaper reporter, you

can dish it out but you can't take it? Just a question or two more and then you can ask away.'

Carl thought, to hell with it, let's leave this jerk be, but then he thought about another jerk from last night, saying those words: goddam quota baby. He said, 'I wasn't drafted. I joined. In 1960.'

Clemmons sat up. 'You joined? You actually joined the Big Green? Why in hell did you do that?'

'Because my dad couldn't send me to MIT, or anywhere else, that's why.'

He took a drag off the cigarette. 'So. Where were you when JFK and his boys toasted half the world?'

'Overseas.'

'See anything?'

'Nope.'

'And where did you go when the good general brought everyone home?'

'California. Relief and recovery. I stayed there until I was discharged, and since I could type, I ended up at the *Globe*.'

Clemmons smiled. 'Lucky you. Wouldn't it be nice if Uncle Sam got jobs for everybody.' He paused. 'Now, fair's fair. Ask away.'

'Your neighbor, Merl Sawson. What did you know about him?'

He shrugged. 'Not much. Sad old guy, mostly kept to himself. I've lived here two years and I saw him maybe a half dozen times. Did some nice things every now and then. Like bringing in the mail if it was raining and shoving it under my door. Or shoveling the sidewalk out front during the winter. Once he complained about my music being too loud, but I could hardly blame him. He didn't sleep well.'

'How did you know that?'

'Nightmares, man,' Clemmons said. 'Every few weeks he'd let loose with a nightmare, start screaming. Sometimes his dog would join him, howling away. Christ, what a mess. Really made you sit up in bed, make your heart pound. One night I was out partying and came in late. His screaming was so loud I thought someone was strangling him. The door was unlocked and I was drunk enough to go in and check on him. The dog was hiding in the corner and he was thrashing around on the bed, and when I flipped on the light he woke up. He was really embarrassed, shocked that I was there, and I kinda sobered up and got the hell out.'

Carl took a few notes. 'What was he shouting about?'

Clemmons scratched at his chin. 'Same thing, over and over again. Something about a guy named Caz. He was yelling at him, something about it was time to go. Yeah, that's right. "Caz, goddam it, we gotta get going. We gotta leave. We're running out of time." Over and over again. And he was really screaming it, his voice all high-strung.'

'And you never found out who Caz was, or why Merl was shouting like that?'

'Nope. In fact, the time I went into his place, that was only a couple of weeks ago, just before he got killed.'

'And did you hear anything the day he died? Argument with somebody in his place? Shouting? Gunshots?'

'Nope,' Clemmons said. 'I was away for a couple of days.'

'Doing what?'

He smiled, and Carl saw that his teeth needed brushing. 'None of your business.'

'You talk to the cops after they found the body?'

'Hah. That's a good one. More like they talked and I listened, even though they didn't talk much.'

'They didn't ask you a lot of questions?'

'Just a couple. Y'know, did you do it? Do you know who might have done it? You selling any drugs? Crap like that. Truth is, it seemed . . . I don't know. It seemed like they were just going through the motions.'

Going through the motions. Sure. If the murder didn't count, why not just go through the motions? He scribbled a few more notes. 'Did he have any visitors, anybody else in his apartment?'

Clemmons took a final drag off his cigarette, stubbed it out in the ashtray, and resumed talking, not even looking at Carl. 'You know, I sure as hell have been talking a lot, and I don't particularly like it. I don't know you and I don't know where you're coming from, and I sure as hell don't know if I can trust you.'

'What do you mean by that?' A motion caught Carl's eye, and he saw the long legs moving again on the bed, kicking off the covers. He saw that the woman in the bed wasn't wearing a stitch of clothing.

'I mean I think I've said about as much as I want, that's what.' Clemmons was looking over at him. 'Got it?'

Carl thought about this bitter young man, and the rest of his equally bitter generation. Their choices were limited: the draft, a connected job, or something with relief and recovery. And to know with a gnawing frustration that just ten years ago there had been more choices, more music, more food, and more freedom.

Carl said, 'Tell you what. Here's something you might use. Then you can decide whether I'm worthy of more information. You know Division Six police station? Well, three Army trucks pulled up there today with a couple squads of soldiers. Looks like a raid might be going off tonight.'

Clemmons seemed to tense up. 'Why are you telling me?'

'Thought you might be interested. You, or some of your friends.'

'You're wrong,' he said, getting up from the floor. 'But thanks for telling me, anyway. Look, here's what happened. It sounds crazy but I heard him talking to someone in his apartment, a week or so ago, his voice real low. I was bringing down a magazine that got delivered to me by mistake. I couldn't make out anything but I heard the visitor say something twice, the same thing.'

'And what's that?'

He looked around, as if concerned the woman sleeping in the next room might hear him, and said, 'He said, "He lives." Twice. Like he was making a point. Strange, right?'

Carl kept his notebook closed, but knew he'd jot this down once he got outside. 'Mr. Townes, the landlord, was he the visitor?'

'No, Townes was outside, sweeping the sidewalk. This guy was somebody else. Somebody different. And believe me, Merl didn't get too many visitors. You know, that Caz character might be tied into it, 'cause I thought I heard Merl mention that name again.' Clemmons walked the length of the room. 'Look, are we done here? I've got some things to do.'

Carl dodged piles of clothing and old newspapers on the way out. 'Sure. Have to study for an exam?'

'Hell no,' Clemmons said, scratching at his beard again, grinning. 'I've got some phone calls to make, some people to see. About a raid tonight.'

Carl sat in his car taking notes. Yesterday Merl Sawson had been just a lump of cold flesh on a bed and a memory of a quick outdoors meeting, a shaking hand holding a list of names, words about dark conspiracies and the future. Now he was something more. Somebody who was once alive, who once talked and breathed, had bad dreams, was a veteran, and knew someone named Caz. And even had a mystery meeting. How convenient. Until someone had pumped a couple of bullets into the back of his head.

He didn't care what Detective Malone had said. He knew messy. Clemmons's apartment was messy. Merl's was messy only because someone had trashed it, looking for something.

Robbery? Then why not take the prewar television set? It had only been the last year or two that television production had begun again. That old Zenith set was worth something. So it hadn't been robbery. Maybe somebody was looking for something. Something connected to that list of names?

Carl made a few more notes. He didn't make too much of the 'He lives' statement. Troy Clemmons seemed to enjoy chemical stimulation, and who knows how trashed he had been when he had listened outside the door, and who knows who Merl had been talking to. 'He lives.' He doubted Merl was part of the JFK cult. He was a vet, after all. But the fact was, he had been talking to someone. And the landlord, Townes. He'd occasionally had lunch with Merl, and had made the call to the police. Surely Townes knew more about Merl and his background, knew if there were any more friends or family in the Boston area.

This murder sure was screwy. The body was pulled out the rear to avoid photographs. His story had been spiked. Clemmons said the cops seemed ho-hum in their questioning, and even Detective Malone had said as much, that this case wasn't going to get worked. And Merl had come to him, had come to Carl Landry looking for help, with that list of names. Now he was dead.

Still, let's be real, he thought. After all, this was another banner year for homicides in the Hub, and at a time when the current national death rates and the results of the 1970 census were both kept secret because of national security, well, if life wasn't cheap, it certainly wasn't worth much.

Maybe that's all. Maybe he should forget about it.

He looked at his watch. It was one-thirty. He had ninety minutes to do a story on a press conference that he had just missed.

FOUR

AN HOUR AFTER RETURNING to the newsroom, George motioned him over. Carl was surprised to see George stand up and say, 'Come along, Carl. If your busy schedule permits. My office.'

The office. Due to George's position and experience, he rated an office with a door but he hardly spent any time there. George always said that the real work was done out in the newsroom. The last time Carl had been in George's office had been months ago when he gave the wrong name to a city councilor and the story slipped through the copy desk. This meeting promised to be just as fun as that one. He took a deep breath, put both hands in his pants pockets.

The office was small and dusty, and the desk was the opposite of the one out in the metro section. It was clear of papers and debris, occupied only by a framed photo of a young girl, her hair done up in braids – George's niece, Tracy. There were no framed *Globe* front pages on the walls. Carl took a chair as George settled his bulk across from him.

George unrolled three sheets of paper. 'I got your story here on the mayor's press conference about the anti-orfie gang initiative. It reads like it was written from a press release and a couple of phone calls to city hall. Doesn't sound like you were there. Am I wrong?'

Carl knew what George was looking for. 'You're absolutely right. I wasn't there.'

'From the time I told you to the time you left the newsroom this morning, did you forget about the press conference?'

'No.'

'So what were you doing?'

'I was working on a follow-up. On the old vet's murder, out in East Boston.'

George scratched at a hairy ear and said, 'Now I'm confused, Carl. I told you to leave the vet murder alone, and I told you to cover the press conference. So what do you do? You cover the murder and leave the press conference alone. Am I missing anything here?'

'There's a story there, George, in the vet's murder, and that's what I was working on. I lost track of the time and I missed the conference, but I didn't do it out of spite. I did it because I was working a story, not because I was goofing off.'

'Even when I told you to leave the story alone?'

'It's still a story.' He knew he was digging himself into a hole, and didn't care. Merl's death *was* worth a story, damn it.

George tapped his fingers on the empty desk and said, 'Carl, you've done fine work for metro. And I hope you'll continue to do good work. But this is a real screwup. Understand?' He motioned to a filing cabinet. 'See that top drawer? It's filled with letters and résumés from newspaper reporters and journalism grads from all over the country. All looking for a job at the *Globe*. Hell, we could fire the entire newsroom every month and still have enough qualified people to replace them. So don't screw up again.'

'I won't.'

'Good.' George opened up the top drawer of the desk and withdrew a sheet of paper. 'I hope you don't have any serious plans for tomorrow night, it being Saturday and all, but I have an assignment for you. See? I have it all written on a piece of paper so you don't forget it.'

He slid the paper across the desk and Carl picked it up, sparing a quick glance as George continued. 'You see, I want to make sure in my mind that I can assign you a story and feel confident that you'll do it. So here's the assignment. Tomorrow night, six P.M. Reception at the British consulate. The British consul's presenting a check to the mayor for the start of the winter campaign of Bundles for Boston.'

'That sounds like a story somebody from features could do.'

'Right you are,' George said, grinning as only a newspaper editor can do when chewing out a reporter. 'Hell, even one of our copy boys could do this story with his eyes closed. But I want you to do the story, Carl. It's all yours. Get there in plenty of time to take good notes. Find out what's going to be in the bundles this winter. See if they're sending over any more of that awful English sausage. Good human interest stuff like that. Think you can handle it?'

Carl folded the piece of paper in half, and then in quarters. He wondered why he wasn't angry at George, and glanced down at the framed photo of the young girl. 'I'll take care of it.'

'Good. Now get back to the newsroom. Sure you can find your way?'

Carl got up. 'Without a doubt.'

George smiled again and leaned back in his chair, arms held wide open. 'See? I'm already regaining my confidence in you, Carl.'

Usually the noise in the newsroom was reassuring and Carl could block it out and concentrate on what was on his desk and in his typewriter. Not this time, though. The sounds seemed to clatter around in his head and make his teeth hurt, and he wanted to leave. But not now. Everyone had seen him enter George's office and then come back, so everyone also knew he had been reamed out. He didn't want to give anyone any satisfaction by seeing him bail out. To hell with them.

He unfolded the piece of paper. A puff piece that he could have handled in the first month of his job, no problem at all. The first month. Fresh out of the Army, wearing the first civilian suit he had owned since joining up in 1960. When he had left he had been eighteen and from Newburyport, a little fishing town up on the northern tip of Massachusetts. Dad worked for the city in public works, his mom was a secretary in the school system, and his younger sister, Sarah, read strange books of poetry and tried to learn to play the guitar. His own grades had been so-so and, like his cousins and uncles, he decided to join up before getting drafted. See a bit of the world and maybe learn a trade along the way. He also felt that with JFK in the White House – he had no doubt he would beat Nixon in the fall – he could be part of something new, something exciting.

He had also had some half-formed inklings of being a writer but both Mom and Dad had laughed at the idea. Get some real-world life before you try any of that, they had said. Sarah shook her head at his joining the Army and said, 'You're too linear, Carl. That's your biggest fault. You don't see the shadings, the story behind the story.' And getting ready to take a bus into Boston, so he could take a train to boot camp, he had said, 'And what's your biggest fault, little sister?' She had said, smiling faintly, 'My fault is that I want to change the world, and I want to do it tomorrow.'

Someone cleared his throat. He looked up. It was Jack Burns, dressed in an orange shirt and blue jeans.

Carl said, 'You look like you're off to another one of your hippie concerts. Or a whorehouse on the South Shore.'

'Matter of fact, I am,' he said. 'Going to a concert, that is. But mind if I have a seat?'

'Go ahead.'

Jack dragged a chair over and sat down. 'Sorry you had a bad time of it with George. But it's not his fault. George is a bit of a goof but he's all right as newspaper editors go.'

'Sorry, I don't understand. What isn't his fault?'

Jack looked around and then looked back and continued, his voice lower. 'I mean the fuss over your story. The one that didn't run.'

It seemed to Carl like the entire newsroom had gone quiet, and that the only thing that existed was the few feet of space around his desk. 'Go on,' he said.

'Your homicide story. It got spiked because of oversight.'

Carl stared at Jack. 'George told me he held it because of space.'

'Jesus, which potato truck did you fall out of?' Jack rolled his eyes in the direction of Cullen Devane's office. 'They always say a story gets killed because of space. Our efficient censor read the story and it got a spike through its heart like a goddam vampire.'

'How do you know this?'

Jack winked. 'Let's say people owe me favors. I get comp tickets to quite a number of concerts, and for those I don't attend, I like to spread the wealth. A friend in composing, um, he and I were having a drink at the Sod last night after you left and he told me that your story was on its way to being typeset when the word came down to pull it. From the good major himself.'

Carl realized that his own voice was as low as Jack's. 'And do you know why?'

'Do you think people would last long at this newspaper if they ask too many questions of the oversight editor? You should go down to the library and see Grace. Read the particulars of the Martial Law Declaration in '62 and National Emergency Declaration back in '63.'

'Jack, I've read them both. Who here hasn't?'

'Then read them again, my friend. Check out the subparagraph on press oversight. Our dear major has this newspaper by its short hairs, and his brothers have similar holds on every newspaper, magazine, and radio and television station in this glowing land of ours.'

Carl spared a glance at Devane's office. The door was closed. 'Funny. This is the first time one of my stories has been spiked by oversight.'

Jack patted him on the arm. 'Well, congratulations on losing your cherry. I've lost track of the times my stuff's been spiked – usually it's over reprinting some half-literate rocker's lyrics for a review, when they're deemed obscene or seditious.'

Carl looked again at the closed door. 'Maybe I should meet up with the oversight editor, see what's going on.'

The other man shook his head. 'You know that's not smart, Carl. Just let it be.'

'Any guess on why my story got spiked?'

Jack shrugged. 'Could have been anything. Maybe the dead vet was a personal friend of someone in the Northeast Military District and the word came down to spare the family and friends. Or, most likely, someone from the Boston police asked Devane to hold it as a personal favor; there are so many homicides this year, maybe the cops are trying to tone down the coverage. Then, of course, there's the least likely explanation.'

'Which is?'

He smiled, leaned forward. 'Maybe it was spiked because of what they always say – for reasons of national security.'

After a quick cafeteria lunch he was back at his desk, thinking about his spiked story. Who would care about a retired vet, killed in his home in East Boston? It didn't make sense.

But someone connected with oversight sure as hell cared. He picked up a copy of the day's *Globe* and searched through the first section, looking for the 'Bleep You' box. In the first years after the war, every newspaper and magazine had a little box explaining that it was being published under emergency censorship conditions. Eventually it became known as the 'Bleep You' box, and eventually most newspapers and magazines dropped it. Censorship – or oversight as it was politely called – became as much a part of newspapers as paper and ink, and no one bothered reporting on that every day.

Except for a handful of what passed as liberal newspapers – the *Globe*, the *Los Angeles Times*, and the reconstituted *New York Times*, published these past eight years from Albany. There. Today in the *Globe* it was on page six:

> To our readers: The stories appearing in today's *Boston Globe* have been cleared by the U.S. Army under the provisions of the Martial Law Declaration of 1962 and the National Emergency Declaration of 1963.

In the ranks of protest, it wasn't much, but there it was. He looked up from his desk. The door to Major Devane's office was open and he was striding across the newsroom, heading to the news desks. Everyone in the room, except Carl, suddenly found their attention focused on their phones or typewriters. But Carl watched the confident way he walked and handled himself, and his utter ease at talking to the editors, deciding on his own which stories would live, which stories would die. Carl thought about getting up and grabbing that man by the arm, to demand an explanation.

Instead, he grabbed his notebook and coat, and left.

Not much of a protest either, but he would see what he could do.

Merl Sawson's landlord didn't want to talk, but Carl wormed his way into Andrew Townes's apartment by using the old 'can I use your bathroom?' trick and found himself standing in the clean kitchen, notebook in his back pants pocket, trying to memorize everything Andrew was saying. The landlord was dressed in gray slacks and an old black sweater with leather patches on the elbows and looked about twenty pounds underweight. His eyes shifted constantly, like he was expecting the police to come barreling through the door at any moment, to arrest him for the seditious crime of talking to a newspaper reporter. As he spoke he had the odd habit of touching his gray-black hair every few moments, as if afraid of looking untidy.

'I'm telling you, I don't think I should be talking to you, that's all,' Townes said.

'Why not?' Carl asked. 'I'm just looking for some information on your neighbor for a story. What's the harm in that?'

Townes looked cross. 'That's what you told me yesterday. And when I looked in the paper there was no story.'

'Space problems,' Carl said. 'Happens all the time. That's what happened to my story on Merl Sawson. They didn't have room.' Which was true, if one listened to George the metro editor and not Jack the music critic.

'Still,' Townes hesitated. 'One does hear things . . . Look. Will you be using my name?'

'Absolutely not.'

'And when we're done, you'll leave me alone?'

'Until it comes time to renew your *Globe* subscription, you'll never see me again.'

Townes was quick. 'What do you mean by that?'

So much for humor. 'It's a joke, that's all. Mr. Townes, tell me what you know about Merl. How long had he been living here?'

'He moved in about four years ago. I've been here since '64, and I was looking to rent out the middle floor. The previous tenants moved out to Washington State, and Merl came in and I took him on right away. I could have rented to some college students, but . . . they get tiring after a while.' Townes looked up at the ceiling, his eyes glaring. 'When Mister Clemmons moves out, I can tell you it'll be a long time before I rent to another student again.'

'And are you keeping an eye on his dog?'

'Merl's dog? No, the dog died some weeks ago. Old age, I think. Poor Merl was quite broken up about it. Couldn't talk about his dog afterwards without weeping.'

'Oh. Well, did he have friends, visitors, relatives?'

Townes slowly rubbed his hands together. 'He made mention once of a sister in Detroit. That's it. And I know he was a widower, from the war, I believe.'

'And he was a veteran, right? Did you know what branch of the service?'

'Army, though he never really discussed it much.' Townes leaned against the sink. 'Funny thing is, I didn't know till a couple of years after he moved in that he was a veteran.'

'He didn't use his veteran's preference when applying for the apartment?'

'Nope, not at all. I asked him later about that and he said something about how he felt better doing things on his own.'

'And you said he never talked much about his service years?'

'Oh, we played cribbage some nights and I asked him off and on. About the most he ever said was that he kept track of some important papers, that's all. Paper and ink. And then he'd just change the subject. Once, though, after a couple of beers, he said that he fought from behind a desk and except for one dreadful mistake, he had done a damn fine job. Later, he said he shouldn't have even told me that, and asked me never to repeat it. Though I suppose it doesn't matter much now.'

Carl wished he had his notebook out but he didn't want to spook Townes. Once a source started talking, you started milking, and you never let up, as much as you could.

Carl asked, 'Did he ever mention a friend of his, a man named Caz?'

'No, not at all. Look, we never talked much about anything, except for the weather and the price of food and the Red Sox. He was a great fan of the Red Sox. We were just a couple of old guys with a lot of time on our hands. In fact, I can only once remember him mentioning anything about politics.'

'When was that?'

Townes's eyes blinked a few times and he touched his hair again. 'You promise never to use my name, right? Oh, lord, I should have kept my mouth shut.'

'Mr. Townes, just this once and then I'll leave. All right?'

He moved away from the sink. 'Last year, when meat rationing was ended, I got a nice piece of flank steak and I asked Merl down for dinner. We watched the news as we ate and there was a segment showing General Curtis getting an award from some veterans group. I said something about the general looking good for his age, and Merl said, why not. He has no heart or soul, so why shouldn't he look good for his age. And that was that.'

'Nothing more?'

'Nothing more,' he said firmly. 'And now you really must leave.'

There wasn't much more he could do. Carl headed for the door, Townes right behind him, and as Carl reached the end of the hallway Townes said, almost shyly, 'Can I ask you a question?'

'Sure,' Carl said. 'What is it?'

Townes glanced up again. 'His belongings. Do you think the police will come for them?'

Carl found he felt sorry for the old man. 'No, I'm afraid not, Mr. Townes. You should just . . . well, after a while, you could take what you want and box up the rest, see if his sister or any other relative shows up.'

Townes's face seemed to darken. 'I see. Yes, I suppose that makes sense. You know, this house once belonged to my mother and father. When I moved out of here I swore I would never come back to East Boston. I worked for TransAmerica Bank in New York City as an auditor, until the war. Then I and everyone else in that bank was out of a job and I came back here and waited. And waited, and waited. My parents, you see, were on vacation in Florida that October. They never came back, and after a year I boxed up their things and put them in the basement.'

Townes gave a quick, barking laugh that was not humorous. 'Lucky for me, there's room in the basement for additional boxes. Ever think of that, Mr. Landry? All the tens of millions of boxes out there, holding personal possessions of people who don't exist anymore. That would be a hell of a day, if this country decided to hold a gigantic yard sale. Think of all those dusty boxes, being opened up after ten years!'

Carl realized that although earlier he had wanted into this apartment in the worst way, now he couldn't get out of it fast enough.

He parked in the alleyway behind his apartment building, tired and hungry and knowing he hadn't gotten much out of his visit with Townes, except for a queasy feeling that had settled into his chest. The fact Merl didn't talk much about his Army days was no big deal. Neither did Carl, unless forced. And as far as Carl knew, he was sure that a great number of people – though probably not a majority – didn't particularly like General Ramsey 'The Rammer' Curtis. As for his own opinion, well, it depended on the day of the week. Sometimes he could see Curtis for what he really was, a puppet master, pulling the strings of the President and the senators and the congressmen. Other times, he remembered the general right after the war started, and how he managed to end it before too much death came to the country. Either way, whatever he thought didn't make much difference.

From the shadows behind a dumpster came a squeaking noise, and he turned and saw a man, dressed in a sweatshirt, an old Army fatigue coat, tattered pants, and knee-high rubber boots, carefully maneuvering a full shopping cart down the brick-paved alley. It was Two-Tone, the homeless person on the block. Everyone called him Two-Tone, but Carl found that he could not say it to his face, not to a fellow vet. He had found out the man's real first name – William – and that was what he used. As he got closer Carl said, 'Evening, William, everything pretty quiet here tonight?'

'Well, it seems to be, though no one ever knows.' Two-Tone wheeled the shopping cart closer. He was smiling as he reached Carl, his eyes wandering aimlessly around, as if he couldn't stand to stare at any one thing for more than a few seconds. The right side of his face was bearded, the black hair streaked with gray. The other side of his face was a furrowed mass of burn scars. Tonight, he had on a black wool watch cap over his head, but in the summer, with the watch cap off, the same was true of his skull: half bald with burn tissue, half filled with hair. Two-Tone's left hand was also withered and scarred. He had been in Cuba in '62, and was one of the few survivors from the invasion that Carl had ever met.

Carl gave him two quarters. 'Sure appreciate you keeping an eye on things.'

The quarters were pocketed with a friendly nod, the eyes still moving. 'My old Army training, Carl. Always keep an eye on the terrain.'

'And what's the terrain telling you tonight?'

Two-Tone looked about for a second and said in a loud whisper, 'There's trouble afoot, that much I can tell you.'

'What kind of trouble?'

'Official-looking, that's what. Some men were here today, poking around the block. Checking things out.'

'Probably just city workers. Tax assessors, building inspectors, that sort of thing.'

He shook his head. 'No, they were too well dressed. And too determined in their work. Not like guys on the city clock. I thought at first they were looking for me, so I hid for a while.'

'And why would they be looking for you, William?'

The cart was wheeled closer. 'They want to know where my shelter is.'

'They do, do they?'

'Sure they do.' Two-Tone gave him a conspiratorial look. 'It's near here, about ten minutes or so. That's how much warning we'd get, if there's another war. Ten minutes and I'm deep and safe and buried when the warheads come. I won't be caught out in the open again.'

Carl tried to be polite. 'You don't think there's going to be another war, do you? It's been ten years since Cuba. A lot of things have changed.'

'Ole mother Russia is a big place, Carl. Just you see. There's hidden forces there, hidden arsenals, and one of these days, some of those Reds are going to get their revenge. You wait and see. You believe me, don't you, Carl?'

He thought of mother Russia, that destroyed and shattered country, where starvation and madness still reigned, and the only people who had a chance to live were those who could make it to a UN refugee camp along the borders of the old country. No more industry, no more large cities, no more government. Just tribes of people, trying to survive in muddy villages that could have existed in the Middle Ages, a decade after an entity called SAC – the Strategic Air Command – had obliterated their nation from the earth.

'Sure, William,' he said. 'I believe you. It's a big place.'

Two-Tone nodded in satisfaction, looking to the right and

to the left. 'That's right. And you should be ready, too.' He leaned in and said, 'I'd let you into my shelter when the time comes, but I think it'd be too crowded. You got some canned food?'

Carl smiled. 'Sure do. And bottled water.'

'Then that settles it. Time the sirens sound, you be on your doorstep with your stuff and I'll take you with me. Deal?'

'Deal.' Carl turned to leave and then something came to him, something he had just been thinking about. No real reason, just curiosity. 'Two— Unh, William?'

'Yes?'

'I'd like to ask you something, if you don't mind.'

'Sure, go right ahead,' he said, leaning on the shopping cart.

'General Curtis. What do you think of him?'

'Hmmm,' Two-Tone said, reaching out to rearrange one of his trash bags. 'The Rammer. Not a bad man, even if he's Air Force. I don't hold that against him. I know that he's not liked for what's he done since Cuba, but you know what?'

'What's that?'

Something a bit terrifying occurred, as Two-Tone stood up and his voice sharpened and his eyes seemed to bore right into Carl. It was like the man who was once an Airborne officer had returned. 'He saved me and a bunch of my buddies, that's what. After the invasion went to the shits and the Russians used their tactical nukes, some of the high mucky-mucks that weren't in DC wanted to write us off. We were contaminated and most of us were wounded, and without prompt rescue, decon, and treatment, we'd all die. But he was acting chairman of the Joint Chiefs then and he ordered the Navy to come pull us off the beaches, and they did, hundreds of us. What a horrible and honorable day that was,

Carl. We were all there, wounded and dying, but we still had our discipline, we weren't going to show the Navy that we were just a mob. So we stayed in line, letting the worst wounded leave first, with guys out on the perimeter, putting down harassing fire so what was left of the Cuban army or the Soviets couldn't get to us. He got us all off, Carl, all of us who were still alive. So you won't hear me say anything bad about the general. He's an honorable man, Carl, one of the last honorable men alive.'

Carl was shocked at the change in Two-Tone's demeanor, and all he could say was, 'I understand, William.'

'Good,' he said, and then it was like a part of his insides collapsed, and the old Two-Tone came back. He started moving away, shopping cart wheels squeaking. 'You have a good night, now.'

'I will.'

He had gone a few yards when Two-Tone shouted after him. 'Carl! One more thing!'

Carl turned. 'Yes?'

'Your canned goods,' Two-Tone said. 'Don't bring any beans. If we're cooped up for a month in my shelter, last thing I want is you and me farting at each other. It would be awful.'

He gave him a half wave. 'Understood. No beans.'

'Good,' he said again, and as Carl went around to the front of his apartment building, the squeaking noise from the shopping cart seemed to get louder and louder.

FIVE

THE BRITISH CONSULATE WAS ON STATE
STREET, and after parking his car he had to walk a couple
of blocks to get there. His wrists itched from the tweed jacket
he was wearing. His reporter's notebook was in an inside
pocket, and his shoes felt stiff as he walked. Besides the tweed
jacket, he owned a lonely black two-piece suit that he had
bought after being mustered out in '68, but that article of
clothing was appropriate only for wakes and funerals.

This part of Boston was relatively thriving, with gift shops,
restaurants, and state offices in renovated brick buildings.
Traffic was backed up at the lights and there were some
Japanese people in a tiny tour group, probably looking for the
Freedom Trail. Everything looked fine for a Saturday night in
the up-and-coming city of Boston – now the largest port in
the northeast – but with his reporter's eye for detail and his
old soldier's habit of surveillance, Carl could see that things
still didn't fit. The shops mostly attracted state workers, port
employees, or tourists – prices were way out of line for the
average Bostonian. Most of the cars were old and rusted,
tailpipes spewing exhaust, and many of the stores had private

guards, on alert for orfie gangs prowling for smash-and-grab attacks. The average Bostonian passing Carl on the sidewalk looked tired, the men's clothes dull and shabby – elbow patches were now the rage – and the women's clothing looked like it came from 1950s New York. Most of the women were bare-legged, but they tried to look like they were wearing hosiery by inking a black line up the back of their legs.

The British consulate was in a newly constructed building, four-stories tall with a brick facade and elegant entrance. A black wrought-iron fence surrounded the yard and a British flag hung from a second-story flagpole. Two Boston cops were chatting it up with a plainclothesman who was probably consular security. Across the street, behind a police barricade, were an older man and woman. Both carried signs – the woman's said BRITS OUT OF NORTHERN IRELAND and her companion's sign said NO MORE COLONIALISM. BRITS OUT OF USA. They were ignored by everyone who walked by them. Boston was an old Irish town, with memories of feuds and revolutions and the iron rule by the British of their home country, but he knew from reading back issues of the *Globe* that the people had other memories as well. Like the grinding and starvation-plagued winters of 1962 and 1963, when aircraft from BOAC and the RAF landed at Logan every day, disgorging food supplies and doctors and nurses to supplement the Boston hospitals, to help treat the refugees streaming up here from Connecticut and New York City.

Dark times, times that were still very fresh in most people's minds, and which almost always crowded out older thoughts of the 1916 Easter Rebellion and the six counties of Northern Ireland, still under British rule. It wasn't that the Boston Irish didn't care anymore; they just had bigger things to worry about: feeding their children, or seeing their husbands or wives treated for cancer.

At the gate Carl flashed his press pass and his driver's license to the security man and Boston cops and then climbed the short flagstone path leading to the white-columned entrance. He knew there were people in Philadelphia and Congress who didn't like the British presence, but the Brits were still quite popular in lots of places. Their assistance after the war had made the difference between life and death for so many. He'd met some British officers in California in '63 and '64, and while he appreciated their suggestions, he, too, found that there was something irritating about their superior attitude, their spit-and-polish dress, the way they took their meals in their quarters. Somehow they couldn't entirely suppress their glee at being needed again by the Yanks, instead of just being the poor relations across the Atlantic.

But to be fair, he thought, there was that one British paratroop officer, the one who had spent a couple of days with his unit in California and then left Carl with a bottle of brandy. His name had been Kenneth something, and he hadn't been like his brethren. He had really seemed to care, had offered some good suggestions on how to do better patrols in the mountains. When he had left, he had shaken Carl's hand after Carl had thanked him. He had said, 'Don't mention it, old boy. Just consider it a little payback for your help with the Hun back in the forties.'

Carl stepped through the entrance and onto the polished marble floor. The room was crowded but he could see a wide stairway that led up to the left. Before him were a row of tables and another double set of doors, leading to a ballroom. It seemed like half of Boston was crammed into the two rooms. Among the guests, he was surprised to see, was Major

Devane from the *Globe*, in his dress uniform, talking to a couple of consulate officials. Carl elbowed his way to a reception desk, where a sweaty man in a red-trimmed British army uniform was passing out guest badges. Behind him on a wall were a set of five photographs – the largest, in the center, of course, was of the Queen. Then there was a picture of Prime Minister Edward Heath and one of Kim Redgrave, the British consul for Boston. The two other photographs were smaller, black-and-white, and trimmed with black crepe. They were photos of the British ambassadors who had been on duty at the UN in New York and on Embassy Row in Washington during that October ten years ago.

'Sir?' the soldier asked, though it came out 'Saaar?'

'Carl Landry, *Boston Globe*.' After a moment, the soldier passed over a name badge, sealed in plastic, which Carl pinned to the lapel of his jacket. He pressed through the double doors to the reception room. The ceiling was high and gilt-lined with elaborate carvings. British and American flags hung on the far wall, next to a larger portrait of the Queen. A string quartet was playing in one corner, and there was a din of conversation and some laughter. He figured the room held about two hundred people, and as he moved through them he spotted a long line of tables, covered with white tablecloths. His stomach grumbled as he saw the food laid out on fine dishware. Slices of roast beef, cheeses, hard rolls, jumbo shrimp, grapes, apples, and pears. It had been a long time since he had seen a spread like this.

He ate three jumbo shrimp and then went back and made a sandwich with a large roll, some slices of roast beef, and chunks of cheese. It was tender and moist and tasted very good. The food he usually ate was either canned or frozen; fresh food, for the average person in Boston, was a once-or-twice-a-week treat, and Boston was doing better than a lot of other places.

He noticed how many people were eating, and it made sense. No wonder it was so crowded. This was the British consulate, after all, and good food in plentiful portions made this a high point for whatever was left of Boston society. While he was trying to decide about making another sandwich, the crowd near him parted and Mark Beasley came up to him, cameras hanging off him as if he were a poorly decorated Christmas tree. He had a sandwich in each hand.

'Christ on a crutch, Carl, will you look at this feast?' Mark said. 'Here I was, I thought I was being punished by George by being sent out here tonight. Man, if I knew how much food was gonna be here, I would've volunteered.'

'Don't forget to put those sandwiches down when picture time comes, Beast.'

'Oh, don't worry about that, and I won't be putting the sandwiches down anywhere; they'll be going into my pockets.' He came closer and winked. 'When I leave here tonight, I'm gonna have two days' worth of food stuffed in my coat. And you should do the same.'

Carl laughed. 'You know, I just might.' The Beast moved down to one end of the long table and Carl saw one of the white-jacketed waiters behind the table whispering something to a companion, both of them smiling. The taller of the two smiled more directly at him as he went up to the serving table.

'Help you with something, sir?' the waiter said, with just the slightest trace of condescension. Carl paused, and then looked back again at the crowded room, feeling again that sense of irritation from his California duty. The British were well dressed, amiable, and barely touching the food available this Saturday night. The Americans had on their best clothes as well, but there was a discreet sense of shabbiness about them, like the clothes had been carefully mended and cleaned for many years. The Americans held full plates and laughed too loudly, like they were doing their best to say thanks to their British hosts. Ten years, he thought. Ten years ago it had been reversed. The Americans had been loud and rich and well fed, while their British cousins had been the ones with the lesser role. He knew the attitudes of the Brits, and while he couldn't blame them, it still rankled.

'Sir?' the waiter repeated.

Carl looked back at him, picked up an apple, and tossed it in the air. He caught it and deftly put it into his right-hand coat pocket.

'For later, if you don't mind,' he said.

'Not at all, sir.'

'Good,' Carl said, walking away, not wanting to see the smug smiles behind him.

A stage with podium and mike had been set up on one side of the room. A press area was marked off with gray duct tape and three television cameras had been set up, one for each of the Boston stations. Photographers were up front – including the Beast, who was still chewing as he unstrapped his cameras – and Carl stood with the print reporters. He recognized a reporter and photographer each from the *Boston Herald* and the *Christian Science Monitor*, and a couple of radio reporters. A few other press types were there that he didn't know, including a woman wearing a black dress cut just above the knees and a string of simple white pearls. She wore hosiery that would cost an American woman a week's wages, and her high-heeled shoes were polished to a reflective gleam. Her dark brown hair was done up in an elaborate knot at the base of her neck. She had a reporter's notebook and a fountain pen in her slim hands. When she turned and smiled at him, Carl blinked hard. She was the most beautiful woman he had seen in a long time.

By the time he thought to smile back, she had turned away and several men were stepping up on the stage. Carl got out his notebook. The show was about to begin.

A youngish man in a light gray three-piece suit announced in a cultured British voice that he was the press attaché for the British consulate in Boston, and that he was pleased to introduce Kim Redgrave, the British consul. When he stopped speaking there was a round of applause and the consul came up to the podium, giving a little half wave. A few steps behind him was another young man, this one carrying a long, wide piece of cardboard that he held close to his body. The consul was in his early forties, with a wide smile and a ruddy face, and the beginning of a pot belly that strained against the gray vest of his suit.

'I would like to thank all of you for coming out tonight to this wonderful event,' Redgrave said. He didn't read from notes. 'This evening marks something special for British residents in America, and for our people at home. For the past ten years, we have done what we could to ease the suffering which has scourged this land. Ten years after that dreadful war, the people of America are still in our thoughts and prayers. And the people of Boston have always had a special place in the hearts of many Englishmen . . .'

He paused for a moment, winked. 'Except, of course, for the matter of that little tea incident some centuries ago.'

Some polite laughter, and then there was a woman's voice

at his ear, the accent the same as the consul's. 'So sorry, but could I trouble you for a moment?'

He turned his head, noting with a pleased smile that it was the woman in the black dress who was talking to him. 'Go right ahead.'

'. . . as you helped us with Bundles for Britain in the 1940s, so we have helped you in return with Bundles for America, and our own local effort here, Bundles for Boston . . .'

She moved closer and Carl caught a whiff of perfume, something airy and wonderful that he wanted to remember for a long time. 'That red-headed man, behind Mayor Toland. Who is he?'

'Ty Keenan, city councilor and president of the Boston city council.'

'And what's he doing here?'

'Besides making the mayor angry?'

She laughed, a sound he decided he wanted to hear again.

'. . . through three world wars, we have formed an unshakeable bond that can only be strengthened as the years continue . . .'

She said, 'Please go on.'

'Ty wants to be mayor someday, and he wants everyone here to know that.'

'. . . so, tonight, on behalf of the British people, I'm pleased to announce the start of our annual winter relief effort, Bundles for Boston. And I truly hope that this will be the last time that the people of Boston and this great nation depend on our help, despite how eagerly we offer it. You have made great strides in the past ten years – we look forward again to having you as our equal partner in the world.'

Redgrave stepped back and his assistant came forward, handing him the white piece of cardboard. The consul flipped

over the cardboard, revealing it as a mock check, drawn on
Barclays of London and made out to 'The People of Boston'
in the amount of £10,000.

As Carl wrote down the amount he felt again a twinge of
anger. The least they could have done was convert it to
dollars, he thought. The consul presented the mock check to
the mayor of Boston, Franklin Toland, who was grinning as he
shook Redgrave's hand. The television cameras panned
across the stage as one, and flashbulbs went off. Carl was
amused at the sight of Ty Keenan trying to get into the photo,
and the way Mayor Toland gently pushed the consul across
the stage, using the check as a battering ram, so that Keenan
wouldn't appear in any of tomorrow's photographs.

Applause broke out and the woman's voice was at his ear
again. 'What do you think of that, what he said about this
being the last year? Do you think he really believes that?'

Carl said, 'Maybe. But other people would say not on your
life.'

'Why do you say that?'

'Some people would say he likes being consul of Boston,
and that the other consuls and the ambassador in this country like having their noses in our business, day in and day out,
helping run their former colony. And that being in charge of
a big chunk of our relief efforts means influence and power,
and people who have influence and power hate giving it up.
That's what some people would say.'

The mayor's jowly face was bright red and, unlike the
consul, he read from a much-folded piece of paper. His
scuffed dark brown shoes were almost obscured by his too-
long trousers, the bottoms of which dragged along the stage.

The mayor began, 'While your forefathers two hundred
years ago may not have been loved in this great country and

in this city, it's now true that their descendants have now won the true battle for the city of Boston, the battle for its citizens' hearts.'

The woman reporter – damn it, he still couldn't make out her name tag – said, 'That's quite a cynical point of view. What's your opinion?'

Mercifully, the mayor was to the point: 'And I am honored to accept this great gift from our cousins across the Atlantic, and I wish you to bring back to your Queen and your Parliament and Prime Minister Heath, our deepest gratitude.'

More applause, and Carl said, 'You can have my opinion, but only if I learn your name.'

'Oh, I'm sorry,' she said, and turned. Her name tag read, *Sandra Price, The Times*. 'But only my mother and great-aunt call me Sandra. Everyone else calls me Sandy.'

'Carl Landry, *Boston Globe*.' He shook her outstretched hand. 'I didn't know the *Times* had a Boston bureau set up.'

'Oh, we don't,' she said, talking louder as the applause continued. 'I'm here on a special assignment.'

'And what's that? Following around the mayor of Boston?'

Sandy smiled. 'Hardly. No, I'm here doing a story on the tenth anniversary.'

'Oh.' No reason to ask what tenth anniversary. 'Well, good luck to you.'

'Thanks,' she said. 'Now, then, you promised me your opinion. Now that you know my name, please go on.'

He looked at her closely, for some reason remembering an old cache of prewar fashion magazines that he had found in his apartment's closet when he moved in. He had spent an evening flipping through the damp and musty pages, looking at the photographs of the models. The American women then were well fed and smiling, their skin flawless, and there had been a sense of energy and eagerness about them, as if they knew they could do anything they wanted. Those American women hadn't worried about running out of food, or having their children fall sick from poor diet or radiation exposure, or finding out that their husbands were sterile. The few fashion magazines being published today emphasized how to create your own makeup from food dyes, and how to check that 'perfect mate's' background to make sure he hadn't spent time in a contaminated area.

Sandy looked like she belonged in the pages and the world of those prewar magazines, and he at once both envied and resented her. He couldn't remember the last time he had seen a woman so healthy and attractive.

'My opinion,' he started slowly. 'For what it's worth, I don't think it's healthy to have a relationship based on one party being a giver and the other party being a recipient. It builds up resentment on both sides, and resentment can lead to conflict.'

'Conflict?'

He remembered that overheard conversation at the *Globe* cafeteria between the two pressmen, about troop transports in Canada. 'Sure, conflict. Maybe it's time for the givers to stop giving, and let the other party make it on their own.'

'But we're just trying to build you up, make you a partner again.'

He smiled at her. 'A true partner, or a junior partner?'

She smiled back. 'That surely is not for either us to say right now, is it?'

She gently touched his elbow. 'I'm not usually so forward, but would you like to come to a consulate party, later on? After all these people leave, there's going to be a little private swank upstairs. Consider it my thanks for your help, and for your opinion.'

'I've got to get back to the newsroom, write up this story for tomorrow's edition.'

Again, that smile. 'Oh, we'll still be here when you've done that. I'll leave your name at the door. Deal, Mr. Landry?'

'Deal.'

He looked at his notebook. It was mostly blank. During the entire speechmaking he had hardly taken a single note. He saw the slim and elegant, well-dressed figure of Sandy Price trying to move through the mass of people around the consul, and he smiled as he saw the delicate woman use her elbows and a well-placed twist to get in front of the crowd.

The newsroom was practically deserted. Before he got to work, he checked his mailbox. Empty. Grace had said it would take a few days to get back to him on the list he had given her, but still, it was worth checking. Maybe tomorrow, but then again, maybe never. He hammered quickly at the typewriter, bringing back from memory the quotes and details of the night's events, doing his best to block out the smell, sights, and sounds of Sandy Price. As he gathered up his sheets to bring it up to the city desk – a weekend editor whose name he always forgot was on duty tonight – a copy boy came by and said, 'Bring those up for you, Carl?'

'Sure, Sam,' he said, carefully straightening out the four pages and handing them over. Sam Burnett was a bit older than Carl, dressed in jeans and a heavy blue T-shirt. He wore a Red Sox cap every day of the week. He was one of the brightest and most personable of the copy boys, and the oldest, though only in chronological age. His mental age was about fifteen.

'How's things,' Carl continued, getting up from his desk and grabbing his tweed coat.

'Oh, not too bad. I've been listening to the World Series on my mom's radio and I still can't believe the Sox lost it to the Tigers this year.'

'Who are you rooting for? Cincinnati?'

Sam frowned. 'Oh, I'm rooting for Detroit. I can't stand the National League.'

'Maybe next year, right?'

Sam nodded enthusiastically. 'Sure, next year, Carl. You bet. See you later, okay?'

'Okay.'

Sam scampered through the maze of desks and chairs on his way up to the city desk. As he watched Sam head out of the newsroom Carl had a grim fantasy; what if he brought Sam back with him to the British consulate and had Sandy interview him for her anniversary story. He wondered if she could keep up the proper British facade, the politeness and sincerity, if she came face to face with this particular veteran, this particular story. Ten years ago Sam had been a navigator aboard an Air Force B-52, directing the bomber to its target. Carl didn't know the details, but he could guess at what happened and how Sam had ended up here, in this veteran-reserved job, working as a copy boy, fetching coffee and sandwiches for the reporters and editors, always the same age, year in and year out.

Because who could blame Sam for wanting to be fifteen again, after helping his crewmates incinerate over a million human beings?

SIX

WHEN CARL RETURNED TO THE CONSULATE he was directed to a crowded meeting room on the second floor, a quarter of the size of the downstairs ballroom. Most of the people were British and he was glad that Major Devane wasn't there. Having the oversight editor so close would have put a damper on the rest of the evening. Even still, he felt odd and out of place as the well-dressed men and women eyed him as he made his way over to Sandy. He had never been with so many British people before, and he had the unsettling feeling that he was some sort of exotic creature on exhibit. He could guess at what they were thinking, and it didn't please him: here he was, the American male, responsible for death and terror in the old Soviet Union, in Cuba, and a half dozen other countries whose only crime was that they were in the fallout path of American-made nuclear weapons.

There was music from a stereo system set up by the bar, and some of the younger consulate staff – the men in mod suits with large lapels and wide neckties, and the women sporting short skirts and large hairdos – danced in one corner. Their smiles, too, were wide and their complexions were clean. He wondered if any one of them had tried to live, week after week, month after month, under food rationing and without any steady electricity.

'So glad you came,' Sandy said. 'Did you make your deadline?'

'With ten minutes to spare.'

'Good for you.'

'That music,' Carl said. 'What is it? I've never heard it before.'

Sandy said, 'Something French. Called disco. Care for some fresh air? It's getting too smoky in here.'

'Lead on,' Carl said. 'After all, this is your home turf.'

Another smile. 'Oh, it's not home, just a little part of Britain.'

She took him to the far wall, where a set of tall French doors led out to a balcony. She partially closed the doors behind her, cutting off most of the sounds of music and conversation. Carl could make out some of the night lights of Boston in the distance and a small, enclosed park below them.

'Oh, that's better,' she said, rubbing at her bare arms. 'All that smoke-smoke and yak-yak gets to you after a while, even if you are supposed to be a reporter and listening to what these people are saying.'

'Aren't you cold?'

'I'm fine at the moment,' she said. 'Right now I'm far too hot and it feels good to be outside.' She turned to him. 'So, Carl Landry, how long have you been at the marvelous *Globe*?'

'Four years.'

'And what did you do before then?'

'Worked for Uncle Sam.'

'Uncle . . . oh, I get it. In the services, then?'

'The Army. And after that, I was lucky enough to get on the *Globe*. And you, Sandy? How long have you been with the Thunderer?'

Even in the semidarkness, he noted her smile. 'Nicely done. Didn't know the *Times* nickname had crossed the Atlantic.'

'Lots of things make it across besides blankets and corned beef.'

'Yes. Well, the condensed version of the dull life of Sandra Pittwood Price. Grew up in London, an only child. Went to a ghastly public school – which you call a private school over here – and then I went to Oxford and spent an incredible amount of time learning about our glorious literary history, from Shakespeare to Milton. Truth be told, I had more fun with American writers, like Twain and London and Kerouac.'

'Sounds like fun.'

'Oh, I had a great time, but I could hardly wait to go down. Oxford is pleasant but also dusty and ancient. Sometimes it's too full of itself and I wanted to get out and start writing in the real world. Daddy, he works in Whitehall, pulled a string or two and here I am, at the *Times* and now in your neck of the woods. Tell me, do you always cover such affairs as our consulate's little bash?'

'Nope,' he said, leaning back against the black iron railing. 'I'm a city beat reporter. Go wherever my editor sends me, whether it's a traffic accident, fire, or police story.'

'And why did your editor send you here tonight?'

Carl smiled, enjoying the give-and-take with this beautiful young woman. 'He was punishing me.'

'What? Punishing you? Whatever for?'

'Because I'm stubborn, and because sometimes I don't do

what my editor tells me to do.'

She laughed at that. 'Then editors are the same, no matter what side of the Atlantic they live on. My editor feels that he can send me to the States for a week, and I'll have a five-part series right away. Fool. He has no idea what it's like over here.'

That sparked his curiosity. 'Tell me, what is it like, over here?'

'Sorry, I don't follow you.'

'Your impression,' he said. 'I don't mean to be rude. I'm just curious what you think.'

She seemed equally curious, but for different reasons. 'You're not joking, are you?'

'Absolutely serious. You're the first overseas reporter I've ever talked to. I'd like to know what kind of impressions you've gotten.'

Sandy rubbed at her arms again. 'Well, this is a first, me being interviewed by another reporter. First impressions. I always wanted to come to America, even after the war. I'm fascinated with your history, your cowboys, your rock-and-roll music. But I must admit, our newspapers make everything seem foul over here. I was half expecting to see rubble and starving people in the streets when I arrived. I was glad to see they've got it wrong, at least in Boston. The city seems small, with twisty streets and avenues, but on the other hand, it's quite busy, as though everyone is trying to get ahead. Please don't be offended, but I'm amazed at how dirty the streets and the pavements are.'

'No offense taken,' Carl said, feeling a temptation to help her rub her cold arms. 'When it's a struggle to feed a city every day, clean streets sometimes come last. What else?'

'Well, everyone I've talked to has been quite polite,

though not very forthcoming. I haven't had much success with any in-depth research. Sometimes, they just want to know things about me. Like what sort of food I eat, how our health system works, stuff like that. Are the streets safe, compared to Boston. Most don't believe me when I say our policemen don't carry guns.'

He found himself looking at her, again and again, and he forced himself not to stare. That was a problem, since she was so attractive. 'What other kind of impressions have you picked up?'

'Not much more than that, since I've not been here long. The highlight so far has been a day trip to Philadelphia. My editor wanted some nonsense about the new capital, and I managed to wangle a fifteen-minute interview with President Romney.'

Carl was impressed. Old George wasn't known for his one-on-one interviews with the domestic press. 'That's quite an accomplishment. What was it like?'

'Pretty mundane, really,' she admitted. 'We were in an office, like any other building in downtown Philadelphia, except for the Army and the Secret Service agents everywhere. He seemed a nice enough man but he was much more interested in talking about the construction of the new White House, and whenever I asked specific questions, he answered in vague terms, though ever so politely. What did he think of the Franco-German alliance? European affairs belong to the Europeans, he says with that grandfather smile of his. And what about Japan's growing influence in the Pacific? As with Europe, Asia can concern itself with Asia, he says. We have much work ahead of us and we need to focus on our own pressing problems, he says. And I ask, what do you say to those who claim General Ramsey Curtis still exerts undue influence in the nation's affairs?'

Carl felt his hands grip the balcony railing even tighter. 'I'm surprised his people didn't toss you out of his office at that one.'

She shrugged. 'Oh, I could tell they thought I was being awfully presumptuous, but he just chuckled and said that General Curtis was a retired and trusted adviser, one among many, and that this country owed him a debt of gratitude for his service during the Cuban War. I felt like he wanted to pat me on the head, and that was that. His chief of staff dragged me out so the President could get his picture taken with Miss California or some damn thing, and in another thirty minutes I was on a plane back to Boston.'

'Sounds like quite the trip.'

'Oh, one I'm sure you've been on before.'

He felt a slightly churlish feeling of embarrassment. 'No, in fact I haven't. Since I've been with the *Globe*, I've never been out of New England. Gas is rationed and all other travel's just too expensive. I don't cover politics or recovery, so I've never been to Philadelphia. Hell, I don't think I've even talked to anyone outside of New England. You need at least a week to schedule a long-distance telephone call.'

'Oh. Sorry. But to tell you the truth, Carl, you didn't miss much. Just a very busy city with too many people and offices. Besides that boring non-interview, the only real highlight of the trip was the flight back. I actually saw one of the New York craters. Eerie.'

Almost reflexively he looked around, to see if anyone was listening. 'Then the pilot must have been off course, to have gotten that close. Sandy, you've done more stuff in the past few days than the best guy we have on the *Globe* staff.'

'Really?' she said, moving closer to him. 'Too bad my editor won't believe me, even if I do use you as a character reference.'

'The crater,' he said, enjoying the sensation of her coming closer. Trying to get warm, he wondered, or just getting closer for closer's sake? 'What did you see?'

'Not much,' she answered. 'I was coming out of the loo. People on the right-hand side were whispering among themselves, and pointing out of the windows. I looked out and could barely make out the buildings in Manhattan. Then to the east, there was a wide, flat spot. Dark gray, as if one of the craters of the moon had been picked up and dropped down here. We passed it and then I noticed this well-dressed man sitting next to the window I was looking out of. He had his fists clenched up to his face, and he was weeping, really sobbing, but completely silent. Then the pilot came on and said something about our estimated arrival time, the weather in Boston, and reminded us that some National Security Act of some date forbids aerial photography. Then he thanked us for flying Pan Am. Eerie, quite eerie.'

'What an experience.'

'Do you think so? I want to do a lot while I'm here. Besides the man-on-the-street stuff, I want to interview General Curtis, I want to talk to some survivors of the Cuban invasion, and I want to visit Manhattan.'

'Why not fly to the moon while you're at it?'

'If the Germans let me, I will.' She moved closer again, and he could tell that she was trembling slightly. 'Don't underestimate me, Carl Landry of the *Boston Globe*. Many people have, and their underestimations have appeared in my paper the next day. You'll see, I won't leave here until I get what I want.'

———

Then it got cooler and Sandy offered to buy him a drink as they went inside. Before joining her, Carl excused himself and went down a side hallway, to a very small men's room. There was one stall and two urinals, and both urinals were being used by consulate officials who were giggling about something and unsteady on their feet. He went into the empty stall, closed the door and sat down. The urinals flushed and the bathroom's door opened and closed. The two men were replaced by two others. More murmurs of voices, and then a brief conversation began. One of the voices was high-pitched and sounded almost feminine. Carl lifted his feet and leaned against the stall, to hear better.

'. . . from Ottawa.'

'How did it go?'

'. . . bloody Canucks are fearful of reprisals, just for a change. Even with our air defense help, they think . . .'

'. . . can't really blame 'em, can you . . . living with these gangsters on your border . . .'

'. . . they should remember their duty as a member of the Commonwealth . . .'

'. . . well, once the Yanks get taken care of, then we can turn our attention to our Canuck cousins . . .'

There was some laughter, and then the urinals flushed and Carl was alone. When he lowered his feet to the floor, he found that they were trembling.

He came back to the party and Sandy was talking to two well-dressed men. When she noticed him approaching, she said something he couldn't catch and the men – the ones in the bathroom? – blended into the crowd and he lost sight of them. Sandy took care of the beer, and with a shout of 'Sandy, darling, there you are!' Carl found himself with the intense young man who was the press attaché – Douglas Harris – and the three of them moved to an end of the bar. The music had stopped so at least they didn't have to raise their voices. Sandy made the introductions and Douglas said, 'Well, Carl, what did you think of our little get-together tonight?'

'It was fine, very nice,' he said, sipping at the dark, warm brew. American beers were still weak and watery – the majority of the grain crop still going to bread and cereals – and he knew if he had more than one of these English beers, he'd end up sleeping under one of the serving tables. He looked around the crowd, wondering which two of these proper British gentlemen had spoken so lightly about 'taking care' of the Yanks. Something was up, something bad, and every instinct in his reporter's blood and his soldier's history told him to leave.

But then what to do? Call up General Curtis and say the British are coming, the British are coming? And had Sandy been talking to those two particular men, or just two other consulate officials? Take it easy, he thought. Enjoy the beer and the presence of this woman, and don't spoil it.

'This is my fourth time for this ceremony, y'know,' Douglas said. 'Four years I've been in the States, stationed in Boston. It's a beautiful city.'

Sandy said, 'Douglas fancies he's a native, don't you?'

Douglas raised his beer glass. 'Hardly, but I do enjoy your country, what little I've seen of it. The White Mountains up in New Hampshire are wonderful, and I can't get enough of Maine lobster, they're so much larger than ours.' He patted his stomach. 'Unfortunately, it all seems to have ended up here.'

'The rigors of a foreign posting,' Carl said. 'Be thankful you're not stationed in Paris. All those frog legs.'

They all laughed and Douglas said, 'Do you cover politics at all, Carl?'

'Nope. Strictly city beat. I'm here tonight' – he looked at Sandy's interested face and found himself liking the look – 'on a special assignment. Filling in for someone who couldn't come.'

'Oh. Quite.' The music started up again, a softer Beatles tune – 'Penny Lane' – that still made talking easy. 'I've always been interested in your politics. Last week Governor McGovern was in town for a rally. Were you there?'

'I don't follow politics that much.'

'And why's that?' Sandy asked.

He shrugged. 'Foregone conclusion. In a few weeks' time McGovern is going to be whipped by Rockefeller, and the Democrats will do poorly in Congress. In four years' time, the next Democratic candidate will get whipped, and so forth and so on, probably until the end of this century. That's why most people in this country still don't vote. What's the point?'

'Sounds like a fairly grim prediction,' Douglas said.

He kept talking, in spite of himself. Maybe it was the beer or the warm room or the fact that Sandy was watching his every move. He had a desire to show her that he was more than just a newspaper hound, that there was more to him than just a byline. Somehow, what Sandy thought of him seemed quite important.

'Does the phrase "waving the bloody shirt" mean anything to you?' he asked. He got blank looks from both of them and continued, feeling fine at knowing something these two Brits didn't. 'It comes from right after the Civil War, the second-bloodiest on American soil and following the assassination of a beloved president. The Democrats were mostly from the South and every time there was an election, some Republican candidate would wave a bloody shirt and point to it, saying, "here is the bullet hole put in here by a Democratic traitor." People had long memories about the Civil War and they voted with those memories. It was twenty years before a Democrat took office, Grover Cleveland in 1885.'

Sandy played with a paper napkin that had been left on the bar. 'So you think the bloody shirt's still effective.'

'Oh, of course it is, but it's not bloody,' Carl said. 'It's charred black and radioactive. Most people still believe that it was a Democratic president and a Democratic congress that got us into the Cuban War, and they still believe that, ten years later, and will keep on believing it for a long time. Oh, the Republicans aren't crass enough to be that direct. They use code words and phrases. They say that the Democrats are internationalists, that they want to get back into the UN and sign the disarmament treaties, give away our sovereignty, that sort of thing. Most people want to leave the world the hell alone, and they vote Republican. They promise continued recovery, more food on the tables, more ways of extorting aid from our British friends.'

Sandy asked, her eyes slightly downturned, 'And why won't the U.S. sign the disarmament treaties? You're the only nation in the world that still has nuclear weapons, those that weren't used during the Cuban War. The world is still afraid of America, Carl. Signing those treaties could go a long way to mending relations with the rest of us.'

He took another sip of the beer, enjoying the smoky taste and being asked questions that counted, questions that hardly came up in the newsroom. 'Because even with gasoline rationing and food shortages and martial law, with nuclear weapons we're still a nation to be reckoned with. Get rid of the nukes and allow UN inspection teams to crawl around our military bases . . . well, then we don't count. We'd just be Albania, with better roads.'

Douglas made to say something but he was interrupted by a shout of, 'Ah, here we go, then!' from a rumpled, older man with a red face and a gentle, slurred accent who joined them at the bar. 'Farley James, at your service,' he said, weaving slightly. 'The *Sun* of London, a real newspaper, not like that establishment toady that Sandy works for.'

Sandy introduced Carl and said, 'Farley, you old goat, at least I get paid well, and my stories don't run next to adverts for breast creams or sex aids.'

'Hah!' Harris said, punching the older man slightly on the shoulder. 'She's got you there, Farley. Don't pick a fight with a bigger newspaper. Your kind will always lose.'

Farley grinned good-naturedly, took a large swallow of his beer, and said, 'Landry, eh? Scribbler for the *Globe*?'

'That's what it says on the paycheck.'

'*Globe*. Not a bad paper compared to the rest, but then again, all of your papers are just so much trash, y'know.'

'Now, Farley,' Sandy started, and Douglas's smile had frozen on his face, like he wished he was back onstage a couple of hours before, worrying only about introducing the consul.

'No, I don't know,' Carl said, taking his time as he sipped from the warm beer, wondering how it would feel to punch this self-satisfied man in the nose. 'Care to elaborate?'

The older man leaned back against the bar, acting almost like he was on the bow of a ship that was rising up and down, and was afraid he was going to lose his balance. 'Look at the facts, ole man. Your newspapers used to be something, in this country and around the world, but now you've got a censor's nose in everything you write, which is mostly pap.'

He quietly belched. 'Fact is, everything here's trash. Can hardly wait to get out of this godforsaken hole and go back home. This place is falling apart, hurts one's eyes to see it, day after day. How can your country be great again if you're still under the thumb of a homegrown Napoleon, even if he is retired? How can you expect to be admitted as an equal among nations? Christ alive, America used to *be* something. People looked up to you. They admired your government, your Bill of Rights, hell, your Coca-Cola. You have to be great again!'

Douglas tried to step in. 'Some would say their greatness is in their recovery, Farley. After all the damage they suffered—'

'Bah,' he said, waving a hand dismissively. 'Look at the Nips and the Krauts, what we did to them last time round. Flattened those bastards from one end to the other, and look who's nipping at John Bull's heels, not more than twenty or so years later. This place is still falling apart, and I don't mean buildings or streets. I mean politics, governance. Carl, you Yanks can't afford to put your head in the sand. You have to go out there, take back your role as world leader. You should be strong. You shouldn't be an object of pity. You've got to lead again.'

He found his hand was shaking as he finished his beer and gingerly put the empty glass back on the bar, afraid that he might slam the glass down. 'Last time we did that, about ten million of us died,' Carl said, staring right into the face of the reporter. 'You might excuse us if we sit this one out. Douglas, nice meeting you. Sandy, thanks for the beer.'

And he turned and left, hearing the older reporter sputter as his countrymen started arguing with him.

———

Outside, the cold air cleared his head, but he still fumed as he strode up the sidewalk, heading back to his car. The streets were empty except for a couple of lumbering taxi cabs, and most of the streetlights were broken. The shadows were black and deep. He knew that he shouldn't have been upset about the old man's words, but still, they stung. And so what if they did? Who elected you, Carl Landry, *Boston Globe* reporter and former sergeant, U.S. Army, as defender of the faith and soil?

He kicked at a crumpled newspaper. It was their damn smug arrogance that got to him, from the way they talked to the way they acted. Then there was the food spread that could feed a half dozen families for a month. The check – in pounds sterling – given to the grateful descendants of the people who fought to toss the British out two hundred years ago. And that muttered conversation in the bathroom. Something was going to happen, something involving taking care of the Yank problem.

He passed a lump wrapped in blankets, underneath a park bench, and someone hidden in the blankets moaned. It didn't look like he had any legs. Carl kept going, crossing over to the next block. He could make out his car, parked on the side of the street, next to a wrecked hulk that had been stripped. He put his right hand into his coat pocket, feeling for his keys, still thinking about what he should have said in reply to Farley.

He was about fifty feet away from the Coronet when he realized there wasn't much he could say. Truth was a hell of a defense.

And he was about twenty feet away from the Coronet when they jumped him.

———

They boiled out from an alleyway, past overflowing garbage cans and boxes, like bats streaming out from a cave, about five or six boys and girls, though their ages could have been anything from late teens to early twenties. Each one of them carried a brick or a wooden stick, which, if dropped when a cop came by, would blend into the background as a piece of trash and not a deadly weapon. The leader was a tall one with a gaunt look on his face, and he said, 'There he be! Let's get to 'im.'

There was laughter as they came closer, and in his mind's eye he filed it all away: the tight jeans, heavy boots, short leather jackets with chains and fake Soviet military epaulets on the shoulders, and the same close-cut haircuts for both the boys and the girls. Orfie gang on the prowl, out on a Saturday night for some fun and crushing, and he was in their sights. He knew the statistics. He knew the gangs didn't like live witnesses. He knew what they had planned for him, and he knew he should be terrified.

But instead, he remembered an old sergeant's words, from the dusty training fields of Fort Bragg over a decade ago: 'Landry, unless they're well trained and well armed, any group coming at you is just a mob, and a scared mob at that.'

The leader turned again, saying, 'C'mon, kiddos, it's time to—'

Carl leapt at him, car and house keys firm in his fist, with one sticking out between his knuckles, jamming the key hard against the young man's exposed cheek. He howled and fell to his knees. Carl pivoted on his weak leg, letting his strong leg lash out and catch another young man in his crotch. Another yelp of agony. The grogginess from the beer had evaporated and he was moving, he was now on the prowl. He grabbed a chunk of lumber from the trash cans and spun around, knocking a brick free from a girl's hand. Then he rapped another boy across the shoulders. In a matter of seconds, they had retreated back into the alleyway, cursing and tossing bricks and bottles in his direction, but still he moved, heading over to his Coronet and this time – praise God from whom all blessings flow! – the engine started on the first try. He made it out of there, yelling his own curses as he raced away from the gang. He felt alive and well. He said a loud thanks into the cold night, to that drill sergeant who had taught him self-defense.

Still, he went three blocks before turning on his headlights, and he took twice as long to get home, choosing a roundabout route.

He lay on his couch, breathing heavily, still trembling. His right hand was wrapped in ice and a dish towel, and he was watching the end of the *Ronald Reagan Variety Hour* on television, trying to ignore his hand throbbing with pain. He had gone home and locked all the doors and pulled out his Colt .45 Army service automatic, one of the few souvenirs he had taken with him when he was discharged. He wasted only a second thinking about calling the cops. The orfie gang was probably on the other side of the city right now, and even if the cops found them, then what? In fact, the orfies probably could have had a case against him. They had not assaulted him. They hadn't really threatened him. If anything, they could argue, Carl was the one who should be arrested. Another crazy vet who lost his mind and snapped. Happens all the time.

The news came on. After a brief piece showing General Ramsey Curtis giving an award to some Air Force colonel, there was a segment that showed Governor Rockefeller speaking to the chamber of commerce in Philadelphia, looking well fed and happy, the tables full of white males in dark suits, applauding and cheering him on. He was smiling widely as he tore into his opponent: 'His election as president would mean the adoption of an internationalist foreign policy. His election as president would mean a slap to the face of the one country that has helped us since the end of the war. His election as president would mean a unilateral disarmament. We learned – to all our great sorrow in 1962 – that we cannot afford to rely on paper treaties for our defense. It is a different world, a different time, a time for us to focus on our own affairs, our own challenges. Through the help of our British friends, we will continue to meet these challenges.'

'Some happy warrior,' Carl muttered, as he went into the kitchen for a fresh set of ice cubes. When he came back the news had switched, and there was Governor McGovern, speaking at a rally in Albany. Had to give the man credit, at least he was bringing his message to the enemy's camp. It was raining and he had on a soaked tan raincoat. A few of his young aides were holding umbrellas over him as he spoke, his flat midwestern twang cutting through the downpour. Carl half listened as the man talked, rearranging the ice and dish towel around his hand, and then he stopped moving for a moment. There was something about what the man was saying. It was like he was talking to him, Carl Landry, and everyone else who had once worn the uniform. He sat back on the couch.

'Often during this last tortured decade, I've reflected on a question from the Scripture,' McGovern said. '"Which of us, if his son asked him for bread, would give him a stone?" Our sons have asked for jobs – and we've sent them to poisoned lands and sick cities. Our sons have asked for an education – and we've taught them to arrest others and we've taught them to kill. Our sons have asked for a full measure of time – and thousands have been lost *before* their time. So let us seize the chance to lift from our sons and ourselves the horror of this administration, this leadership, this so-called recovery, and finally bestow the blessings of peace. Let us give thanks to our British friends, and send them home. Let us give thanks to our brothers, sons, and fathers in the armed services, end the draft, and bring them home. Then, and only then, can we restore our sense of purpose and our character as a great nation, and rejoin the family of nations in this troubled world.'

The news cut away to a commercial for Alka-Seltzer and he saw that he was dripping ice water on some magazines. He moved the dish towel around and thought about McGovern, soaked to the bone, speaking in the home state of his opponent, knowing that all the polls and pundits had not only declared this election over, but also the elections of '76, '80, '84, and those well into the next century. Still, he had labored on, speaking his mind, not giving up. Stones. That was a good phrase. He knew a lot of people who were burdened with stones. There was Two-Tone, living among the trash and tunnels of Boston. There was Sam Burnett in the *Globe's* newsroom, forever fifteen years old. And then there was Merl Sawson, who had been shot in the back of his head. The sons of America, all looking for bread, all looking for fulfillment.

Not to mention one Carl Landry. Overseas duty hadn't been that bad, back in '62, but then there was California . . . Some of the things that went on in that state after the war were not widely known, nor would they ever be. When he had gotten to the *Globe*, years after California, someone had shyly asked him, what was it like out West? And he had said,

'It was a time when the dogs ate the dead, and when the food ran out whoever was left ate the dogs.'

He thought about that for a while, his leg aching in memory, the television having gone into test pattern. So many times he had thought about the years before the war, and so many times he had tried to leave those memories alone. Why torture yourself, remembering full supermarket shelves, clean clothes, steady power, and a government that didn't hunt down draft dodgers and didn't censor the news and didn't run labor camps for the dissidents, the protesters, the ones that didn't belong. That time was gone, was never coming back, not ever.

He thought about that some more, and also thought of something else. The orfie gang leader. When he had come out of the alley in front of Carl, he hadn't simply said, 'Let's get 'im.'

No. His words were quite distinct. 'There *he* be! Let's get to 'im.' He had been set up. By who and why, he didn't know, but it was clear enough. Someone wanted something bad to happen to him.

That night he slept poorly, the pistol under his pillow, dreaming of California. So many gaunt faces, looking at him for bread, and all he had was a bag of stones.

EMPIRE: ONE

A MATTER OF EMPIRE: ONE

ON A SUNDAY MORNING 350 miles northwest of Boston, Major Kenneth Hunt of the British army's Parachute Regiment, 16th Parachute Brigade – known as the Paras – stood on the runway at RCAF Trenton watching the small executive-style jet with the RAF insignia on the side taxi to a halt. It was a crisp morning and he had yet to eat breakfast at the temporary mess that had been set up for his paras at the Royal Canadian Air Force facility. He had someone important to meet first. His stomach grumbled in protest at having to wait.

The regiment's colonel had been in Boston these past three days, and had asked that Hunt – head of 'A' Company – greet him on his return. He wasn't sure what was going on but he knew it wouldn't be good. His unit had been secretly flown over to Canada just weeks before, and they had immediately started training in empty fields adjacent to the RCAF station in Ontario. Their live-fire exercises had fallen into two areas: the first had been assaulting heavily defended storage areas controlled by a foreign force, and the second had been establishing control in a civilian-controlled city environment. Nothing else had been said about what they were planning for, and like the professionals they were, the paras just continued training and got on with the job.

Hunt clasped his hands behind him as the side door to the jet opened and a couple of RCAF ground crew moved a short metal staircase into place. He was one year shy of his fortieth birthday and had been in the British army since he was seventeen. At twenty-one he had entered the Parachute Regiment and had found his home there, in the regimental headquarters at Aldershot. He had been married for a while and had looked forward to starting a family, until outside events ten years ago had taken control of that part of his life. Now he was single and would always remain a bachelor. He had served his sovereign and country in Korea, the Suez, North Borneo, and Cyprus. But now . . . Hell, he wasn't sure what he was doing in Canada, but he and his officers had quickly hazarded a guess: it had to do with the wounded and still frightening giant to the south, and that thought wasn't appealing, not at all.

The colonel stepped out of the small jet, dressed in an ill-fitting light gray suit. He carried a small leather dispatch case in his right hand and he limped slightly as he walked across the runway. He was ten years older than Hunt and had salt-and-pepper hair, cut short, and a face that looked permanently sunburnt, with a squashed nose that had been broken in some long-ago bar brawl in Indonesia. The colonel limped due to a piece of German shrapnel that had struck him in 1944, during the disastrous Operation Market Garden in Arnhem that was supposed to end the war in Europe that year.

Well, Hunt thought grimly as he approached his superior officer, that was a perfect example of how perfect planning went to the shits when it was brought into the field.

The noise from the jet was lessening and as Hunt got closer to the colonel, he suddenly felt uneasy. Something was not right. Something was not right with the colonel. His face was ashen and his shoulders sagged as if he had been awake for all of the three days he had been in Boston. The colonel nodded as Hunt approached.

'Thanks for seeing me in, Kenneth,' he said, his voice raspy.

'Not at all, Colonel,' he replied. 'How was your trip?'

The colonel wearily shook his head. 'Walk with me to my quarters, will you? I feel like I could sleep for weeks.'

He fell in beside the colonel and they strode toward the collection of barracks, hangars, and RCAF administration buildings. There were many questions Hunt wanted to ask the colonel but he had learned long ago to keep his tongue still. The colonel gave him information when the colonel was ready, and he forced himself to keep patient.

'Can hardly wait to get out of this dratted suit,' he said softly, and was just barely heard over the sounds of the transport aircraft and the RAF Vulcan bombers taxiing about on the runway. 'I've never felt comfortable in civilian clothes, not ever. They just don't seem to fit right.'

'Sir,' he replied.

'But I had to wear the damn thing while I was at the consulate in Boston,' he continued. 'They couldn't bear the thought of all their great secrets being learned because someone spotted an out-of-place colonel, so I had to blend in. Even went to some dreadful party last night. Filled with overweight consulate types and hungry Americans. Civilians all. Bah.'

'And how did the briefing go, sir?' Hunt couldn't help but ask.

'Civilians . . .' he repeated, his voice still low-pitched, ignoring Hunt's question. 'They like to think of us as the coldhearted ones, the warriors thirsting for combat, ready to fight and die for Queen and Country, ready to go into battle at a moment's notice. But do you know what I learned in Boston?'

'No, sir, I don't.'

The colonel paused and looked out to the runway and the far-off fields. He blinked a few times, then seemed to shudder. That one movement frightened Hunt as much as anything he had seen while in the paras.

'I learned that the civilians are the truly cold ones, the right bastards who thirst for battle,' he said.

Hunt watched with dread as the colonel shuffled off to his quarters. In a staff meeting just before his trip to Boston, he had been his usual self: calm, cheerful and utterly confident in his abilities and those of his paras. But the colonel who had come off that jet hadn't been the same man.

Boston. What in hell had happened there?

With that, Major Hunt turned to go to the mess hall, and he was halfway there when he realized he was no longer hungry.

SEVEN

ON SUNDAY MORNING Carl moved slowly around the kitchen, his right hand aching, his head fuzzy from not enough sleep and too many bad dreams. That orfie gang from last night was more than just a coincidence. Had to have been. So who hired them? Someone at the consulate who knew he had overheard that conversation about Canada? Or someone who knew that he had met with Merl Sawson before he had taken a couple bullets to the back of his head?

There was a single egg in the refrigerator, a frozen chunk of sausage in the freezer, and if he trimmed away the mold on the last three pieces of bread, he'd have enough for toast. He was rummaging around in a kitchen drawer, looking for a knife, when the phone rang.

'Carl?' There was a pause. 'It's Sandy Price from the *Times*. Look, I wanted to apologize for Farley's behavior last night. He had no right to say what he did.'

He moved into the living room with the phone, trailing the cord after him. 'Sure he did. He could say anything he wanted, and he did.'

'Farley is old and tired and homesick, and last night he had a skinful,' Sandy said. 'You were my guest at the consulate, and I feel embarrassed.'

He smiled, stretching his legs out onto the coffee table. It was nice to hear the concern in her voice. 'Well, apology accepted.'

'Not so fast,' she said.

'Oh?'

'Oh yourself,' Sandy said. 'My apology's not complete until I've given you breakfast.'

'Where?'

'At my hotel. The Park Plaza. Unless you have a better offer.'

He looked over to the counter, where he could just make out the start of his breakfast.

'Lucky for both of us,' he said. 'Yours is the best offer I've gotten this morning.'

When the dishes had been cleared away and they were both on their third cup of coffee, Carl looked around at the quiet elegance of the Park Plaza's dining room. Clean carpeting, tables with white tablecloths so bright they almost hurt your eyes, and efficient and quiet service by waiters and waitresses in clothing that looked neither old nor freshly mended. It was hard to believe he was in America. The food – French toast, sausages, oatmeal, and toast – was hot and fresh, and best of all, as Sandy said with a wicked smile on her face, it was all paid for by a generous expense account from the *Times*. She signed the check with a flourish and leaned back in her leather high-backed chair. Her fine brown hair was down about her shoulders and she had on a simple white turtleneck sweater and black slacks. She looked . . . hell, she just looked good. No other deep and grand explanations. She just looked good. Again, he was reminded of those fashion photos of the prewar American women. She had the fresh, strong look of a woman utterly confident in who she was and what she was doing. He remembered what she looked like in that black dress the night before, and decided he would very much like to see how she looked in other dresses as well.

'So, when they found out I was coming to the States for a month,' she said, 'Mother and Father had a fit. They only know what they read in the press: food rationing, mutated babies and armed gangs, not to mention a quasi-dictatorship that's running things. They'd much rather I spent my time in Europe, covering the UN or the French or some damn thing. But I reminded them of Grandmama – my father's mother – and how she stayed with her husband during the Siege of Mafeking during the Boer War. I said that I had her genes, and that I fully intended to come here.'

'Mothers and fathers are like that,' he said, trying to make his third cup of coffee last. He didn't want this morning to end.

'Your parents,' she said.

'Excuse me?'

'Your parents. You've not said anything about them. Are they in the area?'

He took a breath and struggled to keep his face calm. 'No,' he finally said. 'They're both dead.'

'Oh. I'm sorry. Did they die in the war?'

The coffee didn't taste so good anymore. 'Yes,' he said slowly. 'You could say that.'

'I'm sorry I mentioned it, Carl.'

'Don't be hard on yourself. Look around this room, Sandy. Almost everyone in here lost someone during the war. A child, a brother, a sister, mother or father, and friends. Lots of friends. I'm afraid that's the way of our world. Some died in the bombing, some died of the flu and other diseases after the war, some just died because food or medicine ran out. Some people even froze to death when the power grid failed. This room . . . There's lots of ghosts here.'

'Did . . . did you lose anybody else during the war?'

His hand tightened around the coffee cup. 'My younger sister, Sarah. She was in college at the University of Nebraska. In Omaha.'

'Omaha . . . Wasn't that your Air Force headquarters?'

'Headquarters of the Strategic Air Command, yes, that's right. When I heard that Omaha was bombed, I . . . I just assumed she died. Then, back in '64, I got word from the Red Cross that a fellow student recalled she had been out of town that day. I've been looking for her ever since, in the missing persons registry in the Red Cross, Salvation Army, and a half dozen other charities.'

Sandy said in a quiet voice, 'Do you think she's still alive?'

How the hell should I know? is what he thought. But he said, 'She was my younger sister. I had a responsibility to look out for her. She may be hurt, she may be an invalid some-where. Who knows. But I haven't given up.'

She looked down at her own cup. 'There I go, putting my foot in it. I'm terribly sorry.'

'It's all right.'

She shook her head. 'No, it's not all right. You see, it's been a problem, ever since I got here. I've been bumping into things and asking the wrong questions, insulting people when I don't even know it, and getting odd looks.'

'Part of adjusting, I suppose.'

'Certainly, but beside that, no one wants to talk. I'm

having a devil of a time with this story, but believe me, I'm not one to let obstacles get in my way. Only last Friday I was at Boston City Hospital, trying to talk to the doctors and nurses who were part of the relief convoys to Connecticut in '62 and '63, and no one would talk to me. Not a single one. They claimed they were too busy, they claimed they really didn't do much, they claimed nothing really interesting went on. Why are they so secretive?'

'I don't think it's being secretive,' he said.

'You don't? What else could it be? I've been through masses of magazines and newspapers and I couldn't find a single word that even acknowledges that this is the tenth anniversary. Not a single one! It's all nibbling at the edges. The gas ration might go up next year. Grain imports from Canada might decrease next summer. Five communities in California near San Diego have been decontaminated and cleared for resettlement. Nobody really talks about a damn thing, and you don't think it's secretive?'

'Nope,' he said.

'Then what is it?'

'It's shame,' he said.

'What?' she said, surprised.

'Shame,' he said. 'We're ashamed of what happened.'

She carefully folded her slim hands. 'Please, go on. I want to know what you mean.'

For a second he felt tongue-tied, like he was telling a stranger a deep and horrible secret about his family, and he said, 'Shame. That's all it is. We're ashamed of what we did to ourselves and what we did to the Russians. We were so damn afraid of the Soviets and matching them, bomb for bomb, that we didn't even know the poor bastards had problems feeding their own people. Our bombers, missiles, and submarines were much better than anything they had, and we either didn't believe it or wouldn't believe it. You can see why Khrushchev put missiles into Cuba in the first place. Look at it from his point of view. Twenty years earlier, the Germans came roaring into Russia, killing millions. Then, all of a sudden, the Germans are back and this time they're part of an alliance called NATO, brimming with tanks and troops. There're also missiles in Turkey and Italy, pointed at him, and our bombers are snooping at his borders every day, and U-2s are flying overhead, taking pictures, preparing bombing targets.'

He looked at her quiet face, she nodded, and he went on. 'So Nikita puts missiles in Cuba, to give us a taste of our own medicine, and things take on a life of their own. Threats and counterthreats and blockades, our forces go on alert and then Cuba shoots down one of our U-2s, we retaliate, they retaliate, the invasion is on, and surprise, the Soviet army in Cuba has some tactical nukes, which they use on our landing forces. Once those let go and a couple of the Cuban missiles are fired and we lose a couple of bases on our soil, well, hell came to visit for a while that October.'

'And the shame?'

He was looking at the other people around him, eating and smiling their way through a lovely Sunday morning. He wondered what ghosts visited them at night, wondered where they had been, ten years ago. Wondered if they thanked or cursed God for being survivors.

'When it was over we had suffered a lot,' Carl said. 'We lost Washington, New York, San Diego, Miami, and some bases, but it was nothing compared to what we did to the Soviets. Every major city was hit, every airport, every rail station, anything and everything that had a possible military function was blasted and scorched off the face of the earth. We tore that country asunder and when we were done, we realized it had been a one-sided fight, a fight that never should have happened. It's like having a bully in the neighborhood who tosses trash in your yard, and you respond by killing him and his family and burning down his house. That's what that war was about, and that's why we don't talk much about it. We're ashamed.'

It was quiet for a moment, and then Sandy said, 'In the last three minutes, I've learned more from you than from anything else I've heard in this country. The *Times* certainly got its value from this breakfast.'

'Bully for the *Times*,' he said.

She leaned forward. 'Carl, I have a proposition for you.' Again, that smile that was so alive, so fresh, so unafraid. 'A business proposition. Would you be my traveling companion today? There are some places in this state that I'd like to visit as part of my story, and I would be eternally grateful if you'd join me. You could answer some of my questions and make sure I don't step on any toes, and in return, well, I could pay you a day rate, as a contributor. I do have funds for such matters. What do you say?'

'Just one question.'

'What's that?'

He swallowed the last of the coffee, pushed everything else away in his mind – including the story about Merl. He was determined to make this day a good one. 'When do we start?'

She insisted on using her rental car – or as she said, 'her hire car' – which was a Lincoln that still had the new car smell. Soon they were driving out on Route 2, heading west. The road quickly became two lanes, riddled with bumps and pot-holes. The traffic was mostly trucks and buses. The leaves along the roadside were still in their fall splendor, reds and yellows and oranges, a riotous tumble of color and shapes. Sandy pointed them out and said, 'It's so beautiful here. Is it like this in the rest of the state?'

'Pretty much,' Carl said, enjoying the sure power and handling of the Lincoln, so unlike his Coronet. 'And if you stuck around for a couple of months, you'd see the waist-deep snow that we're also so fortunate to get.'

She laughed but then spotted something and said, 'Your hand. What did you do to it?'

He saw how swollen and bruised his hand looked grasping the steering wheel. He wondered what to say and decided to tell her the truth.

'Had a little tussle last night, right after I left,' he said, try-ing to keep his voice light.

'Oh,' she said. 'I do hope it wasn't someone from the con-sul's office.'

'No, not at all,' he said, pulling behind a convoy of Army trucks. 'It was a bunch of kids. An orfie gang, most likely, out looking for some thrills and excitement.'

'There you go again. That's another expression I've heard but don't understand.'

Carl watched as a young soldier said something to another on one of the Army trucks, and the soldiers both laughed. Carl kept his eyes on them as he drove.

'Orfie gang. Shorthand for orphan gang.'

'You mean gangs of orphans? Are you serious?'

He spared a quick glance at her, and then looked back at the road. 'I'm not saying they're all orphans, but it's a pretty good guess most of them are. Look. Ten years ago, the kids are in school. Right? Mom's at home or at work, and Dad's at the office, too. Then the Bison and Bear bombers come over the North Pole, along with a few Soviet ICBMs. Sirens start sounding. The radio and television interrupt their programming with bulletins. What happens?'

She paused. 'Everyone seeks shelter, right?'

'Sure, that's what the Civil Defense pamphlets said, and every one of them was wrong. Let's say your two kids are at school. Hubby's at work. You're listening to the radio. Your station goes off the air and next you hear the Conelrad message that tells you to seek shelter. What do you do? You do like millions of other people do, and you pick up the phone, thereby frying the national phone system. What do you do next? Head into the basement?'

Sandy's voice was quiet. 'No. I'd go to the school, to get my children.'

'Right you are. And while the children are safe in the school shelter, their parents are on the roads, trying desperately to get to them, just as the bombs hit. So they never make it. A few weeks later, when the kids finally come out of their shelters, they're orphans. There's tens of thousands of them, maybe more.'

'Didn't the schools take care of them?'

'Most tried,' Carl explained. 'But there was such utter and complete chaos back then, Sandy, it's still hard now to believe how bad it was. Kennedy was gone, Johnson was gone, a good portion of the Congress. Government was crippled. Phones and televisions and most radios were off the air. Gas and oil in short supply. Power grid down. Food deliveries stop. Let's say you're a teacher. How long do you stay on the job before your own family takes precedence? It didn't happen everywhere but within six months of the war, you had thousands of kids in cities and towns foraging and fending for themselves. Ten years later, they still depend on each other. Oh, most have adjusted and are doing well, but there's still some who haven't. All they know is that when they were younger, they had a golden childhood. Plenty to eat, funny shows on TV, wonderful toys, and parents who loved them. One day they go into a school basement, crying from fear, and when they come out, their golden age is gone. They grow up knowing hunger, loneliness, and death. They rely on their gangs because that's all they have.'

'And last night one of those gangs accosted you.'

'You could say that.'

'How did you get away?'

He motioned to the trucks in front of them. 'Some of my old training came back, that's all. Once a soldier, always a soldier.'

'I see. Orfie gangs. How terrible.'

In the truck in front of them two of the young soldiers were laughing and waving, and Sandy gave an embarrassed wave in return. More laughter from the troops, but even at this distance he could see the fatigue in their eyes. He thought about McGovern's speech from the night before, the one on the television, and he wondered what stones these young troops were carrying.

'Yes, how terrible,' he said.

Lexington Common was ringed with roads but was still well preserved. Some old homes still circled the place where fighting had broken out almost two hundred years ago, during the first shots of the Revolutionary War between the British and the citizen militia. He and Sandy got brochures from a local tourist office and walked on the close-cropped grass. Dead leaves crunched under their feet. In the center of the Common was a tall flagpole, and the Stars and Stripes whipped in the breeze. He remembered serving in the Army, how seeing the flag flying would fill him with pride, knowing he was doing his duty for a young president who would do anything to save a nation. Now, it filled him with . . . what? A sense of loss? Of shame? He wasn't sure. He just knew it wasn't pride anymore. The country he had once sworn allegiance to under that flag no longer existed.

Sandy looked around and said, 'It looks so small. Hard to believe a war started here, and that your outnumbered troops actually put up a fight. No doubt some of my ancestors were here, fighting some of your ancestors.'

'Then you would be wrong. My ancestors were busy making other relatives of yours miserable in Ireland. They didn't come over here until the turn of the century.'

She whacked him gently with a tourist brochure. 'No hard feelings, I hope?'

'Not at all.'

'Then let's go on to Concord, shall we?'

He walked with her back to where her rental car was parked, and halfway there, she looped her arm through his. Her touch was intoxicating.

In Concord they stood in front of the famous Daniel Chester French statue that showed a Minuteman, musket in hand, striding away from a parked plow. Behind the statue was a gravel path that led to a wooden bridge spanning the slow-moving Concord River. Trees grew on both banks, and high up on a hill across the river was a large house set in a grove of trees. They paused for a moment before the statue, and then walked to the simple bridge made of rough-hewn planks and beams.

'Is this the same North Bridge?' Sandy asked. 'The one the poet Emerson wrote about?'

'You mean "the rude bridge that arched the flood"?' Carl asked. 'No, it's not. Back then it was just another bridge. It's probably been torn down and rebuilt a half dozen times, and this one is just a guess at what the real one looked like back in 1775.'

'It's just like Lexington, so peaceful.'

He nodded in the direction of the far bank. 'This time it was your countrymen who were outnumbered. The militiamen were on this side of the field and saw smoke rising up past the trees. They thought the Redcoats were torching the town of Concord, and they knew what had happened in Lexington. So they decided to march into town and defend it, and that's when they met the British. The Americans and British fired at each other and then the Americans gave chase, and the Redcoats fled. Lexington was a massacre. North Bridge was a battle.'

She was leaning over a rough wooden railing, brochure in one hand, reporter's notebook and fountain pen in the other. 'You know your history.'

'My military history, I guess,' he said. 'I've always been interested in it, especially when I was a kid. I guess that's one of the reasons why I joined the Army. I wanted to see if I could live some of the history instead of just reading about it, and then maybe write about it if things came together. Become another Ernest Hemingway if I was lucky and talented enough.'

'And did you?'

'Hardly. I spent a few months being a military adviser in a little country in Asia that everybody's forgotten about, until we were all called home after the war.'

'Was it Laos?'

He nodded. 'Very good. But, no, a place nearby. South Vietnam. There were several thousand of us there and by the end of '62 we were all out. By the next year there was just one Vietnam.'

She finished scribbling in her notebook, closed the cover, and said, 'Amazing, isn't it, how wars and empires can change because of a few incidents over the course of a single day. After Lexington and Concord, look what happened. All stemming from that park and this bridge.'

'That's true of all wars,' he said. 'One Cuban dictator and one ambitious American president and one scared Russian premier later, look where we are.'

Sandy tilted her head a bit. 'Still one more place to go.'

'It's a long drive,' he said. 'We'll have to eat along the way.'

'You promised.'

'That I did,' Carl said, walking to her parked car. 'That I did.'

Sandy insisted on stopping at a Howard Johnson's for lunch. 'Oh, come on, Carl,' she said when they had spotted the familiar orange roof. 'I've read so much about your fast-food culture. I've got to experience it firsthand.' So he gave in to her entreaties and when she went in ahead of him he parked the car. A man came up to him in the lot, dressed in patched jeans and wearing three or four shirts. His beard was steel gray and his eyes were wide, like he could not believe he was in Massachusetts.

'Spare a quarter?' he asked. 'A quarter for a refugee?'

Carl passed over the coin. 'Where you from?'

'South Florida.'

He whistled. 'You've been on a long trip. Why did you leave? Must be warm there.'

The man leaned forward. "Cuz I got the word, that's why. Next couple of weeks, we're all gonna be killed. Every last one of us. That's the secret plan, and I learned all their secrets.' The man chortled and walked toward a tractor trailer-truck that was pulling in. Carl shook his head and went inside the Howard Johnson's, remembering a book he'd read back in high school, Steinbeck's *Grapes of Wrath*. All those Okies fleeing the dust bowl and heading west, and Steinbeck was there to tell their stories. Now, refugees still fled from the desolate areas near where the bombs struck, most now running away from demons in their minds.

Inside he had a cold hamburger and Sandy gamely worked her way through some fried lumps that claimed to be fish and chips. On the highway again later, she said, 'All right, I've learned my lesson, as indigestible as it might be. Always listen to your native guide.'

'Be thankful I shan't charge you extra.'

'Just try.'

Now they were in the town of Hyannisport, walking across a shaggy field that had once been one of the most famous lawns in America, where parties and touch football games and politics ruled. The pillared gates were in disrepair and the NO TRESPASSING signs were defaced and scribbled over. The shrubbery had grown wild and Carl thought about what this place might look like in another ten years. The wild things would take over. There was a lot of rebuilding going on but he doubted anyone would do anything here. The land was haunted, it was taboo.

'Well,' Sandy said, stopping, sounding almost out of breath. 'There it is.'

Before them was a pile of rubble and beams, broken windows and doors, shattered walls, and burnt wood. A wire fence had been put up around the destroyed home but it was rusting and torn in places. The ocean was near, the sky was overcast, and the wind had picked up, chilling Carl. He glanced over but Sandy looked fine. From the way the wind was blowing, it might have even come from her home country, so perhaps she was feeling right comfortable.

She started writing in her notebook. 'It's hard to believe that I'm actually here, at the famous Kennedy compound. It always seemed such a romantic place. Politicians and movie stars dropping in, swimming and sailing and football. Very elite, very special.'

He looked around at the desolation, feeling melancholy. Damn it all to hell, it shouldn't have happened. All that fighting to build a country two hundred years ago, and for what? So that a couple of newspaper scribblers – one a well-fed and well-dressed foreigner – could pick through the bones of America's once royal family? 'Not much romance here.'

'Yes, I can still feel it. I spent a summer once in Rome, and I felt then as I do now, among the ruins. A sort of bittersweet thought of what was, and what might have been.'

Carl said carefully, 'As a citizen of this nation of ruins, I'm not sure I appreciate the observation.'

She brushed a strand of hair from her face. 'Are you cross with me? I didn't mean to offend you, Carl, honestly I didn't.'

Take it easy, he thought. 'I'm just not sure if you're a reporter or a romantic.'

She said, 'Ah, I told you before, Carl. I became a reporter to become a better writer. I want to write great novels and essays and historical works. And before that happens, as a reporter, I will do whatever it takes to get the story. No matter who gets in the way.'

He looked at the beautiful face and slim figure underneath the coat and noticed the flash of steel behind her eyes. 'Anybody in your way today?'

She laughed, and the look in her eyes softened. 'No, of course not. Now, I'm going to tell you a little secret, and you must promise not to laugh. Hardly anyone at home knows it.'

'Go on.'

'I've always fancied that one of these days, I'd leave the *Times* and do my own writing, become a George Orwell for my generation. You've read him?'

Damn it, why was the woman irritating him so? Did she think every book here was burned in '62? 'Yes, I've read some of Mr. Blair's works.'

'Who – oh, of course. George Orwell was his pseudonym. Yes, and that's what I want to do. Write about the class system, about the government and what we're doing for the people, write about the push for a new empire. I want to write a book that affects me as much as one of his did.'

'You mean *1984*?' he asked. 'Planning to write a sequel in the next decade?'

She shook her head. 'No, not that one, though I did love it. No, I'm thinking about another one, *Homage to Catalonia*.'

'His book about the Spanish Civil War. Let me guess, a "Homage to America"?'

Sandy crossed her arms. 'You promised not to laugh.'

'I didn't. A smile isn't a laugh.'

'If you say so. Well, that's what I want to do, and I know that these few weeks in America aren't enough. I want to come back and spend a lot more time here, go from coast to coast. I want to tell the story of what happened here and what's going to happen in the future, and Carl, believe me, I'm going to do it. In less than 250 pages, Orwell wrote the best book ever about the Spanish Civil War, and I intend to do the same for this place. I won't be scribbling in notebooks like these for the rest of my life, and I imagine you won't either.'

He put his hands in his pockets. The wind had picked up. 'Don't bet on it.'

She stepped closer. 'All journalists have a book inside of them. Are you telling me you haven't?'

'I'm not telling you a damn thing, that's what,' he said, trying to keep his voice light. 'Miss Price, I'll remind you that I'm a fellow newspaper worker. Not an interviewee.'

She shook her head at that and wrote something in her pad. 'I checked some old magazine and newspaper files. It seems that this place burned down shortly after the war.'

He kept his hands in his pockets, staring out at the rubble. 'Yes, just a few days after the armistice. The fire department took its time getting here, and by the time they arrived, it was over. No one knew who set it. Soon people had a lot of other more important things to worry about, like fallout and getting enough food, and here it sits. Year after year there's a debate on what to do with the land and year after year, the debate remains unsettled.'

'Doesn't a Kennedy brother still own the land? Edward? The one who wanted to be a senator?'

'Teddy?' Carl asked. 'After the war Teddy managed to get

back over to Ireland. He's there now with a few remaining
family advisers and his own family, in an old castle on some
land that he purchased. That's all we know over here. You
probably know more about him than I do. He's a nonperson
in this country.'

She folded her arms. 'There was a story about him on the
BBC last autumn. A story about the last surviving member of
America's royal family, and it was all rumors and gossip and a
blurry picture of him, sailing on the Irish Sea. Speaking of
books, supposedly he's writing his own about his brothers,
trying to exonerate them of starting the war. But he's apparently been working on it for the past ten years. No one knows
for sure.'

Carl kicked at some cracked flagstone. 'Well, there's one
thing for sure. He won't be coming back.'

'Hmmm. Does that please you? What do you think about
the Kennedys?'

He opened his mouth and just as quickly shut it. He
looked around. 'Thanks for another quick lesson in remind-
ing me you're from overseas. That's a subject that's not talked
about much. There's even a phrase, "as hard to find as a
Kennedy." A lot of people who shared his last name changed
it after the war. Some people still think JFK was a mass
murderer in line with Stalin and Hitler.'

'You haven't answered the question.'

He looked at the rubble. Ten years ago, he couldn't have
gotten within a hundred yards of this point, no matter how he
had felt about the man. 'Like I said, there are those who think
JFK is roasting merrily in Hell with Hitler and Stalin. Then
there are the others, the small minority who feel that Hitler
and Stalin were dictators, that JFK was freely elected by
Americans who also freely chose a Congress that passed

defense budgets and who built up a system that allowed a nuclear war to erupt over an island in the Caribbean. This small minority also feels it's unfair to scapegoat one man, one family, over hundreds of decisions and choices the American people made with their voices and their votes.'

'I take it you belong to this small minority?'

He kicked at a stone. 'The advantage of being in a small minority is that it never gets crowded, and I do like that.'

Sandy nodded and Carl was pleased to see her finally shiver. 'How about a quick walk around the house and we find some tea to warm us up?' she said.

'Tea? What's that?'

She made a face and he joined her, walking through the knee-high grass, staying near the wire fence. The wind seemed to moan as it went through the rubble, and waves lapped against the rotting wood of the docks. He remembered, too, but his memory was black-and-white footage from television programs. The Kennedy compound. Handsome men and women, playing touch football on the wide lawns. The newly elected president taking his sailboat out on the gray Atlantic. Beautiful Jackie and then the kids, Caroline and John-John. All happy, all secure, all part of what passed for royalty in this country. And now all gone, all burned away.

They were nearing a corner of the large house when Sandy spotted the graffiti. 'Carl, that's the third or fourth time I've seen that. What does it mean?'

Before them someone had left a sign, black crayon hastily scrawled on a piece of creased cardboard. HE LIVES. Carl stood quiet for a moment. 'I'll tell you, Sandy, but please don't use me as a source. Just say you heard it from a taxi driver or something.'

Sandy looked over at him, her face troubled. 'All right, I

suppose I can do that. But would you tell me why?'

He rubbed his fingers together in his pockets, feeling lint roll under his fingers. 'Because it's a touchy subject, that's why. It's like living in a house that has a nutty aunt in the basement, or having a father who is doing jail time for bank embezzlement. Everyone knows it's going on, but no one writes about it, and no one talks about it.'

'Talks about what?'

He gestured to the sign. 'About that. There's a cult in this country, as weird as it sounds. No one knows how many people belong to the cult or what they're up to. It drives the cops, what's left of the FBI, and the military crazy. You see the graffiti almost everywhere, there are leaflets that get passed out and even billboards that are defaced, one day to the next. Occasionally even a black radio transmission. And they just say the same thing. He lives.'

'And who's he?'

Again, that reflex, of looking around to see who might be listening to him. 'Kennedy. President John F. Kennedy, to be exact.'

Her face was mottled white from both the shock and the cold wind. 'President Kennedy? Alive? But he died in the bombing, didn't he?'

'Of course he did,' he said, surprised at how sharp his voice sounded. 'Of course. The last official word, after the invasion went sour and the Cuban missiles were fired, was that he and the First Family were being evacuated from Washington, and that they never made it. Some say he panicked and refused to leave the Oval Office. DC was hit before their helicopter could even lift off from the South Lawn, and Johnson's helicopter crashed and burned on the way to a retreat area in Virginia. At least with Johnson, there was a body and dental records. No one's claiming that he's still alive. But there are people who believe that JFK managed to escape, that he was badly injured, and that he's holed up somewhere.'

'And what's he been doing these past ten years?' she asked.

'Oh, supposedly he's been biding his time, gaining his strength, before revealing himself as the true savior of the country. He'll cashier General Curtis and end martial law, and bring us back into the world community of nations, so forth and so on.'

'That's odd,' she said. 'There's a similar myth in England, that King Arthur is still in some sort of stasis, ready to emerge and save England.' She laughed. 'My father said it was all bosh, that if the story was true, King Arthur would have come out in '45.'

'To fight the war? It was almost over then.'

'No, to prevent Labour being elected.' She laughed again and said, 'You mentioned something earlier, about black radio. What's that?'

'Black radio,' he said. 'Also known as pirate radio or clandestine radio. Unofficial radio stations that pop up every now and then. One particular station comes up for a few minutes every few months, and there's a voice on that station, claiming to be Kennedy.'

'You're joking.'

'I'm not,' he said. 'A couple of years ago, somebody at the *Globe* gave me the frequencies that this pirate radio station uses. Every now and then, I manage to catch a broadcast.'

'And does it sound like him?'

'Of course, but that doesn't mean anything. About half the people in this state can do a fair JFK impersonation, and that doesn't count the true believers. You see, not only does this particular cult believe that JFK is still alive, they believe the war wasn't his fault. They believe it was accidental, or that a nuclear exchange with the Russians was inevitable, and that JFK did his best. They still believe he lives, and they won't give up.'

She swayed for a moment, as a particularly strong gust of wind came across the waters. 'And that's what you believe, Carl, isn't it? That the war wasn't JFK's fault?'

He tried to sink his head into his coat collar. Damn this woman, for bringing up things he tried not to think about, ideas that he had hoped were safely buried and hidden away.

'I believe I'm getting hungry, and I believe I'm almost freezing.'

'Oh, you poor dear,' she said. 'Drive us back to my hotel and I'll treat you to dinner.'

'You or the *Times?*'

She patted his cheek. 'I don't know yet.'

He turned and went with her, holding her elbow as another strong gust of wind came up, flattening the grass and causing a piece of wood to fall among the rubble. Carl looked back and was surprised at what he saw: the cardboard sign, still there, flapping in the breeze.

He lives.

EIGHT

BACK IN BOSTON, as they approached the hotel's entrance, a man skulked out from the shadows. He was wearing baggy pants, shoes wrapped in newspaper, and a knee-length coat. He held both of his hands out to them, his skin bubbly and twisted, and he whispered, 'A buck for a rad vet, lady? A buck for a vet who's been kissed by a nuke?'

Sandy reached for her purse but Carl stepped in front of her and said sharply, 'Forget it, pal. Go peddle it somewhere else,' and he ushered her through the revolving doors. She was silent as they went through the lobby. In the elevator, she punched at the keys and turned to him, eyes glaring.

'So it's true,' she said.

'What's that?'

'That all of you have got used to the pain, the suffering. It's just part of the landscape, a landscape you can ignore.'

He stared up at the ascending lights. 'If you say so.'

'Damn it, why did you overreact? It's not your bloody money.'

The elevator stopped, the doors opened, and Carl looked

over at her. 'Is it permissible to say something in this interrogation, or should I just go back to the lobby?'

She folded her arms. 'Go on, say what you will.'

'You can give your money to whoever you want,' he said. 'I just didn't think you'd want to give your money to a fake.'

'A fake? That wreck of a man was a fake?'

The doors started to close and he punched the open button. 'Sure. Mixture of glue, flour, and food coloring, and you've got fake flash burns. Hang out at the best hotels and scare the out-of-towners. For those who enjoy such activities, you can make a fairly decent wage.'

'And how did you know those burns were faked?'

His voice was even. 'Because I know what the real ones look like.'

'Oh. I'm sorry, Carl. I didn't mean to react in that way. It's just . . .'

'I know,' he said, punching the elevator button again. 'Everything is so different here, you're from out of town, no one ever tells you anything.'

'Oh, for God's sake, stop taking it out on the lift,' she said, grabbing at his arm. 'Come on, let's have a proper drink before dinner.'

She led him down the hallway and unlocked the door to her room. He tried not to let his jaw drop as he followed her in. She had a two-room suite, with couches, work area, kitchenette, bath, and a bed the size of a lifeboat. Sandy moved to the mini-bar and said, 'Beer sound all right? Budweiser?'

'Is it cold?'

She tossed him a bottle. 'Yes, but I don't see why you Yanks have to freeze it so. You can't even taste the stuff.'

'Tell me again, didn't the British conquer the world,

looking for a good restaurant?'

That brought a large smile to her face and she said, 'Ha-ha. Very good. Here,' she said, throwing over a large, leather-bound volume. 'Room service menu. While I'm in the bathroom, you choose what you want.'

'Your tab or the *Times*'s?'

'Will we discuss current affairs over dinner?'

'Yep.'

Her eyes were bright. 'Then the Thunderer will take care of us, I imagine.'

'Hooray for a free press,' Carl said.

'Yes, hooray indeed.'

He looked through the menu and decided it had been a very long time since he had had a baked stuffed lobster.

Hooray for expense accounts, he thought, opening the Budweiser.

She had the rack of lamb and he had the baked stuffed lobster, and dessert was another visit from room service with dishes of ice cream and coffee. By then they had moved to the couch and Sandy had cleared away a pile of newspapers, magazines, and a few paperback books from Britain. One was called *Challenge of a New Empire*. Another was *Avoiding the American Error*. A third was *The Quality of Their Character: How America Failed Itself*.

His face flushed with anger. 'What's this? A little light reading about the barbarians you've been forced to visit?'

Sandy took the books from his hands, put them on the floor. 'Nobody forced me to come over here,' she said defensively. 'I volunteered, because I knew this was going to be important, the story of a lifetime. You know as well as I do that any decent journalist has to use all sources of information, even ones that are repellent.'

'These sources seem to be a bit biased.'

'They do,' she said. 'Unfortunately . . . well, there are a number of people in the U.K., influential people, who take some measure of pleasure over your troubles. They see America as an upstart, a cowboy or rogue nation that almost destroyed civilization because of a president's ego. They get a kick out of what happened here, at your comeuppance. I assure you, Carl, I don't.'

'An impolite person might mention some imperfections of your own nation,' Carl said, remembering something from a couple of weeks ago. 'Like a quiet little scandal here in town. One of your retired generals, found dead in a hotel room with a prostitute that had OD'd.'

She turned her face away for a moment. 'No one says we're perfect, Carl. And every so often, whether it's the general or some randy Member of Parliament with a fondness for teenage boys, we get reminded of it.'

He picked up one of her books from the floor. *Challenge of a New Empire.* 'Mind telling me what this one's about?'

She stretched on the couch, and for a moment her white sweater pulled up, revealing a brief expanse of midriff. He tried not to stare. 'Well. The state of Great Britain from one woman's perspective. Before the Cuban War, we didn't count anymore. It was the U.S. and the Russians. Then the Cuban War ended and NATO collapsed. In some people's minds, it was almost liberating when it became clear that the younger and wealthier brother was gone, and it was our turn to be number one again.'

'Problem with being number one is that you make a big, fat target for people who are number two or number three.'

'True, but the PM and Parliament didn't see it that way, in '62. With Germany reunited and allied with France, trying to keep order in Eastern Europe, we went back to our old stomping grounds. We went back to India and East and West Pakistan, to help them deal with the refugees and fallout. Australia and New Zealand loved having the Royal Navy in the neighborhood, to keep away Asian refugees in boats and junks. We built up our forces in Hong Kong and Ceylon. Canada welcomed us back with open arms, and we started our aid program with you.'

'How generous, to give back to the world the British Empire,' Carl said dryly.

Sandy said, 'Don't get me wrong, Carl. Most Brits are still divided about this approach. Some support it and others feel it's unseemly, that we shouldn't take advantage of such misery to muscle our way back into prominence. But what you mentioned the other night at the consulate, I know it sounded shocking but it's partially true. These aid programs are not just done out of the goodness of our hearts. Some of us want influence and a partnership, no matter what the cost.'

'Even when the cost is preventing people from starving to death?' He realized he had spoken too sharply and was going to apologize when she lowered her eyes and said, 'We can be a coldhearted people, Carl, but it takes a coldhearted people to create an empire.'

'And how coldhearted are you, Sandy?'

'My editor would say not enough.'

A hardcover book on a nearby nightstand caught his eye and he picked it up and looked at both sides of the cover. The front was a stylized painting of the old White House and on the lawn was a fully armored knight, resting on a white horse, his lance held down as if he was exhausted. *An American Camelot* was the book's title. On the rear was the photo of the author, Jack Hagopian, an American expatriate living in London and a former member of the Kennedy administration. Standing in front of the American Embassy at Grosvenor Square, he had a neatly trimmed beard and a serious expression, and was wearing a dungaree jacket.

He hefted the book and said, 'Customs give you any problems bringing this in?'

'No, they didn't, but then again, I didn't bring it,' she said, pouring fresh cups of coffee for the both of them. 'Dougie Harris, the press attaché, gave it to me when we first met. Is it really banned?'

He rubbed the smooth cover. 'Let's just say that bookstores that carry it have been known to have some windows broken. Have you read it?'

'Most of it. I can hardly wait to finish it,' she said, stirring cream and sugar into her cup. 'It's fascinating. It's a "what if" book, what might have happened if there had been no Cuban War, and if JFK and Khrushchev worked out a deal to avoid a war.'

He put the book down. 'And what happens after the crisis is averted?'

'Well, that's what's so fascinating,' she said, balancing the coffee cup in her lap. 'He suggests that JFK and Nikita were so scared about what almost happened that they started working together in secret to reduce tensions. JFK gets reelected for a second term, and instead of trying to fight communism, he gets disarmament talks under way. Nikita tries to soften things in Russia and give his people some economic freedom. Then the military in both countries finds out what's going on and there's a terrific row, since of course each side's military doesn't trust the other. There's some spy-versus-spy stuff and it's all pretty suspenseful, but there's a real somber note, too.'

'What's that?' he said.

'This is where the real potboiler stuff happens,' Sandy said. 'Bobby Kennedy's jealous of his older brother – typical – and he starts planning his own political career. He wants to become president, as well, and he also starts having an affair with Jackie Kennedy. And that's as far as I've got.'

He turned the book over in his hands again, and then gently placed it down on the table. 'I was at his inauguration, you know, back in 1961.'

'You were?' she said, surprised. 'As a guest?'

He smiled sadly at the memory. 'Hardly. I was part of the parade, in one of the Army units. It was cold, cold, cold. Jesus, I couldn't believe Washington could get so cold and have so much snow. It's a southern town, right between Maryland and Virginia, and a lot of the guys in my unit were shivering. But everything went off on time and Kennedy was up there, giving his speech, and we were in front of him, freezing our tails off.'

Sandy said, 'You see, you were a witness to history.'

'So I was, so I was,' he said. 'He gave a great speech. All about a torch being passed to a new generation. Eisenhower was like someone's grandfather, he was so old, and Kennedy was so young and vibrant. Full of energy and ideas. He promised great things, about bearing any price and burden, about defending freedom and fighting communism. Stuff about asking what you can do for your country.'

'Inspiring, was it?'

Oh, yes, he thought. Quite inspiring, right up to that certain October. 'Oh, at the time, it was, though some of the older guys there, they voted for Nixon, and kept razzing JFK as he spoke. One guy said something like, "Hey, Jack, let's see less profile and more courage." The military's a pretty conservative outfit. But there was . . . oh, a spirit to the moment, Sandy, for us younger troops. It really sounded like we were all part of some new crusade. It felt good. You know, for a while, we believed we could do anything. Later, we even believed we could go to the moon.'

He reached out and touched the book once more, a book about a fairy tale that still had a hold on people. 'Of course, less than two years later, it was over. Most of the VIPs and justices and senators and representatives were dead, and that whole area, as far as the eye could see, was turned into black glass. Funny, isn't it. If today I were to be dropped on the same spot where I was, back in '61, I'd be dead in less than a day.'

She held her cup in both hands and looked off at the far wall. 'I know this is all going to sound a bit strange, but bear with me.'

'All right, I will.'

'I've always envied Americans. Even . . . even with the war. There's just something about you that is special. You always believe that you can do something, fix everything, go anywhere. You have this restless . . . oh, I don't know, this restless energy. Not optimism, mind you, but a relentless need to get things done. Even now.'

'You've been reading too many romantic newspaper articles about the new American spirit,' he said, feeling again that touch of melancholy from Hyannisport. 'The only spirit we have left is the one that tells us to feed and clothe ourselves, and stay out of trouble. That's the kind of country we have now, and will probably have for years to come.'

Sandy said quietly, 'And what are you doing about it?'

He almost laughed. 'Me? One reporter? One guy?'

'George Orwell was just one man. And look at how influential he was.'

'Sure. But our fine Mr. Blair didn't live under martial law or press censorship. No, what I'm doing is trying to make do, trying to write the stories I can get away with, and . . .'

And find out about Merl Sawson, he almost said. Find out what I can about that old man with the taped-up boots who died violently and who came to me for help.

She stretched again on the couch. 'See, I told you that we had things in common. We're both trying to write the stories of our times.' .

'Say again? You've lost me.'

'Oh, I know I said earlier that I want to be a great writer. But I also detest secrets. I just don't want to cover stories which say the PM said this today, or the Lord Mayor said that yesterday. I want to reveal what's really happening behind closed doors, what's being planned on military bases, and what's being talked about in Geneva. Expose enough secrets, maybe we won't have any more wars.'

She smiled suddenly, bringing a grin to his own face. He knew it was unfair but he had never met a woman like this, not once during the past decade.

'Good Lord, I'm beginning to sound like a socialist, aren't I?' Sandy said. 'Daddy would pop an artery if he heard me. But what about you, Carl? Are you just a reporter or someone who finds out what's really going on?'

He thought for a moment, about a dead veteran in an empty apartment, bullets in the back of his head. 'I'm still working on that.'

They talked for a while longer and Sandy yawned twice. Carl excused himself and went into the bathroom, which was off of the bedroom. He washed his hands thoroughly, enjoying the feel of the hot water and the fresh soap on his skin. At his own apartment, hot water was sometimes sparse. He dried his hands on thick, fluffy white towels and went back into the suite. Sandy was stretched out on the couch, eyes closed, breathing slowly and regularly.

Carl took it all in. The fine room with the view and the remains of a room service feast that could have paid his grocery bill for a month. On the couch, the most desirable woman he'd been with in a long time. It had been a grueling day, traveling through almost half of the state, but he would not have missed a second of it. Now, the day was coming to a close and the magic would be gone in just a very few seconds. Any other man might have woken her up and taken the night for whatever might happen, but he couldn't do it. She would be gone in a couple of weeks and he refused to think about the 'what ifs' and 'might have beens.'

Instead, he was both grateful and irritated for what she had done to him these past few days. Irritated at once again being reminded that just an airline flight away there was a land with cheerful people and plenty of food and electricity. And grateful for what else she had done: she had shaken him up, she had made him think. He looked again at her peaceful form, imagined how that smooth skin would feel under his touch.

Carl scribbled a note on a memo pad and walked out of Sandy's room. He carefully closed the door behind him, gently so that it wouldn't waken her, not knowing if he would ever see her again.

———

It was 11 P.M. in East Boston and he knew he shouldn't be doing what he was doing, but Sandy had pushed him. She had asked the question. Are you just a mindless reporter, or are you someone who digs and digs? On the way home he decided he would find that out, and so here he was.

A jet grumbled overhead, making the approach to Logan. He got out of the Coronet and crossed the street, feeling lucky when the porch door opened at his touch. He knocked on the first-floor apartment, the one that belonged to Andrew Townes, the old landlord, but there was no answer. Somewhere up the street a door slammed and a drunk hollered. 'What about my cigarettes, you bastard . . .' came the female voice.

He went upstairs to the next landing, Merl Sawson's place. The evidence stickers were still there and the door was firmly locked. He climbed up to the third floor, to the apartment of Troy Clemmons, and stopped, hand still on the banister. The door was open, the frame smashed and splintered.

'Troy?' he called out, and opened the door with his foot. The last time he had been in this apartment, it had been a mess. Now it was a disaster. The room was dimly lit from a streetlight across the way, and he went inside and closed the door behind him. He switched on a small table lamp and saw that the place had been tossed, even worse than Merl's apartment downstairs. Clothes and furniture and dishes and books were piled in a jumbled and broken heap in the middle of the living room floor. He walked carefully through the kitchen and into the living room, then to the small bedroom. Not a soul was home.

He stood in the living room. The antidraft posters had been ripped from the wall and torn to pieces. It looked like

Troy had been on the receiving end of an Army raid, and if he was lucky, he had been away.

Carl looked over at the windows. Like those of the apartment below, they opened onto a small, roofed porch. He thought for a bit longer, as two more jets made their way into Logan. When he heard the low sound of another approaching jet, he went over to the windows, opened them up, and climbed outside. It was cold and the jet noise was louder. He closed the window behind him, careful to leave a few inches open, and then looked over the railing. It could be done. Hell, back in the Army he'd have done it without a thought. Twice he had parachuted out of airplanes as part of his training.

'But we're just a tad older, now, aren't we,' he whispered, as he stepped over the porch railing and lowered himself to the porch below, the one belonging to Merl Sawson.

And then he slipped.

'Damn!' he exclaimed in a loud whisper as he hung by his hands. He couldn't see well and his feet windmilled below him, looking for something, anything to hold on to. He had an awful thought that he would fall and break a leg or his damn fool neck. How would he explain that to George Dooley back at the *Globe*? His legs hit something solid and he realized he was dangling lower than he thought. He lifted his feet up and got them on the railing below him. In a confusing few seconds he tumbled to the floor of the second-floor porch. He lay there, his chest aching, the breath knocked out of him. It had been a long time since he had used these particular Army skills, and it showed.

The smart thing would have been to wrestle his way back up to Troy's apartment and go home and sleep late, but there was that half smile of Sandy's in his mind, the one that had poked and prodded at him. Just who are you, she had asked. And then there was that gaunt and scared look in Merl's face when he had met the man. I have a story, he had said. Something important. Something historic. Something that will affect the future of this country. And a few weeks later, he was dead.

He stood up and managed to get one of the windows open halfway before it stuck. He bent over and forced himself in and then there he was in the dead man's apartment, sweaty and cold and breathing hard. The place still smelled of old things and old violences, and he walked gingerly through the living room and then into the kitchen, thinking about his advice to Merl's landlord. Box everything up. It was obvious the landlord hadn't listened to his advice, because the place still looked the same. Clothes and dishes were scattered across the floors and on top of the furniture. He turned a light on over the stove and, using a dish towel, blocked most of it so that it didn't look obvious from the outside that someone was in the apartment.

His breathing slowed. Well, hotshot, he thought. Now that we're here, what do we do? He decided to go back to the living room. He sat on the floor and carefully went through Merl's books and magazines, checking to see if anything – like a letter or some other personal note – was hidden in the pages. He was sure that the man's mail was in a police storage locker with any other evidence, but he was hoping for a break. As he worked, he tried not to think too hard about what he was looking for. It made no sense. Anything remotely interesting had already been taken by the police. So why was he here?

'Because,' he whispered, standing up and wincing at the

RESURRECTION DAY   **139**

pain in his knees. Because something was going on. And the old man had come to him, had been ready to confide in him, had passed over that list of names. Carl owed him.

The bedroom was next and he frowned as he went through the meager belongings. The bare mattress was on the bed, a large, rust-colored stain at the head. The bureaus revealed socks and underwear and T-shirts. The bedroom closet was musty and the floor was covered with boots, shoes, and sneakers without laces. He idly went through the clothes and spotted a worn New York Yankees baseball cap. He turned it over in his hand. Odd thing for a Red Sox fan to have. Carl was about to leave the closet when his fingers brushed something leathery. He pushed his hand through and touched it again. It felt like a garment bag. He reached in further, unhooked the bag, brought it out, and laid it on the mattress, being careful to avoid the blood-stains.

The thin light from the kitchen was enough to illuminate the bag. He unzipped it and, without thinking, whistled in amazement. It was a class 'A' U.S. Army uniform with the emblems of a full colonel, a Combat Infantry Badge, and a couple dozen service ribbons. He undid the bag even more and saw a looped brassard hanging from one arm. Merl Sawson had been more than just a vet living off his pension. He had been places and done things. But what kind of places, and what kind of things?

He rummaged through the pockets of the uniform and found a small envelope. He pulled it out and held it up to the light. It was made from heavy white stock and the handwriting on the outside, 'Colonel Merl Sawson,' was written in calligraphy. Inside the envelope was a stiff piece of vellum with the seal of the President of the United States embossed in black at the top. It was a formal invitation.

The President and Mrs. Kennedy
request the pleasure of the company of
Colonel Merl Sawson
at dinner
on Friday, September 19, 1962,
at eight o'clock

Behind the invitation was a smaller card:

On the occasion of
the visit of
His Excellency
The Prime Minister of Canada

Now he recognized the brassard looped over one arm. It was a piece of uniform that only a few soldiers could ever claim as their own. Colonel Merl Sawson had been a presidential aide in the White House.

'Holy shit,' Carl whispered.

He didn't think he'd find anything else. He was back in the kitchen, now hot and tired and thirsty, the ten-year-old invitation snuggled in his own coat pocket. He didn't know who he was going to show it to, or why, but he had to have it. It was proof, proof that Merl was more than just a forgotten murdered vet. He reached into his coat pocket and rubbed at the envelope. The White House. Even though there was no such place, and whatever remained of the building had been vaporized years ago, there was still something weighty about those words.

Thirsty. He was quite thirsty. Without thinking he opened up the refrigerator and gagged at the thick smell. Rotten food, sour milk, and who knew what else. He looked behind the refrigerator and saw that it had been moved, probably during the police search, and the power plug had been pulled out. No electricity for several days. Wonderful.

And then, well, he didn't know why, but he opened up the freezer. Among the dripping remnants of a few frozen food dinners and some unidentifiable lumps in aluminum foil, there was a thin package, wrapped in plastic and hidden way back. It didn't look like frozen food. From the amount of dripping water, it was clear that this part of the freezer had been locked in a few inches of ice. Something was here, something that Merl . . . well, Colonel Sawson, wanted hidden. Carl put his hand into the slimy water and pulled out the package. It had been wrapped in several pieces of plastic and taped shut. Inside was a thin brown manila envelope, letter size.

He opened the envelope in the kitchen, standing by the stove. Four objects tumbled out. The first was a standard issue Armed Services identification card that showed a picture of Colonel Sawson. Nothing unusual about that. Carl had his own card buried somewhere in his wallet. He looked at Merl's firm face and steady gaze and he shivered. The man he had seen by Boston Harbor last month . . . He had looked like a POW camp survivor compared to the strong and confident-looking colonel whose picture he held in his hand.

The second item was a much folded piece of paper. At the top it said simply, 'The White House. Washington.' There was a hand-scribbled note:

10/27

Merl—
You seem to be off at an ExComm meeting. Just a
reminder, God forbid, that if this slips away from us all
that my brother's place in Maine is still open for you and
Carla. The address is 14 Sea Breeze Way, York. Hope
not to see you there, if you know what I mean.

I'm off to the Hill to brief some chowderheads. Luck
to us both, eh?

—Casimir

Carl refolded the piece of paper and carefully put it back
into the envelope. The day before the war started, that's
when it had been written. He held the piece of paper gingerly
in his hand, like an ancient relic. And Casimir had to be the
'Caz' that Troy said Merl had dreamed about so often. So
where was Caz now? Was he the mysterious visitor that Troy
had mentioned, who stopped by before the murder? There
were two more objects enclosed in the plastic. One was a
plain white business card, with the name 'Stewart
Thompson' and a Boston phone number in embossed black
lettering.

The last object seemed to be another identification pass,
though larger than the other one. He picked up the lami-
nated card and tilted it toward the light.

There was another photograph of Merl Sawson in his
military uniform, and a gold thread ran through the photo. To
the right of the photo was Merl's name and rank, along with
an identification number and his height, weight, hair and eye
color. The signature of Secretary of Defense Robert S.
McNamara – another ghost from the past – was on the

bottom of the card, just below a thumbprint. In the middle was a string of words, all in capital letters:

OFFICIAL IDENTIFICATION.

FOR BEARER'S USE ONLY.

OFFICIAL U.S. GOVERNMENT BUSINESS.

EMERGENCY TRAVEL AUTHORIZED.

PASS THROUGH ALL CIVILIAN AND MILITARY CHECKPOINTS

AUTHORIZED.

ENTRY AUTHORIZED INTO ALL MILITARY BASES.

ENTRY AUTHORIZED INTO ALTERNATE SEAT OF GOVERNMENT.

As he returned the card into the envelope, his hands started shaking.

NINE

ON MONDAY MORNING Carl went to York, Maine, a coastal tourist town about two hours north of Boston. For the first time in a long while – the last incident involved an Opening Day at Fenway Park – he had called in sick without actually being ill. He had also dialed the phone number of Stewart Thompson, whose card he had found in Merl Sawson's freezer the night before. There had been no answer.

To get to Maine he took I-95, and the further north he drove, the fewer the number of cars and trucks he saw, and the number of horse-drawn wagons with rubber wheels along the side of the road increased. Each time he went under a highway overpass, he leaned forward and looked up through the dirty windshield. Orfie gangs were known to pass the time by hiding on overpasses and dropping boulders on the cars below.

Just before the New Hampshire border, he drove by the exit for Newburyport, his hometown. He clenched the steering wheel and kept his eyes focused north. In ten years he had never taken this exit. He tried not to think of the house where he grew up, with Mom and Dad inside, right after the war, with the power out, the power out for months, for God's sake, the snows rising and rising during that terrible winter . . .

When he crossed over into New Hampshire, he allowed his hands to relax and his eyes to wander. As he shifted in his seat, he felt something pressing into his ribs from inside his coat: Merl Sawson's identification card and the decade-old invitation from the First Family. The invite made him think of his old downstairs neighbor, Slatterly. They had been friendly the first year he had moved into his apartment in Boston. Slatterly had a shaved head and a thick New York accent, and he didn't get into too much detail of what he did in New York before the war. Now, however, he was into post-war collectibles.

One night, Slatterly proudly showed off the items he sold and traded: souvenir conch shells from Key West, old post-cards from San Diego, miniature replicas of the Statue of Liberty, and his prize and joy: a thick, round piece of marble, the size of a baby's fist. 'Know what that is?' Slatterly had asked. 'No? My friend, that is one of a kind. That's a real gavel that was used in the U.S. Senate, before the war. And you know what I paid for it? A case of canned Spam, that's what. Now, for the original Declaration of Independence – you know, it was rumored to have been removed from DC before the bombing – I bet that would go for a warehouse full of Spam.'

Carl was sure Merl Sawson's JFK invite had some sort of value but Slatterly wasn't there to ask about it anymore. One night, two years ago, Carl had come home from the *Globe*, and the downstairs apartment had been cleaned out, and no one knew what had happened to the hustler.

Several minutes after passing through New Hampshire, he

was in Maine. He took the coastal road – Route 1 – into York, where he stopped at a general store and got directions to Sea Breeze Way from an old man who hobbled using two canes.

The street – which was one lane of cracked and bumpy asphalt – was off of the main beach. The day was overcast and the sands were empty except for a couple at one end, walking a dog. Carl parked at the main beach and walked down the lane. The house was two stories with peeling light green paint, an empty dirt driveway off to the left, and a half-collapsed outbuilding at the rear that was probably the garage. Most of the other houses on the street were cottages, with FOR SALE or FOR RENT signs in the unwashed windows. The mailbox in front of number fourteen had a name, in black-and-gold stick-on letters. CYNEWSKI.

Carl hunched his shoulders forward and walked up the crushed stone path. He took a deep breath and knocked on the porch door. A gamble, coming up here and taking a day off from work, but a gamble he had to take. He waited, knocked again, and was going to try for a third time when an old man appeared behind the screen. The man opened the door and Carl was embarrassed when he realized the man wasn't that old. He was just terribly thin with wispy white hair, wearing baggy blue jeans and a green, heavy-knit sweater. There were fleshy bags under his droopy eyes, and his hands wavered.

'Yes?' he said, his eyes dull, as if he had just been asleep. 'Hope you're not selling anything, 'cause you'll be wasting your time and mine.'

'Carl Landry, Mr. Cynewski, from the *Boston Globe*,' he said, passing over his business card. 'I'm working on a story out of Boston and well, I'm actually looking for some information, information about a man named Casimir. Perhaps your brother?'

The man closed his eyes and stepped back, as if he had been punched in the chest. He said in a whisper, 'Are you telling me that my brother is alive?'

Oh, great, he thought. 'No, no, I'm sorry to have made you think that, sir,' he said. 'I'm doing a story about someone who knew him, before the war, and I was hoping . . . well, it's a long shot, but I'm just looking for information. That's all.'

He opened his eyes, tried to smile. 'Information? It's been a while since anyone's asked me anything, except for those damn tourists who need directions or want to use my bathroom. The name is Marcus Cynewski, though you can get away with calling me Mark.'

'Thank you, Mark,' he said, and then Mark opened the door wider and said, 'You're a long way from home, *Boston Globe*. Why don't you come in and I'll fix you a cup of tea.'

The wind whipped against his legs. 'That would be fine.'

They went into the living room. It was dark and musty, filled with old leatherbound books in shelves against the wall, and magazines and newspapers over the furniture and hardwood floor. Carl sat on a couch and Mark sat in a large, overstuffed chair with a plaid blanket over his legs. He could too easily imagine this older man, alone and sitting at night in the quiet house, reading these books and magazines with his trembling hands, remembering better times. Carl knew he was being ungenerous, but he could hardly wait to leave this oppressive house.

Carl glanced down at the couch beside him and saw a few mimeographed journals with hand-drawn covers: *The Nation*, *The Progressive*, and *Ramparts*.

'I see you've discovered my deep and dark secret,' Mark

said, holding his tea with both hands, a slight smile on his face. 'There they are, my oddball politics open for the world to see. I do find them enjoyable, and you know why? Not necessarily because of the politics, but because of the writing. Underground and uncensored, there's a fresh spirit you don't see in any of the newspapers, no offense to the *Globe*. There's even a name for them, a Russian phrase called *samizdat*. Means self-published. Funny, isn't it, that we honor our former enemies by giving our journals of free speech a foreign name.'

'How often do they come out?' Carl asked, picking up a *Nation* and noting the cheap paper and smeared ink.

'Irregular, of course, depends whether the staff's been rounded up or if they've run out of paper.' Mark sat back and looked outside for a moment. 'But enough of marginalized politics, from someone who thought the 1960s was going to be a liberating era instead of a time of food shortages and labor camps.' He sipped from his tea and glanced out the picture window. 'You know, this is my favorite time of the year. The light is different and the ocean looks more real, without the deep blue sky and sunshine. I can walk out on the sands and not meet anyone, which is just fine. Most of the shops are closed and the roads are empty. The tourists have left, including those damn rich Canadians, who think they own the place.'

He laughed and added, 'Who'd ever think we'd be complaining about the rich Canadians? Or the rich Mexicans, for that? Who would have thought they'd be arming their borders to keep out American refugees? Who'd have thought?'

'Not too many, I guess,' Carl said, seeing that the man wasn't quite all there. His hands trembled so much that the tea in his cup slopped over the sides, and the little smile on his face seemed forced.

'So. You're working on a story.'

Carl said, 'Yes, I am. About someone your brother Casimir knew, back when he was at the White House. A Merl Sawson, a military aide. Does the name sound familiar?'

Mark seemed to think for a moment, rubbing at his chin, and said, 'A little . . . yes, it does. I do remember my brother Caz mentioning a friend of his, a man named Merl that he knew while working for JFK. But that's about all I can remember. Sorry.'

'Did he say anything about what Merl did at the White House?'

'If Casimir did, I must have forgotten it.'

'Well, what was your brother's job?'

Again, the smile that wasn't a smile. 'Besides being a war criminal?'

Carl felt the warmth of his teacup. 'Did he really go to trial, or is that your opinion?'

'My opinion, learned as it is,' he said. 'Tell me, *Globe* man, how many men are still in prison from the Kennedy Administration?'

'I don't know.'

'A good answer. We never do know, do we? The Domestic War Crimes trials in 1963 were closed to the public and to the press. All that was announced was the sentences and Caz's name wasn't on the list, but still, in my own mind, he was a war criminal, even though he probably died in the bombing. He worked for that lightweight Kennedy in that evil agency of his, and he helped bring disaster upon us.'

'Do you know what he did?'

A brief wave of a hand. 'Of course not. Everything was top secret, need to know, all that rubbish. He was some high mucky-muck in the CIA, I do know that, and that's all because of Yale. You see, he went to Yale and was recruited by the spies, and I went to Harvard and did something entirely different.'

'And what was that?' Carl asked.

'I started to work towards my doctorate in history. I was fascinated by the First World War and how it happened. None of the princes, kings, prime ministers, or presidents wanted a war, you know. And yet it came, tore the heart out of Europe, and shattered a half dozen empires. Sound depressingly familiar? And what school did you go to, Mr. *Globe*?'

'The one with the funny green uniforms,' Carl said.

'Ah, a veteran,' Mark said, shifting in his seat. 'Did you serve during the war?'

'Yes, overseas.'

'And where did you go after the callback?'

'Southern California. Relief and recovery.'

Mark slowly smoothed out his blanket, though it didn't look wrinkled. 'Southern California. You know the rumors . . . I suppose you could say something about the story I've heard, about Governor Brown being arrested and shot by military police during that first year.'

Carl looked at the far wall, a spot just above Mark's shoulder. 'I really can't say.'

'And the missions you performed in the Golden State?'

He kept on staring. Some interview this was turning out to be. 'Relief and recovery. And that's all I can say. Look, Mark—'

'I know, I know, you're suppose to be asking the questions. I apologize. You and most of your comrades in the service were and are honorable men, following orders and performing your duty. Except for those damnable thugs in the Zed Force.

I, on the other hand, am old and talkative and still angry, after all these years. My friends and I, we were active in letter-writing campaigns, in protests, in marches. We wanted to ban the bomb. That's it. Just ban the bomb and everything would be perfect.' A wave of the hand, probably in disgust. 'We were such innocents, little children, to think we were accomplishing anything. Bah. We were tiny little King Canutes, all of us, standing at the shore and demanding the tide stop coming in.'

He stroked his chin delicately, like he was so frail he was afraid of injuring himself. 'I still see a couple of my friends, here and there, and you know what they believe? That we were lucky. Lucky the war happened then and was relatively minor. Lucky that it didn't happen ten years later, when a much stronger Soviet Union would have destroyed us as we've destroyed them. Lucky that it didn't happen twenty or thirty years later, when countries from India to Israel to Argentina had the bomb, and we could have merrily nuked our way back to the Stone Age. One physicist friend of mine – quite mad, you understand – even said that there could have been a time, not too far in the future, when corporations or gangs of wealthy criminals could have made the bomb. Or where bombs were so small that they could be stolen by terrorists or religious zealots. Can you imagine living in such an insane world?'

'I'd rather not.'

Mark smiled weakly. 'My brother Caz, though. He could have thrived in any kind of world, so long as he was fighting against godless communism. Perhaps his spirit is smiling, you know. I don't think there's a single communist party left, except for maybe in Italy.'

Carl took a sip from his tea. It was now cold. He tried

again to do what he had come here for. 'But Merl Sawson. Did you ever meet him, or hear of him?'

'Just like I said earlier, only a passing mention that he was one of Casimir's friends. That's all I know. You said you were doing a story about Merl. What kind of story?'

'He was murdered a few days ago. I'm just doing a follow-up about his life, who he was, what kind of background he had.'

Mark wrapped the blanket around him tighter, and his voice was quieter. 'Murdered. How? A knifing in a bar? Shot by an irate husband?'

'No. Shot in the back of the head, in what looks like a burglary attempt. Except . . .'

'Except what?'

He decided not to tell everything about Merl, about the list of the names and what Merl had said last month. Mark was looking frightened, and red splotches had appeared on his cheeks.

'Except it didn't look like anything had been taken, that's what,' Carl said.

Mark said nothing and Carl knew what was wrong. It was one thing to talk grandly about politics and being in opposition to the government and have semi-banned periodicals in your living room. It was quite another to discuss blood and dead bodies. It grew more quiet after a few moments, quiet enough to hear the ticking sound of a clock from the kitchen, an occasionally passing car, and the waves of the ocean, sliding ashore at York Beach. Mark shook his head and looked at his hands, and Carl saw that they were shaking again.

'A part of me wishes you'd not visited me, *Boston Globe*,' he said.

'And why's that?'

Mark looked away and said, 'I've been taken in twice by

the Zed Forces, and have gone twice to a decon camp, one outside of DC and the other outside Omaha, sentenced for seditious activities. I've had two tumors cut out of me and I've got half a stomach and one kidney left. What few years I have remaining I want to spend here in York, Carl. I don't want to go back to a decon camp. I want to stay here. I think you should leave.'

It was like the air in the room had gotten thin and hot, all at the same time. He leaned forward and said, 'Please, this is important, what happened to Merl—'

'Of course it's important, you fool. A man who was once military attaché to President Kennedy's been found murdered in his home. Doesn't that tell you anything? You know what they say? That history is written by the victors? But in this case, history was written by the survivors. Those who made it through, including that overbearing general who's actually governing this sad country. And the Zed Force – those military units who so much enjoy enforcing the martial law declarations. But maybe some of the other survivors from the war, maybe they have a story they want to tell, one that doesn't mesh with what's been officially reported. You're a newspaper man. Has there ever been a book written in this country about the war, a real, serious look at the missile crisis and the blockade and invasion. Has there?'

'No, there hasn't.'

'And why's that?'

Shame, he thought, we're still ashamed – he remembered saying that to Sandy a while ago – and he saw Mark's face and said, 'Censorship. Reasons of national security.'

A quick nod. 'Exactly. Yesterday, today, and tomorrow. We worship at the altar of national security, guarded by the acolytes of the Zed Force and aided and abetted by our fine

British friends. Here's some advice, *Boston Globe*. Go back home and drop this one.'

Mark struggled out of his chair and Carl put the teacup down on the coffee table. He followed the old man out to the entrance way. It had gotten darker since he had first arrived, with storm clouds making their way across the water. Mark stopped at the door. 'Back in '62, Caz called me up and said I should come here. This was our family's summer home. I was still living in Cambridge at the time but Caz said I should stay away from the big cities. He said I should store up some food, and that if things got worse, he'd be here with maybe a friend or two. And, I'm sad to say, that was the last time we talked, and I'm afraid I was quite short with him. Blaming him for being part of a system that was about to cast us into the darkness.'

He paused one last time in the doorway. 'You know, I wonder if we could have become friends, if it weren't for the bomb. That damnable bomb.'

Carl was a half hour out of Boston, driving south on 95, when he noticed the brake lights flickering ahead of him. It was dusk and he was now quite hungry. Lunch had been that cup of tea back in York and a half-stale doughnut from a gas station, after fueling up and using his last ration coupons for the week. The hours on the road had made his left leg achy again. As he drove he kept playing and replaying his conversation with Mark Cynewski in his mind, remembering what the man said, especially that one phrase:

History is written by the survivors.

Merl Sawson had been a survivor, but what was his history? Just to end up in a cheap East Boston apartment with his head blown away, not even missed much by his neighbors, who basically ignored him except for sharing an occasional meal or overhearing an occasional howl from a bad dream. What did it mean? And what about that damn list he had passed over?

More brake lights, and then flares in the center of the highway. Figures moved in shadows among the flares, and the lanes of traffic flowed right and left, onto the shoulders. He turned to the left, seeing Army soldiers wearing MP brassards, slowing traffic. Up and down the grassy median strip were Army deuce-and-a-half trucks, two or three armored personnel carriers, and jeeps. Some of the jeeps had .30 caliber machine guns mounted on the rear. There were also a few state police cruisers, their strobe lights giving everything a bluish glare. The cruisers were parked near an area about fifty feet square that was enclosed by barbed wire. A handful of people sat behind the wire, hands on their heads.

Two soldiers approached his car and he rolled down the window. They wore clean fatigues and helmets. One was a sergeant and the other a corporal. Their shoulder patches identified them as the 45th Division, the Yankee Division. The sergeant had a holstered pistol at his side and a clipboard in his hands. The corporal had an M-14 in his hands with a flashlight attachment at the bottom of the barrel. He stood behind and to the side of the sergeant, providing cover.

The sergeant stepped up to him. 'Evening, sir. Could I see some identification, please?'

Carl knew the drill, and knew how to play it. He reached into his rear pocket, took out his wallet, and removed his Massachusetts driver's license, his Boston residency card, and his Armed Services identification card. The sergeant's attitude instantly changed when he saw the green and white military identification.

'Sorry to stop you, Sergeant Landry. We're doing a sweep of this county for draft dodgers. Can you tell me where you're coming from?'

'York, Maine.'

'Did you pick up any hitchhikers along the way?'

'No.'

'Did you see any hitchhikers in your travels?'

'No.'

'And your destination tonight, Sergeant Landry?'

'Boston, and you can stop calling me sergeant. I'm not active duty; I'm in the inactive reserve.'

The man smiled. 'Very good, sir.' He made a notation on his clipboard and handed Carl back his driver's license, residency card, and military identification. 'You're cleared to go.'

And then they left, to check on a semi-trailer truck behind him. Carl glanced in his rearview mirror and noted two other officers talking to an Army lieutenant, near the truck's cab. They weren't wearing standard-issue uniforms. When they moved in front of the headlights, Carl noted the difference. One wore a British army uniform, and the other officer looked British as well, except for the flag patch on the shoulder: white and red, with a red maple leaf in the center. Canada.

Carl was surprised at how prickly he suddenly felt. He wanted to yell out the window, Just go home. Just go back to your own country. And he also felt guilty, although it was hard to know why. Because he'd been away from the newspaper today? Because there was a lonely old man dying in Maine and for a brief few seconds he had given the man the false hope that his brother was still alive? Because he felt like he owed something to Merl, and he had gained almost nothing today?

Then the traffic started moving and he inched his way forward. He saw four young men and a woman on the grass in the median strip, behind the temporary fence of barbed wire, illuminated by the lights from the state police cruisers and a couple of jeeps. They were dressed in jeans and T-shirts and jackets, and the woman was weeping, leaning against a bearded man, both of them with hands on top of their heads.

Guilt. He remembered Southern California and tried to concentrate on his driving.

Back in Boston he grabbed a take-out container of beef stew from Dilligan's Market at the corner and made his way up to his apartment, copies of the day's *Globe* and *Herald* under his arm. He stood at the kitchen counter, the television set on, half listening to *Gunsmoke*, eating the rapidly cooling stew. As he ate he flipped through the newspapers, scanning the headlines. More rallies for Rockefeller and McGovern. A successful launch of the Fer de Lance rocket from French Guiana with two French astronauts aboard. Some fighting among two of the Chinese states. One caught his eye:

PAROLE DENIED FOR BUNDY

LEAVENWORTH, Kansas (AP) – In a secret hearing held yesterday, parole was again denied to McGeorge Bundy, an adviser to President John F. Kennedy, who is currently serving a life term in the Leavenworth Federal Penitentiary.

A spokesman for the Federal Parole Board would not give details of the hearing. Bundy will next be eligible for parole in 1973.

Bundy is one of the highest-ranking members of the Kennedy Administration who survived the Cuban War, having been in New York City at the time of the missile attack on Washington, DC.

In 1963 he and a number of other surviving members of the Kennedy Administration were convicted before the special Domestic War Crimes Tribunal.

Now there was a survivor. What kind of tale could he tell, if he were allowed to speak? He flipped to the back page of the *Herald*, and saw a smaller story about someone who did not survive:

EAST BOSTON MAN DIES IN HIT AND RUN

An East Boston man, Andrew Townes, 59, of Monroe Street, died late last night in an apparent hit and run accident, police say. Witnesses said Townes was walking across the street near his home when he was struck by a dark-colored van, which then sped away. Police had no other details, but an investigation is said to be under way.

Carl threw away the cardboard container from his dinner, turned off the lights in his apartment, and tried to sleep that night in a chair in the living room, dozing off sporadically, his Army-issue .45 in his hands.

No matter what was going on, he intended to be a survivor.

EMPIRE: TWO

A MATTER OF EMPIRE: TWO

IT WAS NIGHT when Major Kenneth Hunt of the British army's Parachute Regiment, 16th Parachute Brigade, threw open the door to his office and sat down at the tiny desk, his legs trembling. He had just come from a regimental briefing that had finally given him and the other officers the word on what they were doing in Canada, and why, and the news had sickened him. He almost ran back to his little office, wanting to be alone, not wanting to talk to any of his brother officers. Not at all.

The only light in the tiny room was an overhead lamp that cast a faint pool of illumination over the desktop and left the rest of the office in darkness. A pencil on the desktop vibrated from the sound of a jet engine out on the runway. He leaned forward and put his head in his hands. Damn them, he thought. Damn them all for planning this awful piece of shit and asking him and his paras to take care of it.

Turnabout, he thought. Operation Turnabout. Such a simple name for such a horrid plan. He reached down, opening a drawer in the desk. Inside, he saw a collection of file folders, a tiny framed photo, and a bottle of single-malt whiskey. He gingerly picked up the black-and-white photo. It showed a smiling woman, wearing a white sweater, standing next to a rose bush in a garden. His wife, Rachel. The photo had been taken eleven years ago, before his transfer to West Germany and the AOR; the British Army of the Rhine. When war had broken out he and his unit had been on the highest stage of alert, waiting for the Soviet and East German tank divisions to start moving west. But except for streams of refugees, nothing else had ever come across the border. When the American warheads had struck in the old Soviet Union, both NATO and the Warsaw Pact had collapsed. The Soviet armies melted away, and soon, so had the armed East Germans.

He remembered breathing a sigh of relief that horrid October and November, thinking he would live after all, live long enough to retire, enjoy life with Rachel and start a family.

But Rachel had been on holiday with her parents in the Punjab in northern India, touring places that her father knew, back when he was in the Foreign Service. No one had known of the fallout that had moved with the winds, but that hadn't made much difference. Rachel and her mother and father had died a month later from the exposure, not even able to leave India to come home.

M'love, he thought, gently putting the photo back into the drawer. I don't know what I can do, but I do know I can't do this. I can't go forward and doom so many others to what happened to you.

I just can't.

He took a deep breath, pulled the bottle out, and put it in

the center of the desk. He stared at it and then finally, reached out and uncorked it.

When he poured the drink into the glass, his hand shook so hard that the bottleneck rattled against the rim of the glass.

TEN

THE MORNING AFTER HIS VISIT to Maine, Carl
drove over to Lane Street Division Headquarters, keeping a
close look at the other traffic as he navigated the narrow
streets, looking for any dark-colored vans. His .45 automatic
– heavy in his hands during last night's fitful sleep – was
under the front seat. He parked at the rear of the station. It
was a cloudy day that was threatening mist, and even on
police station property, he didn't feel safe.

All it would take would be a word from someone – almost
anyone with authority – and he could be detained up to seven
days for questioning, if it involved matters of national security. Then he could be released, and two minutes later, be
picked up again for another seven days. And so forth and so
on. With the deaths of Merl Sawson and Andrew Townes and
the disappearance of the upstairs student, Troy Clemmons,
Carl knew he had entered the murky land of late-night
arrests, 'disappearances,' and closed-door trials. Despite all
that, he felt a tingling energy as he went up the steps, even as
he yawned from last night's lack of sleep. It was a sense of
energy he had felt before in South Vietnam and in California,

when he had perversely felt very much in control and very much alive. Even with everything that was going on, it was a good feeling, a better feeling than what it had been like last week and last month and last year, putting in a day's worth of work and going home to an empty and quiet apartment.

What had changed, he wondered. The murder of Merl Sawson? Or the arrival of Sandy Price?

The inside of the police station was a rolling wave of chaos. There were people sitting on benches and on chairs, some of them handcuffed to railings. Cops and plainclothes detectives wandered about, phones rang, typewriters chattered, and raised voices echoed from a caged-off area in the back. Two Army officers were behind a glass-enclosed office, sitting at a desk with what looked to be a police lieutenant or captain. Just into the entrance was a sergeant's desk. Carl pushed his way forward until he got the attention of a police sergeant with a handlebar mustache and large sweat stains on his uniform shirt.

'Yeah, whaddya want,' the sergeant said, barely looking up to acknowledge him.

Carl passed over his press ID. 'Carl Landry from the *Globe*. Is Detective Malone in?'

'Nope,' the sergeant said, head bent over.

'Well, will he be in later today?'

'Nope.'

'How about tomorrow?'

'Nope.' His head was still lowered, as he wrote with a thick pen on a pad of paper. A sign on the nearby rear wall said CONSERVE PAPER. CONSERVE PENCILS.

He took a deep breath and said, 'Look, have I pissed you off in the past, or are you just having a bad day?'

The sergeant looked up. 'Any day in this freakin' zoo's a

bad day, pal. Look. Detective Malone won't be back for a month or two. He's been called up.'

'Army reserve?'

A shake of the head. 'Nope, Navy.'

'He doesn't seem young enough to be in the active reserves.'

The sergeant's face colored. 'Yeah, and neither does his wife or his dying mother or his three kids think so. The son of a bitch was in the inactive reserve, just like me and half the crew in this station. But for no goddamn good reason, he's been called up. Last I heard, he's going up to Seattle, do some boat patrols on the Canadian border. Shitty duty for a guy that old.'

He thought fast, wondering what in hell was going on, and said, 'Can you tell me who's handling a case of his? The Merl Sawson homicide, over in East Boston.'

The sergeant muttered and made a great production of going through some file folders. Then he said, 'Detective Picucci. Up one floor and to the left.'

Carl followed the directions and spent an unsatisfying few minutes with Detective Greg Picucci, who coughed a lot and looked about one week away from retirement. He looked through a collection of file folders, and peered through thick glasses as he said, 'Ah, here it is. Merl Sawson. Case to be placed within the inactive file.'

'Inactive? Hell, it's only a week old!'

Detective Picucci blinked slowly a few times, like an old tortoise ambling his way home. 'Sorry, young man. That's what the file says. Inactive.'

'Well, can you tell me—'

He held up a hand. 'According to the department rules, you should be placing your request with the press liaison's office, down at headquarters.'

'You know that's a waste of time. It takes a week for them to return phone calls.'

A shrug. 'Not my problem. Them's the rules, and that's why I'm about to pull the pin and get out of this rotten city on full pension. I followed the rules and I suggest you do the same.'

Carl stood up and headed out of the detective's bullpen. 'Screw the rules,' he said, but he was sure that Detective Picucci hadn't heard him.

At the *Globe*, he was scrounging a cup of coffee from the cafeteria when he was ambushed by Grace Hanratty. She shook her head as she approached, her eyeglasses bouncing from the thin chain around her neck.

'Sorry, Carl, couldn't find a damn thing,' she said in a loud voice, and a couple of *Globe* staffers looked up from their tables. 'That list came up with nothing, nothing at all.'

'Are you sure—'

'Don't be telling me how to do my job, boy,' she said, snorting in disgust. 'There's nothing there, nothing. I put the list back on your desk. Don't go bothering me again unless you've got some real work for me to do.'

Damn, he thought, as he left the cafeteria and went to the newsroom. There was a clump of reporters surrounding the metro desk and George Dooley was leaning back in his chair, grinning. Jeremiah King, the city hall reporter and beer trivia expert, was the center of attention, receiving a lot of backslapping and handshaking. Carl looked at the group and a voice echoed in his head: Quota baby. Student killer.

Bobby Munson, one of the other general assignment

reporters, broke away from the crowd. Carl looked up and said quietly, 'Hey, Bobby.'

'Yeah?' Bobby came over, reporter's notebook in his hand, thick fingers smeared with newsprint and ink.

'What's going on over at metro? Somebody's birthday?'

Bobby glanced back and said, 'No, Jeremiah's one happy fellow, that's what.'

'And why's that? The mayor decided to stop asking Jeremiah to suck up so much?'

Bobby smiled, just a bit. 'No. Word just came down from Albany. Northeast Military District's allowing a press tour of Manhattan later this week, first one in five years. Jeremiah's been selected to go as the *Globe*'s representative.'

'Who did the selecting? The *Globe* or Albany?'

Bobby smirked. 'What do you think?'

'Then he must have a friend at city hall.'

'Or an enemy or two who hopes he doesn't come back.'

Carl looked over at the grinning Jeremiah King, wishing he had met the man when he was in the service. Back then, at least, you could take care of jerks in a more direct way. Like an elbow to the jaw. 'He looks pretty pleased with himself.'

'Maybe so, but that's an assignment I'd gladly give up.'

He looked over at Bobby, who seemed almost embarrassed by what he had just said.

'C'mon, Bobby, that's a story anyone would want to go on.'

He shook his head fiercely. 'No thanks. That there is a dead island. I've seen one before, and I have no urge to see another.'

'You've been to Manhattan?'

Bobby glanced down at his feet. 'No. It was when I was sixteen, back in '62.' He looked up, a haunted look on his face. 'My dad was in the Navy, stationed at Guantanamo Bay in

Cuba. My mom and me, we were evacuated from Gitmo on October 22, along with a couple of thousand other dependents. We were on a ship called the *Duxbury Bay*.' His eyes started to tear up. 'We didn't even get a chance to say good-bye. We had one hour to pack and leave. We were placed on the ship, and three days later, we steamed into Norfolk. And when the war started, a couple of days later, we had to evacuate again because they thought the Navy base there would be a target. We went to live with my dad's parents in Kentucky and that's when we heard about the base being overrun by the Cubans and Russians. And that's all we heard, ever. So Jeremiah can have his fucking dead island. I don't want it.'

Bobby moved away and Carl pretended to look at a week-old *Globe* on his desk. Everywhere you go, everywhere you look, he thought, there's those damn decade-old ghosts.

He looked through the papers on his desk, didn't see the list. Damn it, Grace said she had left it here. Carl looked around at the adjoining desks, saw that he was being studiously ignored, and from inside his coat pocket – next to the JFK invitation and Merl's identification card – he pulled out a small square of white cardboard. 'Stewart Thompson,' it said. He dialed the number and after three rings, it was picked up.

'Hello?' came the man's voice.

Carl sat up in his chair, blocking out the sound of the teletypes and ringing phones and typewriters. 'Stewart Thompson, please.'

There was a pause. 'May I ask who's calling?'

Carl thought furiously and said, 'A friend of Merl Sawson's.'

A longer pause on the other end, and the man cleared his throat. 'Could you say that again, please?'

'A friend of Merl Sawson's,' Carl said.

'And what might your name be?'

Carl said, 'Look, my name doesn't matter, could I please speak to—'

Click. The man had hung up.

'Damn it all to hell, you stupid reporter,' Carl said to himself. 'You should have said Caz, Caz Cynewski. Moron.'

The phone rang twenty-five times before he hung up. He looked at the card, double-checked the number and dialed again. This time, it was picked up on the first ring.

'Hello, is this—' Carl began, and then he listened in disgust.

There was an odd-sounding tone, and a recorded female voice. 'I'm sorry, that number is no longer in service.'

He slammed the receiver down. Damn it, if you had only thought this out before calling, you fool, he thought, looking again at the business card. Stewart Thompson, mystery man. Avoiding answers. Avoiding phone calls. Even avoiding repeat phone calls. But there were two things old Stewart Thompson could not avoid.

One was his British accent.

And the other was his distinctive, high-pitched voice, a voice Carl had heard a few days ago, huddled in a men's room at the British consulate.

He had a quick lunch with Jack Burns at the Bel-Aire, an old aluminum-cased diner that had survived the 1950s and '60s, and which got a lot of lunchtime business from the truckers going up the Southeast Expressway to Boston and the North

Shore. As they ate Carl asked, 'You know anyone at the British consulate?'

'I guess the hell I don't,' Jack said. 'I don't think they're in the business of handing out immigrant visas to music critics. Why do you . . . oh. You're working on something odd, aren't you.'

'You could say that,' he said, wondering how much he could tell Jack. 'Let's say I've got a story here that's somehow connected to the consulate.'

'Did George assign you this story?' Jack asked, his voice sharp. 'Oh, Jesus, don't tell me. It's hooked into that murder, right? The one that got spiked.'

Carl noted the fear in Jack's eyes. 'Maybe it does, and—'

'Then drop it, right now. Anything that involves a murder and the British consulate and a story of yours that gets spiked, then drop it. Write a feature about Halloween or ice skating this winter at the Public Garden. It'd be a lot healthier.'

'I can handle it, Jack.'

'Maybe you can,' he said. 'But I like having you around the newsroom, Carl. I'd hate to see you get re-upped and sent to Omaha because of this. Take my advice. Don't piss off the powers that be.'

Carl picked up a fork, thinking again about that encounter he had the other night with the orfie gang near the consulate. 'It might be a little late on that point, Jack.'

There was someone waiting for Carl in the newspaper's lobby as he came in off Morrissey Boulevard. Sandy Price was wearing a long leather coat belted tight around the middle over tan slacks. 'Finally,' she said, smiling. 'You're back. I dropped in to see if you'd like to join me for lunch. If only I had been a few minutes earlier.'

He smiled back. It was good to see her. 'Sorry to disappoint you, and I'm afraid I'm going to have to disappoint you again. I really have to get up to the newsroom.'

'Can I come in with you, then,' she said. 'I've got something to ask.'

They took the escalator up to the second floor. As they went into the noisy room, past the desks and pillars and teletype machines, she laughed. 'My word, newsrooms don't look much different, no matter what side of the Atlantic you're on.'

'It's been said newsrooms are run on beer, butts, and coffee. How about the *Times*?'

'Except for the coffee,' she said. 'We have afternoon tea, with biscuits.'

He steered her through the crowded desks, conscious of the looks they were attracting. To hell with them all, he thought.

She sat next to his desk, large black purse in her lap, and said, 'I wanted to thank you again for spending the day with me on Sunday. It was lovely and I learned a lot, and I had to go and spoil it all by falling asleep. And thanks for that little note, especially the au revoir part.'

'No apologies necessary,' he said, conscious again of her fair skin, her warm smile. 'I'm glad you were able to get some good out of it.'

'Yes,' she said, opening her purse and taking out a thin envelope, which she passed to him. 'Here. Sandy Price always keeps her promises. A check for a day's work for the *Times*.'

He supposed he should have done the noble thing and refused the check, but his bank account had a hard time recognizing nobility. 'Thanks,' he said, taking the envelope.

'There,' she said, clasping her hands back on top of the

bag. 'Now that we've got that out of the way, I have another proposition for you.'

'A business proposition, I'm sure.'

Her eyes were shiny. 'Of course a business proposition. Tell me, can you take pictures?'

'News photos?'

'Yes, of course that's what I meant. News photography.'

All this time, looking at her smile and bright eyes, he realized that more than a dozen people in the newsroom were watching him, and he didn't let his gaze waver from her, not a bit.

'Sure,' he said. 'I've done some shooting with a 35-millimeter single-lens reflex. Most people in this newsroom have. But I don't do darkroom work. I let the magicians handle that one.'

'Don't we all,' she said. 'Well, here's my proposition. I've just been invited to go to Manhattan for a press tour, one of the first ones the U.S. Army has had in years. Remember what I said, at the consulate party? I told you I'd find a way to get to Manhattan before my trip was over. And can you believe my luck, that I was here at the right time?'

He thought of the tears in Bobby Munson's eyes and decided to be polite. 'I know, you must be really happy.'

'I am, and my editors are terribly excited. They are making room for a special report next week, and they've asked me to make other arrangements as well. Visual arrangements. They've given me the authority to hire a photographer to come along and I thought, well, you've done work for the *Times* already, you're vetted as it were, and why not? I think we'd have a wonderful time.'

Damn that smile, that self-confidence, the spirit that this whole trip was just a lark, and not a trip to a dead city. He hated what he was going to say but he saw no other choice.

'I'm afraid I can't,' he said, and something stirred inside him as he saw the disappointment in her face. 'It's not that I don't want to, but I can't see how I can. First of all, the *Globe* will be sending along its own reporter and photographer. I'm positive they won't want me to be there. Second, there's no way I could get the time off to go, even freelance. I'm sorry, Sandy.'

When she frowned, faint lines creased her forehead. 'Well, why don't I talk to your editor? Perhaps we could work it out.' She turned in her chair and said, 'Which one of those characters up there do I talk to?'

He let his fingers brush across his typewriter keys. 'I really wish you wouldn't.'

'Why? Don't you want a chance to go to Manhattan? Most reporters I know would cheerfully give up beer for a lifetime to be in on a story like that.'

Carl wondered how to say it. 'Let's just say that my position in this newsroom is already precarious. Most of my fellow reporters don't think I even belong here in the first place.'

Her hands were quite still on her large black purse. 'What do you mean?'

He slowly turned his head, looked over at the newsroom, saw his fellow reporters either whispering with each other or pretending to ignore him. Up at the semicircle of desks that belonged to the editors, a couple of them were craning their necks, looking over the mess of newsroom furniture toward him.

'Time for another lesson,' Carl said. 'There's a term that's used here, although they try not to use it when I'm around. But sometimes people slip and refer to me and a few others here at the *Globe* as "quota babies."'

'Quota what?' she asked, puzzled.

'Quota babies,' he said, finding it hard to avoid those steady brown eyes of hers. 'When I left the service, because of my veteran status, I was able to get into a rent-controlled apartment in a reasonably nice part of the city, and I was able to get this job as well. Some, well, most people resent that, especially nonveterans. They see us as "quota babies" and the whispers around the newsroom are that if I weren't a vet, I wouldn't be at the *Globe*. I'd be working on a suburban paper somewhere, covering PTA meetings and church fairs. If that.'

'And you're afraid that a trip like this one—'

'Will make my position in the newsroom even worse,' he said. 'Afraid is probably not the right word, but I am concerned. I've also been working on a story that's gotten me into a few scraps, one that I want to wrap up, and well, Sandy, it's a hell of an offer but . . .'

She nodded briskly. 'I understand perfectly. I think some of the most devious politicians I've ever met worked at the *Times*, and not the House of Commons. Some hate the fact that my father's influence helped me get my job, and I continually have to prove myself by always going after better and bigger stories. Like this one.'

She stood up and passed him a business card. 'It will be a unique trip, Carl, and I wish you were coming along. But if that can't happen, I'll buy you dinner when I get back and you can ask me anything you'd like.'

Sandy held out her hand and he shook it gently. 'Deal,' he said,

'Deal.' And then she left the newsroom. He watched every step she made, strolling to the glass doors.

Searching for a pencil in his desk, he found the list of names from Merl Sawson. It was in the center drawer and attached to the list was a handwritten note:

> Carl—
>
> Here's what I found, and I didn't like what I learned. Which is why I pretended otherwise in that very public scene this morning.
>
> Please keep me out of whatever you're doing, but in the meantime, good luck.
>
> By the by, I was a volunteer for JFK in 1960 . . .
>
> —Grace
>
> P.S. Please destroy this note. Thanks.
>
> —G.

Carl looked up to see if he was being watched. He wasn't. He removed Grace's note, tore it into tiny pieces, and then dropped the pieces in a half-empty coffee cup that was on his desk. He poured the sludge into his wastebasket.

He looked at the clippings Grace had supplied, blurry photocopies from *Boston Globes* past, and with every name on the list, there was a clipping from the year listed next to each person's name:

Q. DOOLEY   65

Quentin Dooley, a special assistant to President John F. Kennedy, convicted during the 1963 Domestic War Crimes Tribunal, was shot and killed while trying to escape from Leavenworth Federal Penitentiary last week, authorities said . . .

T. ISAACSON   65

It was reported this week that Thomas Isaacson died of heart failure last month at the Federal Prison on

Alcatraz Island in San Francisco. Isaacson worked for the Department of Defense, and was serving a term for his actions during the Cuban War . . .

C. PORTER   68

Soon after his arrest last night, Clarence Porter – a Deputy Assistant Secretary of Defense during the Kennedy Administration – died in Military Police custody . . .

N. DINITALE   71

Nicholas DiNitale was killed in an auto accident on Route 3 in southern New Hampshire last night, as police officials and members of the Military Police were attempting to arrest him. DiNitale – a counsel to President John F. Kennedy – has been a fugitive from justice since being convicted *in absentia* during the Domestic War Crimes Tribunal of 1963 . . .

F. X. TILLEY   72

One of the last surviving members of President John F. Kennedy's inner circle and a member of the Executive Committee – ExComm – which so disastrously planned the Cuban War, was killed during a prison disturbance this past Saturday.

Francis X. Tilley was an inmate at the Leavenworth Federal Penitentiary when the riot broke out . . .

It felt like something was crawling up the back of his scalp. He remembered his meeting with Merl Sawson last month. Something awful was going on, a big story, maybe the biggest story ever, the old man had said. Carl had covered enough crimes to know what had been going on. Witnesses. Witnesses to the start of the bloodiest war in history were being eliminated, and Merl had been the latest. And it looked like Merl had gone to him, Carl Landry, and then to the British consulate, and now—

He sensed someone coming up behind him in the newsroom. As casually as he could, he pulled an expense report over the clippings and the list of names.

'Mr. Landry?' said the voice behind him, a male voice that was vaguely familiar and sounded very self-confident.

'Yes?' he said, turning in his chair and blinking his eyes quite hard as he saw who was before him.

Major Cullen Devane, oversight editor, nodded with satisfaction. 'I need a few moments of your time, please.'

He walked past Carl's desk and headed to his own office, without looking back to see if Carl was following.

The newsroom seemed awfully quiet. Not many things one could do at a time like this.

He took a deep breath.

He got up and followed the Army major.

ELEVEN

HE CLOSED THE DOOR BEHIND HIM as he went into the oversight editor's office. Devane was already sitting in a plush leather swivel chair, and he motioned to one of two leather chairs before the wide desk. He was wearing his standard work attire of dark gray vest and dress pants, white shirt, and dark blue necktie. The matching suit coat hung on a wooden clothes rack in the far corner. The office blinds were closed and green-shaded lamps were lit. Carl sat down and looked at Devane, who was opening up a manila file folder. His hair was black and streaked with gray, cut quite short, and his ears were small and set against his head. In the faint office light his skin looked smoothly waxed. There were two kinds of officers in this man's Army, Carl recalled. Those who count and those who don't. Those who count were in the field, making a difference, working with their troops and doing their job. Those who didn't count remained in the rear, generating and thriving on chickenshit rules and regulations. In Carl's mind, no matter how much power the man had, Devane didn't count.

On the wall behind the major were framed awards, certificates, and photos. One photo showed Devane in dress Army uniform, getting a medal pinned on him. Another photo showed a smiling Devane – still in dress Army uniform – shaking hands with General Ramsey Curtis.

Devane looked up from the file folder. 'Interesting record you have here, Landry.'

'Yes,' Carl said. He placed his hands on his pants leg, surprised at how calm he felt. So this was what it was like, being in the lion's den. He looked closely at Devane, at the tailored clothes, clean office, tidy desk, and decorations on the wall, and suddenly he felt something, something he had not felt in a very long time, since he was in the Army and facing down other stupid officers. He took a deep breath. This was going to be a hell of a ride.

'Let's see,' Devane said, leaning back in his swivel chair, his voice steady and low, the file folder open before him. 'Carl Martin Landry. Born in Newburyport, Massachusetts, on March 5, 1942. Went to the local schools. Parents deceased. One sister, reported missing after the war. Enlisted in the U.S. Army on May 1, 1960. Successfully went through infantry training and advanced infantry training.'

Devane looked up for a moment, raised an eyebrow. 'Also successfully went through Special Forces training in Fort Bragg, North Carolina. I'm impressed.'

'Good for you,' Carl said.

'After additional training, sent overseas and assigned to the Military Assistance Command, Republic of South Vietnam. Spent several months there, training and advising South Vietnamese troops. Hot as hell there, I'm sure.'

'It had its moments.'

Devane turned a page, snapping it over. 'After the war, you and the rest of your advisers from Vietnam came home. You ended up in Southern California, attached to the 24th

Infantry Division. You spend the next six years there, working relief and recovery. Well, eventually working relief and recovery.'

Carl said nothing, staring intently at the man's face. Devane stared back. 'For a year or two – your records aren't that clear – you were attached to a Special Forces unit. Something called Task Force Coven. Care to elaborate on your duties there?'

'No.'

'It says here, Mr. Landry, that you were involved in a number of interesting campaigns in the Southern California area. Operation Thrasher. Operation Kilroy. And this one, Operation Phoenix. What were those operations like?'

Surprise, surprise. His hands felt fine and his voice was quite clear. 'When I left active duty, I signed a standard National Security nondisclosure form. I'm afraid I can't say anything else.'

Devane merely smiled. 'Operations Thrasher and Kilroy took place in the spring of 1963 at the border with Mexico. Mexican gangs – some of them consisting of off-duty Mexican army officers – were raiding the refugee camps set up east of San Diego. You and your units went into Mexico – illegally of course – and neutralized the problem. Correct?'

Carl said nothing, remembering the bright sun of those days, the wind that came out from San Diego smelling of soot and decay, and the cold nights in the desert, moving south, scared to death that you were going to be seen by the Mexican Federales before reaching your target. Then brief firefights. Explosions and tracers lighting up the night sky.

Devane kept smiling and placed the folder on his desk. 'Now, Operation Phoenix, that's the interesting one. Back then, farmers and rural residents in Southern California were forming armed gangs. Militias, they called themselves. It seems they didn't like the refugee camps being placed in their towns, they didn't like being under martial law, and they didn't like the Army confiscating their crops and farm animals to feed their city brethren. Operation Phoenix targeted the leaders of these militia groups. You were supposed to go out at night and capture these leaders.'

Carl said, 'Is this going anywhere, or are you just the kind of guy who likes to hear himself talk?'

'Oh, it's going places, don't you worry,' Devane said, shifting his weight, the leather chair making a faint creaking noise. 'That's when your career really got interesting. A few discipline problems while engaged in Operation Phoenix, then you're wounded on a night engagement, you receive the Purple Heart, and then you're transferred to Sacramento. There, you're assigned to a desk, performing writing duties. Including the base newsletter. From there you serve out the rest of your term, and then you end up here, at the *Globe*, in 1968.'

Devane folded his hands and leaned forward. 'Tell me, Landry, haven't you learned anything at your time at the *Globe*? Anything at all?'

'I know some great parking spots downtown, if that's what you mean.'

'No, not hardly,' he said, eyes glaring. 'I'm talking about your job. About listening to your editor and completing your assignments. Your real assignments, not ones you're doing on you own. Landry, why in hell haven't you left that Merl Sawson story alone?'

Carl forced himself to keep his voice even. 'Because it's a story, that's why.'

Devane shook his head. 'No, it's not. You know why?

Because your editor says it isn't, that's why. I don't care if you see rogue Russian paratroopers or Cuban refugees dropping into Boston Common tomorrow morning. If your editor tells you that's not a story and sends you to the Boston Garden Club for their annual meeting, then that's all you need to know.'

'Why did you spike it?' Carl asked, wondering how far he could push Devane. 'What is it about Merl Sawson that involves national security?'

'My job doesn't concern you, Landry.'

'The hell it doesn't, when you're spiking stories I write and I don't know why.'

'The fact that they're spiked is all you need to know,' Devane said sharply. 'So listen well. Stop poking around Sawson's death. Understand? There's no story there. Leave it be.'

Carl said nothing, just stared at that smooth and healthy face. Devane looked like he could order the death of the men on that list that Merl Sawson had, men who were on the inside during the first dark days of the Cuban War. All because of those magic two words: national security. What a country.

Devane went on. 'What the hell are you, anyway? One of those crazy Kennedy cultists, is that it? Looking to rewrite history? Here, let me tell you about history.' Devane opened a desk drawer, pulled out a sheaf of papers, clipped together. 'Here, read this when you get a moment. It's a copy of an article I wrote for the *Army Times*, a few years back. We were talking operations back a few minutes ago. Ever hear of something called Operation Mongoose?'

Carl slowly nodded. 'Anti-Castro activities conducted by the CIA and others, right after Castro took power in Cuba.'

'Not quite correct, Landry. After Kennedy came to power. After Kennedy was humiliated at the Bay of Pigs in 1961, he and his brother were determined to get rid of Castro. Back then, you didn't ever humiliate a Kennedy. They always got even. That's what Operation Mongoose was about. It was more than just burning sugar cane fields or sinking patrol boats. It was about assassination attempts against Castro.' Devane motioned to the papers. 'It's all there in my article, interviews with former CIA officers, some Department of Defense personnel who were involved. Hell, the Kennedys were running a Murder Incorporated in the Caribbean, they were so pissed off at Castro. They tried to assassinate him. Several times. And their attitude stumbled us into a third world war. Is that what you're after, Landry? Is that what you are?'

'I'm a reporter, that's all.'

'That's it? Just a reporter? I don't think so. What the hell is driving you?'

Carl felt it coming up, all at once, like a water pipe under pressure. 'That's right, just a reporter. More of a reporter than you're an editor. You know what you are, Devane, don't you? You're what we called a REMF – back in Saigon and Bakersfield and Tijuana. A rear echelon motherfucker, a by-the-book, regular Army toad who doesn't care about his soldiers or his command or anything else. He's just looking to punch his ticket and go places and have pictures in his office of him kissing butt with the general.'

Devane's face was darkening. 'You better shut up right now, Sergeant Landry. I can have you reactivated and next week you can be doing latrine duty at a refugee camp in New Jersey.'

Carl laughed, happy at the reaction he was getting from

the major. 'That's right, another sign of a pure-bred REMF. Someone who isn't afraid to make threats or throw his weight around. Most of the people in this man's Army are trying to do good work in a rotten place, and guys like you are like carrion hovering up there, picking and chewing on them all the time. Must make you real proud whenever you put on your uniform.'

Devane's voice was flat. 'That's enough. You're dismissed. For not following instructions from your editor, you're suspended without pay for the rest of the week. I don't want to see you in this newsroom until next Monday. Understood?'

Carl got up. 'Oh, you've made it as plain as the brown nose on your face.'

He didn't shut the door on his way out.

At his desk he just sat for a moment, letting the tension ease away. He had gone face to face with the Great Ghoul himself, received the Killer C., and he was still here, still an employee, not someone who'd been re-upped and who would have to report to the State Street Armory tomorrow. The newsroom seemed awfully quiet. A typewriter on the other side was being used, the keys hesitantly tapped at, and there was the low stammering murmur of the teletype machines. But that was it. He found he could not look at the faces of his colleagues. He wondered what was going through their minds, and knew it was probably a mixture of fear about what had just happened, and relief that it hadn't happened to them.

'Carl?' said a quiet voice. He ignored it, content to look at his messy desk and feel a vicious sense of glee that well, what the hell, he wouldn't have to worry about this mess for a week. A week's unpaid vacation, that was the way he knew he should look at it, but it still stuck at the back of his throat, along with the thought of what he would do now. Continue to chase down the Merl Sawson story from his apartment? Could it be done?

'Carl?'

He looked up. George Dooley was standing there, looking at him. He almost laughed out loud. Now that was scary. Being inside Devane's office, well, one could expect that might happen, one of these days. But to have the city editor come to your desk? That was frightful, almost unbelievable. George never came to your desk. You went to him, and you went often, summoned by his loud, braying voice.

'Carl, could I see you for a moment?' George blinked and looked around the still quiet newsroom. 'In my office, please.'

He nodded. 'Seems to be my day for office meetings.'

In George's office he sat down, conscious that he was quite tired. George sat across from him and quietly ran his hands across the smooth surface of the desk. He picked up the photo of his niece and replaced it, looking up at Carl. 'I'm sorry for what just happened. Devane told me earlier today what he was going to do, and I did my damnedest to try to talk him out of it, but it didn't happen. I'm sorry it didn't work.'

Carl felt like his head was getting too large for his shoulders. George apologetic was something he had never seen before, and he felt a new sense of affection for the man, even with being suspended from the paper. 'So what's the story. Am I being suspended for not following orders, or because I kept chasing the Merl Sawson story?'

George's hands were flat on the desk. 'You're being

suspended because the oversight editor wants you suspended. I wish I didn't have to say that, but it's a hell of a business.'

'It sure is.'

There was the sound of a drawer being opened, and George pulled out two empty glasses and a Jack Daniel's bottle. 'Feel like a drink?'

Carl didn't feel like much of anything, but an offer was an offer. 'Sure.'

George talked as he poured the drinks. 'I usually hate to say this, because it goes to people's heads and they become worthless, but you're one of my best, Carl. I know you get crap from the newsroom about being a quota baby and I try to squash it when I can, but all in all, you do a good job for me.'

George slid a glass across the table and Carl picked it up, not quite believing what he was hearing. He took a sip from the glass, and then another.

'Tea?' Carl asked. 'Your whiskey bottle is filled with tea?'

His editor nodded, with a smile. 'Sure it is. What do you think, I drink on the job? Those days are gone, along with my liver.' George swallowed his drink in one gulp and refreshed the glass. 'Lot of days are gone. You know, back in the fifties and early sixties, if someone ever told me that we'd put up with daily censorship of the paper, I would've told 'em that they were crazy. Who'd ever think we'd be at a newspaper where a goddam Army major not only tells me what to publish but what to do with my staff . . . Christ on a crutch.'

He looked down at his glass, moved it around a bit. 'Though I gotta admit, it did make sense, at first. Back when the war started. You were overseas, weren't you?'

'Yes, I was.'

'How did you hear the news?'

'We heard it mostly over the shortwave. The BBC and

Voice of America. It seemed very far away, all distant, like it wasn't quite real . . .'

'Hah,' George said, taking another swallow. 'It was pretty real from where I was sitting.' He waved a hand out to the newsroom. 'I was one of the wire editors, checking the AP and UPI copy as it came across. First the word of missiles, the speech by Kennedy, all of those meetings at the UN. The U-2 photos. The blockade around Cuba. Troops being sent south to Florida. Reserve units activated. A very scary time. It seemed like the bells on the teletype would just keep going, hour after hour, telling you when the news was coming in.'

Carl remembered a humid bar in the Thong Qui section of Saigon, a few blocks away from the MACV headquarters, staying up late at night, listening to the news with the other advisers. Remembered a Florida soldier, an overweight, sweaty sergeant, who sat closest to the radio, chewing on a cigar, drinking that awful '66' beer. What was his name? Began with K. Was it Kyle? Yeah, that was it. Kyle. He had sneered a lot about Kennedy, wondering if JFK had the guts to take care of Castro once and for all. Well, ole Kyle had eventually found out, hadn't he.

'We didn't get much sleep back then,' Carl said. 'Our time zone meant that most of the news we got was in the middle of the night.'

'We didn't get much sleep either,' George said, his voice soft. 'Then came that weekend when the U-2 was shot down, and everything went to hell. The bells on the teletype rang so much that they broke. Our bombing raids on the SAM sites and the start of the invasion. Then the word that tactical nukes were being used on our landing forces. Ding, ding, ding. Every time that bell rang, it meant something more awful. Some of the missiles there in Cuba being launched. Soviet bombers coming over the North Pole and down through Canada. Parts of Florida, then Washington and New York City being hit. Our retaliation. All those Russian cities . . . Moscow, Minsk, Vladivostok . . . Obliterated.'

He looked at Carl, eyes blinking again. 'People lined up outside of the *Globe* building that night, and every hour we ran a new front page. It got so that the trucks couldn't even leave the loading docks 'cause people wanted to get the latest news, right there. The television networks were off the air and the radio reception was all screwy, so we were the best source of news, whatever we could get from the teletype. A day or two later we get word that General Curtis was in charge of what was left and that there was an armistice, and when the Army came by and told us what we could or couldn't print, well, it made sense. We didn't want to spread panic, we didn't want to print rumors, and we had to get out a lot of information about emergency shelters and food distribution and lots of other stuff.'

Carl drank some more of the tea. It tasted awful, like it had been in the bottle for a year, but it was a gift from George. He was now seeing a part of George he never knew existed.

'And how long before it stopped making sense?'

The older man shook his head. 'Who knows. All I know is, it's been ten years. A decade. You'd think we could get back to being a real newspaper again, one of these days. But you know what? I don't think it's going to happen, not in my lifetime.' His hand chafed the glass. 'In a few weeks this country is going to elect a New York governor who's going to promise more of the same, more of the same for the next eight years, and when his term is up, the powers that be will select another presidential candidate who'll promise even more of the same, and we'll keep on merrily electing dictators until the next century. You'd think we'd learn.'

Carl finished his glass and put it down on the desk. 'Sure enough. One of these days, but on this particular day, I guess I should go home.'

George nodded. 'Go home, Carl, and for God's sake, do me a favor, will you?'

'What's that?'

'Drop this whole mess, will you? Take a trip or something.'

Carl smiled. He felt good. 'Sorry. I'm not in the mood for favors.'

Outside, the sun was bright and besides the smell of exhaust and soot, there was the sharp tang of dead leaves, something that always reminded him of his home and growing up. He closed the door of his car and the memories came to him, of the small Cape house he and Mom and Dad and Sarah had lived in, in Newburyport. Winter, making snow forts in the backyard, burying Sarah's dolls. Spring, with the melt-off turning part of the street into a pond, making boats out of glued-together Popsicle sticks. Summer, hot and long days and cool nights, and an occasional fishing trip out from the harbor, helping bait the hook for Sarah. Fall, dead leaves and wood smoke and dressing up in a Davy Crockett costume to go trick-or-treating, Sarah beside him, a fairy princess . . .

And back in California after the war, the phone wires down, the mail system overwhelmed and clogged, not hearing anything about Mom and Dad and Sarah, not a damn thing, until that Red Cross telegram in '63 that gave him the news about his parents. That telegram. Two sentences that just bore into him, two sentences that he had to read and reread, because he could not believe what he saw on the Western Union form.

'Damn this day,' he finally said, walking away from the car, turning up the alleyway past the trash cans and dumpsters. He was cold now and felt an odd weight on his shoulders, knowing that he had no work to do tomorrow, or the day after that, or the day after that. He could look at it as an unpaid vacation, but it was all too quick and strange. What would he do with all that time? Shouldn't he keep on after the Merl Sawson matter? Find out who Stewart Thompson was at the British consulate? Work on the book? Hah, now that was a thought—

'Hey, Carl!' a voice whispered to him. 'Hold up for a sec, will you?'

From a set of cellar stairs that descended into the building next door, a man came up, dressed in old clothes and knee-length rubber boots. It was Two-Tone, a very nervous Two-Tone, who kept looking up and down the alleyway as he came over to Carl. He didn't have his shopping cart with him, which was odd, very odd. His good eye seemed nervous, wandering, and Two-Tone sidled up to him and said in a low voice, 'I have to say I'm sorry.'

'Sorry for what?'

He bobbed a bit, like he was anxious, being out in the open. 'Sorry that I couldn't stop the guys from getting in.'

Those little cold traces of feeling that worked up and down his neck back in Devane's office were now back. 'What guys are you talking about? The ones that were snooping around earlier?'

Another bob of the head. 'The same. Dressed nice and polite and in suits. Came through here like they owned the place, started looking through the trash. Can you believe that, them checking out the belongings and leftovers? That's my job! That's what I do!'

'Of course, of course,' Carl said, joining Two-Tone in look-ing up and down the alleyway. Traffic hurled by on Comm Avenue and there was the sound of sirens and horns, but he kept his focus on the scarred old man in front of him. 'What did they do after they checked the trash?'

'Them good-lookin' bastards, they went into your place, that's what, near as I can figure it. They went through the main door – they must've had a key or something 'cause I could tell nobody buzzed them in. And then I saw some movement, up in your windows. I stayed out here for a long time, keeping an eye on them.'

He looked up the brick wall of his apartment building, try-ing to see anything in those dark and quiet windows. 'Are they still up there?'

'Nope, not at all,' Two-Tone said, now stepping from foot to foot, like a first grader seeking permission to go to the bath-room. 'I counted 'em, Carl. Three went in and three went out. They ain't there no more. But they got through and I'm sorry about that, truly I am.'

Two-Tone looked so serious and crestfallen that Carl wasn't sure what to do. He nodded and said, 'Don't trouble yourself, William. It's not that big a deal.'

Two-Tone looked like he was about ready to cry. 'The hell it ain't. You good folks around here have hired me to do a job, and that's what I do, day in and day out. I keep an eye on things and chase away the bad people, but I didn't do it, not this time. Here.' Two-Tone held out a soiled white handker-chief, tied together at its four corners.

'What's that?' Carl asked.

'Your pay these past months,' Two-Tone said, gesturing with the loaded handkerchief. 'All those quarters you paid to me, week after week. All saved and I'm givin' 'em back to you, Carl. I don't deserve them.'

Carl took the bundled quarters and then took Two-Tone's free hand and gently placed the tied-up handkerchief back into the man's scar-tissued palm. 'You deserve them more than anybody I know, Captain. You take them and don't you worry, all right? You're doing a fine job.'

'Carl, you know it's not right, I should be—'

He raised his voice. 'Not true, Captain, and you know it. You remember your basic infantry training, don't you? When meeting a superior force, fall back and observe. That's exactly what you did, and that's exactly right. You earned your pay today, sir, and don't you forget it.'

Two-Tone pondered that for a moment and his eyes filled up. 'You're right, I was trained that. I knew that, I knew that all along.' He managed a smile, showing his yellowed and stained teeth. 'I guess the old training comes back, even when you don't expect it.'

'I guess it always does.'

The bundle of quarters went back into his coat and Two-Tone started to walk away. 'I'll keep on the job, Carl, but you be careful. Some boys are interested in you, are quite interested in you, and I'd hate for anything to happen. Remember, you hear the sirens wail, you be on your doorstep and I'll come get you. We'll ride out the next war together. Okay?'

'Okay,' Carl said.

He took his time going up the stairs and then entering the apartment. His heart was swollen and thumping and he wondered if it was possible that Two-Tone had miscounted or miscalculated. Maybe the all-powerful 'they' were waiting in the apartment, waiting with handcuffs or with the paperwork that got him reactivated in the Army. Could be. He unlocked the door and went in, and in a moment or two he felt a bit better. No one was there. Maybe Two-Tone had been hallucinating some about the visitors.

He poked around, and after a few minutes he knew everything Two-Tone had said had been right. People had been in here and had tossed the place. They had done it well enough so that it wasn't obvious, but he could tell. From drawers partially open to papers on his desk that had been rearranged, he knew he had been visited. But if they were looking for anything incriminating, well, he hung up his coat in the closet and briefly reached into the inner pocket. Still safe. Merl Sawson's ID, the JFK invitation, and the card belonging to the mysterious Stewart Thompson. And the list of names and the attached articles, outlining their fates.

The room felt dusty and soiled so he opened two of the windows and sat down on the couch. What is to be done? He folded his arms across his knees and stared across to the blank wall on the other side of his apartment. Well, he thought, we've definitely caught the interest of some very big people, some very big people with heavy hands and lots of muscle. Enough muscle to do a daylight break-in. Enough muscle to get him suspended from work. And maybe enough muscle to set an orfie gang after him, back at the British consulate when he had first met Sandy. Sounds like the Zed Force, riding out in the shadows.

What is to be done? Stay here in Boston for the next week and keep on working the story? That thought didn't appeal to him, not at all, despite what he knew must have happened to Merl Sawson. Now there were watchers and burglars out there, following him and poking around and doing who knows what. He knew from whispered conversations that the

Zed Force, sometimes they visited a home or apartment first, to get the lay of the land before coming back a day or two later for the inevitable arrest and detention.

What to do? He thought back to his meeting with George. What had George said?

Take a trip. Get out of town and just forget everything.

'Why the hell not?' he said aloud. He reached into his wallet and took out a business card and dialed a local number. It rang just once and he asked to be connected to a certain room, and when she answered after just three rings, he was direct and to the point:

'Sandy, it's Carl,' he said. 'Still looking for a photographer?'

TWELVE

WELL, CARL THOUGHT, standing on the sidewalk in front of his apartment on Comm Ave., it wasn't suppose to be like this. But she had been insistent.

'I'm so thrilled that you're coming with me, Carl,' she had said. 'Let's celebrate. I know, I'll be at your place in an hour, with dinner in hand. How does that sound?'

It sounded horrible, but he couldn't say that. 'Sounds great,' he had said. For the past hour, he had been going through the apartment, performing a blitz clean. Papers and magazines were bundled in a pile and shoved behind the couch. Clothes were picked up and dumped in closets. The sink was emptied of dishes and silverware. He looked at his book-lined office, the papers and pencils on the floor, books half open and piles of notebooks teetering, shook his head, and closed the door. That place would take a week, and he didn't have a week.

As he waited for her to arrive, watching the traffic go by, he tried to remember the last time he had been graced with a woman visitor. It had been a while, a little over a year, right? Monica, the woman from advertising. The one who liked to go to those semi-secret movie houses in Cambridge, see foreign films with subtitles, and who had that awful habit of smoking those dark little cigarettes after making love. He would ask her to open a window, whether at her place on Beacon Hill or here, and that had been a nice five or six months, until she took a job with an advertising firm in San Francisco. Two letters and a postcard later, that had been it. And nobody since then? And why's that?

Because, he thought. Because we're a quota baby and a vet, and people usually either hate quota babies or fear vets. Monica had been the rare exception. A taxi cab pulled up and Sandy stepped out, two grocery bags in her arms. She was laughing, her face flushed and her hair tussled from the wind. 'Oh, this is going to be fun,' she said, handing a bag over to him. 'I hate cooking but the hotel managed to put something together for the two of us.'

Back upstairs the bags were put on the freshly cleaned counter and Sandy looked around and said, 'Well, how about a quick tour of the manor before we eat? The food just needs reheating.' She shrugged off a tan overcoat, which he took and hung in the foyer closet. She had on black flat-heeled shoes, a snug pair of jeans, and a long-sleeved white blouse that had little flowers embroidered along the collars. She was smiling at him and for a moment he tried to remember what Monica had looked like.

'Not much of a tour,' he said. 'You're seeing most of the place right now. As you can see, there's the living room, the idiot box, and the lovely view.' She walked with him into the living room and stood by the tall windows.

'Nice view of the park,' she said. 'My flat in London has a view of a mews.'

'A what?'

'Mews. A courtyard where old stables used to be. At least here, you have trees and greenery.' She leaned against the window glass with her hands. 'Does it get noisy at night, being on the main street?'

'Well, you get used to the traffic and the street sounds after a while. Being three floors up, that helps. Plus I'm gifted.'

'Oh?' she said, turning and arching an eyebrow. 'In what way?'

'I can sleep pretty much through everything. Which takes us to the next part of the tour.'

After showing her the small bedroom, with made bed and bureau drawers and another closet, she pointed to the two closed doors, down a short hallway. 'And what's down there?'

'Bathroom and office.'

'Can I see your office?'

Wonderful. 'It's a rat's nest.'

She folded her arms. 'Carl Landry, I'm a grown woman and a writer, just like yourself. I shan't be shocked, no matter what you show me.' And then she smiled. 'Unless you're a typical male and have a pinup stuck on your wall, like Raquel Welch or Marilyn Monroe or somebody.'

'Hardly,' he said, opening the door and letting her in. It still looked messy. A single window looked out over the alley where he and Two-Tone had stood, a couple of hours earlier. The desk was a battered wooden castoff that he had purchased from a Boston University student a couple of years ago. The chair was surplus from the *Globe*, as was the Olympic typewriter. The bookshelves he had made himself from scrap lumber and Sandy went over to the shelves.

'I love looking at other people's books,' she said, tracing her fingers across the spines of the volumes. 'You find out what a person is really like. That's what my mama always told me. She says someone can always rabbit on about what they've done or where they've been, but it's only when you see their books that you can tell what sort of a person they are. Buying a book for yourself is a very personal business.'

He leaned against the doorway, enjoying the sight of her moving past his bookshelves. 'And what are you learning about me, Sandy?'

Her head was turned but he could still sense the smile. 'Oh, that you're a man who likes history. Most of your books here are about the past. In fact, our bookshelves are quite similar. I have a lot of history books as well, including the complete works of our mutual friend, Mr. Orwell.' She turned, a bit quizzical. 'But here I see mostly books on wars, and two wars in particular. Your Civil War and the First World War. Why is that?'

There, now that was a question. 'I'm not sure I can give you a good answer.'

'Oh, tosh, you could try,' she said, and now she was at his desk. 'Hello, what's this?'

He moved from the doorway, walked to where she was. 'Nothing, really.'

She raised an eyebrow. 'It looks like something to me.' She had her hands around a thick stack of typewritten pages and was riffling through them. He felt his cheeks warm, seeing her going through something so personal.

She looked up, eyes bright. 'It's a book, isn't it?'

'Sort of.'

She hefted it in her hands like it was a piece of fruit she was buying at a market. 'Carl, there are a couple of hundred pages here. That makes it a book where I come from. So, my secretive friend, in the ruins of the Kennedy compound, you wouldn't tell me if you were working on a book or not. And now I know. Your secret's out. What's it about?'

'Suppose I don't tell you?'

She flipped more pages, and then stopped, holding one out. '"A Soldier's Tale, by Carl Landry."' She looked over at him. 'It's not fiction, is it? It's a true story.'

'As true as I think it is.'

She gently put the pages back, glanced once more at the bookshelves. 'These all relate to your book, don't they.'

'A good guess.'

'I've told you, I'm a good reporter, and right now I'm jealous of you.' She gently tapped the side of her head. 'Any books I have are still stuck up here. At least you've got something on paper. But, back to my original question. Why do you have so many history books?'

Damn, that same good question. He had struggled with it himself for a while, coming home from the *Globe* day after day, reading and rereading the history books, trying to get his hands around . . . what? A theme? A message? Something to make sense out of that decade-old slaughter? And his own desire to put down in words, on paper, something that was true, as much as he could remember it.

Carl cleared his throat. 'I chose the Civil War for obvious reasons. Before Cuba, it was the last time that we had a war on our soil, the last time hundreds of thousands died in this country, and the last time cities were destroyed. Richmond, Vicksburg, Atlanta.'

Sandy nodded. 'We did the American Civil War at school. It reminded me of the First World War. There was great cheering and bombast and loud predictions that the war would be over in a matter of months. But four years later, the fighting and the killing were still going on. You even had trenches and mud and rats in the Civil War.'

'Yep. In some ways, the Civil War was a precursor to the First World War. Use of the telegraph. Long-range artillery. Railroads to move troops and supplies. When I looked at what happened in 1914, it reminded me so much of 1962. Two great alliances, armed to the teeth, teetering at the brink of war, just waiting for that push to send them over the edge. And it's always events in a small country that set it off. An assassination in Serbia. Missiles in Cuba.'

Carl reached past Sandy and pulled down a slim book. 'Here. Barbara Tuchman wrote this, just before the Cuban War. Called *The Guns of August*. In it, someone asks a German general how the First World War started and he said, "Ah, if we only knew." Two different wars in this same century, and the same excuse. We don't know.'

She took the book from his hands and gently put it back up onto the bookshelves. 'And what's your book about?'

'Oh,' he said, letting his fingers touch the typewritten pages, as if seeking some reassurance. 'Just a ground's-eye view, that's all. What it was like to witness the war from thousands of miles away, and what was it like to come back home and find everything in chaos. What it was like to leave home to fight communism as part of a great crusade for a young president, and to come back and see your homeland partially destroyed. Food and fuel in short supply, fallout still a problem, Washington gone, most of the political leadership gone, and one brassy and self-confident Air Force general saying he was in charge and would make everything right.'

'And did you believe that general?' she asked, in a slightly mocking tone.

He paused. 'I actually saw that general once, a decade ago. As part of an inspection tour in Saigon. Quite the character.'

'You still haven't answered the question, of whether you

believe him or not,' she said. 'Do I have to wait to read your book for your answer?'

He touched the pages one more time. 'It'll be a long wait, I'm afraid.'

'Oh,' she said, sounding disappointed. 'Still a while before it's finished?'

He gently grasped her elbow and took her out of his office. 'Sandy, no U.S. publisher will ever want to publish a book like that. Now, what have you got planned for dinner?'

'Show me the kitchen and I'll get to work.'

He set some dishes on the wide counter that separated the kitchen from the living room, and she got busy. Soon his apartment was filled with smells and sounds that had not been there in quite a while. Sandy moved about the kitchen, throwing things together, heating the dishes from the Park Plaza, putting a couple of Guinness stouts into the refrigerator. He donated a bottle of California red wine to the cause, and they ate a thick lobster stew with salad and chunks of crusty bread, and he could not remember the last time he ate so well in his home.

As they ate he turned on the radio on the counter, getting an evening jazz show from WBUR radio and the music helped deaden some of the street sounds.

'So,' she said, spooning up some of the stew. 'Tell me more about your suspension from work. You crossed up your censor, did you.'

'That I did. The official reason was that I wasn't being a good boy around my boss. The unofficial – and real – reason is that I won't go away on a story.'

Her gaze was direct, and he wondered what would happen

if he just kept staring back. 'Is it a big story? Something to do with national security?'

Plenty to do with national security, he thought, but he didn't want to say any more. 'It was a story about an old guy shot dead in his apartment. But the story never ran in the paper, and I've been told in no uncertain terms to drop it. And to make sure I got the message, I got my unpaid vacation.'

Sandy dabbed at her lips with a napkin. 'At home we have the Official Secrets Act, and there are some things we're not allowed to publish. They slap a D-notice on the press when we're about to print something that's so-called against the national interest. Like a skirmish last autumn in the Bay of Biscay, when a Royal Navy destroyer shelled some French gunboats, harassing our cod fishermen.'

Carl nodded. 'You're right. That's a story that never made it over here.'

'But at least our editors were on our side,' she said. 'They fought against Whitehall and Number Ten, trying to get the story told. But no, sorry, here's a D-notice. I can't imagine what it must be like, to have a censor in the newsroom all the time.'

'It makes their jobs very easy, and ours very hard.'

'And what will you do when your vacation is over and you're back from Manhattan?'

He finished his wine, thinking about that list of names, thinking about the mysterious Mr. Thompson, the man with the British accent and business card. Merl, the old veteran from the White House who handled papers. 'I'll check for messages, and then I'll get right back to work trying to figure out what the hell happened to get that old man murdered.'

'Good for you, Carl.'

Later, after the dishes had been dried and put away, Carl stood with Sandy in the tiny kitchen and said, 'I'm afraid there's not much in the dessert department. There's some ice cream and frozen yogurt in the freezer, but I'll give no guarantees for its freshness. Or we could take a walk down Newbury Street, find a little café. Though it is cold out.'

Her eyes were bright and she was leaning back against the counter, arms folded. 'Isn't there anything else you can think of?'

Carl smiled, took one step forward. 'Well, there's this,' and he took her in his arms and kissed her, gentle at first, until it was quite clear that she was responding to his approach, moving tight against him and running a hand across his hair, sighing with pleasure. He reveled in her scent, the feel of the fresh and clean clothes, the soft yielding of her skin.

'Oh, how wonderful,' she whispered. 'I was so hoping this would happen.'

She lay on his chest, lightly moving her fingernails across his chest as he nuzzled her hair with his nose and mouth. The scent was intoxicating and he was trying hard to burn that scent and that touch and everything else for the past hour into his mind, so he would never forget it, never forget one second or one sigh or one gasp. From the first fumbling moments in his bedroom, as he drank in the sight of her taking off her clothes, saw the unblemished skin and tasted her warmth, feeling her in his arms, to just the past minute or two, when she had sighed long and loud in his ear and had run her fingernails down his back, he had never thought it could be so wonderful.

Even though it was a cold October night the room was warm and the blankets and sheets were piled up at the end of the bed. Sandy said, 'You're very gallant, Mr. Landry.'

He smiled, her hair tickling his nose. 'Really? I thought I was slow and clumsy.'

She kissed his chest. 'Hardly, dear sir. The few times – and I emphasize the word few – I've done this road before, the men were either so slow you felt like grabbing them and telling them to get a move on, or so fast you thought they had a train to catch. No, this was very, very nice.'

'No, it wasn't.'

She sat up in mock anger. 'And what the hell do you mean by that?'

He winked. 'It wasn't nice. It was bloody marvelous, that's what it was.'

She nipped his nose, and he tugged at her ears in retaliation, and after a few moments of tussling she put her head down back on his chest. Then all of the lights went out and Sandy said, 'Carl, what's happened?'

He reached over to the nightstand, feeling for the matches he kept there, and lit a candle. Another of his country's failings had been highlighted. 'Power failure, that's all. The grid's still not stable, and sometimes things just let loose. Like tonight.'

'How romantic.'

'Well, at first, but it gets tiring after a while. Especially if it's for a week and everything in your refrigerator goes bad.'

She lay back down. 'Hmmm, Carl, can I ask you something?'

'Have I ever said no?'

'Not yet, you haven't,' she said, breathing softly upon his chest. 'Tell me, are you scared? About going to Manhattan?

Because I certainly am. Most of the stories I've covered have been in and around London. That's where I grew up. I know the shops and the tube stops and the parks, and how things work. In Manhattan . . .' She shivered. 'It just sounds so dead. I had an awful dream the other night, about being left behind during the tour. Sitting alone in the middle of a street, with the grass growing up through the cracks in the sidewalks, the night approaching, no lights coming on, listening to wild dogs howling . . . I know I've tried to put on a brave face, telling you about my stout grandmama and how she stayed with her husband during the Boer War, but still, I go cold, remembering that dream . . .'

He let his fingertips play over her soft skin. 'No, I'm not scared. Concerned, perhaps. I'm sure it's reasonably safe or the Army wouldn't be allowing a press tour. And I'm sure they'll be keeping us on a pretty short leash. Hard to see how we can get into trouble.'

'You've been scared before, haven't you?'

He closed his eyes, trying still to remember everything that was going on, feeling that soft skin against his fingertips. 'Yes, plenty of times.'

'And how did you handle your fear?'

'Most times, I took a deep breath and just kept on pressing, hoping it would be over soon. Plus I was younger and well trained, and when you're that young, full of energy and enthusiasm, you think you're invincible.'

She said nothing, but her hand moved down, lightly brushing his skin, until she reached his left thigh, where she traced a ridge of scar tissue. 'And did you stop thinking you were invincible when this happened?'

Something caught in his throat. 'No, by then I was quite sure I wasn't invincible.'

'What happened, then, if I may ask?'

His lips seemed dry. 'I was shot.'

'In Vietnam?'

'No. In California. During the Relief and Recovery mission.'

With her chin on his chest, Sandy looked up at him with great seriousness, the candlelight making her skin look impossibly smooth. 'How did it happen?'

'Do you want the real story or the official story?'

'You decide.'

'Okay, the official story was that I was out on night patrol, trying to arrest the leader of a militia group in San Bernardino County. We had intelligence information that he was in a ranch house at the end of a long dirt road up in some hills.'

'Why were you arresting him?'

'Because he and his people were becoming too effective. They were riling the farmers and ranchers, trying to prevent the Army from feeding refugees from San Diego and other towns like La Mesa and Spring Valley. So that was our mission.'

'Was there a battle?'

'That's what it says on my Purple Heart citation. When we approached the farmhouse we came under fire. Our unit was pinned down. I was trying to get our guys closer, to get to an adjacent barn, when I was hit. More dumb luck than anything else. Even though I was hit, I was still trying to do my job. So there you go. The official story. Shot while leading his unit under intense fire from a militia band.'

She bent her head and kissed his chest. 'And the real story, Carl?'

'The real story?' he said, surprised at the bitterness in his voice. 'The real story was that this militia was one large family: mother, father, sons and daughters, aunts and uncles and cousins. They didn't like being pushed around by the state government and what was left of the federal government, which is a popular American trait. They also didn't like having their cattle and grain confiscated by the relief officials. They saw us as thieves, supporting other thieves, which is why they opened fire. And a very scared fourteen-year-old boy shot me in the leg with a .22 rifle. Not very heroic, not very glamorous. The whole family was arrested and after a thorough trial of about an hour, they were sent to a decon camp outside of San Diego.'

He could feel her breath on his neck. 'We've never known precisely what happened in California, Carl. Just rumors and whispers. Could you . . .'

'Tell you what happened?' he said. 'Depends. Is the *Times* or Sandy Price asking the question.'

Her fingers again, soft upon his skin. 'Sandy. Just Sandy.'

He sighed, remembering the document he had to sign upon mustering out, swearing he would never tell anyone what he saw. To hell with it. 'Chaos. That's all. Just chaos. Before the war, Southern California was this beautifully balanced, jeweled instrument, supplying power and water to millions of people in a desert wasteland. After the war, that instrument was smashed. Imagine London without power for a month, without food deliveries. What would happen next?'

Her voice was quiet. 'People would leave.'

'Exactly. Tens of thousands of refugees from around San Diego start heading north. To Los Angeles. But hundreds of thousands of people there had been without steady power or food for weeks. There was . . . chaos. Shooting in the streets. Citizen roadblocks, refugees hung from telephone poles . . . Mothers selling themselves and their daughters for a loaf of bread. Whole city blocks being burned . . . And then winter came. And . . . well, the official story is that six or seven hundred people died of starvation that winter.'

'Oh God . . .' she whispered.

'Sandy, the real story? The real story is that two or three times that amount were dying every month. Barges were taking the bodies out to the Pacific to be dumped. And the good citizens of Southern California, they were showing their appreciation by shooting at the Army.'

'I'm sorry you were shot, Carl.'

'Don't be,' he said, squeezing her tight. 'By then I was sick of soldiering and this was what we called a million-dollar wound. I was sent away to an Army hospital and after a while I was offered a desk job in Sacramento, working on the base newsletter. I took it and found I had a knack for writing, which got me to the *Globe* and to this apartment and this lovely reporter from merry old England in my bed.' He touched her lips. 'If I had known then that getting shot would have ended me here, I wouldn't have yelped as loud.'

She smiled. 'You're being gallant again.'

'Does that mean being knightly? If so, my armor is rusting in a few spots.'

'Oh, rubbish. Can I ask another favor?'

'What's that?'

'Your book. I'd like to read it.'

'Tonight? Right now?'

'Why not?' She tickled him for a moment. 'Unless you have something better planned, my handsome stallion.'

'It's not finished. Won't be finished for a while.' The lights came back on then and he blew out the candle, a thin wisp of smoke rising up to the cracked plaster ceiling.

'Doesn't matter.' She sighed. 'Oh, damn it, I'm being forward again. Earlier on, you said it would never be published in the United States. But there are always English publishers. They're hungry for American material, since so little of it gets abroad, and I have some friends in publishing. No promises, though.'

He closed his eyes, wondering how in God's name someone like her had come into his safe and gray life, had turned everything upside down, and along the way, had made him do things that he otherwise would never have done. Like that midnight climb into Merl's apartment.

'That's a generous offer, and it brings up a subject that you and I have yet to discuss.'

'My going back to England? Let's not spoil this evening, Carl. I'm here for at least another two weeks. Let's make the most of those fourteen days.'

He moved his other arm, grasped his hands together so that she was encircled. 'All right. Deal. You can read a sample chapter, tell me if you like it. Just don't laugh at the typos and the bad spelling.'

'Promise, no laughing.'

He got up and went into his office, knowing the chapter he wanted her to read, one that had set everything up, ten years earlier. He came back and she was there, sheet now wrapped about her, looking up with a steady smile, a gaze that said things were fine, everything was possible, and he lay down next to her, passing over the small pile of papers.

Carl said, 'One quick question before you get to reading my life's work.'

'Go on,' she said, rearranging some of the typewritten sheets.

'Do you know most of the people at the consulate?'

She grimaced and snuggled up against him. 'Sort of. When I first got to Boston, I had to meet everyone there, as part of an orientation session. Christ, it was dull.'

He tried to keep his voice calm. 'Did you meet a Stewart Thompson there?'

Sandy turned to him, amazement in her voice. 'Carl Landry, how on earth do you know that man's name?'

He looked into her eyes, wondered what he could say, how much he could trust her. 'It came up in the story I'm working on. And I hope we can keep it just between us. Who is he?'

She dug an elbow into his ribs. 'Oh, I shan't be telling your tales to the consulate, don't worry. Us press people have to stick together, especially when we're faced with censors, no matter what they call themselves. And now I know why you got into trouble with your editor, if Stewart Thompson's involved.'

He couldn't move. 'Why's that?'

'Because Stewart Thompson is an assistant agricultural attaché, but everybody in the consulate – and I imagine your local FBI – knows his real job. He's with MI6.'

'British intelligence,' he said, finding it hard to say those two words. My God, Merl Sawson must have gone to them after he met me outside of the *Globe*.

'Exactly. He was at the reception. Tall, dour fellow, with a big mane of white hair. Looks like he spends his free time eating limes and lemons so he can get that sourpuss look just right. Funny thing is, Dougie Harris – the press attaché – said that Stewart was having a terrible time a few weeks ago, over that general's death, the one called Sheffield. It was causing him a tremendous headache with his superiors.'

'The one found in bed with the prostitute?' he asked.

'The same,' she said, holding up the typewritten pages of his book. 'And here's my chance to tell you a little secret, so we're even for the night. Apparently this retired general was more than just some Army officer with a taste for teenage girls. It seems he had quite an interesting past, as military attaché in Washington before the war.'

'Here? That general was the military attaché in 1962?'

Sandy smiled, picked up a single sheet of paper. 'Of course. I didn't mean the Korean War. Luckily for him he got out of Washington just before it was bombed. And how ironic, he comes back to this country for the first time in ten years, and dies of a heart attack in bed with a prostitute.'

Ironic, he thought. In the space of a week in Boston you have the death of the British military attaché in 1962 and the death of an aide to President John F. Kennedy – men who probably knew each other back then – and the name and number of the local MI6 officer is found in the possession of the murdered aide.

'Yes,' he said, not believing a word he was saying. 'How ironic.'

A SOLDIER'S STORY

by
Carl Landry

CHAPTER THREE

It shall be the policy of this Nation to regard any nuclear missile launched from Cuba against any nation in the Western Hemisphere as an attack by the Soviet Union on the United States, requiring a full retaliatory response upon the Soviet Union.

—*President John F. Kennedy*
October 22, 1962

In October 1962, I was one of several thousand advisers in South Vietnam. Most of us were forming training cadres, trying to get the South Vietnamese armed forces into some sort of shape. We were 'advisers,' which on paper meant that we were supposed to stay on base and supervise the training of the ARVN troops before sending them out to deal with the Viet Cong, but that was nonsense. We all went out into the field, and we all went out with enthusiasm. We wanted to be with our troops when they came under fire, we wanted to show them we were partners they could depend upon, and being young and foolish and full of spirit, we wanted to prove to each other that we could be out on the front lines, fighting communism.

It's hard to write these words, seven or eight years later. Fighting communism. It sounded so noble, and yet this noble undertaking took us down some dark roads at a very high cost.

Part of the cost were three advisers who were killed just before the Cuban War, their spotter aircraft shot down by the Viet Cong insurgents while they were providing tactical information for some nearby ARVN units. I'm sure they are forgotten now, except for their families, but this is who they were: Army Special Forces Captain Terry Cordell, Air Force Captain Herbert Willoughby Booth, and Technical Sergeant Richard Fox.

On Saturday, October 20, 1962, there was a memorial service for them at the Ton Son Nhut airfield in Saigon. It was another hot, steamy day, and being on that flat landscape was enough to fry your brain. Our adviser units were there, with a South Vietnamese honor guard, and a chaplain who read some verses from the Bible. You could hardly hear him for the sound of the helicopters and aircraft, and I remember standing there with that odd mix of feelings that all young soldiers share. Sadness at seeing dead comrades. Pride at what they were doing for their country. A self-assurance that it would never happen to you because you were too smart, too lucky, just too something to get killed. And a sense of duty, seeing those flags fly, being in a foreign country and knowing you were there, helping them fight against an outside force of communists.

Another contingent on the field that day were some reporters, one from the *New York Times*, because even in such a small war as this one, even in Laos, there was a sense of a global mission going on, of being in the front lines, sent here by a young and cocky JFK, to hold the line and 'pay any price and bear any burden' for the cause of freedom.

We were sure that's what we were doing, and for the most part, the press agreed. This ceremony was reported in the major newspapers, and it was duly noted that the crew who were killed in the spotter aircraft were the sixteenth, seventeenth, and eighteenth Americans killed in service in South Vietnam.

As we marched off the field that day and headed for the bars, none of us knew those three men were destined to be the last Americans killed in South Vietnam.

The Cuban Missile Crisis – before it became the Cuban War – became public shortly thereafter. Being twelve hours ahead of Eastern standard time made it challenging to keep up with the news of what was going on in Moscow, the United States, and the United Nations. To put this into perspective, as an American family watched President Kennedy's speech at 7 P.M. on Monday, October 22, some of us were trying to listen to it on shortwave at 7 A.M. on Tuesday, October 23. Which meant that news got passed along, from one person to the next, along with some rumors and speculation. Plus we were all busy with our training and trips out to the bush. We didn't have the luxury of catching the Voice of America or the BBC every chance we got.

And it sounds arrogant, but in our minds we were already at war with the communists, and for those of us in the Army at the time, it was intolerable that Eisenhower and Kennedy had allowed a communist regime to set up shop ninety miles from Florida. Many a beer was shared over the general conversation of 'why in hell are we here, ten thousand miles from home, fighting the Reds, when we've got our own Reds back home in our own neighborhoods.' We had been fighting them so long in South Vietnam that it's fair to say most of us cheered when we finally saw Kennedy exhibit some backbone in Cuba, demanding that the missiles be removed. None of us thought that Khrushchev and his boys would get the missiles out, so we knew that eventually, Kennedy would be sending in the Airborne and the Marines to get them out.

And of course, we were all struck by the arrogance that the Russians – the damn Russians! – had managed to sneak bombers and medium-range missiles into Cuba. Most of us thought Kennedy should have sent in the bombers first and not bothered with the negotiation and blockade route. After all, there were promises from the Russians that they would never install offensive weapons of any kind in Cuba, and we saw this as another sign of treachery from the Reds.

I don't think many of us – if any at all – talked about the American missiles in Turkey and Italy, and our bombers in Great Britain and West Germany and Japan and South Korea. After all, everything was black and white. We were good, they were bad. Our nuclear weapons were good, theirs were bad. And of course, we ringed the Soviet Union with bombers and troops and spy planes and missiles and submarines because we were going to 'contain' them. Remember, too, that this was a scarce twenty years after Germany had invaded the Soviet Union and killed tens of millions of its soldiers and civilians. One could see how the Soviets would put missiles into Cuba, to give the United States a dose of the fear that the Soviets had always tasted.

But this is no excuse for what happened, and what had

happened earlier with the Soviets. The Katlyn Forest massacre of the Polish officer corps in World War II. Stalin's own labor and concentration camps from one end of the Soviet empire to the other. And Hungary in 1956, crushed under Soviet tanks because they had the temerity to choose their own government.

No, we didn't have much feeling of charity for the Soviet Union. Which – at the time – is why it made so much sense for us to be in South Vietnam. The struggling governments and democracies, we felt, needed our help, and that's what we were there to provide.

Even a day or two after the missile crisis broke out into the news, I found that my own day-to-day thoughts were more mundane. I would catch a news broadcast or read *Stars & Stripes,* and find out bits and pieces of news. About the block-ade. The preparations for invasion going on in Florida and Georgia and Alabama. The meetings at the UN and the attempt by Secretary General U Thant to get both sides to cool down. But I would just nod and think that the 'guys upstairs,' the ones at a higher pay grade than mine, would figure it all out. Meanwhile, I had my own problems.

At that time I was a training officer with a company of South Vietnamese regulars, who we were training to go out in the bush and fight the Viet Cong on their own terms, instead of sitting tight in guarded villas and hamlets. My counterpart was a South Vietnamese lieutenant, Nguyen Van Minh, who was about my age, though almost a foot smaller and fifty pounds lighter. If he ever had problems of being a lieutenant and taking 'suggestions' from an Army sergeant, well, he always kept them to himself. I would like to think that in the months we worked together, that we formed a cautious friendship – me, a working-class kid from a North Shore town in Massachusetts, he the son of a wealthy rubber plantation owner outside of Pleiku.

Unlike some of my counterparts in the advisory group, I actually took the time to read up on the history of Indochina, about the French colonials who ran the country, the Japanese who took it from the French in the 1940s, and the revolution and civil war that began under Ho Chi Minh. Funny thing, which I didn't believe but which an old 'Vietnam hand' told me one day: that Ho Chi Minh wrote his own country's Declaration of Independence, based it on our document of 1776, and that he was willing to accept American advisers and American aid, if we would only support him against the French.

Of course, we couldn't upset the French, our noble allies from just-concluded World War II, and Ho Chi Minh took to the jungle, until he defeated the French at Dien Bien Phu and the United Nations got involved. By the time I was there, there were two Vietnams, a North and a South, and we were supporting the South while the Soviets and the Chinese supported the North.

Nguyen taught me a lot about his country, and I like to think we were fortunate in being assigned to each other. In getting me (or so I'd like to think) he got an adviser who knew something about the history of the region, and who didn't look down on the 'natives' or 'little brown brothers,' as they were sometimes called. Some of our advisers, mostly the older, drunken ones from the South, even called the allies we were sent to train 'rice niggers.' Even if these words were spoken late at night in bars among other Americans, word got back to the South Vietnamese. It always did.

I was fortunate, too. I got a reasonably trained soldier who wasn't in the Army to gain influence or to make money on the side, through rigged concessions to the armed forces, and who was serious about his job. One night, sharing beers, he looked at me and said, 'Carl, my grandfather fought the Japanese, my father fought the French, and now it is my turn. But I fear I have the much worse job. I must fight my own brothers, just like you did a hundred years ago. I feel sorry for you, my friend. This is not a war of lines and campaigns. It is a civil war, a guerrilla war, and that is a hard war to fight. And one more thing!'

And what was that, I asked.

He pulled himself together, as drunk as he was. 'You must let us fight our own battles. If we cannot defend this country on our own, then we do not deserve it. You take that message back to your superiors.'

I probably promised to do just that, but that was one promise I was never able to keep.

Through the time of the crisis I worried about other things, too, working with Nguyen. One was getting enough ammunition. Nguyen's unit had gotten some M-1s, a great infantry weapon, though pretty heavy and unwieldy for a force that was considerably shorter in stature than the average American soldier. But before sending them out into the bush, I wanted Nguyen's company to get enough ammunition to practice on, until they were confident with what their weapons could do. Only makes sense, right? But it took a lot of begging and work on my part, driving around Saigon to different depots and bases, looking for cases of that damn .30 caliber ammunition.

I guess it's pretty funny, that in the last few days of peace, as missiles were readied in silos, B-52 and Bison and Bear bombers were patrolling the skies, the naval blockade was in place around Cuba and submarines were deep in the oceans, closing in on their targets, this particular soldier in Uncle Sam's Army was trying to scrounge a few cases of ammunition.

I stopped scrounging the weekend of October 27.

On Saturday, the twenty-seventh, a U-2 spy plane was shot down over Cuba and I got word, heading off to breakfast, that in retaliation, Air Force units were bombing the SAM missile sites that had opened fire on the U-2. One old Army vet, Kyle Secord was his name, was listening to the shortwave radio we had set up in a little lounge area in our headquarters building. He was from Florida – Key West – and he was all smiles as he passed on the news. 'That old JFK finally found his balls, boys,' he said, in a Southern drawl. 'Jus' you wait, the Marines and the paratroopers will be hittin' the shores, soon enough.'

Well, Kyle was one of my least-favorite among the advisers (he was one who used the term 'rice niggers' a lot) but on this day, he was prophetic. By the time dinner came around, Marines were storming ashore in the biggest amphibious invasion since Inchon in Korea in 1951, and units of the 82nd and 101st Airborne were dropping in and around Havana, trying to secure airfields. Bombs were being dropped on the Cuban missile sites, and our blockade fleet started sinking the Soviet subs that had been shadowing the blockade line. It was strange to see groups of military men sitting around on wicker furniture, fans moving slowly on the high ceiling, as the scratchy and static-filled sounds of the Voice of America described, with the Saigon traffic roaring in the background, a war that was going on thousands of miles away.

We didn't talk much, as other advisers and even some South Vietnamese drifted in to see what was going on. There was a lot of cigarette smoking and drawn faces, and though there were some attempts at bravado, I could tell that everybody had the same thoughts: worries about friends in the Army units going in, worries about what was going on at home, worries about what the Soviets would do. And I know that we all shared an anxiety about the fact that we were missing out on a major war, a war that promised promotions and decorations and real combat experience, instead of this penny-ante adviser crap of teaching soldiers how not to shoot one another, and how to go through the bush without sounding like a herd of elephants.

It just goes to show you the tenor of the times: we were so confident in ourselves and so ignorant of what was about to happen that we didn't realize just how lucky we were.

Sometime on Monday night, as a late dinner was being eaten around the shortwave, the strained, panicked voice of the announcer came through: Soviet units on the ground in Cuba were putting up a ferocious fight, and small-scale, tactical nuclear weapons had been used against our landing forces and Navy support vessels.

Even now, with the benefit of some years between that moment and the present, I can't adequately express the shock and dismay and horror that we all felt. It was something like a 'quiet panic.' The nuclear genie had been let out of the bottle, for the first time in a war since 1945, and events over the next couple of days cascaded, as one bulletin after another came at us like a full punch to the stomach. Not many of our little group left that room. We smoked and drank and ate a little, some of us caught catnaps on the floor, and every couple of hours, someone would cry quietly into his hands, or one of us would raise our voice, looking to fight with somebody, anybody. Our Vietnamese counterparts were there with us as well, and they had their own selfish sense of horror, I suppose, that their enormous friend and ally was now in a fight for its life, and the problems of this little country were off the table.

The bulletins got worse as each hour went by. When the first nuclear weapons were used in Cuba, our SAC began a response against military targets in the Soviet Union. Our naval forces in the Mediterranean clashed with Soviet ships. Soviet troops were marching into West Berlin. Cuba was in chaos, with no real news coming out of that burning island. Late one night Kennedy came on the air, speaking to the nation and the world, and we could hardly make out the words through the static and interference. He was offering an immediate armistice and stand-down, a summit meeting, trade concessions, anything and everything to stop the war, to stop the war from hitting America. Even through the static, over the thousands of miles, we could hear the panic in his voice.

'Goddam Ivy League Harvard boy,' one of my fellow advisers said. 'If he hadn't fucked up at the Bay of Pigs last year, none of this would be happening.' There were nods and shouts of agreement at that.

We listened closer to the radio, trying to find out what Kennedy would say, but it was too late. At least two or three of the Soviet medium-range missiles in Cuba had become operational, and we heard that Omaha – home of the Strategic Air Command – had been struck. With that, I bent my head into my hands and quietly wept, thinking about my sister Sarah.

Then our naval base in San Diego was bombed – probably by a missile-bearing Soviet submarine – and with our cities under attack, SAC engaged in a full, retaliatory response, and the news of those attacks on the cities of the Soviet Union made us nauseous. At some point – I don't remember exactly when – the Voice of America went off the air. After several long minutes of dial twisting, we got a signal from the BBC, and that's when we learned that for the second time in its history Washington, DC, had been attacked by an enemy force. But there was no romantic story of Dolly Madison racing through the White House to secure valuable paintings and documents in front of the advancing British. Just the numb horror when we realized that Kennedy and Jackie and Caroline and John-John and Bobby Kennedy and most of the Cabinet and Congress and the Pentagon and the Smithsonian and the Washington Monument and the Jefferson Monument and the Lincoln Memorial had been melted away by a weapon as hot as the interior of the sun, and that as we sat in this little lounge in a city at the outpost of the American empire, millions of our countrymen were dying.

Numb. We were drunk and tired and numb, and we didn't even stir much when word came of the New York City attack and the near miss on Manhattan, and the tens of thousands who were killed trying to escape from that island. But it was the destruction of another island that made the horror hit home. The British announcer, in listing the known cities destroyed in the Soviet Union and the United States, also mentioned offhandedly that the U.S. military bases at Key West had been hit by Soviet warheads, and that the entire island had been blasted down to bedrock and was covered by the ocean.

Kyle Secord leapt from his chair, screaming, his hair disheveled, his face unshaven, and just a bit drunk. 'Momma! Murleen! Oh, my girls!'

A couple of us made toward him and he turned away, eyes wide. 'You stay away! All of you. You stay away!' In one hand he held his Colt .45 Army-issue automatic, and his hand was shaking as he waved it around. 'You stay away, all of you!'

So we did, following him in a half circle as he went to the door that led outside and then ran down the middle of Hang Quo Street, dodging past motor scooters, bicycles, and cabs, screaming and waving his hand in the air. We followed, too, wanting to help him but also feeling a sense of relief that we were finally doing something, anything. Kyle stopped, barefoot and partially in uniform, staggering and retching and crying all at the same time.

'Momma, oh my momma,' he screamed, his voice high-pitched and howling. 'Oh, my Murleen . . . All dead . . .'

'Come on, Kyle,' one of his buddies said, a guy named Pope, and edged closer to him. 'Give it up, buddy. Just give it up.'

Kyle stood in the middle of the intersection, a mass of Vietnamese people gathering around, looking to see what this crazy white man was doing. Horns were honking and there were sirens, and Kyle wavered, saying, 'Give it up? Give it up? Jesus, Pope, you're so fuckin' right.'

And with that, Kyle put the barrel of the .45 in his mouth and blew off the top of his head.

After Kyle's body was finally taken away, I couldn't stand the thought of going back to that lounge. I was suddenly exhausted and sick to my stomach. Like every other American in Saigon, I got to a phone and tried to get an overseas line, but everything was hopelessly jammed. I tried to put Sarah out of my mind. I just hoped and prayed that she had found shelter, or had been out of Omaha when it had been struck. My parents were in Newburyport, far away from

Boston if that city ever became a target, but I worried about the Portsmouth Navy Shipyard and Pease Air Force Base, further up the coast in New Hampshire. I was hoping my parents had the sense to either be in the basement or in a car, heading west into rural Massachusetts. I couldn't get a phone line overseas, so I went back to my quarters and, still dressed and fairly drunk, collapsed on my bed.

I had some bad dreams that night. I wish I could forget them.

Sometime on Thursday morning, I heard pounding on my door and I got up, bleary and nauseous, my legs weak and shaky, and one of my compatriots was there. Al Richter, from Idaho. 'Better get ready, we're leaving.'

'What do you mean, we're leaving?' I asked.

'Haven't you heard?'

'Heard what?'

'The war,' he said. 'It's over. We're all going home, first flight out.'

I had trouble getting dressed, but I made it back to the lounge, where some of the other advisers looked like they had never left. The air was sick with the smell of sweat and fear, and on the radio was a man's voice, the very first time I had ever heard him through a speaker, Air Force General Ramsey Curtis, Acting Chairman of the Joint Chiefs of Staff. His voice was strong and calm and confident, and he sounded like a very concerned surgeon who told you that you were desperately ill, and that he would do everything possible to make you better. He talked plain and to the point. The Cuban War was over, the shortest and bloodiest war in American history. Surviving American military units had been pulled out of Cuba, and he offered to assist the United Nations in providing relief to the civilians still alive in Cuba. He had managed to reach an armistice agreement with a Marshal Sergei Lavenkov of the Strategic Rocket Forces, the highest surviving authority – either military or civilian – left alive in what was left of the Soviet Union.

'My heart is heavy, my fellow citizens, as I inform you that President Kennedy and his family, Vice President Johnson, and many of the Cabinet and members of Congress perished in the attack on our capital,' General Curtis said. 'Until the question of succession is cleared and a new president is sworn in, I have assumed emergency – and temporary – command of our military and federal agencies.'

Later, we would learn that it would take weeks to locate the highest surviving Cabinet officer – Secretary of the Treasury Dillon – and swear him into his new office.

The country had suffered grievously. Curtis made mention of Omaha, San Diego, Miami, Washington, New York City, and a few – unnamed for national security reasons – military bases. Civilians were urged to stay tuned to their local radio stations, to learn of fallout conditions in their areas. Civilian casualties were horrific, with the numbers – though he never actually mentioned one – certain to climb. He made only passing mention of the destruction that we had rained down on the Soviet Union, saying only that the 'aggressors had paid a steep price.' Martial law had been declared, all National Guard and military reserve units activated. More news to follow on relief and recovery efforts. And there was one more stunning announcement.

'I am also ordering today that all overseas U.S. military forces, no matter where they are stationed and what their mission, return forthwith to this country, to aid in our relief and recovery efforts,' he said, his voice now tinged with resentment. 'During this terrible war, where we took on the free world's mantle of leadership, we have quickly learned that – to our dreadful surprise – we stood alone. Not a single one of our allies responded militarily at this time of need. Not a single one. My fellow citizens, we have spent dearly in treasure and blood to defend this world from an aggressor nation. We have paid the price. We paid it alone. It is now time for us to come home and rebuild.'

I looked over at Al Richter, who was smoking a cigar and he caught my eye and said, 'NATO collapsed, the moment the Russians used nukes on our landing forces. Can't really blame 'em. Do you think the Prime Minister of England is going to see London destroyed because of some pissant sugar cane of a country?'

'Why not,' came a sour voice from the other side of the room. 'Kennedy and his boys sure as hell did.'

General Curtis signed off and then we heard more news, news directed to a domestic audience. Where to go to seek shelter. Which counties in California, Nebraska, Iowa, Alabama, Georgia, Florida, New York, New Jersey, and Connecticut were exposed to fallout danger. How to build a fallout shelter in your basement. I left the lounge, went back to my quarters and packed, and found myself surprised at how little I had to bring back with me. My clothes, some photographs, a few books and personal belongings, and that was it. Not much to show for my time there. Later that night a bus came by for us and we fought our way through traffic to Ton Son Nhut airport, where just over a week ago I had stood in the broiling sun as the bodies of three soldiers went home to the last few days of a peaceful country.

We were processed in a hangar while helicopters came in from some of the fire support bases out in the bush, bringing with them some of the advisers that had been stationed out with ARVN camps. There was a low roar of talking and rumors spread, about China invading India, American embassies overseas being burned to the ground, and American tourists in Europe being arrested. I tried to ignore what they said. The real news was bad enough. Some of the Vietnamese, taking advantage of what was going on, started looting some of the warehouses and the MPs gave up trying to keep a semblance of order. Like all of us, they just wanted to go home. As I went to get some water while waiting for my assigned flight, there was a tug at my elbow. I turned and it was Nguyen Van Minh. His eyes were red-rimmed and watering, but his uniform was as sharp and clean as ever.

'I wish to say good-bye to you, Sergeant Landry,' he said, formally shaking my hand. 'You are a good man. You taught us well.'

I thanked him and said I appreciated him coming to the airport.

'Ah, but that is the honorable thing to do.' He looked around at the mass of people in the hangar, the crates of supplies and gear piled up and abandoned, the swearing soldiers, the loudspeakers blaring announcements. 'I am very sorry for the losses you have suffered. Your nation has been a good friend to us. I hope truly that you and your brethren will return.'

Maybe I was tired or cranky, but I confess I wasn't that hopeful. I said it was doubtful, that we had more than enough work to do back home.

He nodded, eyes still watering. 'Home. Of course.' He looked around again. 'With you leaving, I am fearful for my own home. I wonder what will happen to our government, to the Viet Cong and the North. I wonder what they will do and it fears me so.'

I didn't know what to say, and he stood and saluted. 'Good luck to you, Sergeant. And please do not forget us, no matter what you do.'

I saluted him back and he turned and I lost him in the crowd. I never heard from him again. A month or so after we evacuated, the Saigon government collapsed and the North invaded. A new government of reconciliation was established a year or so later, headed by Ho Chi Minh. I think they may still call themselves communist or socialist, but the Japanese and French are back there now, investing and making markets for their respective goods, and I hope Nguyen Van Minh is doing well.

A couple of hours after Minh departed, it was my turn to leave, and I walked across the tarmac with a single carry-on bag, which was the only luggage that was allowed. There had been some cursing and complaining about that, but the cargo holds of the aircraft were being filled with food and medical supplies. Piles of luggage had been dumped on the runway and young Vietnamese children were busily looting them. I was quite lucky, having been assigned to a civilian Boeing 707 that was under contract to the military. Some of the other units flew home in unheated military transports, sitting in seats made of canvas webbing.

I looked back at Saigon one last time. It was early evening and the lights were coming on, and the heat and the smoke and the humidity seemed to sink right into my pores. I almost laughed as I entered the plane. My parents' prayers had been answered. They had asked that I would leave South Vietnam alive and well, and that was coming true. I'm not sure, though, that they ever realized the price that would be paid to fulfill those prayers.

The flight back was long and dull. The stewardesses did

their best but you could tell they were fighting back tears and tremors. Some of us tried to get information from them, about things back home, but they had come from Hawaii and didn't know much. There hadn't been much time to stock the galley, so for the sixteen-hour flight back across the Pacific, all we had to drink was water, and we had one meal, consisting of an apple and a peanut butter sandwich. More grumbles about that but I think no one would have grumbled had they known that this was going to be one of the best meals they would eat in the next few months.

We refueled in Hawaii and weren't allowed to get off the plane. Just land and fuel up and that was it. We took turns stretching our legs, walking up and down the aisles, looking out the small windows. 'Look at all the traffic,' someone said with awe, and it was true. Military transport aircraft of all types were landing and taxiing and refueling and taking off, all heading east, to the continental United States.

'Take a good look, boys,' an Army captain with a day-old growth of beard and tired eyes said. 'All those planes are bringing troops and supplies home from Japan, the Philippines, Thailand, South Korea, Australia . . . We're abandoning the Pacific to God knows who, and you can tell your grandchildren that you saw the collapse of the American empire.'

After takeoff we headed east and some of us tried to sleep but the closer we got to the West Coast, the more everyone started to talk. We wondered what was waiting for us, what would be going on, and what we would do. A few of the younger soldiers were cocky, saying stuff like, 'Well, we took our licks but we survived. At least we nuked the Reds and those bastards are taken care of, forever. Just you see. A year or two from now we'll be back, stronger and better than ever.

We're a strong country. It takes more than just a couple of Russian bombs to change that. You'll see.'

When we reached the California coast there were gasps of shock as the plane wheeled in to make its approach into the airport at Riverside. Through the windows and off to the south was a deep red and angry-looking glow, as San Diego and its suburbs continued to burn. The plane fell silent, and not another word was spoken until after we landed.

The next several hours were more chaos. Suffice it to say that we slept on the floor in an airport terminal and the next morning, after a breakfast of cold oatmeal and watery orange juice, most of us were assigned to 'A' Company, 4th Battalion, 45th Infantry, and were sent south. Our job was crowd control, to help move along the thousands of refugees heading north from the area outside of San Diego, to direct them to aid camps being hurriedly set up in towns north of the destruction.

The first day, I stood on the meridian strip of Interstate 15 outside of Temecula, with a loaded M-14 in my hands, a radiation officer with a clicking Geiger counter, watching the frightened and burnt and injured walk by, using both sides of the highway. The lucky ones were in slow-moving school buses and trucks and cars. The unlucky had to walk, and some of the walking were on crutches and many had bandages about their heads and limbs. I saw one father, hauling his son in a little red wagon, the boy's head covered with gauze. There were a couple of horse-drawn wagons, piled high with furniture and mattresses. A little girl went by, staring at us and holding her mother's hand, and the young girl's hair had been scorched and burned. The sounds I will never forget: the low growling of the motors, the shuffling sound of the feet, the coughs and sighs and gasps as the people who had lived around San Diego struggled to get free of the fall-out cloud that was approaching. I was reminded of newsreels I had seen some years before of refugees streaming from battles in Korea and the Congo and other far-off countries. I had never imagined that the fate of being a refugee would fall upon my own nation.

My fellow soldiers and I were silent, and I felt my throat constrict with guilt as the crowds streamed by. We had sworn to protect them, our brothers and sisters and mothers and fathers, and we had failed them, we had failed them all. A few days ago, I had been a self-confident soldier, ready to pay any price, bear any burden for my country and for my president.

Now, both the country and the president I knew were dead.

A woman struggled by, pushing a shopping cart filled with her belongings, her legs bleeding, wearing a dress shoe on one foot and a sneaker on another. 'You bastards!' she yelled. 'It's all your fault! Why did you let it happen? What were you doing? Why?'

I turned, not wanting to see her anymore. Across the way, bulldozers were digging mass graves by a high school football field, a scene I would see again and again in my months of duty in California. And when the screaming woman finally passed us by and I turned and saw the dark cloud in the south that marked a dead city, I knew it would take more than a 'year or two' before we came back.

If ever.

THIRTEEN

THEY WERE SITTING in the crowded interior of an Air
Force KC-135 tanker with some other members of the press.
Sandy had grabbed his hand when they had taken off that
morning from Logan Airport and still hadn't let go. Carl
figured it was part affection and part nerves, or maybe he was
the one who didn't want to let go. Sandy pushed her head in
close and spoke over the roar of the engines, 'I hate flying,
Carl. Lucky you weren't on the flight from London. I would
have crushed your hand by the time we got to Boston.'

He squeezed her hand in reply and gave her a nuzzle but
his thoughts were elsewhere. He no longer believed in co-
incidences. How could he? A murdered presidential aide, an
MI6 contact, a dead British general, a list of names of
Kennedy Administration officials, all dead, all within official
custody. And what was that warning Merl had given him last
month? Carl tried to tease the memory to life. 'You know,
even ten years later, some people still enjoy killin'.' A hell of
a story, Merl had offered.

So, what was he doing in this jet, heading south and away
from this story? Regrouping, thinking. How ironic that for

him, Manhattan would be a sanctuary. There, he couldn't be arrested in the middle of the night. Or have an accident like the one that supposedly killed Merl's landlord. Sandy looked over at him and he squeezed her hand again. He remembered their special night together and the energy that sparked something inside of him. A feeling that there was more out there than just doing your job and staying out of trouble. Sandy. She was making him think again. She was making him care again.

Merl, he thought, if I ever find out what really happened to you, you'll have both me and this woman to thank.

He looked around. The inside of the aircraft was strictly utilitarian. Alone with about a dozen other press people, Carl and Sandy sat on bright red canvas web seats that pulled down from the side of the bulkhead. There were six airline-style seats up forward, and those were taken by the older reporters. The floor was metal, with odd rings and hooks set into it, and the flight was noisy. The KC-135 was an Air Force tanker craft, converted from a Boeing 707 and used for aerial refueling. As the public affairs officer at the military terminal at Logan had said – a woman Air Force lieutenant with a smile too bright for the early-morning hours: 'Folks, this is the best we can do. This KC-135 is returning to Tyler Air Force Station in Yonkers. It won't be comfortable but it will get you there.'

There was a bit of grumbling from the assembled reporters and photographers but not much. Carl was sure that most of them would have gone to New York State in an ox cart if it meant access to Manhattan. One of those reporters was Jeremiah King, from the *Globe*, who smirked when he saw Carl signing in at the access desk.

'Are those cameras in your bag, Carl?' he said, with mock

surprise. 'My, my. I didn't know you were so talented. Who are you shooting for? Some shopper weekly?'

'Nope,' Carl said. He looked over and saw that Mark Beasley – the Beast – was standing next to Jeremiah. Mark looked about as happy as if he were heading into a dentist's office. 'I'm doing some photo work for the *Times* of London. Maybe you've heard of it?'

Jeremiah's eyes darkened. 'Lucky you, to have the spare time for this trip.'

'Yeah, lucky me.'

As Carl left to find Sandy, the Beast had followed. 'Hey, Carl, if you need any spare film, let me know.' Carl had gently slapped the burly photographer on the back.

Now the plane tilted and Carl guessed they were heading in for their approach. A yellow flap near a window was buttoned up against the fuselage. It was scorched on one side, as if it had been exposed to a strong heat lamp. Black letters on the flap said FLASH BARRIER. Sandy followed his gaze and spoke in his ear. 'What's that for?'

The back of his hands felt cold. 'It's a flap to go over the windows. It shields the interior of the plane from a bright flash.'

She nodded grimly. 'From a nuclear bomb.'

'That's right. And from the scorch marks along the side, I'd guess that this plane's been flying for at least ten years. And in some bad neighborhoods.'

The aircraft tilted again and an Air Force sergeant in a green zippered jumpsuit moved past the reporters. 'We're touching down! Make sure you're belted in! Five minutes till landing!'

They heard the thumping of flaps and landing gear being extended and lowered. Carl caught a glimpse of roads and fields and homes as the KC-135 descended into Yonkers, an area about fifteen miles north of Manhattan. The landing was smooth, with just one small jolt that made Sandy gasp a bit. Out the window he could see that all types of military aircraft were on the field, mostly four-engine transports. Some of them bore the roundel insignia of the Royal Air Force. Interesting, he thought. What were they doing here? Still bringing in blankets and relief supplies? And what were their brethren doing, up in Canada? He remembered that overheard conversation from the consulate: '. . . getting ready to take care of the Yanks.'

Two dark green helicopters at the end of another runway took off, like little mechanical dragonflies. The group filed out of the aircraft and went through a jetway. In the terminal a large sign hung from the ceiling, painted in blue and white:

WELCOME TO TYLER AFS

GATEWAY TO NEW YORK STATE

RELIEF AND RECOVERY

There were few civilians in sight. Most of the people walking by were military, friendly but cautious-looking in their jumpsuits or fatigues. Downstairs, luggage and camera bags were lined up on the floor beside a baggage carousel. Carl heard one photographer, from a newspaper in New Hampshire, complaining as he looked for his gear.

'I can't see why we weren't allowed to carry our cameras on board,' he said, picking up a canvas bag that bulged with rolls of film and cameras. 'This stuff's delicate and I'd rather have it riding in my lap.'

Carl saw his own overnight case and camera bag, on loan

from the *Times*. 'Because they were being polite.'

'Polite?' the young photographer demanded. 'What do you mean, polite?'

Carl picked up his things, slung them over his shoulder, and spotted Sandy at the other end of the line. 'They'd rather store your gear than let you have it in your lap, and have to tell you that you couldn't take a picture of the New York crater on your way in. Less fuss that way.'

Carl walked up to Sandy and she held out a mimeographed sheet of paper. 'Bloody efficient, they are. First there's a press conference, then some free time and lunch, and this afternoon, we get shuttled into Manhattan.'

'Just trying to make it easier for the poor overworked press people that we all are.'

Sandy said something else and Carl expressed shock. 'My, how vulgar. If only your friends in Fleet Street could hear you now.'

'Don't worry about me, Mr. Landry,' she said. 'My friends in Fleet Street are being bored to tears by a Labour conference in Blackpool. I'm getting a look at Manhattan.'

They filed into an auditorium with cushioned chairs that could have doubled as a movie theater. On stage was an American flag, an Army flag, and the flag of New York State, as well as a podium with a military crest that had to be the base unit insignia. Three easels with large charts covered by light blue sheets were near the podium.

Carl fumbled with the bag that contained a Nikon 35mm with built-in flash and an adjustable zoom lens. The damn Japanese piece of equipment was light and efficient, and he felt sorry for the French, who were trying to go head-to-head with the Japanese trade monster in Southeast Asia. It had taken him hours of practice and reading and rereading the manual before he felt comfortable. He had taken pictures off and on for the *Globe* when he first started and was fairly competent, but that was about it. He had lots of film and planned to burn through most of it. More film exposed, better chance of having some usable photos for Sandy and the *Times*.

'Excuse me,' he said, as he saw some movement up on stage. 'Time for me to earn my pay.'

'Do a good job, will you?' Sandy said, smiling up at him. 'Or I'll think I just hired you for your eyes and your shapely bum.'

'Leave my bum out of this,' he said, feeling good as he went forward, the camera still awkward in his hands. He wouldn't have passed this up for anything.

He joined about a half dozen other photographers in the front row of seats. The Beast nodded at him as he got his camera gear ready. A slim black man dressed in Air Force blues strolled across the stage to the podium, accompanied by two other officers. Carl noticed their shoulder insignias and was fairly impressed. One hell of a press tour had been put together.

'Good morning,' the Air Force officer said. 'I am Colonel Brigham Jefferson, the base commander here at the Tyler Air Force Station. I'm also one of two deputy commanders for the New York Military District. I'd like to welcome you to this two-day tour of Manhattan and its surrounding communities, and I also welcome your participation and cooperation. Before I begin this briefing about our mission and status, I must settle a couple of ground rules.'

There were a few groans from the assembled reporters. The colonel smiled and held up a hand. 'Please. Before you protest too much, I'm sure you'll see that this is nothing too onerous. First, at all times you will be with a military guide and escort. It is that guide's job to answer your questions, to take you to the places you'd like to go, and to watch out for your safety. If tomorrow your guide says going over to the Roosevelt Parkway will be too dangerous, please listen to him. He knows this area and is looking out for your safety as well as his own.'

The colonel wasn't speaking from notes, which impressed Carl. Most officers he knew – not to mention Cullen Devane back at the *Globe* – couldn't find their way to the men's room without a written map. He took a few photos and then let the camera rest in his lap.

'Second, while you're in Manhattan, you will be issued dosimetry, a device to measure any possible radiation exposure. Please follow the instructions of the radiation safety officers. If any of you are found without your dosimetry, you will be immediately airlifted off the island.

'Third, while we will answer your questions to the best of our abilities, I'm afraid there are a few items which we cannot discuss, due to their sensitive nature. There may also be a few instances where we cannot allow photographs, for the same reason.' Another wide smile. If Colonel Jefferson wanted to enter politics when he left the Air Force, Carl thought, he'd do quite well. 'I apologize in advance for any stonewalling that we will be sending your way.'

A little light laughter and the colonel went on. 'Now. Those are our preconditions for this tour. At the end of this briefing, we will ask all of you to sign a form stating that you understand the ground rules of this press tour. If you feel that you cannot – or will not – agree to these conditions, you may exit to the rear of the auditorium at this time, and we will make arrangements for your return to Boston.'

No one was leaving, and who would? This was one of the

biggest stories of the year, bigger even than the upcoming election between Rockefeller and McGovern.

'Very good,' Colonel Jefferson said, looking pleased. 'Now. Lieutenant Sinclair, the first easel, if you please.'

The chart on the easel was a large-scale map of Manhattan, Long Island, lower New York State, and eastern New Jersey. At the top of the map was the heading: 30 OCTOBER 1962 TUESDAY A.M. Three circles in gray scale were superimposed over the map. In the center of each circle was a caption: NUDET 1, NUDET 2 and NUDET 3. Two of the circles overlapped, east of Manhattan. The third was to the west of Newark, New Jersey. Colonel Jefferson picked up a wooden pointer and began talking.

'It has taken some years of work to determine what exactly happened in the New York metropolitan area on October 30 of 1962, a few days before the Cuban War ended,' he began, his voice firm and low. He sounded like a lawyer, reading the will of somebody's long-dead relative. 'But based on pilot debriefs and ground observations, and even some records from United Nations recovery teams working in the former Soviet Union, we now have a fair idea about what occurred.'

He tapped the gray circle marked NUDET 1. 'We are almost one hundred percent confident that the nuclear weapons dropped in the New York metropolitan district that morning came from a flight of Soviet TU-95 turboprop intercontinental bombers, known by the NATO designation "Bear." Almost all Bear flights from Soviet Asian air force bases that flew against the United States during the Cuban War were tracked over the North Pole through the DEW warning lines in the Canadian Arctic, and were successfully shot down through joint American-Canadian fighter interceptor flights. However—' Carl could hear the steely dismay in the man's voice, even ten years later. 'However, in the case of this particular flight, five TU-95 bombers, flying in from the east at extremely low altitudes, attacked the New York metropolitan district. Our best intelligence at the time said that the Bear bombers had neither the endurance nor the ability to make the long, low-level flights that would arc and bypass the DEW line. We were obviously wrong.'

Carl balanced his camera on his knees, listening with awful attention to the measured, clipped tones of the Air Force colonel. He had heard the basic story of the New York City attack, but never in such detail, never in such deadly thoroughness.

'Three Air Force F-102 Delta Dagger interceptors, part of the 10th Intercept Squadron out of Dover, Delaware, were at New York's Idlewild Airport as part of our dispersion activities during the crisis. Radar installations at Cape Cod and Long Island started tracking the five Soviet bombers, and the F-102s were scrambled to attack. The bombers themselves, once they approached the United States, also dispersed as they began their attack profiles. Other F-102s were alerted, to support the three from Idlewild, but they didn't reach the area in time.'

He raised the pointer. 'Two of the bombers were successfully shot down at about 8 A.M. One crashed into Long Island Sound, and the other impacted here, a mile south of Plainview in Long Island. In 1964, an Army-Air Force Decontamination Task Force excavated the crash site and successfully removed two unexploded one-megaton nuclear bombs.'

The colonel cleared his throat. 'The third bomber, with its engines aflame, began to descend over Great Neck and released its bomb at about 8:10 A.M. The impact point was in

Queens, between Bayside Avenue and Forty-sixth Avenue. Along with the bomber, two of the pursuing F-102s were destroyed in the blast.'

The colonel's voice was getting more strained, and Carl thought he knew why. He was an Air Force man and one of the Air Force's primary missions was to protect the country's skies. There had been no defense against the missiles that had destroyed such targets as San Diego or D.C., but the Air Force had done a lot opposing the Soviet bombers. A number of success stories had come from the Cuban War, including some vicious air battles over the Canadian prairies where dozens of Bear and Bison bombers had been intercepted heading south, but those victories all paled in the face of the one big disaster: New York City. And another single word – SAC – was still a nightmare to many trembling survivors in Europe and Asia. Most Air Force personnel never traveled abroad, for fear of being arrested as war criminals.

'Fifteen minutes later, here, the fourth bomber from the flight dropped its payload over Idlewild Airport, destroying the airport and adding to the damage and firestorm caused by the Queens detonation. The bomber then went on and dropped its second payload, here, in Orange, New Jersey. We believe its original target was Newark Airport. We still don't know why it missed. Perhaps the plane was damaged, perhaps crew members were wounded. We're not sure. The bomber itself crashed a few minutes later, north of Patterson. A few crew members parachuted out but they were killed on the ground by armed citizens and police units.'

The colonel's voice then changed. Pride, perhaps? Maybe a wistful pride. Carl wasn't sure.

'The fifth TU-95 bomber was making its attack approach here, coming south over New Rochelle,' the colonel said, his voice softer. 'The third surviving F-102, which had joined in the attack that shot down the two other Bear bombers, intercepted the TU-95 bomber. The F-102 had exhausted its six Falcon air-to-air missiles, and somewhere north over the Bronx the pilot of the F-102, Air Force Major Conrad Tyler, deliberately rammed his aircraft into the Bear bomber after seeing its bomb bay doors begin to open. The Bear crashed here, on Wards Island. In 1963, an unexploded five-megaton nuclear bomb was successfully retrieved from the island. That bomb, ladies and gentlemen, was to have been dropped on Manhattan proper, and would have destroyed the entire island outright, no doubt along with most of its several million inhabitants.'

Colonel Jefferson paused, and then continued. 'Major Tyler's F-102 crashed in Flushing Bay. His body has never been recovered. In 1963, he was posthumously awarded the Medal of Honor, and this Air Force Station was named for him, in 1964.'

You could hear people breathing, that's how quiet the room was. The colonel nodded briefly and said, 'Lieutenant Sinclair? The next easel, if you please.'

The young Air Force lieutenant pulled the sheet of paper back from the second easel. It had the same large-scale map of Manhattan, Long Island, lower New York State, and eastern New Jersey, but the heading at the top said: NEW YORK MILITARY DISTRICT OCTOBER 1972. Tyler Air Force Station was marked off by a stylized drawing of an airplane. There were irregularly shaped sections of gray-scale shading over portions of the map, along with three black ovals centered in the same areas that had been marked NUDET in the other chart. With pointer again in hand, Colonel Jefferson began talking.

'This is where we are today, ladies and gentlemen. These shaded areas are what's known as RZs, Restricted Zones. The RZs for the New York Military District cover all of Long Island, west from a line stretching from Fort Salonga in the north to Bay Shore in the south. This RZ also covers the New York City boroughs of Queens and Brooklyn. Over here, in lower New York State, the Restricted Zone runs south, from a line east to west that is roughly parallel to the county line between Westchester County and Bronx County. Manhattan, Wards Island, Welfare Island, Ellis Island, Governors Island, and Staten Island all fall within this RZ.'

The pointer moved to the left side of the chart. 'In New Jersey, the RZ contains those New Jersey communities within a boundary marked by Interstates 80, 280, and the Hudson River. Among the cities contained within this RZ are Clifton, Passaic, Montclair, Hoboken, and Orange, New Jersey.'

Colonel Jefferson stopped, the pointer in his hands. 'The Restricted Zones are those areas still affected by fallout from the three nuclear detonations. All civilians left these areas in 1962 and the RZs have been under military control ever since. I am pleased to report that the RZs here in the New York Military District are about half the size they were in late 1962. Each year, as part of our Relief and Recovery efforts, we are able to reclaim more communities and land in these areas. Our planners tell us that by 1982, the RZs should shrink by another half.' Carl noted that the colonel had begun to talk faster, as if ashamed at what he was saying. 'The black areas on the map are of course the areas immediately surrounding the points of detonation. They are known as UZs, Uninhabitable Zones. It is doubtful that these areas will ever again be habitable in our lifetimes.'

The room was still so silent, Carl thought. It was as if the reporters and photographers had been struck dumb. Ten years ago, it happened ten years ago, but for the wide eyes and quiet mouths, you would have thought it happened last week.

Another motion of the pointer, to the top of the map. 'Tyler Air Force Station – formerly a civilian airport – was a temporary field in November of 1962, meant to serve as a refueling point for aircraft coming to provide relief forces for the area. The field quickly expanded and became an official Air Force installation in 1963. We serve as the staging area for most of the relief and recovery efforts in the RZs. Our mission here is the same as it was when it began, ten years ago. To protect private property. To preserve industrial facilities. To recover, decontaminate, and transport out items of wealth or value from the RZs, such as the gold bullion stored in some of the banks, and artworks from the dozens of museums in the RZs. To prevent looting. To decontaminate and recover areas so that civilians who wish to return to their former homes can do so. And folks, believe me, even a decade later, they do. Lieutenant, the last chart, if you will.'

The third chart was a map of Manhattan, and Colonel Jefferson pointed to a rectangular section in the center of the island. 'Your eventual destination, ladies and gentlemen. The Manhattan Air Force Station, located here, at the southern end of Central Park. You will depart here later this afternoon, in helicopters, and arrive there for a briefing and tour of Manhattan. Now. I appreciate your patience in letting me monopolize your time. I believe we have time for a few questions. Who's first?'

Carl turned and looked at the small crowd of reporters. Their faces were impassive and silent, like marble sculptures. Questions. Didn't anyone have a question, anything at all? Maybe it was just too damn big to ask a question about. You could spend a day and a week and a month with this colonel, asking questions, again and again. The most popular one being, of course, why? Why did this happen? Was it inevitable? Why?

A hand rose up, breaking the spell. Colonel Jefferson almost looked relieved. 'Sir. Go ahead.'

'Thank you,' came a male voice, but Carl couldn't make out the face. 'Civilian casualties. Could you tell us what they were for the area around New York City?'

The colonel nodded crisply. 'I'm afraid I can't. That's still classified information, but I'm sure it's evident to all of you that we suffered tremendously on that day. Next question?'

A woman, with a British voice but not Sandy: 'Is it true that civilians are still living in the Restricted Zones?'

'Yes, unfortunately. There are people who refused to leave, and others who have snuck back in past our checkpoints. There are also organized gangs of looters, sad to say, who are still stripping out belongings from many of the homes and businesses.' His voice lowered. 'We still have orders to shoot on sight, and when we encounter these looters, that's often what happens.'

His hands trembled for a moment, holding the camera. Carl had a sudden thought of his sister, Sarah, perhaps trying to survive in a Restricted Zone around Omaha, maybe injured, maybe not quite right in the head, and one day, she runs into an Army patrol that thinks she's looting. A soldier raises his rifle, hell, maybe a soldier Carl knew back in basic training or South Vietnam or California, this soldier aims at his sister, the suspected looter, and begins to pull the trigger—

'Next question?' asked the colonel, and Carl took a deep breath. Back to the world, son, he thought. Let's get back to the world. He recognized the unctuous voice of the questioner. Jeremiah King. 'Colonel, as a member of the Air Force, do you and your fellow officers, well, if you excuse the question, sir, do you and your fellow officers feel any guilt about the Strategic Air Command, and what it did during the war? Sir?'

Lieutenant Sinclair looked like he could have shot King if he had a weapon, while Colonel Jefferson's eyes narrowed as he held the pointer stiffly. 'An interesting question, one I've been asked before. And I'll answer it just as I've done in the past. The Air Force and the Strategic Air Command and all other military departments of this government have been and continue to be under civilian jurisdiction. We follow the legitimate orders of the civilian leadership of this nation. We are here to do a job, whatever job is deemed necessary by our civilian oversight, whether it was President Kennedy in 1962 or President Romney in 1972. You ask if I feel guilt. No. Do I feel sadness at what happened to the people of the former Soviet Union? Of course. But I also feel much more sadness for the people of New York and New Jersey and other communities in our nation. Yes, you, in the second row.'

A male Brit, this time. 'Colonel, if I may, I'd like to ask you a somewhat personal question, not really connected with our tour here.'

A wide smile. 'Now that's a welcome change. Go ahead. I'll see what I can do.'

Some polite laughter. The British reporter said, 'As a Negro and a colonel in your Air Force, do you still think there's room for improvement in the area of race relations in this country?'

Another sharp nod. 'All right, I'll give that question a go. First, I'd like to point out that Negro is a term that's not often used today. Some like the phrase black, others like

Afro-American. Myself, I consider myself Air Force blue.' There was more polite laughter but then the colonel's voice grew serious. 'But I will tell you this, sir. In 1962 I was a tech sergeant at a base in Oregon, and I thought that was about as high in rank as I could get. Cousins of mine were getting beaten as Freedom Riders. Other relatives were being clubbed and teargassed in Southern communities. Then came the war and then the National Security and Civil Rights Act of 1963, written and passed as a result of General Ramsey Curtis's efforts. You can say a lot about General Curtis and his decisions after the war, and his influence in our affairs today. That kind of discussion I will leave to other people.'

Colonel Jefferson leaned on the podium, as if emphasizing a point. 'But I will tell you this. When General Curtis appeared before the surviving members of Congress in Philadelphia in '63 and said it was for the good of the country that we work together as one, that it made no sense for a full 10 percent of our workforce and brainpower and willing hands to be left behind while we were in the gravest crisis of our nation, well, he made history that day, ladies and gentlemen. And he made history that week, when Army units went into Alabama and Georgia and Mississippi and elsewhere, and crushed the Klan and ended segregation. That's a history that I personally am grateful for. Sir, you asked about the state of racial affairs in this country. There is still work to be done, but you can thank one man for destroying segregation and Jim Crow in one day. Who's next?'

A couple of other questions were tossed up to the colonel, mostly about the mechanics of the trip and what one could and couldn't do in Manhattan. Then the colonel raised his hand and said, 'Time for one more.'

Carl's ears tingled when he heard the next voice. 'Colonel, Sandy Price of the *Times*. I see two hours before lunch is allocated as free time. I'd like to make a request, and I think I speak for at least most of my fellow reporters, that we travel a bit south and see the Fence. We've heard so much about it, I think we'd like to see it firsthand.'

There were some murmurs from the reporters and some- one said, 'Hear, hear' in a loud voice. Colonel Jefferson said, 'We thought that after your flight from Boston, you'd like some time to refresh yourselves.'

'With all due respect, Colonel, I feel quite refreshed. And I would be very grateful if a visit to the Fence could be arranged. If it wouldn't be too much of a bother.'

The colonel beckoned Lieutenant Sinclair over, and they huddled for a moment, and then Colonel Jefferson broke free and said, 'Very well. For those of you who wish to go to the Fence, we'll have transportation ready in a half hour. It won't be too comfortable, and for those who'd like to stay behind, there'll be a more in-depth briefing on this base's mission in thirty minutes.'

FOURTEEN

IT WAS LOUD AND COLD in the rear of the Army deuce-and-a-half truck. Carl was at the very back, looking out onto the frigid fall landscape of this part of New York State. Sandy sat next to him. They were rattling their way south along the New York State Thruway, and Carl leaned over and said to Sandy, 'That was very nice, what you pulled back there.'

'Whatever do you mean?'

'I mean how you posed the question. No one else mentioned their name or affiliation. You did. Is that what you wanted, to use the grand and heavy name of the *Times* to get us this trip to the Fence?'

She smiled and wiggled her nose. 'Well, it worked, didn't it?'

He patted her on the knee and looked around. The interior of the truck was plank seating and a wooden floor, and the sides were canvas. The rear of the truck was open, and he could make out the landscape as they moved toward the Fence that separated Westchester County from the southern portion of the Restricted Zone. The road was bumpy and

rough, with potholes and cracks in the pavement. Some of
the cracks even had grass growing in them. The leaves had
started turning colors but his attention was drawn to other
things. Like the abandoned and rusted cars from ten years
ago, pulled or dragged over to the side of the road. Like the
lack of traffic on this thruway. There were a few other Army
trucks and a converted bus, and that was about it. And there
were the horses and wagons, assigned to the left-hand lane.
Sandy tugged at his arm.

'There are so many horses,' she said. 'I didn't see that in
Boston.'

'In the cities it's easier to distribute gasoline and other
goods. The further out you go, the more expensive it is. Plus,
power isn't as reliable, the roads aren't so hot. Horses are
relatively easy to maintain, compared to cars. Horses also
have another advantage.'

'And what's that?'

He smiled at her. 'No one's been able to figure out how to
make two cars breed to make more cars. Horses seem to have
the advantage there.'

'Don't they just.'

The thundering growl of the diesel engine shifted in tone,
and the truck ground to a halt in a large parking lot. Two
soldiers unbolted the tailgate and helped Carl and Sandy and
the others to the ground. Carl stretched his legs, blew on his
cold hands, and looked around.

About a hundred feet south of the parking lot was the
Fence and its gatehouse. They were still in Yonkers but
beyond the Fence was the Bronx, and beyond that,
Manhattan. The lot was filled with all kinds of military
equipment: jeeps, deuce-and-a-half trucks, half-tracks, and
several armored personnel carriers. The Fence stretched to

the east and west, as far as he could see. Brush and trees had been trimmed away, but from this distance, it looked like leaves and branches had gotten caught in the chain link.

'Ladies and gentlemen, could I have your attention please!' said a soldier in fatigues, holding up a clipboard in his black-gloved hands. His face was red and he looked cold.

'My name is Lieutenant Morneau. Here are the ground rules. Feel free to take as many pictures as you'd like. You can go anywhere you want on this side of the Fence. Do not attempt to cross over the Fence or gain entry into the Restricted Zone. If you do so, you will be arrested. In fifteen minutes, the trucks leave. We'll give you five minutes' warning with the horns.'

A voice from the crowd, German-accented. 'Vat if ve miss the trucks?'

'Then it's a long walk back to Tyler,' the lieutenant said. While some in the crowd laughed, Carl saw no humor in the young man's face. Sandy came up to him and said, 'Let's split up and see what we each can come up with.'

Carl lifted up his camera bag. 'Sounds good.'

He went over and took a few photographs of the gatehouse. American and New York State flags snapped in the breeze atop fresh-white flagpoles. The roads heading south into the RZ looked to be in even worse shape than the thruway they had just traveled on, with broken asphalt and knee-high grass growing from the cracks in the roadway.

A couple of soldiers at the gatehouse – MPs in shiny helmets and shoulder brassards – smiled and shook their heads as they saw the group approaching. Carl knew from his Army days what they were thinking: dealing with reporters always meant dumb questions, wasted time, and the possibility of getting into serious trouble with your commander. Therefore, reporters were trouble and were to be avoided at all costs. Sure enough, as the group of journalists got closer, the MPs quietly turned on their heels.

On the gatehouse was a red, white, and blue sign in large letters:

YOU ARE NOW LEAVING WESTCHESTER COUNTY

YOU ARE NOW ENTERING THE

NEW YORK METROPOLITAN RESTRICTED ZONE

ENTRY TO AUTHORIZED PERSONNEL ONLY

USE OF DEADLY FORCE AUTHORIZED

And below, in smaller white letters: 'C' COMPANY, 2ND BATTALION, FIRST DIVISION, 'THE BIG RED ONE.'

Carl took a number of pictures of the entry sign, then walked away from the crowd which was now clustered around the gatehouse. He walked toward the fence and saw that he had been wrong about the leaves and branches in the Fence. It was something else, and his throat caught for a moment.

All along the fence were tokens and talismans, left by the untold numbers of visitors who had come here. Ribbons of all colors were tied on the chain link, and birthday cards and greeting cards, some faded by the weather, had been placed on the ground. Dried flowers and plastic flowers and fresh flowers were stuck through the fence and there were handwritten messages and notes. He took a number of pictures and then stopped. The mementos were placed on and around

the fence as far as he could see. A bottle of scotch. Some playing cards. A Zippo cigarette lighter. A card was stuck in the
fence by his feet and he picked it up. It was a Peanuts birthday card with a picture of Snoopy pretending to be Joe Cool,
and inside was a note: 'Tommy, you were always the coolest.
We still miss and love you so much. Jack.'

Next to the birthday card was a *Playbill* magazine, ten
years old, faded and taped together. It felt brittle in his hands,
like it had come from an ancient Egyptian tomb. A white card
was taped to the front, and he could just barely make out the
handwriting: 'Les, when we get back to Broadway, we'll host
one for you and make sure your name is back in lights. Bill
and the rest of the gang.'

Behind him he heard people walking by and he ignored
them. Everything he wanted to see was right here. He softly
put the *Playbill* down on the ground and nearly jumped when
a man behind him said: 'Pretty wild stuff, hunh?'

Carl turned and next to him was a young soldier, standing
there, rubbing his hands together. He looked to be about
eighteen or nineteen, in Army winter gear, with an M-14
slung to one side. He had on a black watch cap and his helmet was hanging from a utility belt at his side, along with a
canteen and a small field pack. A square piece of plastic that
Carl recognized as radiation dosimetry hung from a clip on
the left breast pocket of the soldier's jacket. His skin was
white and splotched with freckles. Carl looked back up at the
gatehouse and saw that the rest of the soldier's squad was
slowly walking across the parking lot.

'Yeah,' Carl said. 'Pretty wild stuff.'

'You with that bunch?'

'Sort of. I'm taking pictures for a newspaper.'

The soldier laughed. 'No shit, really?'

'No shit, really.'

'What's the story?'

'Well, the Fence for one. And this afternoon, we're going into Manhattan.'

'Far out,' the soldier said, and laughed again. 'Man, that's the deadest place I've ever been. Can't believe anybody would want to get in there to that dead island.'

Carl nodded to the Fence. 'You coming back from patrol?'

The soldier was still smiling but there was something guarded about his look. 'Is this an interview?'

'Nope.'

'It sure sounds like it. You asking questions and all that.'

'No, I'm just curious, that's all. A few years back, I was doing the same thing you were doing.'

'The hell you say,' the soldier said. 'You were in the Big Green?'

'Yep.'

'When were you drafted?'

Carl gave him a rueful grin. 'I wasn't. I enlisted. Back in 1960.'

'Must've seen some serious shit, then.'

'That I did.'

'Where were you stationed?'

'Most of the time I was on detached duty, relief and recovery, from Fort Ord, in California.'

The soldier shook his head. 'I heard that California after the nukes fell was definitely not the place to be. Is it true that Governor Brown was fragged by the military commander and that they covered it up, said it was a traffic accident?'

'Can't say,' Carl replied. 'Truth is, I heard that rumor a lot, and it's the kind of rumor it's not healthy to look into, if you know what I mean.'

The young soldier grinned. 'Yeah, I know that ride. Things are pretty quiet nowadays but you learn quick not to ask too many questions.'

'So,' Carl said, motioning to the fence. 'What was your job today?'

'Pokin' and strokin', that's all,' he said. 'We walk the fence down and meet another patrol, sent up from the Hudson River station, and we make sure that the fence is one piece, that no one's cut holes in it, and that things are fine.'

'And are things fine today?'

'Oh, yeah, things are great. Fence is nice and tight.'

'You still trying to get people going across?'

The soldier nodded. 'All the time, man. You'd think they'd give it up, ten years later, but it's their homes in there, you know? Every few weeks, either we find the fence cut through or we catch some family trying to head south. Pretty sad. And then there're the people that come by to leave stuff at the fence. Brrr,' he said, mimicking a shiver. 'Makes you think this fence surrounds the biggest graveyard in the world.'

'Seems to be a lot of stuff here.'

'Yep. A couple of the old-timers, they told me about a checkpoint commander here a few years ago, a real hard-ass. Every week he made the patrols sweep through the fence and pick up all the stuff that the families dropped off. He wanted this place to look sharp or something like that. So each week, we got piles of this stuff and we started putting it in one of the warehouses, 'cause nobody could bear the thought of tossing it out.'

'And what happened?'

'Oh, he ordered the stuff to be burnt and next morning, he was out taking a dump in the officers' latrine, and the place blew up. Busted his eardrums real good and broke his legs. Funny thing, how that place exploded. Must've been a buildup of methane gas or something.'

'Or something.'

'Yeah, and that was it for cleaning up the fence.' Carl looked again at the soldier's eyes and saw how tired he was. He had seen that resigned look before, during duty in the States. Ten years, he thought. Ten years later and we're still teaching our soldiers not to soldier, but to be policemen in green uniforms.

Carl motioned to the land on the other side of the fence. 'What's it like in the RZ?'

The soldier shook his head. 'Don't rightly know. Only a few patrols get sent in there and that's just for the day. Most of the time, it's just fence watching.'

'I thought the RZ was regularly patrolled.'

A knowing smile. 'Right. And the draft is a fair and equitable way for everyone to serve this wonderful country of ours. Look, besides the regular contamination, the RZ has a lot of crap inside that can bite you in the ass, especially at night, and we leave it pretty much alone unless we have to.'

'Really? So what's in there?'

'Sorry. Rather talk about fence walking, 'cause that's what I've been doing, all these weeks. Pretty boring stuff, but the good thing is, it looks like I'm going to be bored for just another seven months and twelve days.'

'Enlistment's up?'

An enthusiastic nod. 'That's right, pal. Seven months and twelve days from now, my term is up and, can you keep a secret?'

'Sure can.'

The soldier laughed and moved a bit closer. 'Truth is, I

learned a lot about fences and how to cross over in my duty here, and I'm gonna use that in good practice. Day after I'm out I'm gonna screw being in the reserves, m'man, I'm going up North, maybe Michigan or Montana, and I'm gonna cross the Canadian border. Get up to the Canadian Rockies and relax and drink a lot of beer and flush this place out of my system. My dosimetry tells me I've picked up minimal, but since the Army checks the dosimetry, well, I'm still going to flush it out.'

'It probably won't work,' he said, knowing he should be horrified at this tale of desertion, but instead finding himself liking this soldier's spirit.

A shout came from the parking lot, and the soldier waved. 'Yeah, but it sure will be fun. Sorry, man, my sergeant's yellin' at me and it's time to go.'

'Good talking to you. Thanks for your time.'

A brief wave back and the soldier started to the parking lot. 'Always nice, talking to someone who's been there, you know? Don't get too many zoomies while you're in Manhattan.'

There was something about the soldier, as he trudged over to the parking lot, his uniform and gear and M-14 and helmet hanging off his belt. Carl knew what it was. For a moment, it had almost been like looking in a mirror, seeing himself when he was back in California. And he remembered a lot of other things, like the slang for radiation exposure.

Zoomies. Must be lots of zoomies out there, beyond the Fence.

A horn blew twice, from a truck out in the parking lot. Time to get back. He started back and saw something white among the red and orange and yellow of the leaves. It was a prayer card and he picked it up. On one side was an illustration of the Virgin Mary, and on the other was a set of prayers and a handwritten scribble, in Spanish. He didn't know Spanish but that didn't matter. Neither did the Fence.

He put the card back against the chain link and walked to the parking lot.

FIFTEEN

HE CLAMBERED into the dark green U.S. Army Huey helicopter next to Sandy. The interior was shaking with the noise, and then a crew member entered, slid the door shut, sat down across from them, and with an unsteady motion, they were off the ground.

The inside of the helicopter was greasy and stained, and their overnight luggage and camera bags were strapped down in one corner. There were two other reporters on board, from Japan, and they nodded and smiled at him and Sandy. There was also a cameraman from ABC news who muttered to himself and sat with his arms crossed, looking grimly out the window. Carl looked out the other window and caught a view of four other helicopters, taking off, one after another, from Tyler Air Force Station. It was late Wednesday afternoon and they were heading into Manhattan.

Being back in a helicopter with the smells of the oil and canvas and the sounds and motions of being lifted and then propelled forward into the air brought back such a rush of memories that Carl had to close his eyes for a moment. He remembered training missions at Ft. Bragg, in North

Carolina, flying treetop level over the hot pine forests. Back in South Vietnam, heading out to hamlets with other advisers, smiling and nervous and excited all at the same time, flying low over the steamy rice paddies. And back in California, in the tall rugged hills, chasing militia units, dropping off food caches to remote towns still in shock after the war, and making illegal middle-of-the-night raids into Mexico.

There had been one particularly memorable helicopter trip. It had been routine, ferrying three congressmen around the edge of the San Diego crater. Then there came a high-pitched whining noise as something went wrong with the engine and they started spiraling in. Carl had been surprised at how calm he felt. All he could think was, well, this is where it's going to end. He remembered seeing the congressmen hang on to the sides of the bulkhead, eyes wide open. One of them vomited and because of the G-forces, it sprayed the ceiling. Carl had closed his eyes, waiting for impact, when the pilot managed to regain control and they landed hard, cracking one of the landing struts. Another of the congressmen had wet his pants, but the third – some guy named Bush from Texas – had just grinned and said that was the second-wildest ride of his life, the first being when he was shot down by the Japanese over the Pacific, in World War II.

Carl opened his eyes and he looked out the side window. Below was the Hudson River and to the right was New Jersey and further, to the south, was the black and gray streak that marked the New Jersey nuclear detonation zone, the NUDET. There were a handful of boats on the gray water and he could see a few cars and trucks on the roads on the New Jersey side of the river, just north of the Restricted Zone. He wondered how anyone could live and work across the water from such a huge and dead city.

The spires and buildings of Manhattan crept into view as the helicopter tilted and swerved to the left. Off in the day's haze were two more oval gray and black shapes, marking the UZs in Queens and western Long Island. The edges of the ovals weren't sharp, because the borders were marked by mounds of rubble and other debris. They looked like large racetracks or horsetracks or something equally benign, and he felt nauseous at knowing the truth of what he was seeing. The fused graves of hundreds of thousands of Americans. Below him now were the narrow streets and crowded buildings of Manhattan and his chest started to tighten up. There it was, America's first city, quiet and dead. If you took a quick glance the city still looked like the old postcards and photo books – the crowded buildings, tall and proud. It was when you looked closely that you saw all the details, the details that Carl knew he would never forget.

There were jagged, black sections in some of the city blocks, where fires had broken out in some buildings and had been extinguished, but where nothing had been rebuilt. Some of the trees had grown so large that on some of the narrow streets, they had formed canopies of branches and leaves. There were craters of some sort in a few of the streets, from collapsed tunnels, perhaps. Other buildings had lost their brick or marble facades, exposing rusting steel beams into the air. He blinked as the helicopter descended. There was something odd about the streets below, there was traffic down there. A lot. Cars and trucks and buses and . . .

He sat back against the bulkhead. How stupid could you be, he thought. None of the traffic was moving. It was a silent, deadly, rust-filled stillness of vehicles abandoned on that day ten years ago when firestorms and mushroom clouds seared the horizons, and when the city's population began an exodus like none other seen in the world, millions of people taking to their feet, crowding the bridges and tunnels, some even seizing boats at the river's docks in a desperate attempt to leave Manhattan.

Sandy tightened her grip on his hand. They were lowering in altitude. He could see more details of the surrounding buildings. A lot of windows were missing, leaving gaps along the brick and concrete walls. Another pile of burnt rubble. Then there was a large swath of green, regular and rectangular. Central Park. Most of the northern section of the park was still wild and green, but the southern end looked like a military base. There were concrete pads with large, yellow H's painted in the center, and Quonset huts and temporary buildings. There were rows of trucks and armored personnel carriers and jeeps, and other helicopters were taking off from other concrete pads as they came in for a landing. There was a swooping sensation in his gut as the pilot flared down and landed, and the engine noise changed pitch as the engine throttled back.

The crew chief nodded and slid open the side door, and Carl hurried outside, still holding on to Sandy's hand. They hunched over as they scrambled away from the helicopter and its rotating blades. The wind from the rotors kicked up dust and pebbles and he drew Sandy to a grassy area of the park and then turned around.

'What are all those buildings?' Sandy asked, raising her voice some.

'Wish I knew,' Carl said, feeling slightly ashamed that he couldn't tell a foreigner the intricate details of his country's first city, but he'd only been to Manhattan for two brief visits before the war. 'I've got a map but it's buried in my luggage. I know that's Fifth Avenue over there. Used to be some very pricey real estate, before the war.'

He turned around, trying to take everything in. There were trees along the edge of the park and between the buildings, and asphalt paths connected the huts and some older, brick structures that must have belonged to the park. He could make out tall office and apartment buildings beyond the trees. The sky was a brilliant blue and the leaves on the trees had changed, a jumbled collection of yellow, orange, and red. Squirrels ran along the tree trunks and pigeons moved in flocks along the ground. It was all so damn peaceful, if you could ignore the armored vehicles, the helicopters taking off and landing, and the Army lieutenant with a clipboard and swagger stick, trying to get everyone to walk to one of the older brick buildings marked ADMINISTRATION – MANHATTAN AFS. It looked clean and peaceful and orderly, and he knew that this was just a very small refuge of order in a larger sea of chaos, out there in the crumbling streets of this island city. He sniffed the air. There was a smell of aviation fuel and exhaust and something else. The smell of things that had gotten wet and burnt and rotten. A smell of decay, of things falling apart and no one possibly being able to clean it up.

Carrying their luggage, they were led into one of the Army administration buildings and led down a corridor filled with offices. Carl could see soldiers at work behind the glass windows, at typewriters and on the phones. A door opened and two officers in fatigues emerged. Carl caught a glimpse of a soldier carrying a green beret in his hand, while his companion held a red one. As soon as the two officers saw the group of reporters, they spun on their heels and went back into the office.

In the auditorium they were briefed by an Army general with an easel and chart marked U.S. MILITARY DISTRICT – MANHATTAN that showed a map of the island. He was tall, with brown hair cut short and streaked with gray. When he turned to talk to another officer, Carl saw something that reminded him of his neighbor Two-Tone. The general had burn scar tissue on one side of his face. He wondered if he had been in Two-Tone's unit, back in Cuba. Carl took an aisle seat and Sandy whispered to him, 'Another press conference. Time to think up another question.'

He reached into his jacket and pulled out his notebook, scribbled something, and tore off the sheet of paper. Reporters can ask questions. Not photographers. 'Here. Ask this, if the time comes.'

Sandy read it and looked at him, quizzically. 'All right, I think I will. But what do you mean?'

'Shhh,' he said, getting up from his seat and readying his camera. 'Briefing is about ready to start.'

The general went to a plain brown podium and Carl joined the other photographers, kneeling and squatting in the front row. The general cleared his throat and said, 'I am General Malcolm Conroy, and I'm the commanding officer for the U.S. Military District, Manhattan. What we have for you today is this briefing, a meal, another presentation, and room assignments for tonight. Tomorrow, after breakfast, each of you will be assigned an escort and a vehicle. You will be allowed to tour any part of Manhattan, with exceptions made for road conditions or radiological conditions. Following lunch back here at this facility, there will be another news conference, and then you will be flown back to Tyler Air Force Station.'

Carl snapped a few pictures, and then looked back at the reporters and photographers, and Sandy, who was busily scribbling in her notebook.

'. . . first built in the middle 1800s, the 843 acres of

Central Park became the logical location for a military installation following the Cuban War and the subsequent evacuation of the city. Military units arrived in the city shortly after the war's end, and the Manhattan Air Force Station was formally named in early 1963. This station's mission has changed substantially over the past decade. At first, the mission was relief and recovery for the inhabitants of Manhattan and the survivors from the surrounding boroughs, especially the Bronx, Queens, and Brooklyn. Then, in the summer of 1963, it supported the final evacuation of all civilians from the designated Restricted Zones in and around Manhattan.'

The general paced back to the podium. 'Since that time, ladies and gentlemen, our mission has been a unique one in the history of our military. We are engaged in the protection and preservation of the property, buildings, and industry of Manhattan. This includes using our Army Corps of Engineer units to maintain the necessary utilities and make sure that the libraries and museums of this city are protected from the elements and from those remaining few looters. We are also engaged in specific salvage operations, such as the one in 1964, when we removed several tons of gold bullion, stored by the Federal Reserve branch bank. Never in the history of the world has a city that had been home to millions of citizens suffered such a loss of population in such a short time. Never in the history of the world has a large city been occupied by military forces for the sole purpose of protecting its assets. And never in the history of the world has such a city – largely abandoned – been resettled.'

The general allowed himself a brief smile, and even with the burn tissue, it was charming. 'To our friends in the foreign press, and the domestic press, I have a point I'd like to make.

It's been quite fashionable in some newspaper and magazine articles to portray Manhattan as a ghost of a city. Like Babylon, Nineveh, and Carthage. Dead cities of dead empires. Well, I hate to disappoint you folks, but that is entirely wrong. It's the business of my forces here to ready Manhattan for resettlement. And ladies and gentlemen, it will occur, sooner than you think. I guarantee you that.'

There was a low murmur of excitement. So *that's* it, Carl thought. The whole purpose of the trip, the whole purpose of this show. The great announcement that New York City will soon be open for resettlement. And if it happens a few weeks before the presidential election – where Rockefeller is seen as a friend of the military and McGovern isn't – well, what an amazing coincidence.

He missed the first question but didn't miss the general's answer. 'No, no official date has been set, but I would say that spring of next year – say, April or May 1973 – would be a logical date.'

Carl squeezed off a few more shots of the general at the podium, and then bent over to change his film. The other photographers jostled him for positions. The next question was something to do about looters, and the general's voice carried in the hall: 'Actually, looters aren't as much a problem as they were in the mid-1960s. We have maintained a strong presence in the city and those few looters still at work, I believe, are poor and deranged. We are certain that a few hundred residents of Manhattan still live here, and they go to great lengths to avoid detection. Some years ago, any citizens found here would have been arrested. Now, if we do find them, we feed them, give them medical treatment, and evacuate them to a Red Cross facility in Connecticut. All in all, this is very quiet duty. Next?'

Another question that Carl couldn't make out. The general continued. 'Challenges? Well, one challenge is the problem of fires. As utilities are reconnected, some of the wiring in these older buildings fails, and it's easy for a fire to begin and not be noticed. We cannot let a building catch fire and spread to other buildings. It would soon get away from us, especially since water pressure is still uneven in some neighborhoods. So we've established fire spotting locations on buildings throughout Manhattan – on top of the Empire State Building and the Chrysler Tower, for example – that work not unlike fire towers in the national parks out West. We also have roving fire watches and maintain fire houses throughout Manhattan. Some of the soldiers at these fire houses, I'm proud to say, are former New York City firefighters who enlisted specifically to come back here to their old jobs.'

Then came Sandy's clear voice. 'General Conroy, Sandra Price from the *Times*. Could you tell us why we were *flown* to Manhattan, instead of being driven along one of the expressways? It seems quite an expense, all those helicopters. Are the roads not safe?'

The general shrugged slightly. 'Based on their wear and tear, the highways from Tyler Air Force Station are still in fairly good condition. Your flight here was based on your convenience, nothing else. We know how pressed for time most of you are.'

Good girl, Carl thought. Now for the follow-up. 'I'm sorry, General, perhaps I didn't make myself clear. When I asked if the roads were safe, I was talking more about safe from looters, or other marauders. Is there a problem in the Restricted Zones with armed civilians?'

Carl was close enough to see the general's hands tighten on the edge of the podium. 'No,' he said crisply. 'Final question, please.'

Another British voice, this time male. 'General, if I may be so bold. I'm curious about the apparent burn injuries to your face. Are you a Cuban invasion veteran, perhaps.'

'No,' came the clipped answer.

'Then where were you injured?'

The general stared at a point about six feet above the reporters' heads, his voice suddenly bleak. 'I was at home, recuperating from foot surgery. I was outside getting the mail when Maxwell Air Force Base was attacked. My wife and sons were at the base PX shopping. That's it for questions.'

And then he turned and strode off the stage.

Carl stood by the window in his room at the old Blaine House Hotel, which had been taken over by the Army to billet guests and visitors, and which was adjacent to Central Park. It was on Fifth Avenue and the view was of a blank brick wall across the way. He was in room 1410. Sandy was in 1418. He would do something about that later, but first things first. He went to the bathroom, washed his hands and face, and stared at his tired expression in the mirror. Dinner had been in a dining hall attached to the administration building, and had consisted of reconstituted potatoes and some type of canned beef in gravy.

After dinner they went through an underground utility tunnel to the Blaine House and sat through a long lecture from an Army lawyer who went on and on about the legal aspect of leases and property rights in Manhattan. Carl's eyes had gotten heavy and he had started to nod off, and when room assignments had been distributed, Sandy had arched her eyebrow at him from across the lecture room and he was sure of the invite.

But still . . . There was something odd going on, something that he couldn't figure. First, there were the British planes back at Tyler Air Force Station. Then there were the two officers he had seen before the general's briefing. The one carrying the green beret was American Special Forces. How thoughtful of the Army, he mused, to have someone from his old unit here to greet him. But the other officer . . . The fatigues he had been wearing were not American. And he had been carrying a red beret. Which meant British paratroopers.

British paratroopers and American Special Forces. Elite units sent in for special missions.

Not for reconnecting the lights and the sewers.

He turned on the black-and-white television set and found four channels: ABC, NBC, CBS, and the Armed Forces Network. He turned it off and looked out the window again. Not much of a view. In fact, he hadn't seen much of anything since they had landed. Ferried across in a helicopter, sent to the administration building through a tunnel, and now a room that had a lovely view of a brick wall.

Made one wonder what was out there.

He unzipped his worn leather suitcase. Inside was a small knapsack with some old Army rations, a poncho, and spare clothes. Deep inside he felt the touch of something metallic. All right, maybe it was paranoia, but he still felt good, having that Colt .45 along. It was almost eight o'clock. Time to explore. He put on a light jacket and went out into the corridor, locking the door behind him.

In the lobby he saw the bar where most of the members of his press contingent had congregated, sprawled around small tables. He went across the carpeted floor to the glass double doors leading outside. An Army MP was standing there, boots and helmet polished. The MP held out a hand palm up. He was tall and muscled and looked like the kind of guy who enjoyed juggling bowling balls.

'Can I help you, sir?' he asked.

'Thought I'd go outside, walk around the block and get some fresh air.'

The MP shook his head. 'Sorry, sir. That's not allowed without an escort.'

'Well, do you know where I can get an escort?' Carl asked.

The MP's stolid face didn't change expression. 'You'd have to contact the press officer, sir. Tomorrow.'

Carl took out his wallet, removed his Armed Services ID card. 'Look here, will you? I'm not some nitwit civilian. I put in eight years and I'm in the reserve, so I know my way around. Just looking for some fresh air. What do you say?'

The MP nodded and turned back to face the door. 'That's quite nice, sir. I suggest you contact the press officer for an escort. Tomorrow.'

Carl put his ID card away and walked back across the lobby. He passed by the elevators and saw a door marked STAIRS. It led to a concrete landing, where he paused for a moment, and then descended. There was the sound of machinery, of pumps and air-handling units and he emerged into tight quarters filled with overhead pipes and valves and lights. He fixed the location of the door in his mind, and then went exploring. He passed a kitchen area, a laundry room, and a collection of canned food, set on pallets and locked behind a wired enclosure.

Then he smelled something: diesel fuel. He went down a concrete-lined corridor and came to a heavy metal door. He opened it slightly and peered through the gap. An underground parking area. There were Jeeps and $2\frac{1}{2}$-ton trucks, and on the far side of the lot, overhead lights and tool benches. Some soldiers were grouped around the open hoods of several Jeeps and trucks. Something caught his eye, to the left. He opened the door wider.

Now, that's something, he thought. Rolls and rolls of coiled barbed wire, piled one on top of another. Wooden saw-horses and barriers, tagged and numbered. Bundles of what looked like thin plastic strips, held in plastic bags. Other bundles of thick sticks, like thin and long baseball bats, tied together. Against the wall, piled up as if left by the ghosts of Roman legionnaires: rectangular plastic shields. And there, by the barbed wire: cardboard boxes, piled high up to the concrete ceiling. He could just barely make out the stencils on the side:

HANDLE WITH CARE

FOR TRAINED PERSONNEL USE ONLY

CS . . .

He was interrupted by the sounds of booted feet coming his way, before he could make out the whole of the third line on the box. But what he saw had been enough. He closed the door, ran back to the stairway, and in a minute was back in the lobby. A few seconds later, he was in an elevator, heading back to his room.

The corridor was empty. Good. He strolled down the hallway and reached his door, out of breath from what he had done and seen. Call it a night? No, he thought. We're on a roll. It felt good. Let's keep going. At the end of the corridor, a light marked EXIT flickered and glowed. He opened the door carefully and slowly started up the concrete steps.

He was glad he took his time. He had another nine flights to go before he reached the top, and when he got there, he was breathing hard and his chest hurt. There was a sign above the door handle:

BEFORE EXITING, CHECK YOUR DOSIMETRY

Below that, another, smaller sign had been taped.

AND MAKE SURE YOU CHECK YOUR BUDDY'S!

Sorry, he thought. Must have left it at home. He stepped out onto the roof. It was a cool night and even with the sweetsour smell of decay, it felt good to be outside. The door started closing behind him but he grabbed it before it shut. It'd be a hell of a thing if it locked automatically, wouldn't it?

He took out his wallet and propped the door open, and then went out further beyond the stairwell entrance. The stars were out and there was a crescent moon rising in the east. A waist-high brick wall marked the edge of the roof. He rested his hands on the wall and looked around. He shivered. His heart was still pounding and he liked to think it was because of the hard climb up the stairs, but he knew better. What was in that basement garage didn't belong, if all you cared about was changing a few lightbulbs and making sure the toilets worked. So what was going on?

Across the street were the bright lights of the Manhattan Air Force Station in south Central Park. Below him streetlights shone on this part of Fifth Avenue, where several dark green Army vehicles were parked. The surrounding buildings were well lit for the military personnel who lived here, but beyond this one block, darkness. In the light of the moon and the stars, he could make out darkened buildings all about him, like a deserted and empty mountain range. He hugged himself and looked around. Darkened buildings and skyscrapers stretched as far as he could see. All these buildings, and apartments and slums and businesses and offices. Filled with nothing now except dust, old papers, bones and dried corpses, and maybe a few shivering survivors or looters, still refusing to leave this island.

To the north a light hung almost motionless, but then it moved. He could make out the faint sound of a helicopter engine, and saw a bright cone of light emerge from underneath the helicopter. A searchlight. But who was being searched for on this cold night? The same people they were preparing for, a dozen floors below, with the rolls of barbed wire and barricades and plastic restraints and riot shields and batons and CS gas?

He turned and—

'Sir, put up your hands,' came a voice from behind him.

'You got it,' he said, raising his arms.

Light erupted about him, and he blinked his eyes and the voice said, 'Please turn around.'

He did. Two soldiers stood there, in helmets and full combat gear. One had a flashlight trained on him, and the other had his M-14 lowered in the general direction of Carl's stomach. Not a nice feeling.

'Who are you, and what are you doing up here?' the soldier with the flashlight asked.

'I'm Carl Landry, and I'm with the press contingent. I felt like some fresh air and decided to come up here.'

'Do you have identification?'

'In my wallet. Which is propping open the stairwell door.'

After his wallet was retrieved and his press pass checked, the soldier with the flashlight politely passed his wallet back and said, 'Sir, you shouldn't be up here without an escort. And you haven't been issued your dosimetry yet.'

He returned the wallet to his pants. 'No problem, guys. I'm heading right back down.'

As Carl opened the stairwell door, he saw movement over on the other side of the building's roof, overlooking Fifth Avenue. There was a squad of soldiers and two of them seemed to be wearing larger-than-normal helmets. Instead of M-14s, they had long rifles.

He wanted to ask questions, lots of questions. Instead he went downstairs.

At room 1418 he rapped on the door, and when a woman's voice said, 'Who is it?' he said, 'A delegation from the Prime Minister's office.'

Sandy opened the door, wearing a long blue robe and rubbing the sleep from her eyes. 'Oh, come on in.'

He moved some in the bed, her head upon his shoulder. 'Hmmm, why is this bed so comfortable?'

'I don't know,' she said, her lips gingerly nipping at his ear. 'Maybe we broke something earlier on.'

'Maybe we did.'

She snuggled against him some more and he said, 'Quick question?'

'Sure.'

'Why?'

He felt her pause. 'Why what?'

'Why me?' he said. 'Why us? Sandy, the past few days have been wonderful indeed, but I . . . Well . . .'

She raised her head. 'You want to know my feelings, is that it? Why I'm attracted to you?'

He stroked her back. 'If you don't mind. Having you near me is like . . . it's like winning the lottery, and I didn't even buy a ticket. It's been a wonderful and unexpected gift.'

Sandy smiled and scratched at his chest. 'Among a lot of things, dear boy, including your handsome and rugged face, it's that you're different. You've been places, you've done things, you have this quiet sense of energy and intelligence and strength. You're not like any man I know, back home. There, I've grown up with soft English men whose idea of exertion is running after the train, and whose idea of hardship is not having fresh bread for toast. There. Satisfied?'

He hugged her and she said, 'Not so fast! Your turn. I shan't let you get away without you giving me the same in return.'

Carl gently touched her chin and lifted her head. 'The truth?'

'Of course, the truth.'

'The truth is . . . Sandy, you give me hope.'

'Hope?' she said, in mock anger. 'What do you mean, hope?'

'You come into my life and show me what things are like, an airline flight away. You show me that things still work, that there are still good places left. And you give me hope that it's not too late.'

'Too late for what?'

He looked past her and out the dark window. 'Not too late for my country.'

A bit later she said, 'Can I ask you something, my friend?'

'Ask away.'

'How did you come up with that question that got the general so upset? I had the feeling that I was knocking at a very forbidden door.'

He rubbed at her silken hair and said, 'Earlier today, when we were at the Fence, I had a conversation with a soldier, maybe eighteen or nineteen years old. He didn't come right out and say it, but he did tell me that contrary to published reports and public opinion, the Army doesn't aggressively patrol the Restricted Zones.'

She suddenly sat up again, brushing her hair back from her eyes. 'And what else did he tell you?'

'That was about it, except for a roundabout statement that there are some dangerous things in the RZs. I don't believe in monsters and I don't believe in ghosts, and I'm sure the Army isn't afraid of dog packs. So I think it's people.'

'Who? Who would be living there?'

'Survivors, who never left their homes or who came back. And maybe some militia types, the kind of groups that formed in California. Whoever they are, it seems like the Army is fairly cautious when it goes into the RZs.'

Sandy rubbed at her chin. 'Then that was a bloody good question you had me ask, you conniving fellow. Anything else you're hiding?'

He drew her down and she kissed him on the nose, and he kissed her on her lips and cheeks and eyes, and said in a low voice, 'Sandy, when the good general was talking about being stationed in Manhattan, what kind of duty did he call it?'

'Mmmm,' she said, nuzzling and nibbling at his ear. 'I think he called it calm duty, or something like that.'

'Close,' he said, caressing her back in long, looping motions. 'He said it was quiet duty. And that's an important thing to a soldier. Quiet duty means you get your job done, things go as planned, and you don't have to worry about your bed being blown up during the night.'

She made a growling noise, like a frustrated cat. 'Your point being, young man?'

He tightened his hold on her smooth back. 'My point being that if you have a building with a sniper unit on its roof at night, would you call that quiet duty?'

Carl felt her stiffen under his touch. 'You mean this building?' she asked.

'I certainly do. Earlier, I wanted to get some air and I went up to the roof. Spooky sight, all those dark skyscrapers and office buildings. Then a few soldiers stopped me and sent me back down. Two of them had standard-issue gear, but there was a squad over at the other side of the roof that got my attention.'

'What were they doing?' she asked, her soft voice now all business.

'They weren't watching me. They were looking down at the street. And they were wearing night vision gear of some sort, and bolt-action rifles. Sniper rifles. And there's another thing.'

'What's that?'

'Just before our briefing today I saw two soldiers come out of an office and then just as quickly duck back in, like they didn't want to be seen. But before they did that, I made note of their headgear. Sandy, one of the soldiers belonged to you nice folks. He was from a British paratrooper regiment.'

'Paras? Here?' She sat up quickly, sheet drawn to her chest.

'Right. And the other was from my old unit, Special Forces. Both elite units. Not run-of-the-mill garrison troops.'

'And if this island is on such quiet duty, you wouldn't expect to see paras or Special Forces here,' she said, holding the sheet with her fists.

'No, it'd be a waste. If this is just hooking up lights, sewer, and water, then you wouldn't have elite forces here. Unless there's other work to do.'

'Such as?'

He recalled what he had seen in the basement, but decided to save that for later. He didn't like the inquisitive tone of her voice. 'Such as I don't know.'

'Well, tomorrow I intend to find out,' she said, reaching for her notebook on the nightstand. She flipped the pages and made some notes.

Carl rolled over on his back, folded his hands behind his head, and stared up at the ceiling. Foreigners, he thought. Civilians. Not a single clue. She thinks this is one terrific adventure, a lark set up especially for her, for the benefit of a good newspaper article and some stories to tell at the pubs on Fleet Street when she gets home. A moment passed, and then he listened to the sound of her notebook and pen being replaced on the nightstand.

She touched the back of his head, gently stroked his hair. 'Carl, what's wrong?'

'Sandy, do you know what the phrase "Potemkin village" means?'

Her hand stopped moving. 'Something to do with Catherine the Great. A minister fooled her into thinking that a region was doing well. Am I right?'

'Your parents got their money's worth at Oxford. Yeah, that's pretty close. Prince Potemkin was an adviser and lover of Catherine the Great. In the late 1700s, she wanted to tour some new territories that Russia had annexed. Potemkin wanted to make a good impression, so he had the villages rebuilt and repainted, and the sick, elderly, and poor were shunted away. Some villages were nothing but facades. Peasants were supposed to sing and dance for the empress as she traveled by.'

Sandy said quietly, 'You think this whole trip is a Potemkin village?'

'Or something damn close. And you know what worries me?'

'Go on,' she said.

He kept on staring up at the ceiling. 'I'd suggest you don't ask any embarrassing questions tomorrow, Sandy. Everybody in a Potemkin village has their role to play, and that includes the news media. The peasants that were lined up for the empress had their roles. If they didn't dance or sing on cue, they were beaten or killed. What happens if we don't sing or dance on cue?'

She hugged herself. 'Carl, you're beginning to scare me.'

He thought about what she had planned to do tomorrow, to publicly poke and ask questions in the middle of a restricted military zone.

'Good,' he said.

EMPIRE: THREE

A MATTER OF EMPIRE: THREE

MAJOR KENNETH HUNT was working in temporary quarters in one corner of an aircraft hangar at RCAF Trenton, reviewing a personnel roster, trying to keep his mind focused on his job and nothing else, when there was a tapping at the thin wooden door. He looked up, ready to snap at whoever was standing there, and then dropped the papers on the desk.

'Clive!' he exclaimed, standing up and extending a hand. 'What the devil are you doing here?'

His older brother was wearing a rumpled black suit, white shirt, thin black tie, and a tired look on his face. He was five years older than Kenneth, with a thick thatch of black hair, heavy eyebrows, and saggy cheeks that would one day turn into the jowls of a bulldog, though even now, he had that dog's tenacity. Officially, Clive worked in the Foreign Office, but Kenneth knew better, had known better for years.

Clive shook his hand and said, 'Sorry about barging in on you like this, old boy, but I was passing through on my way to Ottawa and thought I'd see how little Kenny is doing. Feel up to a bit of a stroll?'

Hunt was going to protest that he had too much work to do, that he had a meeting with an RCAF liaison officer in ten minutes, and after that, a meeting with the Regiment's Sergeant-Major, but he saw the look on his brother's face and said, 'Of course.'

In the quick stroll across the runway, they talked about their parents and their only sister, Penelope, a producer for the BBC. They reached a grassy area surrounded by a chain-link fence and Clive sat on the ground, letting out a sigh of exhaustion as he leaned against the fence. It was sunny and warm for October, and Hunt sat next to his brother.

About a hundred yards away, just off the runway, was the rusting and picked-over carcass of a B-52 bomber. It had been there ten years, partially buried and collapsed in the soil. Talking to one of the Royal Canadian Air Force officers, Hunt had learned that the bomber – damaged by missile fire some-where over the old Soviet Union – had made an emergency landing here on its way back to the States. The crew had gone home and the top-secret gear had been stripped out, and there it remained. The Canadians had protested and had asked for funds to remove the hulk, and the Americans had said they would get around to it, one of these days, and these days had extended into weeks and months and years.

Clive gestured to the dead jet.

'There you are,' he said. 'Another relic of a dead empire. A Boeing bomber. Built in Seattle, probably based in the Midwest, and then sent over the North Pole to the middle of Asia, to kill people who probably never left their village in their entire life, and whose only fault was that they lived next door to a Soviet military base. The reach of an empire. And

RESURRECTION DAY **281**

here it rests, rusting, never to fly again. But one sure thing about dead empires is that sometimes they don't want to remain dead. Like ours.'

Major Hunt nodded, knowing what was ahead. His older brother was a lecturer, and when he was in the mood to talk, it was best just to listen. Clive reached into his coat pocket, pulled out a thin box of Dunhills. 'Want a fag, Kenny?'

'No, I'm sticking with the pipe nowadays. I find it soothing.'

'Hah,' Clive said, pulling out a cigarette and lighting it. 'Haven't felt soothed in months, not since the stupid bastards upstairs thought up Operation Turnabout.'

Hunt felt himself stiffen at the name of his operation, the one that he had been planning for, the one that was due to commence in less than four weeks' time, the one that gave him nightmares about his dead wife, Rachel. 'If I were you, I wouldn't be bandying that name around too much, Clive.'

His brother waved a hand dismissively. 'Bah, don't worry. That's why we're sitting out here, instead of in your office, which might have an electronic ear or two. There *is* something that I didn't want anybody else to hear, though. Operation Turnabout does not have the full backing of Her Majesty's Government. The PM is still wavering.'

'Is there a chance it might be called off?' Hunt asked, anticipation in his voice. 'I tell you, Clive, it's kept me up a few nights.'

His brother frowned, took a deep drag from his Dunhill. 'Then I'm afraid you're going to have a lot more sleepless nights over the next few weeks.'

'Oh.'

Clive nodded, stared out at the runway. 'Oh, we had a chance, maybe, just a week or two ago, to stop this bloody thing. We had someone in the States, in Boston, who claimed to have some information that would have helped us tremendously in blocking it.'

'And who is "us," if I may ask?'

He rubbed at his face with his free hand. 'Those of us who don't like Operation Turnabout. Those of us who think three world wars in one century is more than enough, thank you very much. And those of us who think that if another British empire is to be created, it will be done because the world wants it. Not because we took advantage of a wounded friend.'

'If that's "us," then who are the others?'

Another deep pull on his cigarette. 'Ah, the others. The ones who are fearful of our French and German comrades across the Channel. Who would have thought that those old bastards, de Gaulle and Adenauer, would form an alliance after the war? And that Pompidou and Brandt would keep it alive? The French and Germans have been moving in on Eastern Europe, opening up those markets, while we, the poor man of Europe, are being ignored, being ridiculed. But here's a chance to bring the empire back to life overnight, with more territory and the most terrible weapons in the world, and then, well, we won't be the poor man of Europe anymore.'

Hunt felt bleak, seeing the angry and tortured expression on his brother's face. 'You're probably right, Clive. We won't be the poor man of Europe anymore. Just the most hated.'

His brother nodded, stubbed out his cigarette on the grass. 'A decade ago, all of us thought we'd seen the last of war, especially after seeing pictures of what happened here and in Russia. But ten years is a long time, Kenny. People forget.'

He was surprised when his brother – not usually a demonstrative man – grabbed his hand and gave it a firm squeeze.

'And when the people and the politicians forget, they tend to do stupid things. Like send their finest young men into battle to do the devil's work. Oh, blast, look what's coming.'

Down the side of the runway, an RCAF staff car was approaching. Hunt and his brother stood up, Clive brushing at the grass on his pants. 'My official escort approaches, Kenny, so I'm off to Ottawa.'

'What happened to the man in Boston?' he asked. 'Who might have helped stop the whole thing.'

Clive sadly shook his head. 'We were asked to send him someone, someone who knew him a long time ago. An old general. Sheffield was his name. And now they're both dead, and Operation Turnabout seems to be unstoppable.'

Hunt suddenly felt chilled, standing next to his brother. 'Both of them, dead. And that's it?'

'So far. Unless we get terribly lucky in these next few days.'

The dark blue car came to a stop and Clive gave him a glum half wave as he climbed in. Hunt watched the car turn around, thinking, I can't. I can't do it. Not with Rachel up there, watching me.

I can't.

SIXTEEN

LIEUTENANT GREG LOOMIS LOOKED like a recruiting poster for the Selective Service. He was tall, and wore clean fatigues, a web utility belt, and black combat boots. Hanging from the utility belt was a holstered Colt .45 pistol and a small handheld radio. His black hair was cut short and his handshake was firm and to the point. Carl and Sandy met him after a breakfast of oatmeal and sausages in a crowded mess hall. Carl had a small backpack with a few odds and ends in it, and Sandy had her large leather purse.

The lieutenant got straight to the matter at hand.

'I'm your escort for today,' he said. They were in a large banquet hall and the other reporters, photographers, and television crews were also in small groups, talking to their respective escorts.

'First things first,' he said, opening a large leather dispatch case and pulling out a shiny tubular object the size of a stubby pencil and a square plastic badge with a clip at the end. He gave a set to each of them.

Something about the young officer bothered Carl, and he

remembered what the lieutenants had been like when he was on active duty. Ninety-day wonders, they were called, because after three months of officer's school, they were considered trained and fit for command. Carl and many of the other sergeants had had a slightly different opinion: after ninety days, they were trained and fit for wiping their bottoms after using the latrine, and not much else. The new lieutenants were eager, proper, and if you weren't careful, they could get you killed.

'Your dosimetry,' he said. 'Clip them on your chest. The square plastic one is called a TLD, stands for thermoluminescence dosimeter. Measures your total dose. After you leave Manhattan you'll get a letter from the Army's Dosimetry Lab in Ithaca, telling you how much you picked up, and don't worry, it'll be minimal, if that.'

He held up the pencil-shaped tube. 'The other piece is called an SRPD. Stands for self-reading pocket dosimeter. Hold it up to the light and you'll see a scale. Each line on the scale marks one millirem of radiation. The needle should be zeroed out to the left. Every now and then, check on the needle's position. If it starts moving to the right, let me know. It'll probably just mean we're near a hot spot and should saddle up and drive somewhere else.'

Carl clipped the dosimetry to his jacket and suddenly felt transported back to California in the 1960s, where such dosimetry was as much one's gear as a canteen and spare ammunition. Like then, it felt creepy. It was one thing to be out in the bush, facing another person who was armed. It was quite another thing to deal with an enemy that you couldn't hear, taste, or smell, an enemy that could kill you just as dead as a bullet to the head.

Sandy followed suit and said, 'Lieutenant, if New York is

ready for resettlement next year, why do we have to wear dosimetry?'

'Regulations, what else?' he said. 'The fallout in Manhattan – like in the other RZs – has decayed to reasonable levels. But we still keep track of everyone's exposure, and the Army moves slow sometimes when it comes to changing regulations. Chances are, next year, dosimetry won't be a requirement anymore. It hasn't been exposure to radiation that's blocked resettlement these past couple of years, you know. It's just getting the utilities and services brought back on line.'

'How many hours will we have in the city, Lieutenant?'

He smiled at her. 'First of all, we can be informal. Call me Greg, all right?

She shouldered her bag. 'If I get to call you Greg, then it's Sandy for you. Understand?'

'Sure,' Greg said. 'I learned long ago not to pick a fight with the press. Because we always lose.'

Not always, Carl thought, but he kept that to himself.

It was a crisp fall day, the sky was blue, and Greg led them out to the street, where a sergeant sitting in a Jeep saluted and gave the vehicle over to the lieutenant. Greg got into the driver's seat and Carl got into the back, letting Sandy sit up front. There were folded Army-issue blankets on the seat, along with two small satchels. Clamped to the dashboard, between the front seats, was an M-14 rifle, and at the rear of the Jeep, two jerricans of gasoline hung from the tailgate. Other Jeeps were parked up and down the street, and groups of twos and threes occupied and then drove them.

'You really can't see as well with the canvas tops up, so we tend to leave them down,' Greg said. 'But it can get chilly, so feel free to use the blankets. Inside each satchel is our lunch and a Thermos of coffee. Sorry, miss, there's no tea.'

'Oh, I'll survive,' she said, turning back to smile at Carl and arrange the blanket around her legs. 'I think everyone over here runs on coffee and cigarettes.'

'Well, not tobacco for me, that's for sure,' Greg said. He opened up the dispatch case again, pulled out a much-folded map, and said, 'We're in luck today, folks. The wind is blowing to the east, so we have pretty much the entire island to look at, just as long as we get back by three P.M. My job is to show you around and answer as many questions as I can.'

He turned in his seat and said to Carl, 'I see by the roster sheet that you're a photographer assigned to the *Times* of London. But where are you from?'

'Massachusetts. Boston.'

Greg nodded. 'I'm from Springfield, myself. Graduated from Dartmouth last year, got my commission through the ROTC program.'

'Sorry,' Sandy said. 'What was that you just said?'

'ROTC. Reserve Officer Training Corps. Pretty good program, actually. The Army paid for my tuition and I also trained as an officer, weekends and summers. Then when I graduated, I got in as a second lieutenant. Avoid putting up with the draft. Boston, eh? Go to college there?'

'Nope.' He paused, and said, 'Went to a little school, back in the early sixties. University of Saigon.'

The smile flickered for a moment. 'I'm afraid you have one on me.'

'No, Greg,' Sandy said, glaring at Carl. 'I'm afraid my photographer is being too clever for his own good. Carl was in the Army, as well. I believe he joined up after high school, and he was stationed in Saigon, in Vietnam.'

Greg nodded. 'You got me there. Infantry, right?'

'Among other things.'

'Well, this man's Army sure has changed a lot since then. When I received my commission I asked for duty here in Manhattan, and I was lucky enough to get it. I've been on this island for almost a year and I haven't gotten tired of it yet.' He swiveled in his seat, reached to the dashboard, and pressed the starter button. 'What do you say, let's go see it?'

The Jeep started up with a muted roar and Greg pulled his radio free and switched it on, holding it near his lips.

'Traffic Control, this is Baker Fourteen. On Fifth Avenue, heading south. Kay.'

A static-filled voice returned. 'Baker Fourteen, have a safe one. Out.'

They started heading south, down Fifth Avenue. Carl spoke up. 'What's your duty here, Greg?'

Greg seemed eager to talk, and it was easy to listen to him, since he kept the speed of the Jeep low. The road was bumpy, with cracks and potholes and even some sinkholes where wooden barriers had been set up. Grass filled some of the cracks and Carl wished the Jeep were still, so he could get a photo. Grass growing, in the middle of Fifth Avenue. Most of the buildings had piles of rubble in front of them from facades and decorative stonework that had fallen over the years.

'I'm in Building Recovery,' Greg said. 'My platoon goes out every day, building to building. We look for structural damage and broken gas pipes. We also disconnect each building from the electrical grid. It's all prep work for when the utilities get switched back on. After ten years we're still not sure how some of the wiring will handle being energized again.'

'It sounds very tedious,' Sandy said, pulling out her notebook.

'Actually, it's not,' he said. Greg spotted the open notebook and slowed down, pulling over to the sidewalk. The only sounds were from the idling Jeep engine and some static chatter on the radio. Sandy looked over, a bit concerned, but Greg was still smiling. He said, 'Look, I apologize but maybe we should clear a few things before we continue. Otherwise we'll be fussing over what's on the record and what's off the record, and we'll waste half the day. Okay?'

Sandy nodded. 'Go ahead.'

'How about everything I say is on the record, but you don't attribute it to me by name. Or by service. Just a military officer assigned to the Manhattan Air Force Station.'

'Won't that narrow it down?' Carl asked.

'Nope, not at all. We have all branches of the service here, except for Marines. We have Air Force and Army, of course, but we also have Navy and Coast Guard units working the harbor and the rivers. That way, if whatever I say causes a fuss, it won't come back to bite me. And if we do it this way, I think we'll have a better day. Agreed?'

'That's fine,' Sandy said, digging out a pen, and Greg said, 'All right, you were asking about building duty. The truth is, I do find it interesting. You never know what you're going to find. It's like being paid to be a burglar, or a snoop. We have guys that would be dangerous if they ever decided to be criminals when they got out of the service. They can pop most locks in under a minute.'

'And what do you do when you get inside?'

'We head up to the top floor and work our way down. Part of the survey work is checking apartments to see if there are any valuables that should be transported for safekeeping, like paintings or antiques.' Another swivel of the head and he smiled at Carl. 'We were in this high-priced co-op once, over on the Upper East Side. Someone had turned an entire room almost the size of a ballroom into a miniature city with model railroads. Very intricate, very detailed, all left in place. Boy, that was one of the few times I've been glad we don't have power. Some of the guys in my squad, they would have spent the day putting that display through its paces.'

'Do you find many . . . many bodies?' Sandy asked, balancing her notepad on a blanket-covered knee.

A shake of the head. 'Some, but not as many as you'd think. Most people did manage to evacuate back in '62. Ten years later . . . Well, nature's taken care of many of the bodies left behind. We have a couple of guys assigned to Graves Registration, and if we find any remains – mostly bones by now – it's their responsibility. We record where we found them and whether there's any identification left. Then that information goes to the Red Cross. Guys in Graves Registration, they get rotated out after a month. That job can get to you, especially when you go through a school's basement . . . Last month, a buddy of mine working on clearing up the subway system came across a bunch of subway cars. Filled with skeletons. Brrr. He says it still gives him nightmares.'

Carl said, 'You've done escort duty like this before, haven't you?'

'Surely have,' Greg said, easing the Jeep back out onto Fifth Avenue. 'Congressmen, senators, overseas visitors, and the occasional VIP who wants to check up on his old Park Avenue place. I've had them all, but you know what? They never come in winter, which is a pity. This place is so beautiful then, all the streets covered with snow, not a sound to be heard. Last winter, a guy I know from Maine, who works in

Deeds and me, we cross-country skied from Battery Park to Inwood Hill Park, up at the north end of the island. Just a beautiful trip. Even saw some deer along the way.'

'Deer?' Sandy asked, incredulous. 'In Manhattan?'

'Why not? Who's going to stop them? A couple of guys've told me that they've seen wolves, but I doubt it. Just dogs, probably.'

Carl said, 'Is that what the rifle is for?'

'Yep. Wild dogs. Sad but true. We still have wild dog packs, that mostly hang around the parks. The Humane Society has an office back at the base but there's not much they can do.' Greg turned his head back and looked ruefully at Carl. 'We still have a standing shoot-on-sight order for wild dogs, because of the rabies problems, but I can't do it. When I see them, I either blow the horn or shoot over their heads.'

Carl looked to the cross streets, which were jammed with abandoned cars, trucks, and buses. 'Are there still a lot of streets blocked with traffic?'

'Most streets are,' Greg said, and he held up the map. 'Which is why this is so important. A lot of the main thoroughfares – like Broadway – are cleared, but not many of the side streets. We chip at it, week after week, but I bet you there'll still be thousands of abandoned cars here next year. Still, we get an updated map every month, showing us which streets are open for traffic.'

Greg put the map down and turned the Jeep right, across East Forty-sixth Street. The sound of the engine echoed among the walls of the buildings, and Carl leaned back and looked up at all the empty windows stretching far overhead. Millions of people, he thought. Millions lived and breathed and ate and loved and fought in these buildings. Now, where were they? Most of the refugee camps set up in Pennsylvania,

New Jersey, and Connecticut had been disassembled, as the refugees slowly moved on, to relatives or friends or jobs elsewhere. There were still a few camps left for those who had no other place to go – the disabled, the elderly, the orphaned – but with every passing year, those numbers dwindled away. For those former New Yorkers with new lives, there were organizations and newsletters to keep track of old neighborhoods and associations, and there were still thousands upon thousands who wanted to come back.

If the offerings at the Fence were any sign, they were still waiting.

Greg slowed and turned left on Broadway. Carl felt his throat clench as he realized where they were heading. Times Square, the crossroads of the world. Greg stopped the Jeep and the three of them got out and stood in the middle of the street, looking around. The streets that merged here were broad and wide and empty of vehicles, save for two Jeeps at the south end of the square, where film crews were filming stand-ups with network correspondents.

Carl unlimbered his camera and took pictures of the abandoned stores and movie houses. He saw a faded poster, still in its frame, for an Anthony Quinn film. *Barabbas*. He turned around, saw Sandy talking to Greg, taking notes, and he felt a faint flush of melancholy at seeing this beautiful and smart and talented woman from a safe and peaceful country calmly jotting down notes about this dead city, America's first city. Sandy was just doing her job, that's all, and at least she didn't have the smug look of some of the German and Japanese reporters. From their attitudes and laughter, he got the feeling of . . . of payback, he guessed. Their cities had been bombed, industries destroyed, civilians killed, all by American planes and weapons back in the previous world war. He knew he was being unfair but it seemed like they were enjoying this visit, gloating at what had happened to American cities and how, even ten years later, the premier city was still abandoned. Berlin and Tokyo were thriving metropolises in 1955. The same was not true of New York in 1972.

He turned and started taking more photos. He went around the corner for a moment, onto West Forty-first Street, and took pictures of the abandoned vehicles. All of the tires were flat and the paint faded. There was a city bus and a number of taxicabs, and he decided not to get too close. He didn't want to see what might still be sitting in the vehicles.

Around the corner was the building – what was its name? – that had had the scrolling news ticker that was always shown in movies. He followed Sandy and Greg north a couple of blocks. Across the way was a fenced-in statue of a soldier dressed in a First World War uniform and the name etched below it said 'FATHER DUFFY,' who was of the famed Rainbow Division of what was known back then simply as the Great War, before it became fashionable to number them. He took a couple of shots of the statue and got a few that he was pleased with, of Greg in his fatigues, with the statue of Father Duffy in the background.

Sandy and Greg came over to him and Sandy asked, 'Where to next?'

'Your suggestion,' Greg said, and Sandy piped up, 'How about the United Nations?'

'Sure,' Greg said, taking out his radio. 'But we can't go inside the buildings. Too dangerous.' He held the radio up to his mouth and said, 'Traffic Control, this is Baker Fourteen, kay.'

'Baker Fourteen, go ahead, kay.'

'Heading east to First Avenue, kay.'

'Copy.'

Greg put the radio back into its leather holder and Carl said, 'Do they like to keep that close of a watch on traffic?'

'Sure,' Greg said, as they walked back to the Jeep. 'First, it's just good sense. If the radio dies or we get into an accident – say, drive into a sinkhole – it's nice to know that somebody out there has a general idea of where we are, and will come looking for us. And if we need backup for something, a radio can be a lifesaver.'

'And what kind of backup are you talking about?' Sandy asked.

'Just whatever kind of backup we need,' Greg said, trying to make light of his answer.

But Carl noticed the way his smooth face tensed up as he answered her question.

They stayed on West 42nd Street, until past Fifth Avenue, which had also been cleared. As they passed a fire house near Third Avenue, Greg honked the Jeep's horn at some fatigue-clad firefighters washing down two firetrucks parked out on the sidewalk. They waved back, and a couple of them whistled at the sight of the woman in the Jeep.

'Those guys have a real tough job,' Greg said, raising his voice. 'If a fire ever gets away from us, it could take out three or four city blocks. Back in '65, during the Great Harlem Fire, they had to bring in special aircraft that used to be used to drop water over forest fires out West, before they got that one under control.'

Twice they passed Corps of Engineer units, working around manholes, and Greg said, 'Utility work. Real grind stuff but it's work that's got to be done.'

He slowed and made a left on to First Avenue, and there it was. A fence topped by barbed wire had been erected around the square that held the two familiar buildings of the United Nations. Even at this distance, Carl could see the broken windows and large, black scars of fire damage along the side of the main building on the right, the Secretariat. The low-slung building on the left, the General Assembly building, wasn't as badly damaged. Greg parked the Jeep up on the sidewalk, next to the fence. Just beyond was a long, curved driveway that led to the two buildings. With the engine off Carl could make out a faint tinkling sound. He wondered what it was. Beyond the United Nations was the East River and Carl saw Welfare Island and, across the river, burned shells of buildings and piles of rubble that marked the borough of Queens.

They got out and Carl took two photos, then stood still. He couldn't get used to the sound of so much silence in such a large city. Sandy wiped at her forehead and said, 'What happened here?'

Greg folded his arms. 'After the bombs were dropped on Queens and Idlewild Airport, tens of thousands of people were making their way through these streets, most of them on foot. You also had refugees coming in from Brooklyn, and people were terrified and angry. Many were angry enough to come here, to the UN building, to kill any Russian diplomats they could find. I don't know if they ever did, but they did succeed in looting the place and burning it.'

Carl asked, 'Any chance of getting in, to get some pictures?'

Greg shook his head. 'No, sorry. First, it's dangerous in there. With the fire damage and the decay, there's a good chance of being injured. And second, well, hard to believe but we leave this place alone. This is United Nations property and when the Army came into Manhattan, they built this fence around it.'

Carl put the camera down and looked at the two buildings, remembering when they were finished in the early 1950s, and how, as a kid, he had thought that this would be the head-quarters of a place that would outlaw war. Well, Korea and Cuba took care of that little experiment in world peace and now the UN was back in Geneva. It was still at work, es-pecially with the UN Disarmament Agency in China and the former Soviet Union, trying to track down unaccounted-for nuclear weapons. The UN also maintained large refugee camps in Eastern Europe and the edges of the old Soviet empire, and helped Spain with its trusteeship of Cuba. But the United States . . . the country that helped form it back in the 1940s had only been granted observer status last year, and that only after months of furious debate in Geneva, London, Berlin, Paris, and Tokyo.

He was trying to figure out where that tinkling noise was coming from, when Sandy spoke, her voice strained. 'Has anyone else noticed a difference in their dosimetry reading? I checked it in Times Square and it was zero. Now it's one.'

He and Greg moved almost as one, holding up their SRPDs to the skies. 'Mine's also on the first scale,' Carl said, and Greg added, 'Well, mine's at two. That's a good sign that it's time to move on.'

They went back to the Jeep and Sandy said, 'Is that dangerous?'

'No, not at all,' Greg said, getting behind the wheel. 'It probably means there are a few hot spots around here, deposited by a wind from last night or yesterday. You'd have to get readings ten or twenty times as high before you'd have to worry about any ill effects. Still, it's a good enough reason to head west. Where to next?'

Before Sandy could speak up, Carl said, 'We asked you to take us here. Why don't you take us to a place you like to visit, someplace that's yours?'

Sandy looked and smiled and Greg nodded. 'All right, deal.' He picked up his radio and said, 'Traffic Control, Baker Fourteen, we're heading southwest.'

'Baker Fourteen, copy,' came the reply.

As Greg reached down to start the Jeep, Carl realized where that tinkling noise was coming from: it was from just in front of the UN General Assembly building, from the flag-poles, where a few ropes still hung, holding up faded rags that were once flags of proud nations, many of which didn't exist anymore.

Along the way Carl began to feel colder and he wrapped the Army blanket around his legs. He had a sense that Greg was in a hurry, for the Jeep was going faster and there wasn't the same opportunity for conversation. Even Sandy seemed to hunker down in the front seat, and Carl felt the same oppressive feeling. It was just too damn big, this large island with buildings and skyscrapers and stores and tenements and subways and parks and streets, empty of life, empty of the living. A pack of dogs ran across a street, a block ahead, and Greg honked the horn a few times. The storefronts and the broken windows seemed to merge in a dark blur as Greg maneuvered the Jeep through the streets, and Carl noticed some graffiti painted on the sides of buildings and abandoned city buses. Some of the graffiti looked quite fresh.

There were a few ARMY LEAVE US ALONE and YANKEES GO

HOME, a host of REPENTs, a RESURRECTION DAY IS COMING, and an old, faded RED CROSS HAS SET UP AT TOMPKINS SQUARE. There were also a bunch of strange symbols and letters in bright colors. One of the symbols, three circles connected by curving lines, was marked on at least three street corners, and looked familiar for some reason. He couldn't understand why.

And on the side of a building on Bowery Avenue, in letters that looked five feet tall:

HE LIVES.

Even here, he thought, finding himself liking the sight. True believers still.

They came to a park with a large arch in the center, and Greg drove the Jeep right up to the arch, which was richly decorated and carved. He shut off the idling engine and leaned back into the driver's seat.

'Welcome to Washington Square Park,' Greg said. 'My favorite spot – because of what happened here, and what will happen here again in a few months. In this square, on April 30, 1789, George Washington was inaugurated as our first president, back when New York City was, for a time, our capital. A year later the capital was moved to Philadelphia. A bit ironic, don't you think?'

He shifted in his seat and said, 'Now, what I'm about to tell you is just rumor, and if you do print it, please don't report it as coming from anybody associated with the Manhattan Air Force Station. All right?'

Sandy said, 'You've piqued my curiosity, Greg. What is it?'

'It's still just a rumor, but the planning's already begun, back at staff headquarters. Next January, Nelson Rockefeller will be returning here, to be inaugurated as president, and to show the world that we really are on the verge of reopening New York City to resettlement.'

Greg moved his arm across. 'Can you see what it's going to be like, in a couple of months? All of these buildings will be rehabbed and connected to utilities, and there'll be flags and bunting and an honor guard, and the world news media, and right under that arch, he'll take the oath of office. It's going to be a hell of a sight, something I'll tell my grandchildren.'

Carl pulled the blanket tighter around his legs. 'There's a little matter of an election that has to take place.'

Greg laughed. 'Oh, he's going to win. No doubt about that.'

Sandy leaned over a bit. 'You seem happy about a Rockefeller presidency.'

The soldier shrugged. 'Most people are. He promises to keep the focus on relief and recovery, on rebuilding, on minding our own business. McGovern wants to cut the armed forces and wants us to rejoin the UN. Put our trust in treaties and other nations. I had an uncle who was in the Army and was stationed at the West Berlin garrison back in '62. When the war broke out the Red Army and East Germans stormed into West Berlin. Not a single one of the soldiers in that garrison has ever been found. It's as if they disappeared. That's good enough reason for me to vote for someone who wants to focus on the home front.'

Then Sandy sat up and said, 'There! Did you see that!'

Greg leaned forward and so did Carl. 'See what?'

'Oh, he's gone now,' she said, her voice rising in excitement. 'Across the park, by that brick building that looks like a university. I saw a man walking along the pavement but then he must have seen us, because he ran down an alleyway. Shall we see who he is? Do you think he's a looter?'

Greg started up the Jeep. 'To answer your second question, I doubt he's a looter. They usually work at night. And to answer your first question, no. We don't chase people anymore. If they surrender into our custody, fine. Otherwise, we leave them alone.'

Carl remembered last night. He remembered a helicopter with a searchlight and the sniper squad on top of the roof of their hotel, and the supplies in the parking garage. He folded his arms and said nothing.

Greg said, 'What do you say, lunch at Battery Park? We can see the reconstruction work going on at the Statue of Liberty. Ever since the arm—'

The radio at his side crackled into life. 'Baker Fourteen, Baker Fourteen,' came a voice different from before. 'This is Traffic Control, kay.'

He halted the Jeep, brought the radio up to his mouth. 'This is Baker Fourteen, kay.'

'Baker Fourteen, proceed to Greenwich Street and Seventh Avenue. A survey team's run out of gas, they need a fuel-up. Kay.'

Greg gave Sandy and Carl an amused look, and said in a loud whisper, 'Happens a lot, when guys are in a hurry to leave the motor pool and don't check the fuel gauge.' He keyed the radio mike and said in a louder voice, 'Baker Fourteen acknowledges, kay.'

Sandy turned her head and said, 'Is it far?'

'Only a couple of blocks. Just delays lunch for about fifteen minutes.'

Carl kept his hands under the blanket as Greg sped the Jeep to the west, to the low buildings of Greenwich Village. They got onto Seventh Avenue and headed north. As he turned onto Greenwich Avenue, Greg braked. The road ahead was blocked by a tangled mass of taxi cabs and a fuel oil delivery truck. He picked up the map and said in a quiet voice, 'That's odd, the map shows this road's been clear for months. These vehicles shouldn't be here.'

Carl felt the hair along the back of his arms creep up into life and he leaned forward and said, 'Greg, get us out of here!'

Sandy said, 'What on earth are you—

Carl shouted, 'Lieutenant, haul ass and get us out of here!'

Greg dropped the map and slammed the gear shift into reverse, as the first shot boomed and struck the hood of the Jeep. The second shot shattered the windshield.

The third shot blew off the top of the head of Lt. Greg Loomis, U.S. Army.

SEVENTEEN

ANOTHER TWO SHOTS RANG OUT and the Jeep continued in reverse, backing up onto the sidewalk and hitting something – a fire hydrant or another crushed car – and tipped to the side, throwing Carl to the ground, next to a screaming Sandy Price.

The sounds of the shots seemed to turn a switch on inside of him, making everything razor sharp, from the echoing blasts of the gunfire to the gritty feeling of the cracked asphalt under his hands. He grabbed Sandy and pulled her into the shadow of the overturned Jeep. He checked Greg, pinned in his seat behind the steering wheel, his eyes staring lifelessly, the top of his head an awful jumble of brain, blood, and bone. He tried to unclip the M-14 from the stand but failed and saw that it was locked shut. He had neither the time nor the interest to going through Greg's pockets, looking for the keys. Instead he grabbed the map, radio, his knapsack, and the two satchels.

'Are you hurt?' he said, grabbing Sandy's arm and whispering harshly into her ear.

'No . . . no . . .' she said, voice quavering. 'Oh, God,

Carl . . .'

'Hush,' he said, not too gently, passing her the two blankets. 'Hold on to these. We're getting the hell out of here.'

'What?' she said, protesting. 'We're being shot at!'

He tossed her the blankets, peered around the side of the Jeep, and saw an open door into a storefront. He looked back and Sandy had rolled up the blankets and was carrying them under an arm. He motioned to her and she crawled over.

'That door, right there,' he said. 'Keep it low.'

They made it across the three or four feet of open space without incident, running into a small grocery store. The shelves were empty and dusty and there was a sour odor, and he didn't care. He was alive. Sandy was alive. They weren't being shot at that particular moment.

He was amazed at how calm he was.

A half hour later Sandy said, 'Carl, please, can we have a rest.'

He checked around the second-floor apartment that they were in, about two blocks away from the ambush site. Sandy was sitting on the floor, back against the wall, head drooping from exhaustion. Carl just nodded, too tired to say anything. The last thirty minutes had been a dirty mess of going through alleyways and across rooftops, crawling and climbing amid the rubble of decaying buildings. They were in a six-story tenement building on Perry Street. Up two blocks was Seventh Avenue, which had been cleared for travel, and he could make out a corner bar and grill. The sign was still visible. OPEN ROAD BAR.

The apartment was small and looked like it had belonged

to an artist. They were in the living room, which had hardwood floors and large windows. In a corner were a couple of easels, some dried-up tubes of paint, dropcloths and paintbrushes, and canvases that had faded to gray. Wallpaper was pulled away from the walls in long strips, and plaster bulged from the walls. There was a small kitchen and an even tinier bathroom. When they had gotten in he had opened the bedroom door and just as quickly shut it. There had been a huddled shape under the blankets, and he didn't want to look any closer.

Sandy's voice was shaking as she raised her head. 'Why are the buildings like this?'

Carl kept view of the street below, hiding behind rotten drapes that still hung to the floor. A couple of the windows had fallen out, and there was a draft moving across his legs, chilling him. Shock, he thought. She must still be in shock, to ask such a question.

'I said, why are the buildings like this? Carl, we nearly fell through those stairs.'

'Imagine a single year here, without anybody taking care of anything,' he said, not turning around. 'Sewers back up, gutters get choked with leaves, and water comes through the walls. Windows crack, wind and snow get into the rooms. Basements leak and roofs leak. Water freezes into ice and damages the floors. Rot sets in over the summer. That's in a single year. It's been ten. It's amazing more buildings haven't collapsed.'

The street below was quiet, gray pigeons moving along the sidewalk and among the dead cars. In the distance he could hear dogs barking. He stepped back from the window and went to Sandy, knelt down and held her head in his hands. 'Are you all right?' he asked.

Tears were rolling down her cheeks. 'Jesus, that was so frightful . . . I . . . I've never been shot at before . . . Carl, can you call for help on that radio? Contact the Air Force station? Can't they come and get us?'

He gently stroked her ears, and looked over at the radio and map, on top of the two knapsacks and the rolled-up blankets. He spoke carefully. 'I don't think that's a good idea.'

She wiped at her eyes with both hands, which were trembling. 'Why the hell not?'

'Because I don't know who's on the other end of the radio, that's why.'

She dropped her hands from her face. Her eyes were very wide. 'Tell me what you mean.'

'I wish that the people who shot at us were looters, Sandy. But I'm afraid they weren't. That was an ambush, a well-planned one. We were set up.' He picked up the dark green radio and looked at Sandy. 'Whoever was on the radio was part of the plan.'

She got up from the floor and walked over to him, staring at the radio now like it was an alien artifact, an object of fear. 'Are you sure?'

'I wish I was wrong, honest to God I do. But what happened back there? Greg was told to go to an address. And when we got there, was there a survey team waiting for us?'

She slowly shook her head. 'No, there wasn't. And Greg said just before he . . . just before the shooting started, that the road was marked clear on the map.'

'Yep. It was blocked. And if you and I had the time and the ways to do it, I bet you we'd see that those trucks and cars were moved recently. That tells you whoever did this had the resources to move wrecked vehicles around and to send out a bogus radio message. Right in the middle of a military reservation. That rules out looters, don't you think?'

'My God,' she said, her voice low, holding her arms together at her chest. 'What do we do now? Try to walk back to Central Park?'

He looked back out the window and down at the street. Nothing. Some papers fluttered by. He looked to Sandy and said, 'It'd be a long walk. More than fifty blocks. And it'll be getting dark soon, within a few hours. I'd hate to see you and me trying to hoof it tonight. Especially if we ran into a pack of dogs. Or our friend the sniper.'

She shivered, rubbed at her arms, eyes filling up. 'Carl . . . Jesus, this is just like the dream I had, the one I told you about. Abandoned in Manhattan, alone at night, hearing the wild dogs get closer . . .'

'Then stop dreaming,' he said, trying to keep his voice calm. 'Just like your grandmama in South Africa, you're not alone. And I'm not going to let anything else happen to you. We've got a couple of options.'

'Such as?'

'Option one.' He held up the radio. 'We call for help and tell them that we're someplace else. We watch that someplace else, see who turns up. If it looks like regular Army, then we can run out on the street and make a fuss. Maybe that ambush was a one-time deal.'

'And if it doesn't look okay?'

'Then we go to option two.'

She rubbed at her eyes again, and a hint of a smile appeared on her lips. 'Typical American. Always full of plans and ideas. Go ahead. Give it a go. Where are you going to send them?'

He motioned out the window. 'There's a bar and grill down the street. I'm going to send them there.'

She nodded in agreement and Carl switched on the radio. 'Traffic Control, Traffic Control,' he said. 'Please come in, Traffic Control.'

The reply was instant. 'This is Traffic Control to unknown radio traffic. Who's calling, kay?'

'Traffic Control, this is the *Times* contingent, assigned to Lieutenant Loomis.' He looked over to Sandy. 'There's been an accident. Lieutenant Loomis is dead. Over.'

The voice sounded skeptical. 'Say again, *Times*, kay.'

'I said, Lieutenant Loomis is dead. We're holed up in a bar and grill in Greenwich Village. We need help.'

'Your address, kay.'

He looked out the window, double-checked against the map in his other hand, and said, 'We're on the first floor of the Open Road Bar, corner of Seventh Avenue and Perry Street. Repeating, we're on the first floor of the Open Road Bar, corner of Seventh Avenue and Perry Street. Over.'

'Understood, *Times*. Help is on the way. Traffic Control out.'

He switched off the radio and looked at Sandy. 'And now we see what happens.'

Carl emptied one of the two satchels into his knapsack and fastened the blankets to the pack. He pulled out his holstered Colt .45, unbuckled his belt, and slipped the holster onto it. Sandy stared at him, and then the weapon.

'Where did you get that?'

'From my years of service to this country, that's where. Hold on, will you?'

He stood behind the drapes, near the open window, holding a pair of small binoculars. Sandy stood with him. 'How much longer?'

They heard the sound of an engine. A couple of engines. 'Not long at all, I think.' The binoculars gave him a good view of the bar's entrance. In a very few seconds, he felt quite sick to his stomach.

A squad of armed soldiers tumbled out of two Jeeps, in plain fatigues with no insignia, billed fatigue caps, and black ski masks over their heads, automatic rifles in their hands. They moved whip-fast, into position, using hand signals to communicate to each other. They hunkered down as one of their number nudged open the door and tossed something into the first floor of the building. A hollow *boom!* echoed up the street, and broken glass spewed out from the bar.

Sandy said something he couldn't make out. He continued to stare at the scene up the street, at the cool professionalism of the soldiers as they went about their task. Damn it, they were good, they were quite good.

Carl heard the soldiers yell as they poured into the building, and then the rapid fire of gunshots, the flat sounds of the explosions causing pigeons on the sidewalk below to fly off in terror. He lowered the binoculars, turned his head. Sandy was trembling at his side, tears streaming down her cheeks, hand held tight against her mouth.

He stroked her cheek, just for a moment. 'Time for option two.'

They were out of the apartment in less than a minute, leaving the radio behind them on the floor, switched off. She motioned to take it and he said, 'No. They might be able to triangulate the signal if we use it again, figure out where we are.'

'But—'

'If they do that, we're dead. Let's go.'

———

Two hours later they had moved three blocks to Barrow Street. His head ached and Sandy's face was gray with fear and exhaustion. It had been slow going, traveling from one building to another, scurrying across alleyways, over rooftops, and through tiny enclosed backyards. He would pause occasionally, raising his hand and then holding his fingers to his lips. Twice he heard the sounds of engines, as Jeeps crisscrossed the open streets around Greenwich Village. He tried to keep to the streets that were blocked with traffic, to give themselves an edge, however slight, over the men that were patrolling in Jeeps.

Along the way they lost their dosimetry, and secretly, he was glad. Pausing to check on the dosimeters wasted a lot of time, and getting a slight dose of radiation was the least of their problems. At one wide alleyway they froze at the sound of barking. A pack of five or six dogs, ribs showing, fur mangy and tangled, slowly advanced on them, growling.

He thought of the pistol and the noise it would make, and picked up a scrap piece of lumber instead. He threw it at the pack and one or two of the dogs flinched, but they didn't stop. They came closer, teeth bared. Carl pushed Sandy through an open door and closed it, just as the dogs lunged. They were in a dark stairwell. More barking and claws scrabbling at the closed door. Sandy sobbed. 'It's okay, Sandy. Let's find a place for the night.'

They walked up the stairs by the light of the flashlight, staying close to the wall. He ignored the two apartments on the first floor. Too easy for animals to get in. After breaking in each door with a well-aimed kick, he found that the windows in both apartments on the second floor were broken. On the third floor, he found one that looked all right. He switched off the flashlight and Sandy joined him in the living room. She rubbed her arms and said, 'What now?'

'We hunker down for a few minutes and eat. And then we decide what to do next.'

'Carl—'

'Sandy, the sun will be setting in a few minutes. I want to make sure this place is okay before the daylight is gone.'

She just nodded and turned and he knew he had been short with her, but he couldn't help it. All of his training, experiences, and old memories were coming back, demanding attention. In his four years of civilian life, he thought he had built up a barrier, an insulation against what it had been like to be out on the line with a weapon at his side, but that barrier had been washed away like a dike made of sugar during a flood.

The living room was reasonably sized, with a couch, three chairs, and a window seat that looked out onto the street. He went to the rear of the apartment, to the kitchen. The floor was dirty and the counter was covered with dust and tiny animal tracks and droppings. He didn't bother with the bathroom, but nudged open another door, to a bedroom. The bed had collapsed and in briefly shining his flashlight over the mattress and blankets, he saw where rats had made their nests. He shivered and made sure the door was closed. Another door – probably to another bedroom – was wedged shut and he decided not to force it open.

He went back through the kitchen, closing the door behind him, to the living room. It was getting darker. Except for the satchel he had given Sandy, their gear was in the center of the floor, on an old braided rug. The door to the stairway was open.

There was no Sandy.

'Sandy?' he said. And again, louder: 'Sandy?'

The Colt .45 was in one hand and the flashlight was in his other, and he went to the open doorway and almost bumped into her as she came back up the stairs.

'Oh, there you are,' she said, her voice a tad too cheerful, like she was trying to force herself to see this as one large adventure. 'I checked a couple of the other apartments and found these.' She held up a handful of candles, her purse over her shoulder.

He wanted to grab her arms and ask her why in hell she had left the apartment without telling him. He wanted to ask her what would have happened if she had fallen through a weakened floor. Or if rats or another dog pack had gone after her. Or if she had run into a squatter or a looter or one of the armed men out there who were trying so hard to kill them.

Instead he took a deep breath and said, 'Thanks, Sandy. We'll need them.'

Using a small hammer and some nails that they found in a tiny tool kit in the kitchen, he hung a blanket over the window, and then lit a couple of the candles. He spent a scary moment, standing alone on the dark street, checking the window to make sure no telltale glow could be seen from outside. They sat cross-legged on the floor, the candlelight flickering on the walls. Now that they weren't moving around, he began to notice little things about their shelter. The built-in bookcases. The family photographs on the wall. A music stand in one corner and a violin case. The little pile of mail on a table to the side of the front door. Sandy handled the mail briefly, looking at a couple of bills and a *Time* magazine from October 1962. On the torn cover was a painting of a man, the headmaster of Phillips Andover.

'Look at that,' Sandy said. 'A week before a nuclear war, and on the cover of the largest news magazine is a story about prep schools. What were they thinking of?'

'They weren't,' he said.

She touched the mail again. 'We have to talk, Carl. I need to know what happened, why we were ambushed. Could Greg have been the target?'

His head still ached and there were a lot of things he wanted to do, like recheck the apartment and inventory their supplies, but he saw that look in her face, the face of a reporter who needed to know something, right away.

'No, I don't think they were after Greg. Which makes us the probable targets. And Sandy, I apologize, because I think it was my fault.'

'What do you mean? Apologize for what?'

He got down on the floor, started opening his knapsack. 'Apologizing for being an idiot. Last night . . . well, among the other delightful things you and I did last night, we had a conversation, about secrets and Potemkin villages and special forces from my country and your country being here in Manhattan. Less than a day later, we're almost killed. Twice, if you count that raid on that bar. Hell of a coincidence, don't you think?'

She clasped her hands before her, like she was afraid they would start shaking. 'Our rooms . . . they were bugged, weren't they?'

He opened up her satchel. 'Yes. I was too stupid to think of that. It makes perfect sense, so our hosts would know what all the reporters were talking about in the privacy of their rooms. We should have passed each other notes but instead, I ran off at the mouth. And someone heard us, someone with secrets that they wanted kept.'

'Secrets worth killing for,' she said, her voice just above a whisper. 'Carl, what do we—'

He laid out a blanket on the floor. 'What we do now is eat. We've got to keep our strength up, because we've got a long night and a longer day ahead of us.'

'Carl, but what about—'

'Sandy,' he said, feeling again that he was slipping back into his Sergeant Landry mode. 'We can talk later about anything you want and what happened back at the ambush scene, but right now, we're going to eat. So please sit down, all right?'

Her eyes downcast, she did just that.

After they finished eating – roast beef and cheese sandwiches from the Army box lunches – it was now dark outside, and he could feel the apartment get cooler. There were rustling noises coming from the walls, and while he tried to ignore them, Sandy couldn't. They had taken cushions off the couches and were sitting up against a coffee table, and she turned to him and said, 'Rats?'

He nodded. 'Rats. I checked the walls in this room and I didn't see any holes or openings. I'm sure we'll be all right.'

'Brrr,' she said, burrowing closer to him. 'Vicious little creatures. Do you remember the rat scene towards the end of *1984*, when poor Winston Smith is being tortured? The wire cage pressed against his face with the rat on the other end? Still gives me nightmares.' She turned and brushed some hair away from her face and said, 'It's time for another talk, Carl. What kind of secrets are worth killing the two of us for?'

He took a deep breath, reached out and held her hand. 'I

don't know. All I do know is that someone probably found out we weren't content playing our roles in this little press tour charade. And that someone decided to do something about it. The bigger the secret, the bigger the response. What happened to us and Greg means this secret has got to be huge.'

'Carl, your own Army, doing this—'

'No, I don't think it was regular Army,' he said. 'That wasn't regular Army back there, not by a long shot. Look out there, at the walls.'

He saw her head move. 'See the shadows? See the darkness? That's where things happen in this country. My guess would be rogue Special Forces units or intelligence agencies. People working for the powers that be. And the powers that be must have something planned for Manhattan, something involving our Special Forces and your paratroopers. Something more than just turning on the lights and inaugurating Rockefeller next January.'

'What could those plans be?'

'I have no idea, and right now, I've got more important things to worry about.'

'Like what?'

'Like getting a good night's sleep. And getting us out of Manhattan.'

She sat up. 'Are you joking? We're on an island, and the Army controls the bridges and the tunnels. How do you expect us to get off it?'

'Remember the briefing yesterday, about looters still at work on the island?'

'Yes, I do.'

He squeezed her hand again. 'If the looters are still busy looting buildings, then they have to get off the island somehow.'

'And how do you intend to contact these looters?'

'Just wait and see.'

Although it was risky, he saw no other way of doing it, but he made sure he had his flashlight in one hand and his pistol in the other as they went out the back of the building to a small yard that was choked over with trees, shrubbery, and grass. With no running water and no water to spare, Carl dug small holes in the yard with a piece of wood which they both used as outdoor latrines. Again, the old Army training: don't leave evidence out in the bush that you've been around. It was clumsy and awkward, but when they were finished, Sandy stood next to him and said, 'Switch off the torch for a moment, will you?'

He did and she said, 'All right. Now, look up.'

The stars above were bright and hard, brighter, he was sure, than they had ever been before, except when this land had been occupied by Indians. Around them and in the distance, the dark shapes of the buildings blotted out parts of the sky. She leaned in against him. 'If you can ignore the fact of how terrible this place is, it's a beautiful sight. Where else can you stand in a city built for millions, and see the stars as bright as if you were in the wilderness?'

Then there was the sound of a motor, far off into the distance. He looked up and saw a cone of moving light that began swiveling back and forth. The air seemed colder. 'Time to go back in.'

'What's the light?'

'Helicopter with a searchlight. Looks like we're still being hunted.'

———

Back in the third-floor apartment, he closed the door behind them, blocked it shut with a bureau, and then made another sweep of the apartment, making sure nothing four-legged or furry had moved in since their bathroom break. He sat down on the cushions on the floor and pulled blankets over their legs. One of the candles was still burning.

'We should take turns sleeping tonight, just so . . . well, just so one of us can keep an eye on things,' Carl said.

'That sounds fine, but look at these first, will you.' Sandy was going through a musty pile of magazines and newspapers. She had pulled a few *New York Times*es out of the mess. 'Here,' she said. 'Some historical artifacts to look at.'

The full-banner headline for Tuesday, October 23, 1962, said:

U.S. IMPOSES ARMS BLOCKADE ON CUBA

ON FINDING OFFENSIVE MISSILE SITES;

KENNEDY READY FOR SOVIET SHOWDOWN

'Here's another,' Carl said, gingerly placing another newspaper on top of the first. The date was Saturday, October 27. Its headline:

U.S. FINDS CUBA SPEEDING BUILD-UP OF BASES;

WARNS OF FURTHER ACTION; U.N. TALKS OPEN;

SOVIET AGREES TO SHUN BLOCKADE ZONE NOW

Sandy said quietly, 'It's like looking at a time capsule. Or seeing a film that you've been to before, one that ends horribly but you want to try to change the ending and you're powerless to do so.'

'It sure does,' he said. 'Look at this one.'

From Monday, October 29:

AIRBORNE FORCES AND MARINES LAND IN CUBA;

MISSILE SITES BOMBED AFTER U-2 IS LOST;

KENNEDY WARNS OF 'GRAVE DAYS AHEAD'

Then, Carl pulled out of the pile a *New York Times* that was just four pages long, a single folded sheet. 'I don't believe it,' he said, awe filling his voice. 'They actually have a copy of this.'

'What is it?' she said, moving closer to him.

He held the sheet up to look at it, gently moving its pages. 'It's the very last issue of the old *New York Times,* published on November first, two days after the city was attacked. My God, there are damn few of these left. A lot of the people who put this together died later from radiation exposure. It's worth a lot now, to collectors.'

It seemed like the entire front page was made up of headlines, and the lead one stood out:

SOVIET BOMBERS ATTACK CITY, MILLIONS PERISH;

WASHINGTON, SAN DIEGO, MILITARY BASES BOMBED;

KENNEDY AND MOST OF CONGRESS BELIEVED DEAD

'What they had to do to get this out,' she said, reaching out to gently touch the pages. 'Real newspapermen. And women.'

'You're so right, the last of a breed, before the censors started working,' he said, looking over the other headlines, urgently telling a story, urgently announcing the end of a way of life:

FIRES RAGE OUT OF CONTROL IN QUEENS AND BROOKLYN

EVACUATION ORDERED FOR ALL CITY RESIDENTS

SUBWAYS, MOST CITY BUSES OUT OF SERVICE

MAYOR ORDERS 'SHOOT ON SIGHT' FOR LOOTERS

And a smaller, almost plaintive headline, on the rear page: TIMES TO HALT PUBLICATION FOR FIRST TIME IN ITS HISTORY.

Carl gently folded the paper in half. 'Put this in your satchel, will you?'

EIGHTEEN

SANDY NUDGED HIM, spoke his name in an urgent whisper, and he woke up.

'My turn already?' he asked, feeling groggy. He rubbed his eyes, thinking he could hear something, maybe he and Sandy left a radio on. He blinked and cleared his throat, he knew better. They had no radio.

'Carl, listen to the music,' Sandy said, holding on to his shoulder. 'Can you hear it?'

'I do.'

'Where's it coming from?'

He knew he should probably go outside and investigate, but damn it, he was tired.

'Sounds like live music, coming from up the street,' he said.

'You mean, a band?'

'That's right.'

'Amazing,' she breathed. 'Who'd be playing music at night in Manhattan?'

He reached out and touched her face. 'The stubborn residents of New York, the ones who never left. The ones who live in cellars or abandoned apartments, who manage to make a living out here somewhere. The ones who never gave up.'

'And the Army?'

'Despite what happened to us yesterday, the Army can't be everywhere, I imagine.'

'Carl, do you think—'

'Do you think we should go out there for a visit? No, I don't. First, we're safe here, and I like that. Second, I don't like the thought of fumbling out there in the dark.'

She snuggled in closer to him, and said, 'Anything else?'

He kissed her on the nose. 'Yeah. We weren't invited.'

She kissed him back, full on the lips. 'You said something special the other day, about me giving you hope. Does that still count, here in this depressing place?'

He hugged her back. 'Especially now, Sandy. Especially now.'

After a while, he could tell that she had fallen back asleep. He gently freed himself from her arms. He sat up and lit another candle, as he listened to the echoing sounds of a jazz band, still gloriously alive in this dead city.

Carl woke with a start, wondering for a moment where he was. The room was bright, Sandy was sleeping at his side, and it all came back to him, making him queasy. He gingerly moved himself off the couch cushions and stood up, wincing at the stiffness in his legs and the back of his neck. He walked over to the window and carefully moved the nailed-up blanket to one side.

Outside it was a bright blue day, and the buildings and distant skyscrapers looked clear and sharp. Somewhere out there the hunters were probably still looking for them. Why?

What had happened in Manhattan? Or earlier, in Boston?

He shivered, rubbed at the stubble on his face. He hadn't thought about that connection. Back in Boston he had been poking around, finding things out about Merl Sawson and British intelligence and about old members of the Kennedy Administration being eliminated. Maybe that's what set up the sniper. Not the loose talk about Potemkin villages. No, maybe it was all because of that old vet, the one with the taped boots and the warning that more death was being planned.

He heard movement behind him, then the smooth brush of lips at the back of his neck. 'Good morning, love,' Sandy said, yawning. 'How did you sleep?'

'I did all right,' he said, looking back at her for a quick smile. 'Tossed and turned a bit, and had bad dreams about rats in the walls. And who could forget about the musical entertainment? How about you?'

'Better than I thought,' she said. 'But you know, I had a hard time getting to sleep. I kept thinking about . . . well, all the people. The people who lived here. The orfie gangs. Parents, trying to find their children in the city after the bombs dropped. And that reminded me of something. Carl, did your parents . . . were they home during the war?'

He looked down at the empty street and cocked his ear listening for the sound of vehicle engines, hearing only barking dogs in the distance. 'Yes, they were. And that's where they died.'

She cleared her throat. 'How, then?'

He didn't look back at her. Just out at the great and empty city, and thought again about how he was going to get the both of them off Manhattan.

'Sandy,' he said, 'they starved to death.'

Breakfast was leftovers from their box lunches. Cookies – or biscuits, as Sandy called them – apples, and some chocolate. Carl fashioned a stove out of some pans and carefully heated yesterday's coffee, using old newspaper and wooden kitchen utensils to build a fire. After they ate they repacked and Carl said, 'I was too sharp back there, at the window. You asked me a reasonable question and I bit your head off. I apologize.'

She squeezed his hand, her eyes moistening. 'Apology accepted.'

'Whatever you want to know about me and my parents, I'll tell you.'

She shook her head. 'No, it's not necessary, Carl.'

'Oh, yes it is. It's quite necessary. You have a right to know.' He sat down next to her on the couch cushions and held her in his arms as he talked. 'I was in California and I got a telegram from the Red Cross in March '63. Just two lines in the telegram, two lines that I'll always remember. "Regret to inform you that Andy and Matilda Landry of Newburyport, Massachusetts, perished this past month from starvation. Contact J. Fletcher, Newburyport Red Cross Office, for more information."'

'And did you?'

'Yeah, I did,' he sighed. Even nine years later, thinking about it made the back of his throat close up in grief. 'A week later, I managed to get a phone hookup from our base to that Red Cross office. It was hard to do but my company commander arranged it for me. The line was all crackly with static and the guy on the other end, the J. Fletcher, sounded exhausted.'

'What had happened?'

He shrugged, hearing again the sound of barking dogs

outside. 'Something so simple, it's hard to believe that it could have happened. There had been a number of blizzards in Massachusetts and New Hampshire. There was no fuel for snow plows, and phone and power lines were out. My parents were stuck in their house for days. Food was already low, and later, I learned that residents had had to go to city hall for ration distribution. The snow was just too deep for my parents to get out. Some neighbors found them, after it had melted. That's about all the news I could get out of Mr. Fletcher.'

Sandy squeezed him and he said, 'There I was, doing my duty for God and country, and I couldn't feed my mother and father, Sandy. I couldn't do that one simple thing for them . . .'

'Carl . . .' she began, and he touched his finger to her lips.

'Come now, we have work to do, if we plan to get off this island.'

She kissed him, hard, and said quietly, 'You do your parents proud, my friend.'

They spent a few minutes putting the place back into order. He took two dish towels from the kitchen and put them in his knapsack, and then he piled up the old newspapers and put the couch cushions back where they belonged. Sandy looked at him with a quizzical expression.

'Two reasons,' he explained. 'First, I don't want to leave any evidence that we've been here.'

'Makes sense,' she said. 'And what's the other reason?'

He looked around the quiet and dusty collection of rooms that had been empty for at least ten years, and wondered if it would be another decade before someone visited them again.

'Respect,' he said. 'I want to show some respect.'

Sandy nodded, and then tilted her head. More barking

from outside. 'I've been hearing those dogs for a while.'

He froze. Listened again. Barking dogs. But . . . something was different. They sounded strange.

They sounded disciplined.

He grabbed the binoculars and ran to the window, flattening himself against the wall and pulling the blanket free again. Up the street, a number of blocks away, there was movement. Vehicles. He raised the binoculars and focused them.

Two Jeeps, parked at a street corner. Soldiers were moving up and down the sidewalks and chained German shepherds were barking and straining at their leashes as they sniffed and pawed the doorways and alleyways.

A tall man was out there, talking angrily to two uniformed officers. He was in civilian clothes, a gray suit with matching vest, and the way he strode and pointed and—

It was Cullen Devane, oversight editor of the *Boston Globe*. Here in Manhattan. Looking for Carl Landry.

Jesus, he thought.

Sandy said, 'Carl, what's—'

He rushed past her, grabbed his knapsack and her satchel.

'We've got to get going,' he said. 'They're still after us. And my damn censor from the *Globe* is right there with them.'

She nodded, her face the color of the old plaster walls.

When they reached the bottom of the stairs and the tiny lobby of the apartment building, Carl stopped, his heart throbbing, his hands itchy, and his old wounded leg aching. He wished that he had managed to get that M-14 out of Greg's Jeep. It'd be a heavy sucker to lug around, but it had great stopping power and a longer range than the Colt .45. Sandy stood near him, and he could hear her breathe.

'What do we do now?' she asked.

'Give me a sec,' he said. Cullen Devane. Damn it all to hell. So there was a Boston connection to the shooting. Had to have been. Damn that blackhearted son of a bitch. He leaned out of the doorway, looking down the street. He could hear the barking but couldn't see anything. An abandoned city bus was blocking the view. He grabbed Sandy's hand. 'Come on, let's get moving.'

She said, 'How far do we have to go?'

'Until we don't hear those damn dogs.'

He made sure that they ran quickly, dodging debris and trash on the sidewalks, ducking into doorways. Once they went into the doorway of a wrecked and looted clothing store, and Sandy shrieked at what she saw on the floor until he calmed her down and told her that they were only mannequins.

Eventually, the barking of the dogs faded away and there were no sounds of engines. They rested in a shaded area by the steps of a row of brownstones and he examined the map that had belonged to the dead lieutenant. He had to get them off this island, and soon. They were still being pursued and Carl was sure that Major Devane could be quite persistent. And in another day or two, they'd be out of food and clean water.

'What does the map tell us, Carl?' Sandy asked, sitting up against a brick wall. 'Is there a magical ferry you're taking us to?'

'No, but it shows which streets are clear and which ones are blocked. We stay on the streets that are blocked, that means Jeeps can't follow us. Just like yesterday. Not much of an edge but it's the best we can do.'

'So what exactly are we doing?'

He refolded the map. 'We're looking for graffiti.'

'What? Scribblings on the wall?'

'Yep.' She followed him on to the sidewalk and pointed to the side of a wall. 'You mean like that?'

A granite facade carried a message in black paint that had faded over time: MOOREHOUSE FAMILY – GUYS, JOIN US IN HARTFORD. GOOD LUCK. THE AARONS.

'Nope,' he said.

Sandy's voice took on a threatening tone. 'Listen, my friend—'

'Quiet,' he said, yanking her down and behind a pile of rubble. He had seen something move. 'More soldiers?' she asked.

'I don't think so. Looks like just one person, down at the end of the street. It looks like he's coming up here.'

He peered through a jumble of broken and burned wood, again seeing the odd motion that had caught his attention, a swaying movement. It looked like a man yet . . .

'Damn, I'm stupid,' he whispered.

'What did you say?' Sandy whispered back.

'Hold on. You'll see yourself.'

The man rode by on a bicycle stately and proud-looking. His hair and beard were long and a large gray blanket, worn as a poncho, hung over his shoulders. Bags hung from the handlebars, and the man was whistling something as he ped-aled by, moving in and around the motionless cars and trucks.

Sandy made a motion to get up but he grabbed her arm and pulled her down. 'What are you doing?' she demanded, her voice low. 'I wanted to talk to him, find out why he's still living here. Do you realize he's the first civilian we've seen in Manhattan?'

'And do you realize that we're trying to get out of here alive?' he said sharply. 'Damn it, there are soldiers back there with guns and dogs. And we don't know who this bicyclist is or what kind of shape he's in. He might just be an eccentric who stayed behind, or a guy who collects skulls in his bike bags.'

He stood up and saw that the bicyclist had turned a corner. Sandy was next to him, brushing dirt and soot off her hands and knees. 'I hear you, Carl, but don't tell me how to do my job. I'm still a reporter.'

'If you're not more careful, Sandy, you'll still be a good reporter. But a dead one.' He looked down the street and grasped her arm. 'Come on, I've got something to show you.'

Carl ran across the street with Sandy right beside him, cursing under her breath. At the corner – Washington and West – was a brick building. The rest of the street was lined with more rows of brownstones and apartment buildings, torn awnings flapping in the breeze. Over the main door of the brick building were splotches of red paint, in the same pattern that he had seen yesterday. Three filled-in circles, joined by curving lines. He looked up and down the street, and then at Sandy.

'See anything unusual?' he asked.

'Carl . . .'

'No, I'm serious. Look around. What's different?'

Sandy did as he asked, and then looked up at him. 'The street's clean. Like someone cares.'

'Exactly.'

She pointed to the brick building. 'That graffiti. Is that what you were looking for?'

'Yep.'

'What does it mean?'

'I'm hoping it means the same thing here as it does everywhere else,' he said. 'Ever hear of pawnbrokers, Sandy?'

'Of course I have, people who pay for – Damn it, that's a pawnbroker's sign, isn't it? The three balls.'

Carl nodded. 'That's right. I saw it a couple of times yesterday on other buildings, out near the UN site, when we were going to Washington Square. Think, Sandy. A pawnbroker makes sense if there are people still in the city, going through buildings and stealing things. They need someone to sell to, someone who'll give them something in return.'

'And what are *we* selling?'

He took her hand and walked across the street. 'We're in the market to buy. A trip off Manhattan island, to be exact.'

The front of the building was a mess, littered with faded beer cans, torn paper, and other debris, but nothing compared to the other streets. There was a massive wooden door in the center of the building, painted black, and it looked in good shape. He leaned back and looked up at the windows. 'See there, Sandy, the windows?'

'They're all covered with wood.'

'That's right,' he said. 'This place is under management, that's for sure.'

He reached to the doorknob, which was polished brass and didn't budge.

She noticed the look on his face. 'What's wrong?'

'Door's locked.'

'Oh,' she said, and then she smiled slyly. 'Maybe this has something to do with it.'

He went over to where she was standing. There was a portal of some sort near the stairs, which might have held a mailbox at one time. Now, it contained a wooden sign with neat, block lettering:

GREENWICH SQUARE TRADERS

OPEN DUSK TO MIDNIGHT

WEAPONS *MUST* BE HOLSTERED

Carl looked around. After seeing the Jeeps and soldiers and Cullen Devane at work earlier, the deserted street here in Greenwich Village looked downright friendly.

'We need to find a place to hole up for a while,' he said. 'Those soldiers and dogs . . .'

She ran a hand through her hair. 'Oh, please shut up. I used to think I hated rats most of all, until I heard those dogs, barking because of us.'

They were in an apartment across the street from the pawn shop. It was in foul condition and nearly everything had been smashed or looted. They sat on the living room floor, on chairs that were torn and stained. The windows had been broken and a cool breeze blew in as they shared another sandwich. There was one more left for tomorrow. They had blankets wrapped around their legs and Sandy said, 'It's going to cost us a hell of a lot to get out of Manhattan, isn't it.'

He swallowed, thinking how good a roast chicken would taste. 'Yeah, it is. How much money do you have with you?'

She rummaged through her purse for a minute and said, 'Thirty dollars American, and about twenty pounds. Do you think they'll take the pounds?'

'They just might,' he said. 'I've got about twenty-five dollars, so that gives us fifty-five.' He looked over at his knapsack and said, 'Trade goods.'

'What did you say?'

'Trade goods. This is probably a barter society. We might do better by offering them something valuable. Do you think the *Times* will mind giving up a 35 millimeter camera?'

'If a camera will get us out, that's cheap enough,' she said, opening her water canteen and taking a sip. Then she changed the subject. 'What does it mean, that your Army censor is out with the rest of those soldiers?'

'I think it means that the story I did back in Boston, the one about the old guy getting killed, has a Manhattan connection. Something big enough to get the oversight editor down here. And to answer your next question, I don't know what the connection is. Yet.'

'Here's another one. Tell me what happens when we get to New Jersey.'

If we get to New Jersey, he thought. 'Well, let's worry right now about getting off Manhattan, Sandy, and—'

Her voice was brisk. 'Don't be coy with me, Carl. It's going to be tough, isn't it?'

He looked into her sharp brown eyes and said, 'You're right. It might be very tough. We might be robbed along the way. Those soldiers with the dogs might find us first. Hell, the pawnbroker down there might have been closed for years. I don't know. But if the pawnbroker is open and is relatively honest, this might work. And that's the only chance we've got.'

'All right. Let's say it works. What then?'

'Then we're in the middle of the New Jersey Restricted Zone. And we'll worry about that when we get there.'

In the distance, a sound of a helicopter engine.

'Well, get me out of New Jersey, Carl, and I'll make sure this story about our ambush and the paras in Manhattan gets to the *Times*. I'll get it sent out through diplomatic pouch if I have to. I'm sorry, and I know if it sounds self-righteous, but I don't like being chased, I don't like being lied to, and I certainly don't like being shot at.'

He kept looking at her, the fine and proper Englishwoman in a dead city, with armed men looking for her and her companion. Carl said, 'Your grandmama would be very proud of you.'

She blushed. 'That's high praise indeed, Carl. She was quite a woman. I wish she were still alive so you could meet her. She smoked cigars and was a suffragette and she caused a number of scandals in her time, but her husband was a British army officer who loved her dearly, even though it caused problems in his career.'

'I think when we get out of New York, you'll have a story to match her tale of the Mafeking siege.'

'I haven't thought about that. Did you know who she got to know at Mafeking when the Boers were attacking?'

'Tell me.'

'Lord Baden-Powell, the man who founded the Boy Scout movement.'

'And what did your grandmama say about him?'

Sandy smiled. 'It's like your official and unofficial story about how you were wounded in California. Well, the official story about Lord Baden-Powell is that he was the boyish, stiff-upper-lipped, ingenious defender of a British garrison that held out for nearly seven months against the Boers. The unofficial story, told to me by Grandmama Price, is that he was a cruel man who made up his rules as he went along and killed starving natives for stealing food. I suppose that's the mark of this century, Carl, isn't it? Official and unofficial stories, and trying to find out which one is true.'

'And living to tell about them, Sandy. Living to tell about them.'

The afternoon dragged on and Sandy went through a pile of magazines and old newspapers that she found, most of which had faded away to a musty sludge. Then she pulled out a pamphlet and wordlessly passed it over to Carl.

'"What you should know and what you should do,"' he read aloud, looking at the faded cardboard cover. '"How to survive a nuclear attack and live for your country's recovery."'

Sandy was hunched over, her arms around her knees. 'They really thought they could survive, didn't they?'

'We all did,' he said quietly. 'We all did. Maybe a few hundred people in all the world knew what a nuclear explosion looked like, and they weren't working in the White House or the Kremlin. I don't think anyone could have even comprehended what was going to happen, what could happen with just a few dozen bombs. So why not plan for survival? It probably wouldn't happen, but it would make you feel good.'

Sandy nodded slowly. 'There are friends of my father, old Tory types, who thought that Great Britain should have its own nuclear capabilities. But after the Cuban War . . . everyone was happy to give everything up to the UN. Everyone.'

He looked back at the pamphlet and said, 'A few days ago I was talking to an old man who had been a peace activist, back before the war. He was saying that some of his friends thought that we were lucky. In the United States, that is. Lucky that the war had occurred in 1962 instead of five or ten or fifteen years later.'

'That's a horrible thought,' she said.

'True, but it does make a crazy sort of sense,' he said, rubbing at the rough cardboard cover of the pamphlet. 'If nothing had happened, then both the United States and the Soviet Union would have acquired tens of thousands more bombs. Other countries would have the technology as well. Could you imagine the Israelis and the Arabs, both with nuclear weapons? Or India and Pakistan? Or El Salvador and Guatemala? We could have bombed ourselves back so far in time that cockroaches would rule the earth.'

Her voice was quiet. 'It might not have happened that way. The UN might have found a way for all the countries to give up their nukes.'

'A nice thought,' he said, leaving his doubts to himself. He read more of the pamphlet:

> The purpose of this booklet is to help save lives if a nuclear attack should ever come to America. The foreign and defense policies of your Government make such an attack highly unlikely, and to keep it unlikely is their most important aim. It is for this reason that we have devoted so large an effort to creating and maintaining our deterrent forces. However, should a nuclear attack ever occur, certain preparations could mean the difference between life and death for you . . .
>
> There is no escaping the fact that nuclear conflict would leave a tragic world. The areas of blast and fire would be scenes of havoc, devastation and

death. For the part of the country outside the immediate range of explosions, it would be a time of extraordinary hardship – both for the nation and for the individual. The effects of fallout radiation would be present in areas not decontaminated. Transportation and communication would be disrupted. The nation would be prey to strange rumors and fears. But if effective precautions have been taken in advance, it need not be a time of despair.

Unbelievable. It need not be a time of despair, he thought, looking around the empty apartment, looking out at the dead city. Who would have thought that the despair would continue, year after year, until it just became part of life, part of the landscape. You try to secure and defend what you can, but how can you defend against despair? He closed the pamphlet. Another artifact to join the old *New York Times* in his knapsack. He found that he was having difficulty keeping his eyes open. 'Sandy, do you mind if I take a nap?'

'A nap? You think you can sleep?'

'I'm sure I can, if only for an hour. You'll wake me when it gets dark?'

She smiled, pulled the blanket up around his chest. 'You bet I will.'

He put the pamphlet down and closed his eyes and Sandy was by his side, snuggling and kissing his cheek. 'Carl?' she murmured.

'Hmmm?'

'Just one question, before you go to sleep?'

'What's that?'

'The old vet that got killed, the one you did a story about. Why do you think he was murdered?'

'Sandy, I don't know. But I intend to find out.'

And then he closed his eyes and suddenly found that he wasn't quite as tired as he had been, because as hard as he tried to remember, he was quite sure that he had never told Sandy that Merl Sawson was a veteran. Her body in his arms, which only a few seconds ago had been a comfortable joy to him, now felt like a dead weight.

He kept his eyes closed but was wide awake. The danger had seemed blocks away, with the barking dogs and the soldiers and Cullen Devane.

Sandy shifted in his arms and sighed.

But now the danger felt much closer.

NINETEEN

SANDY'S VOICE was in his ear: 'Carl, there are people out there.'

He opened his eyes and was quickly awake. He had slept neither deeply nor well, worried as he was about the next few hours, about where they would spend the night, and most of all, about what Sandy had told him just an hour or so ago. The old vet. So. How did she know?

How sure was he that he hadn't told her? They had talked about a lot of different things in the past several days. And besides, almost everyone in the country had some sort of military service in their background, so maybe she was just assuming that the old man had been a veteran—

'Carl?' she asked again, voice quavering.

'Yes,' he said, sitting up. 'I heard you. There are people out there.' He yawned and scratched at his back and saw the look on her face, a look of concern and affection. Not now, he thought. Keep it in mind but focus on getting out of here.

'What have you seen?' he asked.

'A couple of people, going in and out of that building. It was so damn spooky! I mean, the only other person we've seen on this island was that loony-looking chap on the bicycle. Now I've seen other people . . . I don't know. It makes me wonder what's really going on here.'

They slung their knapsacks over their shoulders and Carl led the way down the stairs, using the flashlight. When he reached the lobby he turned it off. 'No need to draw attention to ourselves,' he said. 'Let's just go across the way and do our business.'

She slipped her hand into his, and he squeezed back. 'That sounds fine.'

He reached under his jacket and unbuttoned the flap to his holster. He would follow the posted rules of the building, of keeping his weapon holstered, but that didn't mean he wasn't going to keep it within easy reach. Out on the street it was getting dark, and a wind was blowing in from the west. A block away he saw two men carrying something between them. He wondered how anyone could live on this dead island.

At the brick building he took a deep breath and said, 'Well, here it goes,' and this time, the brass doorknob turned easily in his hand.

It took a moment for his eyes to adjust to the darkness. Sandy was next to him, squeezing his hand so hard it almost hurt. They were in a large room, lit by candles at each corner. The floor was dirty tile and the plaster walls were a dull yellow. Peepholes of some sort had been chopped into two of the walls and empty wooden benches and chairs were lined up on the far side of the room but in the wall to Sandy and Carl's right was a window that looked into the next room. As they got closer, Carl saw that it was thick glass, like from a banker's workplace. Below the window was a counter and below that was a metal drawer. To the right of the counter, a barrel-shaped contraption was installed in the wall. It was a type of dumbwaiter, something that could be used to rotate goods in and out of this room, into the adjacent one.

He took a few more steps, Sandy right next to him. Behind the glass were a man and a woman, in their late forties or early fifties. The man was balding, with thin black hair combed back over his scalp. He had a sallow complexion and wore a white shirt that looked gray, a skinny black necktie and a wrinkled leather jacket. He had wide sideburns and he smiled for a quick moment, showing bad teeth. His voice was dulled by the thick glass.

'You're not from here, are you?' he said.

'That's right,' Carl said. The woman was wearing a flowered dress, knitting slowly, and Carl realized by the way her head was cocked and from her unblinking expression that she was blind. Her gray hair was pulled back in a bun, and her forearms were shiny with burn scars. The room the couple was in was lit with candles, revealing rows of shelves behind them, stretching out into the darkness.

The man said, 'Well, what are you, freelance?'

Carl looked at Sandy and then back at the man. 'Sorry, I don't understand. What's freelance?'

The man said something low to the woman and she laughed. He said, 'Freelance salvage, that's what. You thinking you can start work here, without the Village Council having a say-so? Think the two of you can sell me stuff and get your grubstake started, and then have me blackballed? Think again, kids.'

Sandy spoke up. 'No, you don't understand. We're not here to sell anything. We're not even—'

The woman stopped knitting. 'Albert, that woman, she's British.'

The man smiled again. 'Melanie, you're right. She's a Brit. What are you doing here, hon, trying to save us starving savages? Well, you're about ten years too late!' He laughed, a bitter sound that had no humor.

Carl spoke up. 'Listen, we're journalists. We're with the *Times* of London. We're looking for a way to get off this island.'

'How did you get here in the first place?'

'We came in, with the Army.'

'Then why don't you go back with them?'

Sandy interrupted. 'There was an incident, and we can't go back to the Army. We need to leave on our own.'

The older man sagely nodded. 'Pissed them off, right?'

'You could say that,' Carl said.

'Happens all the time,' the man said. 'People in this city, trying to make an honest living, and the Army's out there to harass 'em.'

Sandy spoke up. 'Then how do you keep going, as public as your business is?'

He shrugged. 'At night the streets belong to the people. Army just does a few patrols to pretend they're in charge. Plus, this whole place is hollowed out, lots of lofts and ladders and tunnels. I got a kid or two up on the roof, to see what's coming down. We get word the greenies are on the way, we're down and out. They take our stuff, we open up somewhere else. No matter. So. What's your business? You trying to get off this lovely island paradise?'

'That's right,' Carl said. 'And the sooner the better.'

The man opened a ledger in front of him and ran his fingers down the columns. Next to him Melanie continued to knit, the needles moving slowly. He looked up. 'That's not my business, you know. I deal mostly in trades. But I got a good lead with a group a few blocks out, I know they do regular transport. They can be pricey, but they're reliable.'

Sandy squeezed his hand and he said, 'That will be fine.'

'Let's talk price, then. I'll want a finder's fee before you get the name and location.'

Sandy looked troubled. 'How can we . . . how do we know this is reliable information?'

He smiled, revealing discolored teeth. 'That's not what you were going to say, now, was it? You was going to say, how can I be trusted? Lady, truth is, if you can find anyone else out there that can do better, be my guest. You talk to anyone, you'll find out I've been here two years, and I may drive a tough bargain, but I'm honest. If I weren't honest, then I wouldn't get the business, and I'd have to close up. So. You kids ready to deal?'

'Go ahead,' Carl said. 'What's the price?'

'Depends what you got. You got batteries?'

Only if we strip the flashlight, he thought, and he said, 'No, we don't.'

'How about a portable radio? Shortwave would be nice, but I'd settle for a transistor.'

He shook his head.

'Weapons? Ammunition? Flashlights?'

Carl said, 'No, nothing like that.'

The man tugged at one of his ears and said, 'Well, unless you can rustle something up—'

The camera came to mind but instead he said, 'Chocolate.'

The woman stopped knitting. Albert's eyes seemed to narrow. 'You serious?'

'Yep.'

'What kind?'

'Hershey's. Regular size.'

The man tapped his fingers on the ledger. 'I'll give you the name, for six bars.'

They only had three. 'One.'

The man laughed again. 'I can see you kids aren't from around here, the way you go insulting me like that. Five.'

Carl tried to conjure the face he used to use, back when he was playing poker with his Army buddies. 'Offer still stands at one.'

From behind the protective glass the older man made a show of sighing and shaking his head. 'That isn't dealing, you young buck. But all right, I feel sorry for you two, all alone and not knowing the territory. Four.'

Sandy tried to say something but he didn't let her. He shrugged the knapsack off and lowered it to the floor. He opened the top flap and after a few moments of rummaging, came up with two Hershey's bars. He held them up to the window.

'Two,' Carl said. 'And I throw in a pack of smokes. Camels.'

The woman, knitting still silent in her hands, spoke up. 'Albert, do you know how long it's been since I've eaten chocolate, a real Hershey's—'

'I know, I know,' he said, irritation tinging his voice. 'It's just that—'

She picked up her yarn and needles, jaw set. 'Then close the deal. Now.'

He ran a hand through his thin hair and said, 'All right, all right, it's a deal.' He turned to glare at her. 'And you wonder why I don't like having my wife at my side, when I work. You close too early.'

She resumed knitting, a thin smile on her face, her sightless eyes staring. 'And if it wasn't for me, you wouldn't do anything at all. You always try to close too late, tick people off. That ain't no way to run a business.'

The man managed a smile, moved his right hand, and the metal drawer underneath the window slid open. Carl tossed in the Hershey's and the pack of Camels, and the man moved the drawer back and slowly picked them up in his thick hands and looked at them. 'Very nice,' he said. 'Very nice. We'll make these last a couple of weeks, just you see.'

Then he bent down and wrote something on a piece of paper, slapped a rubber stamp on it, and slid the drawer back around. Carl picked up the torn sheet of paper and read it in the dim light:

PS 19 gang, Houston and Varick Street subway stop, ask for Jim. Show him the stamp and you'll be fine. A.

Below the handwriting was a red ink stamp mark: 'Village Traders. Fine Deals Since 1970,' it read, printed inside a circle.

Carl looked at the man, who had opened the pack of cigarettes and was counting each one. 'Who's the PS 19 gang?'

'They're the ones that own that part of the subway line, and they got connections across the river to New Jersey,' he said. 'They're a couple of blocks east. Easy to find. But trust me, they sure as hell ain't going to ferry the two of you across for a couple of chocolate bars. They'll ask a heavy fare.'

Sandy leaned over and looked at the paper in Carl's hand. 'You've been here for two years?'

'That's right, Brit girl. Been at this location since 1970, and never left the island, even after the war.'

'What's it like here?' she asked. 'You mentioned a village council. Do you mean there's some sort of government?'

'Of course there is,' he said, marking an entry in a ledger. 'Whaddya think we are, savages? Oh, it took a while, after the evacuation, but the traders got together and there's councils everywhere. SoHo. Midtown. Harlem. The councils give licenses to the salvage workers, and they can either trade with us, or try to get stuff off the island on their own.'

Carl looked around the tiny room. 'You mean you didn't leave after the bombing?'

Melanie spoke up. 'Why in hell should we? This is our home, always will be. Even after I was hurt in the bombing, I wouldn't let Albert take me away. I can't live anywhere else but New York, and there's plenty of people who think just like we do. Plenty.'

'But . . . isn't it tough?' Carl asked, wondering how they did it, year after year.

Albert shrugged his shoulders. 'Oh, we make do. There's plenty to eat, if you don't mind the boring food most of the time. Fish, some goat meat. And squab, which is just another fancy name for pigeon. Plus we do well enough trading, and there ain't no goddam city health inspector or tax collector or anybody else who can tell me how to run my business.'

As Sandy spoke up, Carl saw she was quietly taking notes. 'And what about the Army?'

Melanie answered the question. 'This is a big city, little girl. The Army does what they have to do during the day, and we do our business at night. They stay out of our way, and we try to stay out of theirs.'

'And you don't have any trouble?' Sandy said.

Albert smiled again, showing off his poor teeth. 'You kids didn't see the holes in the walls, just when you came in?'

Carl looked back at the crudely cut marks and saw movement behind them. 'You've had us covered, since the minute we came in.'

'We sure did. Two of my sons, both with shotguns. Had a bead on you every second. Oh, it's not as bad as it was back in the early sixties, but I'm a careful man. I've got a family to support.'

The door opened, and a man and woman entered, their clothes old and patched, their boots held together with string and masking tape. They were carrying bundles of clothing and their hair was long, and they went over and sat down on one of the wooden benches.

Albert leaned closer to the window. 'And if the two of you'll excuse me, I've got work to do. This ain't no bus station, and I've got customers a-waiting.'

Outside, Sandy slipped her arm through his and said, 'Carl, I can't believe what we're hearing. This place is extraordinary!'

It was cold and he debated zipping up his coat. He moved away from the storefront, wanting to get to the subway station as soon as possible. Who knew what wandered the dark streets, crowded with the abandoned vehicles that were so much of the familiar fabric of this city. There were lights in some of the windows, and bonfires burning in fifty-five-gallon drum containers at a couple of the street corners. There were some faraway shouts and some music, and Sandy leaned into him and said, 'This isn't a dead city, not at all!'

He swiveled his head around, not feeling well at all. 'That's what I'm afraid of.'

'Why?' Sandy asked.

Carl was going to say something about the city reverting to some form of barbarism. He was going to make a cogent remark about what Rome must have been like, after the last legions had died or been disbanded. He was going to say something about how frontier cities – like this New York City – could never be relied upon to have a police force or any other agency that was dedicated to order.

He was going to say something like that, and would have, but three men swarmed out of a cellar and attacked them.

'Yee hah, look what we got!' one of them shouted, and Sandy screamed. Carl stepped back and stumbled as he tried to get a free hand under his coat. It was too late. Two of the men grabbed his arms and slammed him against a brick wall and Sandy screamed again.

Something sharp was held to his neck and he tried to move his arms. There was a dim light from a burning trash barrel up the street and furtive movement in the shadows. Part of him desperately thought, there really never was a cop when you needed one.

The men's clothes were ragged and all three had beards and stringy hair. One of them held Sandy, his arm across her throat and his hand over her mouth, his other hand holding a knife to her chin. Her captor wore a wool coat, filthy and with buttons missing, and he was laughing. Sandy was struggling and her satchel was on the ground.

'Man, another great one,' he said. 'Pop 'em right after they get out of Trader Al's, great idea. Let's see what they got.'

The man at Carl's left said, 'Zeke, what you got there is pretty good. Am I gonna get seconds this time, or what?' and the man to Carl's right giggled and said, 'Let's get rid of this burden first, 'fore we get to the fun times.'

Sandy squirmed some more. The man called Zeke laughed and said, 'She's a newbie, guys. Man, I don't feel no bones and she smells great!'

More laughter, more shouts, and Carl clenched his fists, then stomped down hard on the nearer man's foot. He yelped and Carl broke free and spun, jamming an elbow into the second man's face. Carl moved again, grabbing his pistol out of its holster and then Zeke was before him, eyes skitterish, the hand still across Sandy's mouth, the knife still at her chin.

'You move any closer, man, I'll cut her,' he warned.

Carl moved out into the street, flicking his gaze back and forth from Zeke to his two friends, who were slowly getting up from the dirty sidewalk. He kept his arm out straight and cocked the hammer of the Colt .45.

'Any closer!' Zeke said louder. 'Any closer she's cut!'

Carl took a few steps, the pistol still out, an extension of his arm. He could hear whispers from the two men he had just thrashed, and whimpering noises from Sandy, but he kept his focus on Zeke, making him the center of his attention.

'I'm warning you!' Zeke said, voice wavering.

Carl cleared his throat. 'And I'm telling you, sunshine. That hand with that knife gets any closer, I'm going to shoot you.'

Zeke laughed sharply. 'You're talking to a true Gotham rat! You think I'm afraid of dyin'?'

Another step closer. 'No, I didn't say I was going to kill you. I said I was going to shoot you. I'll blow off your left leg and let you bleed out here on the sidewalk. How many doctors do you know?'

He moved his eyes, one more time. The other two were

keeping their distance. He looked back at Zeke, who for some crazy reason almost looked like he was about to cry.

'Listen,' the man said, talking in a blur. 'Listen here, I got a good deal. Lining of my coat, near the rear, I got some gold coins sewed in there, coins I lifted from the First Mercantile Bank, up on Broadway, before the Army came. You let me have her, the gold is yours.'

'No deal,' Carl said, taking another step. Even in the dim light he could see that Sandy's eyes were wide and tearful.

'But it's not fair!' he said, his voice louder. 'Not fair! Do you know how long it's been since I've had a woman like this?'

Another step, and the barrel of the Colt .45 was pressing gently against the man's bearded face. 'I don't care how fair it is,' Carl said, trying to keep his voice even. 'Let her go. Now.'

Zeke clenched his eyes and keened an awful noise, and then he pushed Sandy at Carl. Carl grabbed her with his free hand and pulled her behind him. Zeke scampered down the street, now joined by his friends, but he stopped and shouted back, 'I hope you two puke! I hope you suck in some hot spots and die, you fuckers! Puke and die!'

Carl put his arm around Sandy, feeling her tremble, and he looked around. He could see candles and the lights of other people across the way, walking about now that the fracas was over. 'Are you all right?' he said. 'Sandy?'

The trembling increased. 'I . . . I'm afraid I've wet myself, Carl. I was so frightened.'

'I was scared, too,' he said, not letting his eyes rest. 'Look, let's get going. We've got a couple of blocks to go, and maybe we can get you cleaned up there.'

She shivered again, picking up her satchel. 'You . . . you were very brave, back there . . . taking on those men.'

Something in the air tasted sour. 'No, I wasn't. Not brave at all.'

They walked past another fire, burning in a small grate. There was a door and a blackboard that said 'BOGIE'S RESTAURANT – NOW OPEN' and two men sat on the granite steps, baseball bats across their knees. 'What do you mean, not brave?' she said. 'I saw what you did. You were quite—'

'I was too strong for them,' he said, keeping the pistol in one hand and holding tightly onto her with the other.

She stopped, looked over at him. 'What did you say?'

'I'd rather we keep going and talk about this later.'

'No, I want to talk about it now. What happened back there?'

They could hear more music, up the street. He looked around. This was unbelievable. The island wasn't dead, wasn't empty, not by a long shot. It was two cities. One during the day when Army patrols and helicopters went up and down the deserted streets, and one at night, when the Army pulled back into its bases and armed hotels and buildings, and the other people, the ones left behind or the ones who came back, ruled the land.

'Sandy, they were skin and bones. Probably hadn't had a decent meal in weeks. It was like fighting with ten-year-olds, that's what it was like.'

'But you saved my life, Carl.' She reached up and touched his face, shivering again. 'Don't sell yourself short, Yank. Those men were going to rape me and . . . God knows what else, and you took care of me. And I'm damn glad you were too strong. I'd hate to think of what would have happened if it had been otherwise.'

Carl felt something wet on his neck and a burning sensation. Sandy lowered her hand and said, 'You've been hurt.

You're bleeding.'

He gingerly touched the wound, felt the sticky blood. 'It's not too bad. Just a scratch. Let's get to the subway station.'

She touched his face again. 'You're still a brave man, Carl.'

'Hardly,' he said, taking her hand. 'I'm a smelly man. I need a shower and change of clothes.'

'And what about me?'

He tugged at her hand. 'You've got your best clothes with you, always.'

She tugged back. 'That sounds like something my grandmama would have said.'

The next two blocks were easier going, and it looked like someone – though probably not the Army – had made progress in at least getting some of the cars and trucks and buses to one side of the street. Carl looked at the lights ahead of them and wondered what these people would do, once the power came back on and the Army opened up the barriers. Was it true, what Greg had said – God, it seemed like weeks ago! – that Rockefeller would be inaugurated here next year? Could things have progressed so far? Or was it just a fib, one in a long series of lies?

Speaking of lies . . . there were probably a few hundred people out, in this area alone, on this cool fall night. So how many people were in Manhattan in total. Thousands? Tens of thousands? There was life in the air, a sense of electricity, something he had not felt in a long time. He looked at the people passing in the dim light, at the way they walked and they conducted themselves, and listened to their conversations. Something was different here, yet familiar, something that he could almost just—

Yes, he thought. That was it. They walked past another storefront, and inside, jazz was playing – horns and saxophones – and there were the sounds of clapping and shouting. He knew what was different.

They were alive. They weren't afraid. Concerned, perhaps, about getting enough to eat and staying out of the Army's way. But they didn't worry about censorship or decon camps or the police checkpoints for residency permits. Nope. They were just free Americans, living secretly in an open city and—

Oh, no, he thought.

The parking garage basement. The supplies. The barbed wire. The barricades. The riot sticks and shields. The crates of CS gas. And the British paratroopers? Sure. Now it made sense.

And he knew, it struck him so hard it made him nauseous, what was being planned for these brave survivors before next year's inauguration.

'There,' Sandy said. 'That looks like the right place.'

Up ahead, at the street corner, was a lit subway entrance. Sandy added, 'You don't think it's a trap, do you?'

'No, I don't,' he said, bringing his attention back to the here and now. 'It'd be bad for business. But keep behind me anyway, okay?'

'All right.'

The steps were clean, the letters 'PS 19' had been spray-painted in bright red, over the old IRT sign. They descended, and the light grew stronger. The stairs turned to the left and he saw that the light was coming from lanterns, set along the walls and the floor. Ahead of them was a barrier, made of sandbags and scrap metal, and behind it, two young men lounged on high stools, rifles across their laps. They wore

Yankees baseball caps, patched blue jeans, and heavy corduroy coats. Both looked like they were trying to grow beards, but still had a way to go.

One of the men stood up and casually raised his rifle. 'You guys got business here, or you looking for somebody?'

Carl looked again at the piece of paper he held in his hand. 'We just came from the Village Traders, from Al's. He said to ask for Jim.'

The man stepped around the barrier, rifle held loosely in his hands, and Carl guessed that he was in his early twenties. 'Can I see the pass?'

Carl held it out. The man looked at it and handed it back. 'Yep, that's Trader Al's mark, all right.'

The man still behind the barrier laughed. 'Bet you he didn't give you that for free.'

Sandy spoke up. 'No, he didn't. He was a demanding fellow.'

The closer man said, 'That he is. You're not from here, are you?'

'No, we're not,' Carl said, changing their story just a bit. 'We're journalists. She's from the *Times* of London and I'm from the *Boston Globe,* and we'd like to see Jim.'

'Sure,' he said, turning. He snapped his fingers and said loudly, 'Hey, Paco. Get over here, we got a little escort work for ya.'

From the gloom emerged another man, younger than the other two, but dressed like them and with a rifle slung over his shoulder. At first Carl had thought that the barrier was a bit silly, not really strong enough to hold anyone back, but now he saw how it made sense. It was a checkpoint, and there were probably more armed men and other barriers, deeper within.

Paco was dark-skinned and working on a mustache, instead of a beard, and he was doing better than his friends. He came around the barrier and Carl was surprised when he stuck out a hand and shook with Carl, and then with Sandy.

'Did I hear you right, you two are newspaper reporters?' Paco asked, his face friendly and eager.

'You certainly did,' Carl said.

'Oh. Well, welcome to New York.'

Sandy laughed. 'Thank you. That's the first time anyone's said that.'

TWENTY

AS THEY WENT DEEPER into the old subway station, Paco kept up a running commentary, talking and asking questions, and Carl found himself answering in one or two words. There was so much to take in as they walked along the old cement and tile corridors that he could hardly keep everything straight. It was like the dead husk of New York City had been peeled back to reveal a busy and thriving world that no one knew existed. There were shops set back in the walls, selling everything from shoes to kitchenware, and people moved by in polite lines looking at what was for sale.

Walls of plywood and lumber had been erected, with names painted on the sides, and it looked like there were residences behind them. He looked into an open area and saw school being taught, children sitting down with tattered books in their hands, a male teacher gesturing before a blackboard. In another area a weaving workshop had been set up, and he realized with a start that, like Trader Al's wife, every man and woman at the looms was blind.

The corridors were noisy with talk and music, and were lit with oil lamps and an occasional electric light that wavered in strength. He found it hard to grasp and could not believe, again, and again, what he was seeing. They took a moment, to check on the injury to his neck – the bleeding had already stopped – and Sandy spoke up, awe in her voice.

'This is like the Blitz,' she said. 'People living underground in the tube system during the war.'

Paco spoke up. 'London, right? I thought you was British. Accent and all that. Not that I've ever met someone from Britain. I just hear the announcers' voices on the radio.'

'The Beeb?' Sandy asked. 'You listen to the BBC?'

'Sure,' he said. 'I like the way them guys talk, all nice and proper. And the news is better than the States' stuff. Most of the time, the domestic news is boring crap. Can't half believe what you hear anyway. Whaddya guys doing here in New York?'

'Working on a story,' Carl said. 'And working on trying to get out of here.'

'That so? Well, you came to the right bunch of guys, that's for sure. We'll be there in another minute or two. Hey, speaking of news, how are the French and Germans doing?'

Sandy said, 'In doing what?'

Paco stopped, an amazed look on his face. 'The trip to the moon. Don't you guys know about that?'

Sandy looked slightly embarrassed, and in a way, so did Carl. Here was a young man, in his late teens or early twenties, living in an underground world, unknown to anyone in the United States, and he seemed oblivious to his surroundings, only curious about what was happening out in space.

Carl spoke up. 'The Germans and the French are sending rockets up from South America, at Guiana. They're building a space station, called Eagle's Nest, and in a couple of years, they're going to try for the moon. If the money holds up.'

Paco nodded. 'Cool. Hope we get television in here by then.'

They went down another short corridor, this one lined with metal desks and chairs and typewriters salvaged from the city overhead. Paco talked briefly to a man sitting outside a wooden door, who was also dressed in a New York Yankees cap and corduroy jacket, and had a sawed-off shotgun across his lap. The man was older than Paco and had an even more impressive mustache, and when he looked at Carl, Carl recognized the attitude. A gatekeeper, suspicious of everyone and anyone who came to see his boss.

'Can I see that pass from Trader Al's?' the man asked. Carl passed it over and the man looked at it, and then at Paco and said, 'No weapons beyond the door. Paco keeps an eye on your knapsacks as well. You'll get five minutes with Jim, that's it.'

Carl said, 'I'm sorry, but who is this Jim?'

The man snorted. 'Man, you must be out of touch. This here's Jim Rowley, head of PS 19 and one of the most important guys on this island. You're two lucky folks, to see him on such short notice. But we like to do favors for Trader Al, whenever we can.'

Sandy looked down the dark corridor and said, 'I don't want to sound ungrateful, but I'm just a tad wary of letting our stuff out of our sight. It's all that we have right now and—'

Paco interrupted. 'I'll keep an eye on it, miss, honest to Christ. This is PS 19 – we do things straight around here.'

Carl also felt uneasy but he wasn't sure what else they could do. He undid the belt that held the Colt .45 and they set their knapsack and satchel on the ground. Paco took an empty chair and sat down, a wide smile on his face. 'Not to worry,' he said, 'they'll still be here when you get back.'

The guard knocked twice on the door, and then opened it. 'Jim,' he said, 'two guests of Trader Al's, looking for some business.'

Carl and Sandy walked into the room and the door slammed shut behind them.

The room was small and smelled damp. There were two large bookshelves, filled with leatherbound volumes and paperbacks. A metal desk stood in the center of the room, on a frayed rug, and two empty chairs were set before it, their split leather coverings fastened together by gray tape. Two electric lights swayed from an overhead cord. A young man in a heavy green wool sweater, also wearing a Yankees cap, looked up from a ledger book he was examining and motioned them to sit down. His face was heavily scarred on one side, and Carl noticed the collection of wrinkles around the eyes. He tried not to stare at the man's face, or what was set on the wall behind him: a framed photo of John F. Kennedy, with HE LIVES printed at the base.

'Have a seat, have a seat,' he said, gesturing before him. 'The name's Jim Rowley, and I'm in charge of PS 19. I'm told you've done business with Trader Al's and you want to work a deal with my guys. What's the proposal?'

Carl reached into his jacket and pulled out a dirty business card. 'I'm Carl Landry. I'm a reporter and photographer with the *Boston Globe*.'

'And I'm Sandy Price, from the *Times* of London,' Sandy said. 'I'm afraid I don't have any business cards. You'll just have to trust my accent.'

Jim looked at the *Globe* card and leaned back in his chair. 'Boston and London,' he said. 'You two sure are a long ways from home. What the hell are you doing here?'

Carl looked at Sandy and Sandy looked at Carl, and he

said, 'We came here to do a story about New York City.'

'By your lonesome, or with the Army?'

'With the Army,' Carl said.

'What happened, you run away from your escort?'

'You could say that,' Carl said.

He grinned. 'I could, but I won't. Yesterday there was some gunfire, up on Greenwich Avenue. Jeep got shot up, a bar messed up. You guys know anything about that?'

Sandy said, 'That was us. We were ambushed and our escort was killed.'

The grin remained. 'So why are you here? Why didn't you go back to the Army?'

It was Carl's turn. 'The way the ambush was set up, we're not too sure who's out there. If they're with the Army or not, well, I don't think we care that much. We just don't want to run into them again. Which is why we thought going out on our own made sense.'

Jim put his hands behind his head. 'Yeah, that does makes sense. Regular Army's an okay bunch of guys. They're just here to do a job. They leave us alone and we leave them alone. It's the Special Operations guys that give us a hard time, the Zed Force.' His eyes narrowed a bit. 'That's one little problem with you two. If you are Zed Force, well, you're going to be in for a rough time of it. We don't like those guys.'

'Why?' Sandy asked.

'Too true blue. The regular Army, they're live and let live. They figure if and when this crappy island is ever open for business, they'll let the city and the cops deal with us. The Zed Force guys, though, they want everything cleared out. Make this place nice and pristine. Not let anybody know that we're here.'

Carl thought again about the supplies he had seen. Barbed

wire and CS gas and plastic restraints. Not now, he thought. Save it for later.

Carl said, 'Truth is, Jim, I don't think anybody out there knows you're here.'

'Of course they don't,' he said. 'Army controls this place, controls your newspaper, right? Don't have to say more than that.'

Carl looked around the small room and said, 'A school, right?'

Sandy looked confused. 'What did you say?'

He felt more confident, seeing the smile still on Jim's face. 'That's why you're named PS 19 – for Public School Nineteen. Am I right?'

'Quite.'

Sandy asked, a tinge of confusion in her voice, 'You mean, you're schoolchildren?'

Jim came forward in the chair with a start. 'No, not children,' he said, his voice more harsh. 'You want to hear a story? Write this one down, miss, about how a bunch of us in PS 19 grew up overnight, ten years ago, when the grown-ups screwed up big time.'

She did as he suggested, opening up her notepad and uncapping her fountain pen. 'All right, I'm writing. Tell me what happened.'

Jim spoke clearly and carefully, like he had practiced this for years, waiting for the chance to tell his story to an outsider. 'It was in October. PS 19 was an elementary school, a few blocks from here. Couple of hundred kids. I was in sixth grade, the oldest class level. The sirens let loose and the teachers brought us down to the basement, where we ducked and cowered against the walls. We were crying and we were scared, and right then and there, I knew things were wrong, 'cause a couple of the teachers, they weren't there with us. They had run away, to go back home to their own families.'

He rubbed his fingers along the edge of the ledger. 'At first we thought it was another drill or something. We knew about the missile crisis, we knew that things were scary. But things were always scary back then, you know? Crisis and summit meetings and air-raid drills. And then, just a few minutes after we got into the basement, there was a loud, rumbling boom, followed shortly by another, and then a while later, a third. Each time, the floor shook and things fell off shelves and part of the ceiling even collapsed. We kids were screaming and even the teachers and the principal were scared.'

He looked up, a faint smile on his scarred face. 'That's something else, you know. Kids are so tough that I think we would have been fine, except that the teachers were scared. When you're a kid and the teacher is scared, then you know you're in a very bad place.'

'Was anyone hurt in the basement?' Sandy asked and Jim touched his face, saying, 'I guess you're asking politely about this. No, it didn't happen in the bombing. My face got this way 'cause some hungry dogs thought I'd make a great lunch, a few years back.'

'What happened after the bombing?' Carl asked.

'Well, we were crying and a lot of kids had peed themselves, and then the power went off, so we were in candlelight for a while.' His face darkened at the memory. 'Those next couple of weeks were tough, very tough. Some parents made it to the school to pick up their kids, and you had some kids leaving, and their friends staying behind, crying. Those of us who waited for our parents, God, we missed them so much. After a while the teachers started drifting away, one by one. Can't hardly blame them for wanting to find out what happened to their families, though we did blame 'em at the time. But a couple of them stayed on, Mrs. Bouchard and Mrs. Callaghan. Two real old-timer teachers. They tried to keep us organized but it was tough. We lived in the basement, scared of the fallout, scared of what was going on up on the streets. We lived on awful canned water and some biscuits and hard candies, and one day, Mrs. Callaghan, she said she was going to go to the local precinct station, maybe five or six blocks away, to see if we could get some help from the police. She left and never came back.'

Carl realized he was hanging on every word, watching the young man's lips move, trying to see what was going on behind those dark eyes of his. Jim cleared his throat. 'Then, a few weeks later, when we were getting low on water, Mrs. Bouchard got dressed in her hat, coat, and gloves. She must have been near retirement age, but she was there for us, day after day. She was the last one. We were about sixty kids left from the school and she looked at me, 'cause I was the oldest. She said that she was going to the local fire station. Her dear departed husband, as she liked to say, he had been a fire-fighter and she was sure that the firefighters had stayed behind to take care of their city. I remember that's what she told me.'

Jim paused, and looked down. 'Sorry. Bringing back some killer memories, as you can see. Well. We were in the base-ment and she looked at us and told us to be good, to keep on studying and helping each other, and not to worry. Then she patted me on the cheek and said that since I was the oldest, I was now in charge. She put her hat on her head and walked up the stairs outside, and that's the last any of us saw of her. And I've been in charge ever since.'

Carl said, 'This whole place, this is all yours?'

Jim smiled, a sad expression. 'Well, it sure as hell didn't happen overnight. It came later, after we started expanding some. Other kids, a few adults, they joined up with us 'cause we were organized, and we took care of each other.'

Sandy glanced up from her notepad. 'Why didn't you leave the city with everyone else after the bombings?'

He shrugged. 'I guess the word never got to us at first. You see, we were living in the school basement and we spent most of our time there. We were afraid of fallout and we were scared of whatever was out there that had gotten Mrs. Callaghan and Mrs. Bouchard. So we only went out for short periods of time, late at night, scavenging for food. You see, it's less windy at night, less chance of fallout coming from Queens and Long Island. After a while, that's the way of life you get used to. Then we did hear about the evacuations, but we also heard other things as well. That they were shooting the sick, or the ones that had been exposed to a lot of radiation. Crazy stuff like that, but we believed it. By then we didn't trust much of anybody or anything, and we decided it was better to stay on. Plus, you know, we were still kids. It was like some sort of adventure. Better to be in a gang in the city than split up in a bunch of foster homes if we did get off the island.'

Carl looked around the room. 'How did you end up here?'

'Just outgrew the school,' Jim said, toying with a fountain pen on his desk. 'After a while we were the only real organized group in this part of the Village, and we started trading with other gangs, mostly kids like ourselves, or people in other blocks, who never left. We like being underground, you know. Keeps us out of the Army's way, it's a way of life that we're used to, and . . . well, if the bombs ever come again, we feel like we'll already be protected.'

Sandy said, 'You know, of course, that there's no more Soviet Union. Or even Red China. It's a fairly remote possibility.'

He smiled back at her, though he didn't look particularly happy. 'I'm sorry to say we're not as trustful as you, Miss Price. We thought the grown-ups would take care of us, as kids always do, and we got a quick lesson that they didn't know what the hell they were doing. You tell me that we don't have to worry about the Russians or the Chinese. That's true, and you don't have to lecture us. We get the shortwave and a couple of times when I've been over to New Jersey, I've seen the TV. I know what's going on out there, even if you didn't know about us. I know about the English and the French and the Germans. They think they're first on the world stage again, and I know most of 'em don't like us. So one of these days, if the French or the Germans or even the English get tired of us, you can bet that they'll strap a few bombs on their rockets and finish the job the Russians started.'

Sandy was writing furiously and Carl noted the red flush on her cheeks, and stepped in, saying, 'You said you didn't trust grown-ups or adults, Jim, so why the picture of Kennedy?'

He swiveled in his chair. 'JFK? The only president I really knew as a kid. I can't half remember Eisenhower. My mom and dad, they were . . . well, they were lifelong Democrats. Loved Roosevelt. They told me during the missile crisis, before the war started, that JFK would do good, that he wouldn't allow the Commies or the generals to take us to war. I guess I believed my mom and dad, and believed in JFK. I've even heard him a couple of times since the war, on the radio. Or at least some guy who claims to be him. Nice to think that he didn't get killed in the bombing, and it sure would be somethin' if he came back to run things.'

Jim turned back to the desk. 'Plus, it's good for business.'

Carl asked, 'How is it good for business?'

'The old Kennedy folks, the true believers, the ones that worked in his administration. Some of them live here.'

Sandy snapped up her head with surprise. 'Here? They live in this subway station?'

'No, no, most of them live in the Upper West Side. I meant they still live in New York City. Still a bit snobby, after all that happened. We do some trading with 'em and they like to see the picture. Makes them think about the good old days.'

Sandy said, 'You mean they never left in the evacuation.'

'Well, you could say that . . .'

Carl spoke up. 'They came here, didn't they?'

Sandy stared at him, not saying a word.

Jim nodded slowly, as Carl went on. 'Sure. After the war, with the pressure on about the Domestic War Crimes Trial, and arrests and lynchings and all that, they had to go someplace safe, someplace where they could drop out of sight. Why not here, in the largest and most empty city in the world? Guarded on the outside by the Army, left pretty much alone. How many of them are here?'

'Hard to tell,' Jim said. 'But they are certainly the true believers. I've had grown guys, old enough to be my grandfather, in this office and crying in their hands, saying how sorry they were about what happened. The first time I heard that, I felt bad about everything, but at about the tenth and fifteenth time, I just cut 'em short and get right to business.'

Then he opened up the ledger and said, 'Which is what I want to talk about. Business. You said something earlier, about wanting to get out of Manhattan. Still true?'

'Very true,' Carl said. 'Is it possible?'

'Surely is,' Jim said, nodding at them both. 'We run this part of the subway system, and we've explored a lot of places over the years. You'd be surprised at how many water mains, conduits, old subway tunnels, and inspection tubes there are underground. Some of the guys are real explorers, they like to find where some of these old tunnels end up. And we found one that we've used for a while, that ends up in New Jersey. You interested?'

'Very,' Sandy said.

'It's pricey,' Jim warned. 'And pricey for a reason. We can't have everybody traipsing back and forth. It takes a lot of upkeep, and that means resources, and we have to be choosy. So. The earliest you could leave is about five A.M. tomorrow. Whaddya got?'

Now, he thought. Now's the time. 'Information,' Carl said.

'Information?' Jim said, like he couldn't believe what Carl had just offered. 'It had better be pretty important, to pay your fare across the river. So, again. Whaddya got?'

'The Army. They're getting ready.'

Out of the corner of his eye, he could see the questioning look on Sandy's face. He kept looking at Jim. The young man said, 'Getting ready for what?'

'Getting ready to clear every one of you out.'

'They've tried before,' Jim said bitterly. 'They failed, and they'll fail again.'

'They won't, this time,' Carl said.

'Why?' came the question.

'This time, they'll have help,' Carl said, not wanting to see the expression on Sandy's face when he said the next sentence.

'This time,' Carl said, 'they'll be using British troops.'

Sandy said, 'Carl, what do you mean—'

Jim held up a hand. 'Hold on, miss. I want to hear more of what your friend has to say.'

He kept his eyes on Jim, wanting to know what was going on in that young man's head. 'Up at the Tyler Air Force Station, there's British transport aircraft. I've also heard reports of other British troop transports, up in Canada, and there are British paratroopers and Army Special Forces – maybe the Zed Force – working together here, in Manhattan. And I've seen a supply dump.'

Jim's voice was steady. 'What kind of supplies?'

'Rolls of barbed wire. Plastic handcuffs. Wooden barricades. Riot sticks. Shields. And crates of CS gas, also known as teargas.'

Sandy remained silent. Jim was staring right at him. 'Anything else?'

'A few things,' Carl said. 'We've heard that next January, Rockefeller will be inaugurated in Washington Square. Couple of months after that, Manhattan will be open for resettlement. We were part of a press tour, Sandy and I. My guess is that they wanted to publicize the fact that the island is ready to be resettled, and to let everyone know that the island is empty.'

He added, motioning with his hand, 'They want the press to go back and say that this place doesn't exist. That you and PS 19 don't exist. And that opens the way for the troops to come in and clear you out, and soon. My guess is, maybe after the election, just before the inauguration. Maybe before the first snows fly.'

Jim said nothing, though Carl noticed his free hand was toying with the old fountain pen, rolling it back and forth, back and forth. It was quiet enough that Carl could hear someone whistling outside in the corridor, and the faint music of a flute.

The head of PS 19 cleared his throat. 'Mister, you just got you and your friend a ticket off this island.'

A few hours later they were in a tiny room built from scrap lumber and plywood, part of a boardinghouse that had been built over a stretch of rails in the subway tunnel. The only light came from a tiny bulb set in the wooden wall. The older woman who ran the boardinghouse and wore a patched jumpsuit that had a faded New York City Sanitation Department badge on the side had given them two keys and told them what to expect.

'It's clean and that's about it,' she said. 'There's some cold running water from a faucet over there, and there's a chamber pot under each bed. No open fires. That means no smoking and no candles. We find you folks using any flames, you get sent up top and we take whatever we think is of most value from ya as a fine. Got it?'

Carl looked at the two cots with blankets, a small table, and an even smaller sink in one corner. 'It's gotten.'

She left and Sandy dropped her satchel and went over to the little sink, ran some water, and began washing her face. 'We've got to help them, you know.'

He sat down on the other cot. 'I know, but we've done what we could. We've warned them what's going to happen.' He was tired and his left leg ached, but he was also trembling with nervous energy. After leaving Jim Rowley, with Paco as their guide, they had spent the next couple of hours talking to people and taking photographs. His mouth was still dry from talking so much, his fingers ached from scribbling notes and taking picture after picture, and his head throbbed from trying to reason through all of the things that they had been shown. The small businesses that thrived in the underground community, protected by PS 19. The storerooms of canned food and other supplies, guarded by sharp-eyed young men with weapons. The infirmary, dealing with the sick and the dying, especially those men and women suffering from fallout-induced cancers. The classroom where children – some of whom had been born after the war – were taught, not unlike a one-room New England schoolhouse.

And then there had been a meal in a cafeteria-like setting, with thick black bread and bowls of soup that neither he nor Sandy wanted to know the ingredients of. There was a low chatter of voices in the cafeteria, about fifty or sixty people, and most eyes were on them. The outsiders. The reporters. The ones who came from the world of real hospitals and electricity and hot water and safe food. They had not been unfriendly looks, but neither had they been friendly. Cautiously curious was more like it, he thought. But there had been other things as well, and he noticed Jim a couple of times, speaking urgently and quietly with other members of PS 19.

Now he watched as Sandy dried her face with a small dish towel that he had salvaged earlier, and she said, 'When we get out of here, I'll run the story in the *Times*. Maybe we should go to Philadelphia first, so the two of us can find refuge in our embassy. Then I can get the story and your pictures out through a diplomatic pouch. Don't take it personally, but I know your newspaper wouldn't be allowed to print anything. Especially with your censor out there in Manhattan.'

'That might make it worse for Jim and his folks,' Carl said. 'All that publicity.'

She turned, still wiping her face dry. 'Could it be any worse than what you predicted for them? Teargassed in these tunnels? Brought out like animals and sent to some camp out West, so that this place is nice and empty for Rockefeller in January?'

He stifled a yawn. 'Face it, Sandy. Your instincts are good, but they're wrong.'

'What do you mean?'

'You mentioned it before. The Official Secrets Act. A D-notice. You think your story will get published, once your editors find out what's involved?'

She turned to him. 'But it's a story, an important story, a—'

'Damn right it's an important story, but it's a dangerous one as well. Look at the facts. You have troops here, and troops in Canada. They're coming over on someone's behalf, someone's invitation. That means a very powerful high-level agreement. A secret agreement. I'm sure that your Official Secrets Act will cover that.'

Sandy threw the towel on the cot in disgust. 'Damn it . . . You're right, you know that? You're right.' She sat down, rubbed at the side of her temples. 'The paras . . . I had an uncle who was in the Parachute Regiment in World War II. Very dashing, very cocky. A nice man who brought me sweets every time he visited us, but a man who once punched a bloke in the local pub because he insulted the Queen.'

She looked up at him. 'I can't believe they'd do something like that, like coming here and helping your Special Forces arrest these people, destroy their way of life.'

'The paras are a fine, special, elite force. They follow orders. It's what they're trained to do, it's what they have to do. The people who give the orders, the people who reached this agreement, they're the ones who deserve blame.'

'We must be able to do something.'

'We've warned them,' Carl said, his own mind tossing out options, thinking of what he might have missed. 'That has to be enough.'

'I don't like it.'

'Neither do I.'

Later, he lay next to her on the cot. After looking at the gray sheets and black blankets – 'the easier to hide the grime, I suppose,' she said – she had climbed inside fully clothed. She was tired, but he felt terribly awake, so he offered to hold her until she fell asleep. A lot of things were racing through his mind, from Sandy to Merl to this crew of kids running things, kids looking jaunty in their Yankees baseball caps . . .

You idiot, he thought furiously. You should have noticed that before.

Yawning and rubbing her head against his shoulder, Sandy said, 'Promise me something, will you?'

'All right,' he answered mechanically.

She sighed and her hair tickled his nose. 'When all this mess is taken care of, come back to London with me. I want you there, in a safe city. Rooms in the Savoy, a walk by the Serpentine, tea at Harrods. It'll be lovely . . . so lovely . . .'

'Of course,' he said, 'Of course.'

He stroked her hair for a while, until he was sure that she was asleep, and then he gently untangled himself from her arms and stood up. The little light set in the wall was still lit, and he left it on. He scratched at his hair and looked at his own cot. He knew he should get some sleep. He knew that they had a long day ahead of them tomorrow. He knew what he should do.

And he went to the door and outside into the subway tunnel, gently closing the door behind him.

Fifteen minutes later, he was back in Jim Rowley's tiny office, and Jim was looking at him with a mix of suspicion and confusion. 'I'm sorry, I don't understand your request. Look, you're leaving here in about five hours. Shouldn't you get some sleep?'

'I know I should, but I have a couple of things I want to do,' Carl said. He scribbled something in his notebook and passed it over to Jim. 'This person, could she be here in Manhattan?'

He looked at the name. 'Sarah Landry. A relative?'

'My sister.'

'Missing?'

'Since the war. She was a student at a college near Omaha. I got word after the bombing that she might have survived. I've tried all the regular channels, Red Cross, Salvation Army. Nothing.'

'Why do you think she might be here?'

How to explain it, he thought. How to explain the way Sarah thought and the way she talked, her loud opinions about politics and life and women. 'I don't think she'd like it, out there in the Midwest. I think she'd like it better here.'

Jim looked down at the name on the piece of paper; when he shook his head, Carl's hands felt cold. 'Sorry, don't recognize it at all. And you know, it's a hell of a long way from Nebraska to Manhattan.'

Carl just nodded, knowing he couldn't say anything for a moment. He scribbled another name and passed it over. 'All right, then. Does this name sound familiar? I'd like to meet him before we leave. It's very important.'

Jim didn't look at the paper. He kept staring at Carl. 'Important for your story, or for something else?'

'Both,' Carl said.

'I don't like it,' he said. 'Those guys outside, I don't like dealing with them that much. They've got a lot of history behind them, a lot of people who'd like to see them dead.'

'I'm sure,' Carl said. 'But it's important. It's important to something I'm working on, back home. And it might even be connected with what I said before, about the Brits.'

With distaste on his face, Jim unfolded the slip of paper, and briefly nodded. 'Yeah, I know him. But I don't know if he could get over here in time. Do I tell him you're asking for him?'

Another scribble of the pen on paper. 'No. Give him this name.'

He cocked his head. 'You're not going to hurt him, are you?'

'No, I just want to talk to him.'

'All right, all right,' he said, sighing. 'Jesus.' He raised his voice. 'Hey, Manny!'

The man with the sawed-off shotgun opened the door. 'Yeah?'

'Take our guest to conference room one, will you? And see if you can't get me a cup of tea. And send Gordo in here, I got a quick courier job for him, uptown.'

The conference room was another concrete room, with a single table that was old and scarred with graffiti and cigarette burns. A collection of chairs – not a single one matching another – were grouped around the table, and on the near wall was a worn blackboard, an eraser, and some chalk.

Another HE LIVES photo was also on the wall. Carl sat down in the chair and put his head in his hands, and he must have dozed off for a while, because he woke up when the door opened.

A thin man stood there, a gaunt look on his face. He wore patched jeans and a heavy workshirt and wool vest, and his few white hairs were combed sideways over his head. His eyes were wide and darted back and forth, as if he was terrified that at any moment, at any second, something bad might happen.

'I'm sorry,' the old man said. 'You're not the one I'm looking for.'

Carl stood up, suddenly conscious that his knees were quivering. 'Oh, but you, sir, are who I'm looking for. That is, if you are Casimir Cynewski, and your nickname is Caz.'

The man paused for just a moment, swallowed, and then nodded.

TWENTY-ONE

CAZ TOOK ANOTHER STEP into the room. 'But you're not Merl!' he protested. 'I was told that I was meeting Merl Sawson!'

Carl stood up, hating what he was going to do next. 'That's my fault, and I'm sorry. Mr. Cynewski, my name is Carl Landry and I'm a reporter for the *Boston Globe*. I was assigned to do a story in Boston that led me to find out about you and Merl. Mr. Cynewski, I'm sorry to tell you this, but Merl is dead.'

The old man closed his eyes and wavered, as if suddenly out of breath after a very long race. He grasped the back of a nearby chair with a bony hand and said, 'I was afraid of that.' He opened his eyes, which were now tearful, and sat down. 'How did he die?'

'He was murdered,' Carl said. 'Shot in his apartment, just over a week ago. Soon after he gave me information about the Kennedy Administration members, the ones who were being eliminated, year after year. And soon after you visited him, I believe. Am I right?'

Caz moistened his lips and looked around the room,

avoiding Carl's eyes. 'What do you mean?'

'Someone visited Merl just before he was murdered, and Merl's neighbor heard voices coming from the apartment,' Carl said, then added a lie. 'And he also saw an older man like yourself leaving the building.'

'I don't know what you're talking about,' he said, carefully crossing his arms.

'Sure you do, Caz,' he said, remembering his search of the apartment. 'In fact, you brought him a gift from here, didn't you. A Yankees baseball cap, part of the uniform of PS 19. Correct?'

A slow and fearful nod. 'It sounds silly, I know. But I told him if he came back with me, he'd be protected. All it would take for him was to wear that cap at a certain time and place in Boston, and he'd be brought back here. Part of the new underground railroad.'

'To come back with you, right?' he said. 'You two were friends, back in 1962, back at the White House. You worked for the Central Intelligence Agency and he was a military aide to the president. You two were there, right up to the end, weren't you?'

Caz chewed on his bottom lip, his eyes still wandering. 'Oh yes, we were there, right in the thick of things. We were both New Frontier men, right to the bone. The best and the brightest. Fighting the communists, freeing the Negro, helping our South American friends. We intended to do a very lot, because we knew we only had eight short years to do it in. The sixties were going to be a great decade for the nation and the world, and we were in charge.'

His eyes finally focused on Carl. 'You do understand, don't you?'

Yes, he thought, remembering hearing those same words

on a cold Washington day in 1961. I understand very well. 'I do,' he said. 'I do.'

Caz refolded his arms again, as if afraid they would grow brittle if they stayed in one place too long. 'I remember the oddest things, you know, at the oddest times. Women. I think of women a lot. My mother. I don't know to this day what happened to her. Jackie, at the White House. I only saw her a few times, from a distance. So graceful, so beautiful. She and her daughter Caroline, and that poor little boy, John-John . . .'

He tightened his arms against his chest. 'I remember another woman, you know. I don't know her name, though. It was the last day of October, and I was giving up, I was surrendering. I could sense that everything was falling apart, and I had to leave the capital. I couldn't stay, not for another moment.' He looked up at Carl and said, 'That's abandonment, isn't it? Running away? Do you think I'm a guilty man, Mr. Landry?'

Carl chose his words carefully. 'I think you're a survivor.'

'Hah. That's a good one. A survivor.' Caz started to slowly rock back and forth in the chair. 'This other woman . . . I saw her the day I left the capital. I had been at the White House all morning. People were crying and scrambling around, screaming down the hallways. Merl was there, saying, we're out of time, we don't have the time, we've got to go, we've got to go. There was a fight over the helicopters, the ones coming to pick up the First Family, they were late, and I couldn't take it anymore. I got in my car and drove away. I was driving like a maniac, just like everyone else, heading west into Virginia. People were going seventy, eighty, a hundred miles an hour. The radio was filled with the most awful news, about the invasion suffering horribly, the loss of San Diego, bombers being spotted on our radar, our own SAC retaliating.'

Caz was silent for a moment and then lifted his head until he was staring at a point on the far wall. 'This woman. She was on the side of the road. Her car had a flat tire. It was a Chevrolet, an Impala. Light blue. She was frantic, waving at the cars, begging for someone to stop and pick her up. I think there might have been children in the car. I'm not sure. It could have been luggage.' He rubbed at his chin. 'Yes, I want it to be luggage. But of course, no one would stop. We were all looking at our odometers, thinking a mile a minute. At sixty miles an hour we're going a mile a minute, and every minute, we're one more mile away from ground zero. I looked at her, her crying eyes, the white handkerchief she had grasped in her hand, and my foot on the accelerator wavered, just for a moment. The briefest of seconds. And then I went on, Mr. Landry, I kept on driving. And so did the others.'

Carl felt like he was looking at a man who had been dead for a decade, but didn't know it yet.

'You know what happened next?' Caz asked.

'Tell me,' he said.

Another movement in the chair, back and forth. 'She was at the base of this slight hill. The road went over the hill and when I came down the other side, there was this tremendous flash of light behind me. Everything was lit up, like the world's biggest flashbulb had gone off. The back of my neck was burned, and so were the back of my hands. Bubbled right up to second-degree burns, even with the hill shielding me from the rear. The car shimmied and shook, and other cars and trucks went off the road, but I dodged them all and kept on driving. And if I had stopped to pick up that woman . . . Well, here I am.'

'You did what you had to do,' Carl said, horrified at what he had just heard.

Caz said, 'Yes, yes, I did do what I had to do to survive, and look at me now.' He leaned forward and lowered his voice. 'You know, of course, that I'm completely insane.'

Carl shifted in his seat, conscious that he was getting tired, and that in a few hours, he and Sandy would be leaving Manhattan. He didn't have much time to spare with this man.

'But you must be somewhat sane, Caz, to go up to Boston and to see Merl. What was that about? And who might have killed him? It has something to do with the list of names, right?'

Caz smiled, a rictus grin that gave Carl a brief shiver. 'Ah, but would a sane man leave the relative safety of this isolated island, to go back into the world of the truly insane, the national security state that is running things out there, with roadblocks and identity checks and midnight searches? Hmmm? A sane man would stay here. Would stay here underground and work on his memoirs and forget everything that's out there.'

Caz nodded his head. 'But I didn't do that. No, sir. I saddled up and used some of my contacts here, among my fellow exiles, and I found myself back in Boston. A quaint little town, trying to become another New York City, and a pity it will never happen. You folks in Boston are like little boys, trying to run things in the family after the big, strapping father has died. You're trying to fill some mighty big shoes, and it's not going to happen.'

'Why were you seeing Merl?'

Caz tilted his head, kept on smiling. 'You. You say you're a damn reporter. How do I know you're telling the truth?'

Carl reached to his pants pocket. 'I've got some—'

'Identification, right?' Caz interrupted, and then laughed, an unpleasant high-pitched sound. 'If Langley was still there – and I guess it isn't, because I heard some time ago about the mobs burning and looting it – I could have shown you a workshop where I could have made you any type of identification you desired. You could have been a reporter from Reuters. Or Agence-France Presse. Or Tass . . . If there was still a Tass anymore.'

'Then there's nothing I can do to prove it, is there. Except for stating the truth, which is that I'm a reporter for the *Globe*.'

'And you came here to see me, is that it?' Caz said, disbelief in his voice.

'No, not at first,' Carl said. 'I came here as part of an Army media tour with a reporter friend of mine who's with the *Times* of London. We were . . . Our Army escort was shot and killed in an ambush. We escaped and we're trying to get out of Manhattan. When I heard about the ex-Kennedy folks still living here, I made a guess. And I got lucky.'

'Ah, I see. Such luck, too, that you've gotten the attention of our nation's real rulers, haven't you. Not a good feeling. I'm fearful of them and Merl was afraid as well. Some time ago I told him he should come live here. Not a comfortable life but at least if you're careful, you don't have to be afraid of that midnight knock on the door. But he was a stubborn old man, said he wanted to grow old in some measure of comfort. My last visit to see him . . . I tried to convince him to leave. But he wouldn't. He said he had one more mission to accomplish, one more task to finish. You said he showed you the list of names?'

'Yes, he did. He handed them over, said more killing would

happen. That something had to be done.'

More quick nods of the head. 'Yes, yes, always something to be done. Missions to be accomplished, secrets to be kept. My boy, I know so many old secrets that my head buzzes at night, when I try to sleep. That's what my job was about, you know, finding out secrets and meeting with JFK and his boys, and then – like we were kids in a treehouse in a fun neighborhood – planning what we would do. Problems in Laos? Send some M-1 rifles. Problems with Castro? Try to kill the son of a bitch. Problems in South Vietnam? Send some advisers. Then break for a three-martini lunch at Sans Souci or sandwiches at Duke Zeibert's. Then . . . well, then came Cuba. So much for being the best and the brightest. Tell me, Bundy, is he still in prison?'

'Yes. He won't be up for a parole until next year.'

'Pity, I rather—'

Carl interrupted in frustration, knowing important minutes were slipping away. 'You know, your brother was right. You're a snob and a pain in the ass.'

Caz's eyelids fluttered, then closed, and slowly reopened. 'You saw my brother Tom?'

'Good try,' Carl said. 'I saw your brother Marcus, or Mark. I saw him last week, when I was trying to find out more information about Merl.'

'Mark . . . how is he?'

He shook his head. 'Tell me about Merl, and then I'll tell you about Mark.'

Caz stayed silent for a moment, and then Carl saw that his hands were trembling at his sides. Then Caz clasped his hands together and placed them in his lap. 'We became friends out of the oddest circumstances. We were in the Rose Garden attending some damn function, waiting to see the President when he was free. I noticed a ruby-throated warbler in the bushes and made mention of it, and Merl heard me. It turned out that we both had a passion for birding. We started talking and became friends, which is unusual, him being in the military, and the fact that they've always loathed those of us in the CIA. When we got to know each other, we learned that we were both quite similar, quite the same, under our skins. We were patriots and honorable men in the truest sense of the word, trying to help our country through some difficult times.'

'Difficult times, like right now?'

Caz rubbed his hands together. 'We . . . we face certain decisions,' the next few weeks, don't we. Decisions that will affect where we go, whether or not we abuse this second chance that we were given, a second chance at living. We were so close to world destruction back in '62. Millions died but the world got another chance when the war ended so quickly, when it didn't spread to Europe and beyond. And Merl told me he would not let this second chance be threatened. He told me what he was going to do.'

'What was that? And why Merl?'

Caz seemed to hunch up in the chair, like he was trying to reduce himself as a target.

'Because Merl was important. Merl had the key. Merl had it all.'

'The key to what?'

Caz nodded to the picture up on the wall.

'To him,' Caz softly said. 'Mr. Landry, he lives.'

Carl took a deep breath. 'You mean to say that John F. Kennedy is still alive, and Merl knew where he is?'

Caz said, 'Documents. Merl had very important documents, the key to it all. The key to stopping the killing. I've told you quite enough. And that's all I'll say.'

Carl remembered his interview with Merl's landlord, Andrew Townes, who had said something about paper and ink. Merl worked with important papers back at the White House. 'So who killed Merl?'

Caz shook his head, pursed his lips, his voice now crisp. 'My brother. How is he?'

He wondered if he could keep on pushing the old man, but something had happened, like in that conversation he had had with Two-Tone, weeks ago. The trembling old man had changed somehow, like he was now back to his previous self; Casimir Cynewski, of the former Central Intelligence Agency.

'Your brother . . .' he started, wondering what to say, and then decided to tell the truth. 'Mark is hanging in there. He's been arrested twice for seditious activities and has been sent to decon camps, and has been treated for cancer. When I saw him last, though, he looked old and crusty, like he had some years left in him. He talked some about you—'

'He did what?' Caz asked, his voice tinged with amazement.

'He talked about you. He said that he regretted the harsh words that you shared, and he said if it hadn't been for the bomb, that the two of you might have become friends.'

Caz put his hands together again and resumed the slow-motion rocking back and forth. 'That's what it must have been like, back in the Civil War. Brother against brother, friend against friend. Instead of the question being slavery or states' rights, it was the bomb, the bomb, the all powerful and holy bomb. Mark and his folks wanted to dump them all in the ocean and say, fine, we'll all be peaceful and happy forever and ever. Of course, forget about the divisions of Soviet troops in Eastern Europe and the Chinese and Russians raising hell in Laos and Vietnam. Those problems didn't exist in their minds. It was either us or them, the bomb or no bomb. If you weren't one of them, you were evil, you were doomed, you were a murderer.'

'Maybe they were right,' Carl said, growing impatient with the man's verbal wanderings. 'Did you ever think of that?'

'Of course I do . . . every single day, every single night,' Caz said, eyes blinking. 'When I pass through these tunnels, I look at these young people and they stare right at me, like I'm a living relic, a living connection to a past they could only dream about, when there was plenty of food and safety. Sometimes . . . I feel sometimes that they would like to murder me for my sins, of which I have plenty. And that was another reason I went to Boston, you know. To see if I could atone, to see if I could give something back to these young people who let me live.'

Caz looked around again and leaned forward, tapping Carl on the knee, and he tried not to flinch. It was like being touched by a dead man. 'That's why you must find those papers, you know. You have to find out where Merl hid them. Only then, only then, will he truly live.'

The Caz he had first met, the scared old man, was back now. 'Do the papers tell how Kennedy escaped? Or do they tell where he's still being hidden?'

The old man folded his arms, rocked back and forth some more, and shook his head. 'That's all I can say.' He whispered. 'You haven't shown me that you have the need to know.'

He was going up the corridor outside the conference room, when Jim Rowley stepped out of his office, a mug of tea in his hand. 'How did the visit go?'

Carl stopped, rubbed at his eyes. 'It went all right. Sort of around in circles.'

Jim said, 'Did you get what you needed?'

'Honestly, I don't rightly know.'

Up and down the corridor, the true residents of New York City went about their business. Jim looked at Carl, and Carl had the odd feeling that he was being tested, that he was being evaluated. Jim cleared his throat and handed his tea mug to one of the guards outside his door.

'I know you've got just a few hours to catch some sleep before you leave, but could you give me some time? I have something I want to show you.'

Carl didn't feel as tired as he did before. 'Sure. Go right ahead.'

Jim stayed silent as they walked, and Carl followed along, watching how the tunnel residents dipped their heads in respect as he passed. It was like young royalty, he thought, moving among his people. They went into a dark part of the subway station, past another barricade where a couple of young men were sitting, holding what looked like police revolvers in their hands. The way was lit by flickering oil lamps in the wall, and there was a steady dripping of water.

'This used to be one of our upcoming projects,' Jim explained, as he went to a closed door that was fastened shut with a combination lock. 'We had plans to fix the leaks, lay down foundation work for more housing, expand some in here.'

'What happened to your plans?' he asked, his eyes adjusting to the dark.

Jim unsnapped the lock and opened the door, which led into a well-lit room. 'Like all plans,' he said. 'Sometimes they change. Go right in, will you?'

Carl did, and Jim closed the door behind them. It was another meeting room, but it was in better shape than the other one, with polished wood furniture. There was a man sitting at the end of the table, and as he stood up, Carl froze, not able to move at all.

The man wore the uniform of the U.S. Army, and in his hands, he held a green beret, the headgear of Special Forces.

Carl turned on Jim. 'You bastard, is this a set up? Is this what it is?'

Jim laughed, the skin of his scarred face stretching into a grin. 'Jesus, Carl, relax. I want you to meet someone. This is Sergeant Paul Picard of the U.S. Army. Paul, this is Carl Landry of the *Boston Globe*.'

'Sir,' the soldier said, holding out a hand. Carl grasped it and gave it a quick shake. The young soldier's uniform was worn and mud splattered, not spit and polish. He had short-cropped blond hair and he looked muscular and fit, unlike most of the residents Carl had seen in the past few hours.

'And another thing,' Jim said, sitting down and motioning Carl to a chair. 'Paul is also a proud member of PS 19. Right?'

Sergeant Picard grinned and sat down. 'You've got that right, Jim.'

Carl took the chair, staring at the soldier in disbelief and then looking over at Jim, who was sitting there looking self-satisfied, with his hands clasped satisfactorily against his chest. 'You . . . PS 19, you've got intelligence sources in the military?'

Jim grinned again. 'Well, we've seen the ads from old newspapers and magazines that get smuggled in here, about how it's every young man's duty to respect the draft and serve their time. Some years back, we figured we ought to do our civic duty, Carl, and some of our fellows volunteered to go out into the world and join up. The Army's so eager for bodies, they don't look too hard into backgrounds. All our guys had to say was that they were orphans, that Mom and Dad had been in Miami or Omaha back in '62, and that was enough for the recruiters.'

Carl said, 'Not all of them would end up in Manhattan, would they?'

'No, but enough,' Jim said, and then his smile vanished. 'Enough to give us some sleepless days, and change some plans. What you said earlier, about the British troops and the supplies being stockpiled, we had some inkling about that. You confirmed it, though, and for that, we're grateful. But there's something else, something else I want you to hear from Paul here.'

Carl looked over at the sergeant and for a moment saw himself sitting there, wearing the same uniform, having the same confidence of being in good health and being an elite soldier.

'I appreciate the offer, but why?'

Jim looked at the sergeant and then at Carl. 'Because we might need your help.'

He looked into Jim's face, a young man who had listened to his teachers and who had taken care of his classmates, all these years, and who had built this underground city.

'Go right ahead.'

Sergeant Picard nodded. 'Thanks. Like I told Jim earlier, I'm sorry I didn't get better information. But I figured I had to get here soonest with what I did have. You see, last week, I was in Fort Drum, up near Watertown. I was working late in our quarters, and a couple of colonels came in. They were drunk and looking to find a place to take a piss, which is why they were in my building. They were arguing, too, and at first

I couldn't hear what they were saying. Then it got real clear and . . . well, I asked for a quick emergency leave, so I could get back here.'

Jim kept his hands clasped together. 'Tell Carl what you told me, Paul.'

The soldier stared at Carl. 'There's a deal, some secret deal, between London and the people backing Rockefeller. I don't even think those two officers knew all the details . . . But what they did know, really pissed them off. They weren't happy.'

Carl looked over at Jim. 'The British who are coming in. Their government must be charging a stiff price indeed. Is that right?'

Jim slowly nodded. 'That's right.'

'And what's the price?'

'Paul?'

The soldier looked nervous. 'The price is our nation.'

Carl rubbed at his eyes, not wanting to believe what he was hearing. 'What do you mean, our nation?'

The soldier looked at Jim, as if for reassurance, and Jim gave a slight nod. Paul pressed on. 'Again, I'm sorry, but I don't know enough of the details. What I do know is that the troops are coming in soon, before the election. And after the election, Rockefeller, he's gonna make an announcement. Something about the new relationship between the States and Great Britain. That was making the colonels real angry. They said, we're giving up our nation for this, can you friggin' believe it. And one of them said something about having to bow to the goddam Queen when this was all over.'

'What kind of relationship?'

Paul was twisting the beret in his hands. 'I'm sorry, I just don't know. They were pretty drunk. But they were saying something about it being 1938 again, and about how the slush is coming.'

Carl said, 'The what?'

Paul's face reddened. 'I know it doesn't make any sense. They just said, 1938. And that the slush is coming.'

Jim said, 'That's it, right?'

The soldier nodded. 'Sorry, Jim. I know it's not much. But I figured you had to know about the troops coming in. Hell, the election's only weeks away and—'

'Thanks, Paul,' Jim said abruptly. He stood up and so did Paul, and Carl slowly followed. 'You heading back north?'

'Yep. My pass expires in about twelve hours. It'll be tight but I'm sure I'll make it back to Fort Drum in time.'

Jim went over and shook his hand, using a two-handed grip. 'You've served your people well, Paul. Thanks again. Carl? Time for one more visit?'

'Sure,' he said. The slush is coming. The slush from 1938.

Earlier, he had spent time with an old man who had said he was insane.

Was everyone here insane as well?

They went through another locked door between two of the bookshelves, and into a long corridor. Jim grabbed a flash-light from a shelf and switched it on. The tunnel was narrow, made of brick, and went uphill at a slight grade for several minutes. It stopped at a rusting, metal ladder. Carl followed Jim up the ladder, wondering where in hell they were going, and thinking about all that had just gone on. Merl, the old vet with the list of names – now he was more than that. He was an old soldier who had gone on one more mission, one more mission armed with . . . secrets, according to Caz.

Secret documents that would reveal that JFK still lived.

Caz, an old and frightened CIA man, talking in circles, but talking about something real, something bad that was coming in just a few weeks.

And then that young soldier. PS 19 had spies, spies in the U.S. Army, and the best intelligence that they could get was that it was 1938, and that the slush was coming.

Jesus, he thought. And Jim was asking him, Carl Landry, for help. It seemed like the leader of PS 19 was adding a pretty stiff tariff to his and Sandy's fare off this island.

Sandy . . . He hoped she was sleeping well, not wandering around, looking for him. It'd be hard to explain and—

Jim lifted an overhead door of metal and wood, and Carl felt a cool breeze come down from above. He followed Jim up and found himself standing on the roof of a small building, closed in on both sides by taller brownstones. A quarter moon was up, illuminating the night. Covering half the roof was a structure with a closed door on its side. Jim rubbed his hands together and said, 'I've got a serious question to ask you, Carl.'

'Go ahead.'

'Caz, the guy you just talked to. To tell you the truth, we know him well. Did he say anything about some old documents, documents that could mean a lot in the next few weeks?'

Carl stared at Jim. He would not have been more surprised if Jim had told him that JFK was living in the basement of Grand Central Station.

'The conference room,' Carl said. 'You were listening in?'

'No, we weren't. But could you answer the question, please?'

He thought of telling Jim to go to hell, that the conversation he had had with Caz was private. But then there was that look in Jim's eyes. Something bigger was going on, something that he wanted to know more about.

'Yes, Caz did. A friend of his in Boston supposedly had some dramatic information that would change things. Something that would stop the killing.'

Jim said, 'Did you ever find out what he had?'

'No, he was murdered before I could do that.'

Jim blew into his hands, rubbed them again. 'Then Caz was right, the old fool . . .' Jim made a funny little wave with his right hand. 'You ever play the lottery, Carl?'

'What?'

'You ever play the lottery?' Jim said.

'No, I don't.'

'Well, you should,' Jim said, gently grasping his arm and leading him to the door on the other side of the roof. 'My advisers, they said I shouldn't bring you here. They said I shouldn't talk to you. And I said, well, I said I had a feeling about you, that you were a straight shooter, that you knew some important stuff and that you would help us. I was glad I was right. And you should be, too.'

Carl felt something itchy between his shoulder blades, knowing a hidden sniper was keeping an eye on him, a sniper from PS 19. 'That little wave of your hand. From a Kipling poem, right? About the tribal leader who meets with a British officer.'

'Yeah,' he said. 'And if it hadn't gone well back there with our little talk . . .'

'There would have been no wave, and I'd be dead.'

'Yep. No offense, all right?' Jim asked, as he reached for the door handle.

The night air felt cold, quite cold. 'No offense,' Carl said.

The door opened up and he had to cover his eyes to shield them from the glare.

Jim allowed him a moment to take it all in. The large room was smelly and noisy, and, as elsewhere, was lit with a mix of flickering electrical bulbs and candles. To the left were a row of shortwave radio receivers, with young men and women sitting at them, wearing earphones and studious expressions, either jotting down information on notepads or sending out signals with Morse code keypads. To the right were rows and rows of cages, with pigeons cooing and preening and fluttering about. At the far end of the room he could see other young men and women, gently working with the pigeons, placing little capsules on their feet and setting them free out a large window.

In the center of this space was a tiny cluster of desks and typewriters, and a couple of well-armed men, staring at him with a not very friendly look.

Jim cleared his throat. 'Welcome to Radio Free Manhattan, Carl.'

'This . . . this is all for PS 19?'

Jim laughed and went over to a small table with a couple of mismatched chairs. A man dressed in overalls placed two cups of tea on the stained tabletop, and Carl and Jim sat down.

'No, not really, Carl,' Jim said, taking a cautious sip from the tea. 'You see, back there, when the three of us were talking – us two and your Brit reporter friend – well, I didn't feel like giving up too much. But when you gave me that info about the British paratroopers and the supplies that have been prepared for our benefit, and when you came back later and said you wanted to talk to Caz . . . well, I gambled that I could take you a little further.'

'Nice gamble,' Carl said sharply. 'Gambling with my life.'

Jim shot back, 'And I'm gambling with a hell of a lot more lives. Tens of thousands here, and other places. You see, PS 19 is just one group here in Manhattan, Carl. There are others. And we work together, to keep everyone fed and healthy and out of the Army's way. Every two years, we select a leader.'

'And you're that leader. The mayor, is that it? Are you the mayor of New York City?'

He grinned. 'Why the hell not? Titles don't mean much. Call me the chairman of the Manhattan councils if that makes you feel better. But there's a lot more going on than just running this city.'

Carl looked over at the radios, the homing pigeons, the communications setup. Pretty elaborate for a small island like this. Too elaborate, in fact. He turned and looked back at Jim.

'You're not alone, are you?'

Jim looked steadily back at him. 'Go on.'

Carl felt like he was on the edge of something.

'There must be other communities out there, just like in Manhattan,' Carl said, the words coming to him quickly. 'Army's got a half dozen Restricted Zones set up around the country. Around San Diego. South Florida. Omaha. Around destroyed Air Force bases like Maxwell in Alabama and Moody in Georgia. There're people there as well, right? Just like here, the dissidents and the hunted, the deserters and draft dodgers, everyone and anyone who's on the run from martial law, they end up inside an RZ, in hiding. And you're in contact with them.'

Jim glanced around the room. 'We have been, for years. Trading information, news, tips on how to survive without getting in the way of the Army.' He turned and looked directly at Carl, the scarred face serious. 'We communicate through couriers, homing pigeons, brief coded messages on the radio. We have quite a little network of free communities set up, a network we're proud of. In some ways, we see ourselves as the legitimate government of the people of the United States, Carl, because we have real, free, and open elections. More free than the ones on the outside. But it's been ten years, ten long years, and we're getting tired. You can only survive so long and so much on salvaging ten-year-old leftovers.'

Carl thought back to the meeting they had just had with the soldier from Fort Drum. 'You're planning something, aren't you? That's why Paul was so upset that time was running out, with elections coming in less than two weeks.'

Jim stood up and said, 'Come on, let's go outside for a moment, all right?'

Carl followed him to another door that led to a narrow balcony overlooking a dark street. Outside, there were a few lights and some music, more jazz from a hidden club. Jim held onto the balcony railing and said, 'The election's coming up shortly, am I right? First Tuesday in November.'

'Yeah, Tuesday, November seventh.'

'Today is October twenty-fourth, Carl. You know the anniversary date that's coming up, October thirtieth?'

The wind picked up, bringing the scent of Manhattan, of smoke and wet decay and things still rotting away, year after year. 'Everybody does. When the bombs started hitting home, in the United States.'

Jim stared down at the street. 'October thirtieth. Just six days away. The day before Halloween. Some of us are calling it Resurrection Day. Carl, six days from now we're coming out, all of us, and we're going to demand our rights as American citizens, rights that were taken away from all of us – everybody in this nation – after the war.'

He thought of the troops coming in, the barbed wire, the CS gas. 'Jim, you've got to postpone it. Hell, you have spies in the Army, they must—'

Jim turned and said, 'Of course they do. Everybody has spies in this city. The Army, the Navy, the Air Force, the French, the Germans, the British. And someone who's been on the edge of starvation, you give him a steak dinner and you can get a lot of information. All those people, they all know the secret, that there are free people here, and elsewhere in this country, free people that aren't going to give it up. Damn it, we're tired of living on scraps, tired of dying when it's too cold or because we don't have the right medicines. This is my city and my country, and we're going to stop hiding.'

Carl said, 'Your timing. You want to impact the election.'

'Yeah, we do,' he said. 'It doesn't matter to us who is president, who's running against whom. It's the people behind the president that matter. If Rockefeller is elected, it's status quo. Not because he's a bad guy, but because of the people behind him. Same thing with McGovern, but we know if he gets in, it won't be status quo. Things will have to change.'

He was thinking furiously, trying to take it all in, trying to show this young man that while politics and marching in the streets were fine ideas pre-1962, it didn't work that way now. 'Then that's the point,' Carl said. 'When word got to certain people that you were planning to come out, they had to come up with contingency plans. Bring in troops and clear you out before the election. But maybe . . . maybe some of the Army generals, they said there was no way American troops would fire on American civilians.'

'So they bring in outside help. Sure. Makes sense.' Then Jim swore and pounded a fist on the railing. 'Sure. Lots of sense. Shooting civilians. Easy to do after a war where millions of innocent people got killed, right? And you want to hear something hilarious? An old guy who had a hand in working with Kennedy and killing civilians back in '62, he said he could help us prevent the same thing this time.'

'Caz.'

'Yeah, Caz. He's one loopy son of a bitch, but he told us he had a contact in Boston, a guy who had some important documents that could stop Rockefeller and the British cold in their tracks. We thought we had a chance, so we helped him get to Boston. Caz came back empty-handed, but said the man promised to do something, real soon.'

'But he never did it. He got killed.'

'Yeah, and it's too late. We can't back away. Planning this took months, coordinating with the other free zones. It's like one big damn boulder. You start it rolling, it can't stop. We're coming out in six days, Carl. All of us.'

'You'll be fired on,' Carl said, thinking of the men and women and children down below, in the subway tunnels and basements. 'They won't let you get far.'

'Then they'll be surprised. We're not unarmed. We've stolen a number of weapons, over the years. Remember the expression? If they want a war, then let it begin here. And if it takes a second American Civil War to let everyone know we're here, free and alive, so be it.'

'Earlier, you said you needed my help,' he said, putting his hands in his pockets from the cold. 'Maybe I can do something.'

'Put something in your newspaper about this, before it happens? Sorry, I know about your censors. I'm sure your British friend would have the same problem, if she tried to write about

British troops preparing to kill American civilians.'

'No, I was thinking of something else. Before I came to Manhattan, I was doing a story about that man's death, Caz's friend. I met him, just briefly, before he died. If I can get back to Boston in a day or two—'

Jim turned suddenly and stepped up right to him. 'Can you do it? Can you find those documents, before Resurrection Day? Find out what they are?'

It was like the entire weight of Jim's dreams and those of Manhattan and the other free zones and the nation were weighing down his shoulders. He found it hard to breathe, hard to keep his eye on Jim's eager face. A hell of a thing. He remembered that Harvard voice, more than ten years ago on that cold January day. Promising to pay any price, bear any burden, for the cause of liberty. What a hell of a price. What a hell of a burden.

'I can try,' he said. 'Best I can do.'

Jim nodded, reached out and gently slapped him on a shoulder. 'Then that's all I can ask for, Carl. Look, take a look down there. What do you see?'

He peered over the side. 'Just an empty street.'

'Sure. And in six days, the streets of this city and other empty streets across the country, they're going to be filled with people, marching and carrying banners, heading to the RZ fences, announcing that they are alive, that they are survivors, and that they are Americans. Carl, you've got to find those documents.'

Carl clenched his fists inside his pockets. 'I know.'

As he went back to his rented room – hell, for just a few more hours – something was nagging at him. When he looked at the empty street and listened to Jim's description of what was going to happen in a few days, about the people marching and the banners, it had jogged a memory.

A black-and-white memory. A snippet of an old movie newsreel. People marching, people waving . . . Troops. Troops in odd, coal-scuttle-shaped helmets . . .

He stopped outside the room, took out the key.

1938.

The slush is coming.

German troops, on the march. In 1938.

Come on, come on . . . remember.

1938. Czechoslovakia?

No. Someplace else.

The slush is coming. The slush.

Anschluss. The German word for union.

'Holy Christ,' he whispered. In 1938 Germany marched its troops into its neighbor, Austria, swallowing the country whole, making a greater Germany. Austria was no longer a nation, no longer independent, its laws and its rules were made in Berlin.

Britain was going to move into America?

Here? It's going to happen here?

He couldn't believe it. Didn't want to believe it.

Inside, he thought of what he was going to do next. He had to wake up Sandy, tell her what he had just learned. Maybe she could do something with her contacts overseas, maybe if she got to her embassy in Philadelphia, something could be done, something could happen before the British troops came into the restricted zones in the next few days, squashing the very last independent voices in this nation. Getting Merl's notes . . . Come on, that was a very long shot, not much of a chance of that happening at all.

But maybe Sandy could do something. He knew she would, after seeing the look on her face while they toured PS 19. He knew she would help out. She would have to. Hell, earlier she had even said she would, before he snuck away to his meetings with Caz and Jim.

Sandy was on her side, facing the wall and sleeping gently. The light was still on but he didn't mind. He was so tired that he was sure he could fall asleep if it was an inch from his nose. He walked around his cot and stumbled for a moment, as his left foot caught one of the satchels, tumbling it over. 'Damn it,' he whispered, hearing things falling out onto the floor.

Carl got down on his knees on the cold, dirty concrete and started putting items back into the satchel. It was Sandy's, and he replaced her notebooks, a water bottle, and her purse. As he put them back into the open sack, his fingers touched something hard and plastic. He wondered what it was.

He looked up. She was still sleeping. He dug into the satchel, pulled out the object, and held it up to the light. It was a small Sony tape recorder, black and shiny. That was odd. Sandy had never mentioned she had a tape recorder, and had never used it in the days he had been with her, either here or in Boston. Odd. Nice little piece of machinery, though, and he pressed a couple of buttons.

Nothing happened. The tape didn't move, no tiny red light came on, nothing.

He turned it over in his hands. The back plastic plate seemed loose. It looked like it was held fast in each corner by tiny screws, but when he pressed down on it he found it was loose, and that he could slide it off—

—and see a keypad, a small display screen, and other

switches. In one corner was a knob and he pulled it free. It extended and became an antenna, an antenna for a radio, made up to look like a Sony tape recorder.

His chest felt cold and empty, and his mouth was terribly dry. He put the antenna back into place and slid the cover back where it belonged. In another minute everything was back in the knapsack and he was lying on the bed, staring up at the plywood ceiling. Someone had marked in red paint, KILROY WAS HERE '71 and below that, in black paint, HELL, JFK WAS HERE '72. He wondered who was telling the truth.

There was a rustling noise to his left. 'Carl?' came the soft voice.

'Yes, Sandy.'

She coughed a few times, and then yawned. 'Where've you been, love?'

He licked his lips, found that they were still dry. 'I couldn't sleep, so I went for a walk and talked to a few people. Just to pass the time.'

'Oh.' She yawned again. 'I wish these beds were bigger.'

Carl put his hands behind his head. 'So do I. So do I.'

'Do you want to talk some, Carl?'

A pause. 'No, I don't.'

He listened to her breathing slow down and then he just lay there, the rest of the night, not sleeping, not even daring to think.

Just staring.

EMPIRE: FOUR

A MATTER OF EMPIRE: FOUR

MAJOR KENNETH HUNT STOOD at the end of the airstrip as dusk approached, smoking a pipe. He sat down gingerly on a large concrete block, part of some construction project going on at the air base, RCAF Station Trenton. Behind him, in a collection of hangars and barracks about a half mile away, his paras of 'A' Company were getting ready for a mission. In just over a week, a mission, he grimly thought, that could be the opening salvo of the next world war.

But this time, he thought, this time, it will be in Europe. And that awful atomic sun will burn above Paris and London and Berlin and Amsterdam and Rome. All thanks to you, he thought. Damn nice thing to put on one's headstone when one's time is up. He wondered what Rachel would have thought.

There was the constant noise of engines up toward the center of the air base, of lorries moving in supplies, of aircraft engines – the props of the C-130 troop transports and the jet engines of the RAF Vulcan bombers – and of other engines as well. He stared out into the darkness, at the few lights of the civilian homes that were adjacent to the west, and he glanced up. There were too many base lights to see any evening stars. Beyond the lights at the base perimeter there was a thin line of dark. He was sure that it marked Lake Ontario, one of the six Great Lakes. Beyond that was the United States of America, and in that battered nation this evening were the eventual targets for his company and the other companies of the British army, stationed up and down the length of Canada, and in Bermuda and Jamaica as well.

A slight breeze rose, causing something metallic to rattle. He turned and looked at the shape beyond the end of the runway. Even in the dark he could make out the form of the old jet bomber's tail, pointing up sharply to the sky. He remembered what Clive had said about the carcass of the B-52. A relic of a dead empire.

He stretched out his legs and grimaced as a cramp gripped his left thigh. Empires. He had served his sovereign and country across the world, and now, they were asking him and his paras for one more mission, against a nation that had been a friend for almost a century. In spite of his years of service and duty, it troubled him. It wasn't just the memory of Rachel, though that did play a part. He knew that some sort of agreement had been reached with American officials, but he also knew that the true nature of his upcoming mission was being kept secret from them. He thought again of when he was a boy, seeing his first Americans at that Eighth Air Force Base back home during the Second World War. He wondered if he would have to kill some of those same airmen who had befriended him, more than twenty-five years ago . . .

There was the sound of boots on the tarmac and he turned, seeing a figure approach, holding a small torch.

'Major?' came the familiar voice, and Hunt said, 'Over here, Paul.'

His second-in-command, Captain Paul Heseltine, switched off the torch and sat down next to him. Paul was a squat man, hard muscled and only an inch above the required height, and had served with him for more than two years. 'Enjoyin' some peace and quiet, Major?'

'Yes. Anything to report?'

'No, sir. The lads are ready, as ready as they can be. And they're eager to get on with the job. But . . .'

Hunt puffed at his pipe and stared out at the few lights of Trenton, the nearest town, about three kilometers away. 'Go on, Paul.'

'It's just where we're goin' that's botherin' the lads, Major. They like the Yanks, as most of us do. Raising arms against them . . . It just don't seem right.'

'I see,' he said, holding the warm bowl of the pipe in his hand. 'When's the last time you were in the States, Paul?'

'Let's see . . . that would be '63. I was in Georgia, helping them set up camps for the refugees from Florida. Hell of a time. Beautiful country down there, hotter than blazes in summer, but I made out all right. Met some lovely birds. And you, Major?'

He took out his penknife, scraped the pipe's bowl clean. 'The first time was in early '63, in California. Bad times, back then. The state was almost in open revolt. We were attached to an infantry unit. Poor buggers. They were trying so hard to keep everything under control, but they didn't have enough food or equipment. I remember one young officer, a sergeant who had a field promotion. Can't remember his name. Gave him a bottle of brandy when I left and you'd have thought I'd given him the Crown Jewels. So. Now we're going back, you and I, to New York. Who would have thought?'

'Not me, that's for sure, sir.'

Hunt refilled the pipe from a tobacco pouch he kept in his jacket pocket. 'It will be tough, very tough, dealing with Manhattan. But I know B and C Company will do the job.'

'Beggin' the major's pardon, it's our company I'm worried about. And what we're going to be doing. Sir.'

'I know.'

He sensed the captain shifting his weight on the block of cement. 'I thought you might have some more info about our mission, with your brother Clive and all that.'

Hunt flicked the lighter to life, the sudden flare of light bringing everything into focus. The stunted grass. The flat tarmac. He and the captain, sitting next to each other.

'No, nothing like that,' he said, not liking what he said one bit, not liking having to lie to his second-in-command.

'I see,' the captain said, his voice betraying his skepticism.

Major Hunt drew on his pipe and tried to change the subject. 'You know, I was a young boy when I first met some Yanks.'

'Really, sir?'

'During the Second World War. The little village I grew up in was right next to an Eighth Air Force Base. Filled with B-17 bombers. Do you remember how it was back then? Food and coal rationed. Clothing mended and re-mended. You wore shoes until they fell apart, and then you kept them together with cardboard and string. And no sweets, of course, no sweets for a young boy.'

'I remember, Major.'

'Then the Yanks came in, like cowboys. And they would hold socials for us, and we'd get some of their food, some of their excess clothing, extra blankets . . . It was like having

Father Christmas living right next door. They helped us so much, those long months until the war ended.'

He clamped down on the pipe stem with his teeth at another memory, one that still angered him. 'I was at a function last year, at a regimental mess. I shan't embarrass them by repeating their name. But I had to walk out during a toast. It made me ill, Paul. It made me sick to my stomach. They gave a toast to the ghosts of Kennedy and Khrushchev.'

His captain sounded uncomfortable. 'I'm afraid to say, sir, that I've heard the same toast.'

'I bet you have,' Hunt said, wincing. 'Something like, "To Kennedy and Khrushchev, for giving us a second chance." For a second chance to be great again. For bigger budgets for our troops and planes and ships. To mobilize and be strong and to go back to our old haunts in India and Hong Kong. To matter again. Of course, our good fortune has been built upon the corpses of millions.'

He took the pipe out of his mouth, waved it in the air. 'Over there, Captain, across that lake is America. They helped us survive three times this century, kept us from falling into the dustbin of history. And how are we repaying them? By betraying them. By coming in at night, like thieves. By killing some of their civilians and some of their military. That's how. And we should be ashamed. They deserve better.'

He let his hand fall to his lap. 'They deserve better,' he repeated softly.

TWENTY-TWO

IN AN INSTANT HE HEARD BELLS RINGING and someone was shaking his shoulders.

'Carl!' came Sandy's urgent voice. 'Wake up! Something's wrong!'

It felt like all of ten seconds had passed since he had put his head down on the pillow. Jumbled images came back to him: Caz, the old CIA man, talking at length about secrets and conspiracies. He lives. Jim Rowley and the real secrets of PS 19 and Manhattan, and the biggest secret of all: Resurrection Day. And that awful burden put upon him, Carl Landry, to somehow prevent the incipient anschluss, the British troops coming here to—

'Carl, are you awake?'

'Yes, yes,' he said, rolling unsteadily out of bed. From outside the little room he could hear the bells again, cowbells, it sounded like, being rung over and over again. Sandy was in front of him, holding a flashlight.

'The power's gone,' she said, voice trembling. 'I heard the bells and woke up and the light had gone off.'

He stood up, wiping at his beard-stubbled face and looked

over at Sandy. He remembered what he had seen earlier, the radio in the satchel that she had hidden from him these past days. What to do, what to say, what was going—

A pounding at the door. 'Shine the light on the door,' he said, picking up his holstered .45 and freeing the pistol with one swift motion. 'And when I open it, shine the light on whoever's there. Make sure you point it right at their face.'

He pulled the door open. 'Hey!' came a voice. 'Lower the light, will you?'

Carl lowered the pistol. 'Sandy, it's okay.'

The beam of light pointed to the floor and Jim Rowley strolled in, holding up a hand to block the glare. He still wore his Yankees baseball cap and corduroy jacket, and he quickly motioned to the both of them. From behind him, Carl could see the outside corridor. There was movement there, of people rushing by, carrying hand lanterns and small flashlights.

'Get your stuff, right away,' he said. 'We've got to get you out of here.'

He went back to his bed, and Sandy did the same, as they both grabbed their knapsacks. Alarms, Carl thought. So many times in the past we've been woken up by alarms, by alerts, by signals that something was wrong. He turned to Jim and said, 'Army?'

Jim nodded, looked behind him. 'Yeah. A Zed Force unit just came in, about two subway stops uptown. Couple of squads. They're moving fast, heading this way. And . . .'

'And what?' Sandy asked, her voice high-pitched. 'What's going on?'

Jim stared right at Carl, his tired eyes unblinking. 'They're not making arrests, they're not slowing down to process prisoners, they're just moving in. Like they're looking for someone in particular.'

Carl picked up his knapsack, knowing almost with certainty that Major Devane was among the squads of soldiers, heading this way. 'Someone like us?'

Sandy whispered, 'Oh no,' and Jim said, 'I'm afraid you're right.'

Jim talked to them quickly as they made their way through the groups of moving people, the lights from the flashlights and lanterns making crazy and jerky shadows on the concrete walls and floor. Two men with sawed-off shotguns flanked Jim as they went through the tunnels, the sound of people's feet moving echoing along with shouts and yells and the ringing of the bells.

'That's our early warning system, the bells,' Jim said, raising his voice. 'One bell sends out a signal, and the others pick it up and repeat the message. Then runners are dispatched to find out what the hell is going on, and to spread the news. You'd be surprised at how far the sound travels down here.'

'What do your people do when the bells ring?' Carl asked, keeping an eye on Sandy, and what was going on around them.

Jim said, 'Everyone has a job to do or a place to go. We have barriers that we put up, help slow down the soldiers. Or we flood out portions of the tunnel. Or we hide stuff. Those who don't have a job to do, they spread out, go to shelters, hide out in groups of five or six. Then they wait for the all-clear signal.'

They were going up a slight incline as a line of children went by, each with a small bundle of belongings, each one holding another's hand. A young girl with a blond ponytail was bringing up the end of the line, and she looked at them wide-eyed as they passed. Carl felt a quiet taste of horror. This was what it must have been like, ten years ago, when the sirens sounded in this city. Groups of children, holding each other's hands, trying to hide their fear, seeking shelter underground, seeking someplace to hide from the madmen up above.

Six days, the voice came to him. You've got six days to do something about it.

'Look,' Jim said, 'we've got to—'

His words were drowned out by an ear-cracking *boom!* that took Carl's breath away as the concussion pounded at them. He thought he heard Sandy scream but he wasn't sure, his ears hurt too much, and he grabbed her hand. Jim tugged at his shoulder, dragging him somewhere, and he shook his head, trying to shake off the explosion's impact. The two men with shotguns followed behind them, guns raised to their shoulders, pointing straight and level. They went through a small maze of plywood cubicles and barriers, to a small ladder set against a tiled wall. 'Go, go, go!' Jim yelled, as he climbed up. They were in an airshaft of some sort, a metal enclosure that echoed and banged as they moved through on hands and knees. He and Jim both had flashlights and Carl stopped for a moment to look back. Sandy was behind Jim, not looking at him, her head trembling, and beyond her were the two armed men.

'Go on,' Jim said, breathing hard, the flickering light making his facial scars seem even deeper. 'That was one of the Zed Force's calling cards, a concussion grenade that makes a hell of a lot of noise. Shakes you up so that you can't do a thing.'

'That was damn close,' Carl said.

'Not close enough. Go on, there'll be an opening and another ladder in a couple of minutes. Mind you don't tumble.'

They crawled for a few long minutes, until Carl felt a draft of air on his face. True to Jim's word, there was a square opening ahead and another ladder, and he climbed down about a dozen feet, exhausted. Jim came next and then Sandy, and Carl helped her stand up. The two quiet men followed, eyes scanning their surroundings, shotguns at the ready.

They had emerged onto a small departure platform in a narrow utility tunnel and four or five people stood at the edge of the platform, next to a pile of boxes and rolled-up rugs. Jim looked back, then at his two guards and said, 'Your transport will be here in a minute or two. You two be right careful once you get over to New Jersey. It's wilder there, and sometimes they get raided by outsiders.'

'Orfie gangs?' Sandy asked, and Jim made a face and shook his head. 'That's just a popular word used by the newspapers, miss. Some might call PS 19 an orfie gang, but you've seen what we really are.'

Carl shouldered his knapsack. 'So who's doing the raiding over there?'

Jim shrugged. 'You got kids and even adults, they're in New Jersey or Pennsylvania, they got bored with things. There's rules, rationing, and the draft. They need to raise hell and blow off steam, so they go someplace where there's no rules and that's the nearest Restricted Zone in New Jersey. Raid a couple of houses, burn a few buildings, rob a few people, and then go back to your safe and boring home. And – oh, good, here comes your transport.'

Carl turned, not quite believing what he was seeing, but also knowing it made perfect sense. A team of four horses was coming up the tunnel, hauling a large wooden wagon that had steel rims for tires, and rolled along an old rail track. Gas lanterns hung from poles on either side of the wagon, and two bearded men were up front in the wooden seat, dressed in long cloth coats and wearing Yankees baseball hats. The man on the left had a shotgun across his lap, and the man on the right carried the reins in his hand. The man on the right yelled out, 'Come on, Jim, we don't wanna get caught here!'

There was a quick bustle as cardboard boxes and rolled-up rugs were tossed from the platform onto the wagon, and Jim said, 'Even when the Zed Force comes, we keep business going. It's what keeps us alive.'

In a matter of seconds, the platform was cleared, and the people doing the hauling faded into the shadows, leaving behind Carl and Sandy and Jim, along with his two escorts, who were nervously fingering their shotguns as the bells continued to toll. Another, fainter-sounding explosion and another concussion grenade. Carl felt sick at what those scared children must be thinking.

'Here,' Jim said, passing him a piece of paper. 'This is a letter of introduction to the mayors of Hoboken. We get along pretty well and I told 'em to give you some help getting out of the RZ. You can probably catch a bus in Morristown, if you're still looking to get to Philly.'

'Mayors?' Carl asked. 'There's two mayors in Hoboken?'

'Yep,' he said. 'Two ex-pilots who got together years back and decided to run things. They did such a good job that the people still out there reelect them, year after year. Look, I've got to get back to my people. Good luck to the both of you. Understand?'

Sandy shook Jim's hand and then so did Carl. He looked into those young and old eyes and said, 'Understood.'

They clambered into the rear of the wagon and as the horse driver said, 'Hah!' and they started moving, Carl continued to hear the sound of the bells. Then, the faint sound of gunfire. Jim gave a brief wave and, with his two guards, moved quickly into the darkness.

Sandy moved next to Carl. 'We've got to do something, Carl. We have to.'

He stared at the now-empty platform as they went deeper into the tunnel.

'Yes, we do,' he said.

It got dark quickly in the tunnel, the only illumination coming from the lanterns on the side of the wagon. Their knapsacks were jammed into a corner and Carl quietly took out his pistol and laid it in his lap. There wasn't much room and the boxes between them and the front meant that besides a muttered 'how you doin',' they didn't talk with the wagon drivers.

He leaned back, exhausted. Maybe he'd had an hour's sleep, if he was lucky. The horses' hooves sounded loud in the narrow confines of the tunnel, and the flickering light from the lanterns only illuminated a few feet in front of the wagon. He could only see where they had been, not where they were going. Could be a metaphor for this entire miserable trip, he thought. Never quite sure of what the hell they were getting into, only sure of what was behind them.

'Carl?' she asked.

'Hmmm?'

'You're awfully quiet,' she said. 'What's wrong?'

Everything, he thought. Everything is wrong, and everything I've thought about you seems to be wrong. From knowing that Merl Sawson was a vet to the hidden radio in the satchel, it's all wrong. Just who in hell are you, Sandy Price? And are you here, like your countrymen, the paratroopers, to do a job? And what kind of job? To report back on what you've learned about the hidden city, about where the people lived, what their defenses are like?

He squeezed her hand, managed a smile. 'I'm all right. I'm just tired, that's all.'

She squeezed back, and he kept on looking behind them, at the narrow railway and the shadows that played on the curving cement walls.

As when they had been in the airshaft, he sensed the change in the air at first – a slight breeze or draft coming their way. He sat up and turned his head, and saw lights ahead. He could also hear the faint hum of machinery and the sound of people's voices. The pace of the horses picked up, as if they could sense that the end of the trip was near. Sandy said, 'Are we there?'

'I think so.'

She yawned. 'It must be five A.M. My God, I can hardly wait to sleep a full eight hours in a real bed.'

'Soon,' he said. 'Soon. But first we need to get out of here.'

And quick, he thought. How long before we're back in Boston? A day, maybe two, if everything goes right? Then a few days left, a handful of hours, to stop the killing that was going to happen next week. Jesus. And no sir, we're not going back to the *Globe*. Imagine what it would be like, seeing Cullen Devane again after this trip. He was sure the major had lots of interesting plans for Carl Landry, none of them good.

The handler to the right turned back at them and said, 'Almost there, folks. You get ready to step lively. The depot's a busy place and they like to unload us quick.'

The wagon drew closer to the lights and Carl saw a hand-made sign bolted to a rusting girder, illuminated by electric lights. WELCOME TO HOBOKEN. THE CITY THAT WOULDN'T QUIT. Then they were surrounded by a rush of activity, and they entered a wide place in the tunnel, with platforms, wagons and handcarts, and people moving around, unloading boxes and moving them onto the platforms. A couple of men with rifles were posted at the tunnel entrance, and they nodded to the wagon drivers. The wagon halted and he helped Sandy off, both of them stepping down onto the dirty concrete floor. There was a set of stairs built into the platform, and he helped her up.

About four or five men unloaded the wagon. A heavyset man with a coat that flapped about his ankles, holding a clip-board, directed the work. Carl went up to him and passed over the folded piece of paper that Jim Rowley had given them.

'We'd like to see the mayors,' Carl said. 'The sooner, the better.'

The man grunted and handed the piece of paper back. 'So do about half the nuts in this RZ. Hey, Mickey!' he yelled. 'Bring these bozos up to the mayors' office, will ya?'

A young black girl came over, wiping her hands on her jeans. She wore jeans and a much-patched sweatshirt. 'Shit, I've got work to do.'

'Yeah, ain't it the truth. And this is your new job. Get along.'

She made a face and said, 'Follow me, you two. And don't run off.'

They walked with her, and as before in Manhattan, he was stunned at the milling amount of work and activity that was going on in these tunnels and subway stations. And Jim had said it was happening elsewhere in the country as well, in the supposedly empty Restricted Zones that surrounded the blast areas where the bombs had fallen. A hard life, of course, but one that was more free than in the rest of the country, if you stayed out of the Army's way.

It made sense. The RZ communities were a safety valve, a place were the misfits and the rebellious and the draft dodgers and Kennedy Administration survivors and those who really believed in the Constitution could live. And the powers that be let them stay here, because it made everything else easier if all the dissidents were in one place. This type of existence could last another decade or two, except for one thing.

Resurrection Day. These Americans were deciding to rejoin the nation, and the nation wasn't ready to accept them.

He kept his eye on Sandy, seeing the bright look in her face as she took everything in. He felt something cold inside of him, something he had not felt since California, when he was exposed on a hillside, alone, with gunfire tearing up the ground around him from a barricaded ranch house. Exposed. A hell of a feeling.

It wasn't a long walk, and after a few minutes up concrete tunnels and pedestrian ways, and showing the paper from Jim Rowley to two more frowning men, and leaving their belongings and the holstered pistol behind, they entered an office that was luxurious compared to Jim's. There were two wooden desks with leather chairs, an Oriental rug, and a side bar. Bright lights illuminated the office and there were two men sitting behind the desks, both wearing white shirts and skinny black ties. It sure was amusing, he thought. They were the first clean shirts and ties he had seen in days.

The man on the left was smoking and drinking a cup of what looked like tea, and his black hair was cut in a fine crewcut. His companion was balding, but sported a thick black mustache. The man with the mustache looked at their letter of introduction. 'That's good words from Jim,' he said. 'And that counts for somethin' over here. I take it you're Carl Landry and you're Sandy Price. It says here you're both writers, and Jim's asked me to help you folks.'

'That's right,' she said. 'We're on an assignment from the *Times* of London and we're trying to get to Philadelphia.'

The other man was silent, and the man with the mustache scratched at the back of his head. 'Well, I think we might be able to pull something off. Feel like a walk?'

'As long as it gets us going.'

'It sure will. Let's head out.'

They left the office and Carl and Sandy retrieved their gear and shouldered their knapsacks. 'By the by, my name is Tony Sculley,' one of the two men said as they retraced their earlier steps. 'I'm co-mayor of this burg.' He hooked a thumb at his companion, walking with a teacup in his hand. 'The strong silent type over there is my partner in crime. Yuri Malenkov.'

Yuri nodded. 'Pleased, I'm sure,' he said, with a trace of a Russian accent. Carl stopped and found himself staring at the Russian. If Tony had said the co-mayor had come from the moon, he would have found it as likely.

Sandy spoke up, her voice almost squeaking. 'I'm sorry, are you Russian?'

A tired nod and a sip from the teacup. 'Da. And congratulations, my miss. You are probably the ten thousandth person to ask me that since I arrived here.'

Carl found his voice. 'Embassy. Were you on the embassy staff in New York City when the war started? How in hell did you end up as co-mayor?'

Tony held up his hands. 'Folks, here's the story, but you've got to promise not to print it. It'd cause too much problems. Do I have a deal?'

'Well,' Sandy began cautiously. Carl nudged her with his elbow, not wanting to upset anyone or hold up their trip for any reason. 'You've got a deal,' he said.

Tony smiled and they resumed walking, heading down the concrete corridor. He said, 'You'll see why we'd like to keep things quiet. I'm a former Air Force captain, and most people would probably consider me a deserter. You see, I came back from my mission and I sort of ended up here, looking for my family instead of reporting to a superior officer. Yuri here is a former lieutenant in the former Soviet Air Force and a hell of a nice guy, but there are a lot of people out there – not in this city but elsewhere – who'd probably like to kill him, just for the hell of it.'

Even a decade after the war, Carl was surprised at what was struggling inside of him. Part of him saw the thin man as the enemy, the source of all that had happened, the source of the destruction and the death and disease and starvation. But another part of him was looking at the tired and lined eyes, realizing this man was a horrible living example of the character in the Philip Nolan story, a man truly without a country.

'What was your mission?' Carl asked.

Tony laughed and said, 'Even ten years later, it's hard to believe. I was in Europe, in a top secret squadron called 510. We flew F-100s, single-seat jets.'

'Fighters?'

'Nope,' Tony said. 'Bombers.'

'Oh,' Sandy said, her voice quiet.

'Ah, yes, "oh,"' he said, shaking his head. 'The favorite

phrase of someone meeting a bomber pilot for the first time. Well, lady, I hate to use an old and dishonored phrase, but we were following orders. And my target, at least, was a military target. I wasn't a city buster.'

'Tony, please,' Yuri started, but the other man waved him off as they started down a set of stairs.

'No, no, these are reporters and, this being the tenth anniversary of that fuck-up, maybe they can use this as background. You see, our F-100s each carried a single bomb, a lovely little five-megaton device. You know what our mission profile was? We were stationed at a base in West Germany, and when the balloon went up, we went deep into the Warsaw Bloc, flying about fifty to a hundred feet above the ground, trying to evade their radar. Then when we got near the target point we'd pull back on the stick, fly straight up, and release the bomb. It traveled about two miles in a big arc, if you can believe it, and while that happened, I turned tail and headed back west, before the explosion. Barely made it, but I did. Pretty sure I took out the target.'

'And what was your target?' Sandy asked.

He shrugged his shoulders and opened a set of double doors that led into the ground floor of a warehouse filled with shelves and bustling people. Some were moving handcarts of crates and boxes. 'Hell, it wasn't much of anything. A reserve Soviet Air Force base in northern Ukraine. Probably nothing there except some old propeller bombers from World War II, but it was a target nonetheless. Had to have targets, you understand. You know how many nuclear warheads we had in our arsenals back in '62? Care for a guess? No? Well, try more than twenty thousand. And if you had twenty thousand warheads, you had to find a place to use them. We had planners in the Air Force back then, they were targeting cow pastures, calling them alternate landing fields. That's how crazy it was.'

Yuri spoke up. 'But at least you survived, Tony. Not many in your squadron could say that.'

Carl said, 'I've read about the Soviet Air Defense system. It must have been tough.'

Tony laughed. 'Didn't see a damn part of the Soviet Air Defense system. Everything that happened was according to plan. You see, our jets, we didn't have enough fuel to get back to base. That was also part of the plan. After we delivered our warhead, we'd fly back west as far as we could, staying away from major population centers and military targets, and when we bingoed – ran out of fuel – we'd eject and start walking home, using escape and evasion techniques.'

Carl was speechless and Sandy, too, was quiet. Tony laughed as they strode across the warehouse floor. 'You guys look like you've seen a ghost. Well, a couple of times, I sure as hell thought I was going to become a ghost. I survived the ejection, which was thankful in and of itself, and then I landed in a forest in Poland. Started walking west, and kept going. Ate a lot of potatoes, slept in a few hay fields. Got rid of my flight clothes and got some civvies. Made it through Poland and East Germany, and thought I had it made when I got back to West Germany. Just get back to base and head into debriefing. But by the time I got there, everything was gone, and I mean everything. General Curtis had brought everyone home, and being an American right about then – especially an Air Force officer – was not very popular. So I walked a little more, to Denmark, and took myself on a cargo ship bringing Americans out of the country. By then I had long hair and a beard, and I convinced everyone I was a beatnik who'd lost his passport. Got to Maine and then decided that the months I spent walking used up my term of service, so I came south here, to try to find my wife.' His eyes furrowed and he frowned at the memory. 'I guess you could say I'm still looking. But one thing I did find' – and he smiled as he gestured to the man walking next to him – 'was this guy, an ex-commie running some of the neighborhoods in Hoboken. Can you believe that?'

'I can, but it's hard to,' Carl said, hearing the disbelief in his voice. 'You . . . you were on the Bear bomber that was shot down over New Jersey, right?'

Yuri nodded. 'True. My story is not as exciting as Tony's.' He smiled weakly as they approached another set of doors. 'All my life, I wanted to come to America, to see it for myself. I learned English in school and practiced with my brothers, in Moscow. Then, in 1962, my dream comes true. I come to America. But it is not how I planned it, for I came over as a navigator for the TU-95.'

He repeated himself, emphasizing the words as he opened the doors which led outside. 'You understand that? The navigator. Not the bombardier.' Yuri glanced over at Tony. 'Like my friend Tony, here, I was a young man following old men's orders. We had our mission to do, and we did it. And I will not speak of it further. I am sorry for what happened here, just as I am sure Tony is sorry for what happened to my country. When my bomber was shot down over New Jersey, I was separated from the rest of the crew, which was later to prove to be a blessing.'

They were outside now, on a wide loading dock. Yuri grimaced at the memory. 'The copilot, he was not a good man. His name was Leonid. A cruel man. But he did not deserve to die the way he did, hung from a tree. Those weeks and months after I parachuted out, I lived by my wits here in this Restricted Zone, until I began organizing the people in the blocks of houses nearby. They were sick and they were starving, and they did not care much of where I was from. They only cared that I helped, that I was able to do things for them.'

Tony spoke up. 'Yuri was an organizer from way back, a Young Communist. True?'

'A Komsomol member, true, but everyone then was required to join the youth groups. I was no different.' He sipped from his teacup and said, 'Now there are no more communists. Just survivors. I helped one survivor, and then another. We got food, medical supplies. We started trading with other buildings, other towns. When they saw who I was, face to face, they were no longer scared of me or my country.'

His eyes suddenly betrayed him. 'My country. One of these days, I will return. I may be an old man and there may only be a square kilometer of unburnt ground, but one of these days, I will return to my Russia.'

About fifteen minutes later Carl helped Sandy up on the tailgate of an old Ford pickup truck, its fenders rusting and dented. The windshield had long ago been broken, and the doors were dented and stained with rust. Yuri had left but Tony was still with them, in the shadow of an old brick warehouse. Seagulls hovered overhead in the gray predawn. Two trucks were being loaded with bundles and crates. Tony shook their hands and said, 'Sorry we couldn't do better for the transport, but this is all we've got here. They're making a delivery through the RZ fence and they have to be on the other side by dawn, before the Army patrols start. They'll drop you off by the delivery spot. Nearest place to catch a bus will be Morristown, and it won't be much of a walk. You could be in Philly by noon.'

'We appreciate your help,' Carl said. 'Have you heard anything from PS 19 since we've gotten here?'

Tony grimaced. 'No, not a word. We have a telegraph line set up between us. We heard about the Zed Force raid but the wire's been dead since after it started.'

Sandy said, 'Those poor people . . .'

'Jim and his folks, they're smart and tough,' Tony said. 'Have to be, to live on that island. You'll see, they'll be all right. I'm sure we'll hear from them in a couple of hours.'

Two young men came up to the truck, dressed in short leather jackets, dungarees, and work boots. They had reddish-brown hair and both had stubble on their faces. Revolvers were holstered at their sides and they nodded politely. Carl looked at them and thought they belonged someplace else, in a different time. Dodge City, perhaps, a hundred years ago.

Tony said, 'This here is Sam and Drew Cooper, your drivers for today. They're originally from Virginia but came up here after they had some problems with the Treasury folks in their home state. Something about illegal whiskey stills, right? They've been doing the out run for almost a year now and know the towns and roads better than most. Guys, you'll get 'em there in one piece, won't you?'

Both men grinned and the one on the left said, 'Does this mean we get a bonus, delivering livestock?'

Tony smiled back at them. 'Not hardly. Now get your butts out of here. This here's important cargo.'

The brothers got into the truck and after a few grinding tries, the engine finally turned over, belching out a thick cloud of smoke. Then the truck sped away, leaving Tony at the loading dock, waving. Carl and Sandy waved, too.

————

The truck made its way slowly through the deserted streets, heading west, and Carl undid one of the blanket rolls from the pack and spread it across their legs. Sandy moved so she was sitting next to him and she said, 'I don't care about the Official Secrets Act, I don't care about my editors. I want to get this story out, Carl. We've got to stop the paras from going in.'

Do you, he wondered, thinking again about the radio. 'Even if you do get the story out, what then? Official denial, Sandy. Your government will deny anything is going on, if it suits them. You know how governments work. Don't be naive.'

She shot back, 'I don't like being called naive, Carl.'

He kept silent as the truck made its way through the deserted streets. The roads weren't as crowded with abandoned vehicles as Manhattan, which made sense. There were more roads leading out of here than there would be on an island with a handful of bridges and tunnels. They passed shuttered factories and brick warehouses, faded signs that advertised storage and electrical motor works and plastic manufacturing. A few dogs scampered by, one limping on three legs.

Sandy spoke up. 'You know, you must be proud.'

'Of what?'

'Of what your people have done, all of the things that they accomplished,' she said. 'When we were debriefed by the generals, the way they talked about the Restricted Zones, you would think that they were deserted, that no one dared live there anymore. But we found quite the opposite, Mr. Landry. These places are alive, they are vital, and they're not giving up. When all is taken care of, you should put this in your book. About the generals' lies.'

Carl said nothing, his hands clenched underneath the blanket, and the truck bumped along on its way. The sky grew lighter, and dawn was only a few minutes away. He looked again at the deserted streets but saw something else in his mind. He thought about streets filled with uniformed soldiers with gas masks, crowds of civilians gasping for breath and being herded forward into trucks or buses for the long trip to a decon camp. Snipers on the rooftops, firing back, the opening shots of another civil war. He was very tired, he finally realized, and he didn't want to talk or listen anymore.

'You're not saying anything,' she said.

'That's right.'

'And why is that?'

The truck hit a pothole, and they bounced against some of the crates. 'Proud? What's there to be proud of? Oh, what everyone has done here, in this part of New Jersey and Manhattan, in getting some sort of life together, that's admirable. But in a few weeks, probably, the people who are in charge of this country are going to crush them. With your country's help.'

'Not if I can prevent it,' Sandy said.

The radio. He knew he should confront her about it but he was concerned about her agenda, what she was really doing here. She might deny it all and when they got out of the RZ, the both of them would be picked up by British intelligence. And then what? How could he help Jim if he was being held prisoner?

'You're still not saying anything,' she continued, brushing her hair out of her face. 'I thought you said we were going to do something to help them. And now, nothing. Are you giving up?'

'What do you think this is?' he said suddenly, his exhaustion and fear and suspicions of her all boiling together. 'Some sort of adventure, put on for your benefit, so that you can get material to write about? Like your grandmama, sent into the deepest wilds for a wonderful safari among the poor natives? These are real people out here, people who've survived ten years of poor food, little medicine, and lousy shelter. They're not here for your entertainment, so the *Times* can print a glowing story about "our correspondent" who saved them.'

They were now in a residential area, with small houses separated from each other by nicely sized yards. Walls of shrubbery – free from years of pruning – nearly overgrew some of the houses, and the lawns were a brown, waist-high tangle of weeds and saplings.

'You're not being fair,' she said sharply. 'I've never said anything of the sort, not once. Why are you so angry? Can't you trust me to get things done?'

'Trust,' he said, feeling his voice get louder. 'Let's talk about trust, all right, let's—'

And an explosion at the front of the truck blinded him, and his world turned upside down and went black.

TWENTY-THREE

HIS HEAD HURT. His back hurt. And his legs . . . God, how his legs hurt.

He heard voices and opened his eyes. Everything was blurry and gray and black, and he blinked a few times.

'Carl? Carl, can you hear me?'

Sandy and one of the two brothers were looking down at him. He tried to move and said, 'ah, shit,' before falling back again. Something big and heavy was pinning his legs. He was on his back in a drainage ditch, rocks and tree branches digging into his back, and in front of him was the overturned shape of the pickup truck, its front end crumpled and torn. Boxes and crates were scattered around on the roadway and the side of the truck was jammed into the ditch, resting on its side, and holding his legs firmly in place.

'Christ, what a mess,' he said. 'What the hell happened?'

One of the brothers had his revolver out, his voice quavering. 'We was ambushed, that's what. A charge in the road knocked the truck clear off. Raiders, they must have set it, and they gotta be around. They'll be here real quick.'

The other brother came down into the ditch, a handkerchief held to his bloody face, a revolver in his hand. 'Drew, man, we gotta get the hell outta here. The raiders'll be here any second.'

Sandy yelled, 'We can't leave!'

'Miss—' one of them said, and she scrambled up the ditch. 'Come on, there's got to be something around here to get that truck off of him! Some rope or a lever, something!'

Drew ran up after Sandy and the other brother, Sam, knelt down beside Carl, blood dripping down his wrist. Carl took a breath, tried to tell if anything else besides his legs and back ached, but couldn't.

Sam said, 'Your legs broke?'

'Can't tell,' Carl said, his voice labored. 'They sure as hell are stuck, though.'

'Ain't that the truth,' Sam said.

'You okay? What's with your face?'

Sam said, 'I hit my head against the steering wheel when the charge lit off. I must've broke my nose.'

From up on the roadway he could hear Sandy yelling at Drew about going back for help. Sam sighed and said, 'Mister, I'm sorry, but there ain't no way we're getting this truck off of you. We'd need a tow rig or a couple of horses. And the raiders—'

Carl nodded, gritted his teeth at the pain. 'Yeah, I know the raiders, they're probably coming. And I also know that this truck isn't going anywhere. How far are you from the RZ border?'

'Oh, about a half hour, an hour if we be extra cautious.'

Damn, that hurt, he thought, as spasms raced up both legs. 'Then be extra cautious. Take Sandy and get her the hell out of here. She's a reporter and a British subject. She doesn't belong here. You protect her and get her to Morristown safely, and I'll see that you both get rewarded.'

Sam coughed up some blood. 'That's a hell of a thing to say, and I'd try to argue with ya, but I can't. You're making a lot of sense, and I'm sorry about that.' He turned away and yelled, 'Drew! Hey, Drew! Get on back here!'

The other brother came skidding down the side of the embankment, trailed by Sandy, her face set, her hair in disarray. Carl tried to move again and gritted his teeth. Sandy knelt down by him and he took her hand. 'Carl,' she started, 'look, there has to be a way—'

'Sandy, please—'

'No, no, there has to be—'

'Damn it, shut up!' he said, not liking the look on her face at all, the shock of being yelled at.

Drew and Sam stood by, almost shuffling their feet in embarrassment at what was going on in front of them. Carl took a deep breath and squeezed Sandy's hand tight. 'There is no time. Do you understand, Sandy? There is no time.'

She bit her lip and lowered her eyes, tears trembling down her cheeks. Carl continued, feeling the weight on his legs, the weight everywhere, the burden of what he was trying to do and of being with a woman that he was beginning to love and couldn't even trust.

'You've got to get going. These guys will get you over the fence and into Morristown. When you're in a safe place – like the bus depot – call the local Army station. Tell them I'm here and they'll send in a rescue squad. I'm sure of it. Tell them I'm an on-duty Army sergeant, and they'll take care of the rest.'

'But that'll take hours!' she said, tears streaming down her cheeks.

He squeezed her hand again. 'And the longer you stay

here, the longer it will take. Now. Where's my pack?'

Eager to do something, Drew came forward, holding out Carl's knapsack. He reached in and took out the camera and exposed rolls of film. 'Here's what you need. Get going, will you? I'll be all right.'

Sam spoke up. 'He's right, miss, you know he's right. We gotta get going.'

Carl reached into the pack again and moved his hand around, feeling for a familiar object. He pulled out his pistol and rested it on his chest. 'I'll be just fine. Now, go, Sandy, will you? You don't belong here.'

She brought a hand up and tucked her hair back behind her ears. Her voice was a whisper. 'Oh God, Carl, I think I'm falling in love with you.'

She kissed him gently on his lips, and he raised his head just a fraction, returning the slight pressure. A moment passed, as he thought about the hidden radio and all his questions about her, but he let it go. There was no time.

'And me with you, Sandy,' he said. 'Now. Please.'

'The Savoy, remember?' she said, her voice still quiet.

'I remember. And Harrods, too. Now get going.'

The brothers gently grasped her arms, not only to help her get back up the embankment, but also to get her on her way. He watched as they clambered up the steep, grass-strewn bank, and at the top, she made a motion to look back one more time, but the brothers wouldn't let her wait, and in a moment or two, they were gone.

Even with the sun rising, it felt cold but with some difficulty, he managed to get his blanket roll free from his knapsack and draped it over his chest and waist. He tried to move his legs, grimacing each time he failed. He clawed at the dirt, trying to dig himself out, but the soil was cold and hard-packed, and he ended up scraping the tips of his fingers raw and not achieving anything else. He lay back, breathing hard. He moved the pistol out from under the blanket and put it within easy reach.

So. He felt cold anger and dismay and sorrow, and he wondered about Jim Rowley, back at PS 19, hiding in the tunnels and hoping and praying that Carl Landry was going to do right and come to the rescue. Sorry, Jim, he thought. Ten years ago you placed your trust in grown-ups, and look what happened. Ten years later, you again trust an adult, and here he lies, an easy target, unable to help you or anyone else among the free people left in this country.

Another spasm of pain raced up his legs, and he closed his eyes, imagining what was going on elsewhere. Somewhere, the plans were being finalized, the decon camps were being prepared, and the British troops were practicing, again and again, how to subdue a civilian population. In a matter of weeks, it would be over, Rockefeller would be elected and the anschluss would take place, and this country would be ruled from London instead of Philadelphia.

George Dooley, he thought. Good ole George Dooley, back at the *Globe,* upset that every four years, a dictator continued to be elected again and again, until such time as the voters never knew anything else, never knew a world without martial law and decon camps and censorship. And soon, they would never know that this country – for all its problems and faults – was once independent. As Caz's brother had put it, the survivors write the history books, and soon no one would ever remember the words of that dead president, that this country was once a beacon of freedom for so many.

There had been one last opportunity, a small chance, to prevent this continuing journey into darkness, and it had been destroyed just a few minutes ago, with that damn explosion.

What a waste, he thought, trying not to move, trying to ignore the steady pressure on his legs. In the Army he had sometimes wondered – especially in Vietnam and in California – if this day, if this particular day, was going to be his last. If on this day, the Jesus bolt at the top of the helicopter engine assembly would let loose and he would die in a rice paddy as the copter crashed in. If on this day, a hand grenade from a Viet Cong sympathizer would be tossed into an outdoor café in Saigon. Or if on this day, a sniper from a farmer's militia unit would drill through his forehead as he patrolled the high hills of San Diego County.

Well, he never thought that last day would be in New Jersey, and he allowed himself a small laugh.

He moved again, trying to find a more comfortable position, and after a while, decided there was no such thing as a comfortable position. To pass the time he wondered how long he had been lying there, how many minutes and hours, and where – at this moment – Sandy might be. If all went well, she should be in Morristown by now, making that phone call. And how would the call be received? An anonymous tip that an Army sergeant was trapped in a Restricted Zone. Would that mean a fast and furious response, an APC and a couple of Jeeps roaring down these dead streets?

Or would the guy on the other end of the phone make a few scratches on a notepad and pass it along to someone else, who would pass it along to someone else, and then – maybe today or maybe tomorrow – the regular patrol would be asked to check things out if it had enough time.

Time. He wondered what time it was. His watch had stopped.

And he thought about something else, something that chilled him even more. He imagined Sandy going to a pay phone, and instead of calling the Army, calling her embassy. Or maybe she would use her radio. And report that their plans had been discovered, the plans to bring in British troops to suppress civilians, and instead of this awfulness being prevented, it would happen even faster.

And then she might hang up the phone or switch off the radio, and try to forget about Carl Landry, slowly dying of thirst under a truck in the New Jersey RZ.

Something moved up at the embankment. His hand went to the holster and he unsnapped it and brought out the pistol.

A head appeared, and another. Two skinny dogs looked down and growled.

'Go away,' he said, putting the pistol down and throwing a rock up at them. 'It's not your time, not yet.'

The dogs moved away. Time. Of course, everything he had just imagined, about how long it would take for Sandy to get out of the RZ, that all revolved around one big assumption. That everything had gone well. That the brothers had indeed brought her out of the RZ, and hadn't retreated back to Hoboken, or been hung up on the fence anywhere. And if Sandy had only made one phone call, to the British Embassy . . .

Voices.

Carl heard voices up on the roadway, and the sound of an engine. He grabbed the pistol and then brought it under the blanket, letting it rest on his chest. Two, and then three men appeared at the top of the embankment, and they started laughing, and then everything was even more uncomfortable.

The taller of the three seemed to be the leader. He scampered down the side of the ditch like it was a fun little obstacle course. He was dressed in black jeans, knee-high boots, and a large cattleman-style coat. He wore a Western-style holster that held two holstered revolvers low about his hips, his dark brown hair was pulled back in a ponytail, and his goatee was neatly trimmed. His eyes had the merry look of someone who enjoyed collecting freshly chewed animal bones.

'Well, my good friends, it does seem like our trap has caught something today, hasn't it?' he said. He walked around, nudging the crates and bags that had been loaded onto the back of the truck. His companions were shorter and not as neatly dressed, with untrimmed beards and patched coats. They wore fingerless gloves and had long rifles slung over their backs. They laughed along with their leader but their humor was not as confident.

The tall man squatted down near Carl and rubbed at his chin. 'We heard the boom, of course, but we were engaged in other . . . in other business a while back, so we couldn't get over here as quickly as we should have. Sorry about that.'

Carl cleared his throat. 'Well, you could make up for it by getting this damn truck off my legs.'

Now all three of them laughed, and the tall man stood up and said, 'I'm sorry, we can't possibly do that. You see' – and he spread his arms out for emphasis – 'this happens to be our little playground, to do with as we please, and what we please to do is show no mercy. You understand? This is where we can do anything, anything we want, and nobody can stop us. My word, the stories I could tell.'

He stepped back and drew his coat back, reaching for a revolver. 'I hope you do understand, that I don't have time for you or any of your stories.'

Carl watched as the man raised the revolver. Carl said, 'Sure, I understand,' and he shot the man in the chest, pistol still hidden under his blanket. The man's eyes bulged and his mouth opened in a wide O. Carl threw the tattered blanket away and tried for the two other men, who were racing up the embankment, slung rifles bouncing on their backs. He shot one more time, the pistol bucking in his hands, but he was tired and his aim was off and the other men got over the edge of the embankment and were gone.

He looked back at the raider, who was on his back, arms splayed out, not moving. A breeze fluttered his coat flaps. Carl coughed and said, 'That's what you get for talking too much, you nitwit.'

Carl looked around, the pistol in his hand, trying to see if the two other men had really left, or if they were coming back for revenge. Couldn't hardly blame them. Looking again at the dead raider, he wondered who the real nitwit was. Shit. That hadn't been too bright, not at all. He didn't feel guilt for what he had just done – too many other feelings were fighting for attention, from a dry mouth to an empty stomach to a full bladder that was demanding release, to the worsening throbbing in his lower legs – but he did feel pretty stupid.

'Idiot,' he whispered, moving his head around and looking from side to side. Didn't have to shoot him right off. Could have drawn him down, could have talked him out of what he was about to do, could have bribed him and his hairy companions to get the truck off of him for a big payoff. Wouldn't have been hard to do. Wouldn't have been hard to follow through. But no, he had to overreact, had to go for the pistol, right off the bat.

Damn it, was that the curse of his people, to always reach for the weapon, whether it was a stick or a pistol or a nuclear-armed B-52 Stratofortress?

He closed his eyes. Suddenly he felt faint.

The sound of a shot and the *wheee!* of a ricochet near his head got his attention. He responded automatically, firing twice up at the embankment. There was laughter in response.

'Hey, asshole!' came a voice. 'Start counting your breaths, 'cause you ain't got too many left!'

He blinked his eyes, he blinked his eyes again, and still, everything was blurry. It felt like the damn earth under him was starting to rotate at a slow and heavy speed. Everything was moving off-kilter. Damn, was this it? He got off another shot and then another. There was a loud roaring noise and a long, rattling fusillade of shots erupted all around him, and he closed his eyes and willed his body to stop spinning.

For a while, it seemed to work.

There were voices in the darkness. Then came the sweet feeling of his legs being released and then a bouncing sensation. He blinked his eyes open and saw what looked like giant bugs staring down at him. They were dressed in green with large, bulbous heads. One of them extended a black claw at him and gently probed his mouth. He suckled at some water and blinked again. The scent was what brought him back, of old and worn canvas and aviation fuel and the sweat-smells of men who had worked and flew in this machine, this great green and wonderful helicopter.

He closed his eyes again.

He awoke in a bed, with clean and white and crisp sheets against his body. He coughed and wiped at his eyes, grainy with sleep and debris. He gingerly moved his legs, felt the sheets scratch against his skin. He slowly sat up and flipped the blanket and the sheets off. His lower legs were there. They were bruised black, blue, and green, and had bandages on them, but they were there. He swung them off the bed and stood up unsteadily. His stomach grumbled and he was thirsty and he wondered where in hell he was, but he looked down at his legs. They were still there.

He was wearing his shorts, and he saw that the rest of his clothes were folded in a chair by the bed. The room was carpeted and good sized, with beige wallpaper and a framed print of some trees and a meadow. There was a bureau and a nightstand, and on the nightstand was a phone. He picked it up, but there was no dial tone. He tried the door. Locked. There was a window by the other wall, and another door. That door opened to a bathroom, complete with toilet and shower. He went over to the window. He couldn't open it. He could see that he was on the first floor of whatever building he was in, and that it was sunny outside. The window overlooked a green lawn, bordered by white fences. It looked like a farmhouse somewhere, maybe in upstate New York, and there was a low roaring noise as he saw an Army helicopter swoop overhead and head out to the far woods, rising in altitude.

Well, the Army had sure done and got him, and for that he was grateful.

But then he glanced back at the locked door and the silent phone.

He stayed in the shower for almost a half hour, not even

remembering the last time he had bathed. It must have been back in the hotel room in Manhattan, the morning of that disastrous tour through the empty streets. The hot water and soap felt wonderful on his skin as days' worth of grease and dirt washed away. He was careful of his legs, though. Then he shaved, and enjoyed seeing the stubble disappear from his face.

Carl was surprised at what was waiting for him in the bedroom: a meal cart, not unlike that from a hotel. He raised the metal dish covers and found scrambled eggs, toast, pancakes, sausage, and bacon, along with a tall glass of orange juice and a small pot of coffee. He supposed he could have done the noble thing and ignored the meal. Or the paranoid thing and ignored the meal.

Instead he did the reasonable thing, which was to sit on his bed and eat everything, too hungry even to get dressed first. And as he ate, he looked carefully around the room, looking for the telltales, the little signs that he was under surveillance.

When he was finished and had dressed, Carl checked the phone again. No dial tone. He tried the door. Still locked. He went over to the window. It was sealed on all sides. Fair enough. Carl went back to the bed and tore off the sheets and flipped over the mattress and box spring. The metal frame was not screwed or bolted together and he managed to kick one of the side frames out and picked it up. It was metal, heavy, and about six feet long. Perfect.

He went to the window and drew open the shades and then crossed back to the other side of the room, pacing off where he would start and how far he would get before he could punch the metal frame through the glass. He held the frame firm in his hands, took a series of deep breaths, and—

The door opened. A man's voice. 'Please, Sergeant Landry, you can put that down.'

Carl turned, the frame still in his hands. A young man in an Air Force uniform stood there, smiling at him. He wore glasses, dark blue trousers, and a blue knit sweater, and had the door propped open with a hand. Carl remembered the soldier he had met, back at the Fence, the young man whose term of service was about to expire. He was about the same age as this airman, but there, the similarities ended. That soldier had had a tired look about his eyes from working among the dead for a long time. This airman had the bright eyes of someone who knew he had comfortable duty, and rather enjoyed it.

Carl didn't smile back. 'I will if you tell me who the hell you are, and where I am.'

'I'm Senior Airman Taft, Sergeant, and—'

'You can call me Mr. Landry,' he said, his tone sharp. 'I'm not on active duty. I'm a writer for the *Boston Globe* and I was working on assignment with the *Times* of London. I want to know where I am, and why I've been kept prisoner.'

The smile didn't fade. 'Last question first, Mr. Landry. You weren't kept prisoner. It was decided that it would be easier for all concerned if you stayed in this room until your appointment was ready. And as for your first question, it will be revealed to you, quite soon.'

He dropped the metal bar to the floor, just to see Senior Airman Taft's reaction, and was pleased to see the young man jump. 'Appointment. I didn't realize I had an appointment.'

'You certainly do,' the airman said, opening the door wider. 'And if you come with me, I'll take you there.'

'Suppose I don't want to go?' he demanded.

Not a waver, not a blink. 'You're a newspaper man now, correct? I'm sure your curiosity will get the better of you. Please, Mr. Landry. Won't you come?'

This time, Carl smiled. 'Sure. Why the hell not.'

He was sure he was in some type of military base, either Air Force or Army, and had expected to see the usual tiled corridor with offices. But the hallway was narrow and paneled and wallpapered, as if he were in some sort of expensive country home. There were old chairs and antique tables set against the wall, and a few tasteful paintings. This was a warm and comfortable place, and in these days of gas rationing and food shortages, Carl was surprised it existed. But then again, why not? This sure had been a week for learning secrets.

'Hell of a prison you got here,' Carl said.

'Oh, it's not bad duty, once you get used to it,' Airman Taft said. 'And the food – as you probably could tell – is pretty good.'

'How long was I out for?'

'Some hours after your rescue this morning, that's all.'

At the end of the corridor was an elevator, and the airman took out a key and opened the sliding door. Carl followed him in and Taft slid shut the metal grate. With another key, he switched on the elevator and they glided up two floors. The door slid open and they went down another corridor, almost identical to the first, and Carl said, 'This is a very nice tour, but it sure isn't telling me anything.'

They stopped at a closed door. 'Oh, you'll see, in about another minute or two,' Airman Taft said. He knocked twice at the door, opened it slightly, and motioned to Carl. 'Go in, why don't you.'

'Somehow, Senior Airman, I think that decision's already been made for me,' he said.

He stepped through the doorway and found himself in a study or a library. There were two walls of built-in bookshelves, and one wall was covered with framed pictures and certificates. In the center of the study was a large desk, and in a corner of the room, near the desk, stood a large globe of the earth. There was a fire crackling in a small fireplace, leather couches and chairs, a wet bar, and another door, set into the wall by the far bookshelf. A floor-to-ceiling window by the desk overlooked the meadow that Carl had seen from his window. He stared at the man who got up from behind the desk and walked toward him. He wore a white turtleneck sweater, khaki pants, and brown loafers, and he was smoking a cigar. His thick hair was black, streaked with gray, and he had thick eyebrows, also streaked with gray.

Carl took a deep breath. He had seen this man before, just a few days ago, on the television, back in Boston.

General Ramsey Curtis, U.S. Air Force, Retired.

General Curtis stopped before him, stuck out a hand. 'You're Landry, right?'

Carl shook the man's hand. 'Yes, sir, that I am.'

He motioned to a seat. 'Sit down, why don't you. We've got a lot to cover.'

Carl nodded. 'I guess we do.'

TWENTY-FOUR

THE GENERAL MOVED BACK BEHIND HIS DESK. 'Welcome to Pennsylvania, to my retirement home and final duty station. How're the legs?'

'They're all right,' Carl said, not taking his eyes off the older man. 'They feel pretty sore. But I'm lucky to still have them attached to my knees.'

General Curtis nodded as he sat down. 'When my boys got there, I think you were pretty lucky to still have a head attached to your shoulders. There were a couple of raiders up on the road, taking potshots at you. And I'm told that you took care of one of them yourself. Good work.'

'Wasn't work,' he said. 'It was just something I had to do.'

The general ashed his cigar in a large crystal ashtray. 'Probably wondering why you're here, and why we kept you under such close watch. Door locked, no phone, crap like that. Am I right?'

'That you are, sir.' Carl found it hard to keep focused, with everything that was going on in his mind. This was the infamous General Ramsey Curtis, the man who had once led SAC and the forces that had killed millions. And this was the famous General Ramsey Curtis, the man who helped end the Cuban War before it spread further, and who had helped the country in its first years of recovery. One man, two stories, many contradictions.

General Curtis. Who was supporting Nelson Rockefeller in the upcoming election. And who must know about the plan to bring in British troops to clear out the RZs. And who was focusing his attention on Carl Landry. Carl now knew what it was like to be a tiny field mouse and see the shadow of a descending hawk appear.

'First, standard procedure,' the general went on. 'Wanted to give you time to clean up, shower and eat before we got down to business. Second, you're here because you're a valuable man, Sergeant Landry. A very valuable man.'

He swallowed, his throat quite dry. 'I'm afraid I don't see your point.'

The general nodded. 'You've been a man in trouble, ever since that Merl Sawson case, back in Boston. Am I right?'

'I don't know if I'd use the word "trouble"—'

'Oh, I would,' the general said, tapping another bit of gray ash into the crystal ashtray. 'You poke around where you don't belong. You didn't listen to your city editor, and you didn't listen to your oversight editor. You were suspended. And if that isn't trouble enough, you get on a trip to Manhattan and damn near get yourself killed and a British national along with you. Not to mention a fine young Army officer. All because you wouldn't let the Merl Sawson matter drop. I tell you, if you were in SAC and had tried that shit, you would have been up at a radar station in Point Barrow so fast it'd make your ears bleed.'

Carl tried to keep his voice even. 'I was just trying to find out why he was murdered.'

The general puffed on his cigar. 'Good God, man, don't you think that's what we want to know, as well?'

His head was starting to pound. 'General, I don't mean any disrespect, but what do you mean by "we"?'

A thin smile. 'I've been retired as chairman of the Joint Chiefs for more than a year, but I still get called in now and then for advice, and my advice is very nearly always taken. Much to the dismay of the people at your newspaper and others, I know. Still, I revert back to form when I talk, and that's what I meant by we. Members of the military and intelligence community, who want to know more about you and Merl Sawson.'

His head pounded louder. 'Sir? What was that?'

'Merl Sawson. Don't you think we want to know what the hell was going on with him up in Boston and in Manhattan?' The general leaned over the desk, eyes flashing. 'Damn it, man, Major Devane back at the *Globe*, he was trying to save your ass when he got you pulled off that story. And then you had to go to Manhattan, where your ass almost gets shot off again by the same people who killed poor Colonel Sawson. Major Devane even went to Manhattan to look for you.'

Carl kept quiet, his eyes staring straight ahead at the general, knowing the proper nature of his answers was going to be his only way out of this place.

'I suppose that wasn't what you were thinking, Sergeant, am I right?' the general asked. 'You probably thought that Colonel Sawson was killed by the so-called dark forces within our government. The same dark forces that chased you around Manhattan. The same dark forces that that fool McGovern says he's running against this November. Am I right?'

'In Manhattan,' Carl said, his voice quiet. 'After the sniper.

We were ambushed a second time. By what looked to be a Special Forces or Zed Force unit.'

'You're an intelligent young man. How hard would it be for you or anyone else to get uniforms on the black market. A day? Two days?'

'If that.'

'Right. And if you're in the hire of certain foreign governments, it'd probably be sooner, correct?' the general asked.

'Colonel Sawson's death and the shootings in Manhattan, they were done by foreign intelligence agencies? Why?'

Another tap on the ashtray. 'If I tell you, Sergeant, then you're back in the active reserve, I'm afraid. This is highly classified, highly restricted information. But I need to bring you into my confidence, because of what you might know, and I'll only feel comfortable if you agree to be back in the active reserve. Temporarily, of course.'

'Of course,' he said, wondering if the general could sense the sarcasm.

Apparently not.

'Good,' he said, wiping a bit of errant ash from the immaculate desktop. 'What do you know about Colonel Sawson?'

Carl shrugged. 'He lived alone, was retired from the Army, and worked at the White House during the Kennedy Administration.'

'Have you heard that he might have been in the possession of . . . of some sensitive documents?'

'No, I haven't,' Carl lied. A voice was telling him to be on guard. This is a man who is a veteran of World War II and Korea, and thinks he fought and won a nuclear war all by himself, saving the nation and the world in the process.

'Well, he was, and that's what got him killed. First, forget Colonel Sawson always being at the White House. He was there for a while, temporarily, but he had other duties in the DC area, duties that eventually got him killed this month. And that's why we believe you were almost killed in Manhattan. Our adversaries seem to believe that you either know what Colonel Sawson has, or where he has it hidden.'

'Adversaries? Who are our adversaries? France? Japan?'

A sage nod from the general. 'And Germany. And even some of our so-called friends in Great Britain. They like to call themselves the First World, don't they? The once mighty Soviet Union is nothing but a giant refugee camp, and the once mighty United States is barely among the Second World countries.' He leaned forward over the desk, and his eyes flashed. 'And they want to keep us that way, for a very long time. And what Colonel Sawson had was something that could help us regain our proper role in the world.'

'And what did Colonel Sawson have?'

The general leaned back in his chair, holding the cigar in his hand, like a loaded pistol. 'Before I answer that, indulge me for a moment, will you?'

What choice do I have, he thought, and he said, 'Go right ahead, General.'

A satisfied nod. 'Fine. I always find I make myself more clear when I'm conducting a briefing. So. Your own personal treat. A one-on-one briefing by the old mad general himself.' He grinned and took a satisfied puff from his cigar. 'I know reporters from the Los Angeles Times and the New York Times and the Chicago Tribune who would love to be in that chair right now.'

'Lucky me,' Carl said, wondering what was going on behind the cigar smoke and the glassy eyes.

'Yes,' he said, without a trace of irony. 'Lucky you, and lucky us. During the Cuban War, we were as damn lucky as any country in this world, but you wouldn't know it from what people write and say, even ten years later.'

Mom and Dad. Sarah. Two-Tone and Caz and Jim Rowley and PS 19. Carl found his voice. 'Several million Americans dead in the space of a week, that's really hard to assign the word luck to it, don't you think?'

'No, I disagree,' the general said, his voice lower. 'I still think it was pure luck. Look at what might have happened. Khrushchev could have outmaneuvered Kennedy and left the missiles there, and within a few years, the peasants in the Kremlin would be deciding our foreign policy.'

'There might have been an agreement, an understanding to get the missiles out,' Carl said, wondering why he was bothering to debate with a man who had already made up his mind. 'I've heard stories that—'

General Curtis dismissed the sentence with a wave of his hand. 'I've heard the same stories, and they're bullshit. Oh, the eggheads at the State Department were working on something, but all of us knew – every single one of us in the Joint Chiefs – knew that it would eventually come down to a shooting war. A diplomatic agreement would not have worked, not for a moment, and even if it did, all it would have done is to postpone the inevitable, at a higher cost.'

He swiveled in his chair, to allow himself a glance outside. 'War with the Soviet Union was going to happen, one way or another. We were lucky that it happened then, before they had made more progress with their missiles, submarines, and bombers. We took them on and we won. I don't think we could have done that three or four years later. It had to happen. It's unfortunate that it did, but we shouldn't be ashamed at what action we took.'

Carl found that there was a throbbing sensation in his legs

and his temples. 'Millions of Russian civilians died during the war. A lot of people are still ashamed about that.'

A flick of the head. 'Those poor bastards in Russia, they died because they had the unfortunate luck to have been born there instead of someplace else. Millions of Russians died in the First World War, millions died in the Second, millions more were killed by their own government in the 1920s and 1930s. The Cuban War was just the latest in a series of their misfortunes. I'm sorry, I can't change history. But look at what did happen, Sergeant.'

He pointed the cigar for emphasis. 'Where is the menace now, ten years after the war? Is there a Soviet empire, holding down satellite nations in Eastern Europe? No. Is there a communist China, threatening its neighbors in Vietnam, Laos, Burma, Thailand, or India? No. Hell, even Korea is getting back together. You see, we took it on the chin for the world, we made it safe so now everyone can play at business and expanding markets. Good for them. And give us a few more years, and we'll be right back there, cutting deals with the best of them. But something *is* wrong. Something is missing.'

'And what's that?'

'Our history,' he said, his voice now soft. 'Our nation is healing, Sergeant, but we don't have our history. Philadelphia is a fine city and President Romney a fine man, but he's not in the District of Columbia. Washington was much more than our capital. It was the center that held this nation together, and we're still missing that center. And that's what was so important about Colonel Sawson.'

Now the throbbing seemed even worse. 'Sir?'

'His other duties,' the general said. 'He was a Civil Defense liaison officer, working with different departments and agencies, and part of his work was dealing with the

National Archives. One of his last jobs was securing two important pieces of paper, documents that are priceless to his country. Securing those documents before Washington was attacked.'

Carl looked back at the general, remembering again what Merl's landlord had said, about Merl and important papers. Paper and ink. 'The Constitution and the Declaration of Independence?'

A slow nod. 'The same. They were taken out of the National Archives before the bombing, they've been lost for a decade, and Colonel Sawson knew where they were hidden. Lord knows why he kept it secret all these years. There are other pieces of our history from Washington, still scattered across this country, mostly in private hands or second-rate museums. A draft of the Gettysburg Address, in Lincoln's own writing. A wheelchair that once belonged to Roosevelt. Trinkets and bits and pieces of our past. We need to get our history back, our sense as a nation.'

Carl remembered that onetime downstairs neighbor of his, the one that had a gavel used in the U.S. Senate. 'And Colonel Sawson's death . . .'

'Was because of those two documents. And that's why people are after you, Sergeant.'

'So, who are these people?' he asked.

The general put his cigar in the ashtray and opened the top drawer of his desk. He took out a light brown manila envelope and removed several eight-by-ten black-and-white photos and fanned them out in front of him. Carl blinked and looked down and then looked away. A host of emotions were racing through him, emotions of betrayal and distrust and affection and shame, all at once.

'Do you know this woman?' the general asked.

'You know I do.'

'And who is she?'

'She's Sandy Price, of the *Times*,' he said, still refusing to look for any length of time at the surveillance photos, showing Sandy departing from a BOAC airliner, Sandy checking into her hotel, Sandy walking down the streets of Boston, and, finally, Sandy in front of Merl Sawson's apartment building. 'And . . .'

'And what, Sergeant?'

'She's a spy.'

A nod. 'That she is.'

General Curtis put the photos back in the envelope and returned them to his desk drawer. 'This Sandy Price is on assignment from their foreign intelligence service, MI6. We believe she came to Boston to meet with Colonel Sawson, to set up some sort of exchange where he would pass the Declaration of Independence and the Constitution over to MI6 for some sort of consideration. Money and travel out of the United States, most likely. But I don't have to tell you what went wrong. Either the British played rough, or the French or the Germans got to him first.'

Something in Carl sickened at hearing the general. 'And what would the British, or the French, or even the goddam Belgians want with the Declaration of Independence and our Constitution?'

The general picked up his cigar, carefully examined it, and then relit it with a bulky lighter that had an Air Force emblem on its side. 'What they want to do is to influence the next election, that's what. They can read the polls just as well as everybody else. Everyone knows that Rockefeller is a shoo-in,

(

and some of our so-called friends overseas don't like that.'

'Including the British?'

He snapped the lighter shut with a self-satisfied click. 'Some British – including your newspaper friend – and most of the Germans and French. Let's face facts, shall we? The success of our relief and recovery efforts these past ten years has depended on the generosity of succeeding British governments. It's not been easy for them, spending money on us, year after year. Some in their government want to cut us off. And it's not been easy for us either, playing little brother to a big brother. No, not easy at all. But we do what we can to survive.'

The general put the lighter down on the desk. 'With a Rockefeller election, our special relationship with the British will continue. With a McGovern administration, it won't.'

I'm sure, Carl thought with some bitterness. I'm sure you're right. 'And how do the Constitution and Declaration play into that?' he asked.

The general shook his head. 'Can't you see it, Sergeant? Two weeks before the election, McGovern appears on television, holding up the original Declaration of Independence and Constitution, secretly delivered to him by those in Britain who want to leave us alone. Says it's a sign from above that we should return to our roots, return to a time when we were equal among nations, respected for what our nation stood for. To stand alone again. That it's a time to join him in a new crusade, to come home, America. Hell, Sergeant, you're a writer. You could probably do his speech with your eyes closed.'

'And what's the alternative? To have Rockefeller make the same speech, except he'd ask for people to vote straight Republican?'

'No, he'd never do anything like that. If those documents do get found – thanks to you, we hope – nobody would say anything, not until the election was over. Then Rockefeller'd just announce that the government now had them, and that they'd be on display in Philadelphia. We cannot allow the British government to choose our next president. Which is why we need to get those documents first. We need your help in preventing them from falling into the hands of McGovern's campaign.'

Carl blinked hard. First Jim Rowley and now General Ramsey Curtis, all asking for his help. Damn it, Merl, it would have been a hell of a lot easier if you had told me everything right up front, he thought. Out loud he said, 'I think you have the wrong man, general. I've been out of the service for four years. I'm a newspaper reporter now, that's all.'

General Curtis leaned forward, stabbing the air again with the cigar. 'And that's the point, Landry! You're a reporter. You can ask questions, keep on asking questions, when you get back to Boston. You won't have any problems with Major Devane – in fact, he'll be your ally once he knows that you're engaged in a matter of the utmost national security.'

Carl clasped his hands together, mostly to keep them from shaking. 'In other words, go back and look into Colonel Sawson's death again, to see what I can find out.'

A firm nod. 'That's exactly what we want you to do. You can remain in the shadows and do your work, and nobody – not MI6, the German Security Service, or the French Foreign Bureau – will know you're working for us.'

'But there's one other thing,' Carl said.

'The matter of the *Times* woman?'

'Yes.'

The general shrugged. 'That matter is already out of our hands. We've notified her embassy in Philadelphia that she is to depart the country in seven days, for conduct not compatible with her job as a journalist. I understand she's now back in Boston. And I can't see the value of you trying to contact her.'

Again, that conflict of emotions. Betrayal and love, all at the same time. 'I understand.'

The phone on his desk buzzed and the general picked up the receiver. 'All right, I got it.' He put the phone down and stood up. 'Excuse me for a moment, will you?'

'Of course.'

The general went to the nearby side door and opened it up, and Carl could hear some low voices. He leaned forward in his chair and looked through the open door. It led into a sitting room, where a low fire crackled in the fireplace. Men in dark business suits were sitting on leather chairs and couches, talking among themselves, by another large, empty desk. General Curtis stood by the nearest chair, where a man was looking up at him, talking animatedly, moving one hand – the one that didn't hold a brandy snifter – back and forth.

Carl couldn't make out what they were saying but he could see what was going on. The man in the chair glanced through the open door. Dark-rimmed glasses and a ready smile: it was the governor of New York State and Republican presidential candidate Nelson Rockefeller. Then the door gently closed.

Carl took a deep breath. Curtis was an overwhelming presence, a man who seemed to take away all the excess oxygen in a room. He rubbed his hands, got up, and walked around the small office. He was too nervous to sit still, and if he thought he could, he would have run out of this building as fast as possible.

Sure. Escape from one of the most heavily guarded compounds in these United States. How far do you think you'd get?

Instead, he looked around at the photographs, plaques and

certificates that hung on the walls. There were pictures of General Curtis when he was in the Army Air Force in World War II, both in England and in the Pacific, and there were photos of him at the controls of B-17 and B-29 bombers. Another showed him on an airfield in South Korea. Later photos showed him at SAC Headquarters in Omaha and at the controls of B-47 and B-52 jet bombers. And there were formal, color photographs, as well: General Curtis with President Eisenhower, General Curtis with President Dillon, General Curtis with President Romney.

But there were no photos of General Curtis with President Kennedy.

One corner of the room had been blocked off by a waist-high wooden railing. Inside the railing and near the wall was a stand, and on top of the stand was a small chunk of what looked like brick, embedded in a cube of heavy glass. Small plaques set every eight inches or so along the railing said DO NOT CROSS. In the center of the railing was a larger plaque:

PRESENTED IN GRATEFUL APPRECIATION

TO GENERAL RAMSEY 'THE RAMMER' CURTIS

FOR HIS YEARS OF SERVICE TO HIS NATION

UPON HIS RETIREMENT, AUGUST 1, 1971

A PIECE OF RED SQUARE, MOSCOW, USSR

RETRIEVED MAY DAY, 1971, BY THE

177th RADIOLOGICAL SURVEY SQUADRON

STRATEGIC AIR COMMAND

'PEACE IS OUR PROFESSION'

Carl felt sick to his stomach. Sure, peace. The peace of the grave, the peace of the dead. Some peace. He wondered who would mourn for them, centuries from now, the dead Americans, Russians, Cubans, Chinese, Indians, Ukrainians, Poles. Nobody, that's who. Who, after all, now mourned the ancient dead of Rome, Egypt, Assyria, and Greece?

That voice again, from Caz's brother: history is written not only by the victors, but by the survivors.

Carl looked down at the general's desk. It was clean, save for the crystal ashtray, the cigarette lighter, and a blotter. Off to the side was a phone and an intercom system. There were three switches for the intercom: off, one-way, and two-way. He took a deep breath, flipped the switch to one-way, and bent over to listen through the tiny speaker.

Voices, a mix of men's voices, but he could make out the general's clear enough:

'. . . he'll do an okay job. I've just put the fear of God and the Rammer into him . . .'

And other voices as well:

'. . . can he be trusted?'

'. . . not an issue of trust. It's reliability, it's getting the job done . . .'

'. . . and damn it, trust brings me back again to those Limeys. In a short time there's going to be tens of thousands of them in this country . . .'

'. . . know you don't like it, but what's the alternative?'

The general again: 'You know the alternative. Chaos and riots in every street. We have to keep the lid on, and the Brits are the key . . .'

'. . . suppose they don't leave when they're done? Suppose they do something else while they're here?'

'. . . like what . . .'

'. . . shit, maybe arrest us all . . . who knows . . . foreign troops on our soil, they can do what they damn please . . .'

The general, again: '. . . any funny business, there'll be consequences . . . see what we did to Moscow . . . lobbing one down the chimney at Buckingham Palace should take care of things . . .'

Some laughter, and Carl quickly flipped the intercom switch off and went back to his chair, legs quietly shaking. He thought about what he had just learned, about what was going on, and realized with a start that not once in the discussions had he heard the voice of Governor Rockefeller.

After another minute or so, General Curtis came back into his study and said, 'Well, Sergeant, I have something to show you, if you don't mind wasting an hour or so with a retired old fart like myself.'

Carl stood up, wiping his hands on his pants, feeling like he was trapped in an asylum not only run by the inmates but inmates bent on dragging everyone on the outside into their way of life. 'Go right ahead, sir.'

He kept pace with the general as they went out of the study, down a hallway, and then outside into the cool fall air. Two Air Force officers in dress blues stayed behind them at a respectful pace, and the general kept up a running commentary as they walked down a gravel path that was flanked on both sides by white picket fence.

'This is my retirement farm, though I don't get much time off, as you can see,' the general said, walking with his hands in his pockets, puffing away at the cigar. 'But I never complain.' He stopped and looked around, at the farmland and buildings and the grass and trees. 'Ten years ago, I was in an airborne command post, watching everything go to the shits, and I didn't know if I'd live to the end of the hour, never mind the end of the day. Remember earlier, we were speaking about luck? Lucky for all of us that we were able to get a comm link to the Soviets, and end the damn thing. I knew that whatever I had remaining of my life, that I would dedicate it to rebuilding this nation and its people. You were overseas during the war, weren't you?'

'I was, sir. In South Vietnam.'

The general kicked at a pebble. 'South Vietnam. I was there once, for a briefing and tour.'

That you were, Carl thought, remembering that same day from a different vantage point, as the general went on: 'Little shit-ass country, we had no business being there. That's what I told everyone, everyone who listened, but Kennedy and his boys had other plans. Like Cuba. He and his brother and his clan, they were humiliated at the Bay of Pigs, a couple of months after the inauguration, and who could blame them? It was Eisenhower's job, Eisenhower's plan, Eisenhower's boys who put that fiasco together. But when the shit hit the fan, old Jack wouldn't provide air support to the rebels, and they were slaughtered on the beaches. Poor bastards. But you could tell, the moment the news hit that missiles were in Cuba, that JFK didn't have the balls for seeing the job through right. We should have gone in early and fast, with the element of surprise. That's what we needed, but how the hell could we surprise them, with him blabbering all over the airwaves and that pantywaist Stevenson up in the UN, showing off our U-2 photos?'

Carl felt that he should stay quiet and let the general rave. He spared a quick glance at the two Air Force officers behind them and saw knowing smiles on their faces. They had heard these remarks before, he was sure. Over and over again, refined and reedited, making sure that this particular survivor's story made the history books.

The general took a deep puff of his cigar, resumed walking. 'JFK was just a rich kid, playing at being a grown-up, but the last time he tried to play grown-up, it blew up all around him. He had help all his life, you know that? When his PT boat got run down in the South Pacific, any other Navy commander would have been court-martialed. But his father the booze smuggler and ambassador, along with the Kennedy machine, they got him off. They also got him a seat in the House of Representatives, and they helped steal the election in 1960.'

The general stopped and stared at him. It was an uncomfortable feeling. 'Funny, isn't it? They say the dead voted that November night in Illinois, the dead voted to put Kennedy over the top. Makes you wonder if the dead were lonely and wanted some companions. A few million more companions. Well, they certainly got their wish, less than two years later.'

'General,' Carl said, staring right back, thinking suddenly of Caz and the others, the ones who had kept an old dream alive for a decade. 'I have a question.'

'Shoot.'

'You still have connections, still have resources. You know about the "JFK Lives" cult. What's the real story? Could Kennedy have gotten out of DC in time?'

The general's eyes narrowed and his bushy eyebrows bunched together. 'For ten years I've had to hear about those nutty stories, and I'm quite sick of them.'

'I'm sure.'

'Well, let me tell you, Sergeant,' he said, his voice growling around his cigar. 'I know for a fact what happened that day. It was a foul-up, another in a series of foul-ups. There were helicopters at Andrews Air Force Base whose sole job was to get Kennedy and his family out of DC. First, JFK dithered too much and didn't allow the request to go out until nearly the last minute. Story I heard is that he was having a nervous breakdown, weeping in the Oval Office. Then there were communications problems between the White House Signals Office and Andrews Air Base – someone didn't have the right authentication code. That ate up a lot of minutes. And when the helicopters finally got into the air, they were halfway there when the first warhead struck. We had minute-by-minute communications logs, and we know for a fact that JFK was in the White House, waiting to be airlifted out, when the city was hit.'

A defiant puff on the cigar, and the general continued, walking down the path. 'I know it's a nice fairy story that some people like to tell, that the wounded young President still lives, waiting to come out of hiding at the last moment to save his country. But that's all it is. Fairy tales, and we don't have time for them. All right, here we are.'

The path had emerged into a large clearing, where a barn had been transformed into an aircraft hangar. Near the hangar was a concrete landing pad, and a dark green Huey helicopter stood in the center. When the general was spotted by the crew they clambered aboard, and the engine started with a slow whine, as the blades began to turn.

'Just a brief ride, and then we'll have you on your way to Boston,' General Curtis said, raising his voice and tossing aside his cigar.

Carl followed him into the cabin of the helicopter, wincing at the pain in his legs. A crewman settled him and the general into their seats. They put on a pair of earphones and a mike system, and did a quick comm check with the general as the helicopter lifted off and banked to the right. Carl settled back into his seat, folded his arms, and knew with a cold sense of dread that if the general suddenly decided that this sergeant wasn't trustworthy, it wouldn't take much to toss him out of the helicopter at five thousand feet or so.

Considering what the general had done ten years ago, Carl was sure he could do it without a moment's hesitation.

Less than a half hour later, the general's voice, crackly through the static, came over the headsets. 'Take a look out the side, will you, Sergeant?'

Carl leaned and looked out the Plexiglas, down at the landscape moving beneath them. There were small towns and roads and trees and grasslands, and off by the horizon, a larger city.

'That's Frederick, Maryland,' the general said.

Carl nodded, knowing with a heavy sensation in his feet and hands and chest what was coming next. Below them the landscape started to change, started to become wilder, with fewer homes and buildings. Cars were lined up on the highways and sunlight glinted from some of the windshields, but none of the cars were moving. None had moved, in the past ten years. Then there was the distant sight of a city, and even from miles away, Carl could see the burnt rubble and empty windows of the buildings.

'Rockville,' the general said. 'Nobody's sure when we'll start rebuilding there. Same old story. Too many demands, too little money and too few people.'

The engine noise of the helicopter grew louder, and Carl noticed that they were gaining altitude. The remains of the cities and towns became clearer. Trees and brush were growing among the ruined buildings, and there were still rows of dead trees, their leaves and small branches burnt away. Then there were fields of gray and black rubble, hard to make out anything in detail, and then, incredibly, a lake. They were flying over a lake, the shores of which were fused gray earth.

'Lake DC,' the general said, sighing. 'Once the warheads struck, the whole landscape and geography of this place changed. What's below us is one of the three craters in this zone, and this one's been filled by the Potomac River.'

The helicopter circled and Carl looked down, nauseated but unable to look away from the gray soil and water of the dead lake, or the rubble, the endless fields of rubble. Even this high up, he could smell the deadness of this place, this center of what was once called the American Century. Once Carl had stood proudly here, at the inauguration of a president who had promised great things, great crusades. Now, in his second visit to this city, all that was left was rubble. He knew why flights over these bombed-out areas were forbidden; one could be driven to madness thinking of what had happened here, ten years ago. Carl looked over at the general again, and thought: madness.

'Think of everything that used to be down there, Sergeant,' General Curtis said, his voice sounding strong in the earphones. 'Jefferson walked to his inauguration down there. Lincoln saved the Union. Roosevelt fought the Nazis and the Japs. Eisenhower served his two terms down there with honor. Think of the Capitol, the Lincoln Memorial, the White House, the Jefferson Memorial, the Smithsonian, all of the memories, all of our history, everything that was dear to this country. Gone.'

Carl was startled when the general leaned over and grabbed his arm. 'Except for those two documents, Sergeant

Landry. That's the soul of our nation, a way of finally binding our wounds. Get them for us, Sergeant. Give us back our history.'

Carl said nothing, looking down at the miles of devastation below him, and eventually the general let go of his arm and the helicopter turned north and flew back to Pennsylvania.

And again, he thought: madness.

TWENTY-FIVE

CARL STOOD IN FRONT of his apartment building and let his luggage fall on the sidewalk. He listened to the evening traffic race by, ignoring the people around him heading home or over to Newbury Street for a night of shopping and dining. He looked at the brick building, his head still aching from all that had happened that day. It was late evening and just a few hours ago, he had been flying over the rubble that used to be this nation's capital. Then, after a ride north on an Air Force jet to Logan and a hired car waiting for him outside the terminal, he was back home, exhausted and terrified of what lay ahead.

Six days. In six days Jim Rowley and PS 19 and all the other free communities in this country, they were coming out from the tunnels and basements and refuges, coming out to demand their rights. At the same time – if not earlier – troops would be in place to either arrest them or gun them down. And then after the election, there would be the formal announcement of the anschluss. He could imagine the speech Rockefeller would make. A closer alliance. A return to a special relationship. Nothing to worry about, more food and assistance and maybe a representative from Her Majesty's government sharing the Oval Office.

Six days.

He had less than a week to find Merl Sawson's hidden documents, documents that were going to have an impact on the election, documents that could decide whether or not Jim Rowley and his comrades were going to live or were going to end up in decon camps.

Could he do it?

He had to. There were no other options.

He picked up his bags and went inside.

His apartment was musty with stale odors, and he opened the windows overlooking Comm Avenue and the park. The traffic noises sounded good after the silent streets of Manhattan. He went into the bedroom, unpacked his bags, and saw that the Air Force crew at General Curtis's retirement home had been neat and efficient. All of his clothes had been washed and pressed. Even his pistol had been cleaned, though the clip was empty and there was no ammunition. Very thoughtful, indeed.

A pile of mail had been waiting on the floor near the door, and he spent a few dull moments sorting through it. A *Newsweek*, with a cover photograph of Nelson Rockefeller, grinning and waving at a campaign event. A Boston Edison bill and a mailing from the American Cancer Society. 'Fall Appeal,' it said on the outside of the envelope in bright red letters. He put it aside with the electric bill, to pay later. Another envelope, inviting him to join the Veterans of Atomic Wars. He tossed that one in the trash.

An advertising flyer decorated with drawings of a crystal ball, stars and planets, and with a local phone number and address, caught his eye:

Madame Bolivar
Readings and Predictions
You Can Contact a Lost Relative in the Other World!
Thousands Have Done So. Why Not You?

One of the few growth industries in this country after the war. Mediums and spiritualists, for the millions of guilty survivors out there. He threw that away as well.

The last envelope was a thin one from Searchers, Inc. He knew the drill, knew what a thin envelope meant. He opened it up and saw the invoice, as well as the familiar form letter with the familiar words: 'Sorry to inform you that no progress has been made in locating YOUR SISTER, SARAH LANDRY . . .'

He almost tossed that away as well, but instead went to the refrigerator and took out two bottles of Guinness – gifts from Sandy from their dinner – and then sprawled out on the couch. He didn't feel like watching television or going out for a newspaper, so he sat there, drinking. After a half hour or so, he got a couple more beers, and soon he was lying on his couch, staring up at the cracked plaster ceiling. Maybe he should go into the bedroom. Maybe. Did serious drunks ever make it to the bedroom? They ended up on the floor or on couches or in easy chairs. If he could make it to the bedroom, then he really wasn't a drunk.

He got up, staggered some. His head felt heavy on his shoulders and his legs didn't quite go where he wanted, but in a minute he had collapsed on the bed. He was still dressed, he still had his shoes on, but by God, he had made it to bed. He wasn't a real drunk, after all.

Sometime in the middle of the night he woke up, terribly thirsty. He went to the bathroom, and then to the kitchen to get a glass of water. He drank two glasses and then stopped, feeling nauseated. He put the empty glass into the sink and sniffed the air again. The apartment still smelled odd and then he realized why. Tobacco. Someone had been smoking in his apartment while he was away. He shivered and went out into the living room, and then to his office.

He switched on a light and looked around. Sure enough. Just as before, before he had left on his trip to Manhattan, he could tell that visitors had been in here. Books had been taken out and rearranged in the bookshelves, and he could see that some papers had been moved around. He sat down at his desk and turned on a table lamp. His head still hurt. What does it mean, he thought. Sloppy spies, coming in and looking at whatever they could get their hands on. Amateurs? Or so slickly professional that they didn't care if he knew that they had been here.

He checked the time. It was two A.M. on Wednesday. He now had five days left. He yawned, knowing that later today he'd do some things and on Thursday, back at the *Globe*, he'd get down to serious work. Merl Sawson. If the general had been telling the truth – and that was a mighty big if – then the police and the probable Army searches of Merl's apartment had turned up nothing.

So. Where would an old vet like Merl hide something of importance? And how would he find them? And what the hell was in those papers anyway?

Jim Rowley thought the papers could help prevent the crackdown on the free communities by influencing the election.

General Curtis said they were the Constitution and the Declaration of Independence.

And Caz Cynewski, the old CIA employee, said they were the key, the key to He Lives.

JFK, still alive?

Jesus. Carl was under no illusions. Whatever those papers were, the general and his comrades needed them for their own plans, their own futures. And if Carl did them the favor of locating them, he would probably be graciously thanked and then be sent to the outskirts of San Diego, to decontaminate topsoil or some damn thing.

Never to come back to Boston, never to work again at the *Globe,* never to see or hear anything more about Sandy.

Damn that woman.

He looked at his book manuscript. What was it that she had said, before the truck blew up back in New Jersey? Something about writing another chapter, about what they had seen and about the lies of the generals. He ran his fingers across his manuscript. That was an idea, especially if he only focused on one particular lie, and one particular general. Something the general had said about a visit to Vietnam had brought back an old memory. He knew he should get some sleep but he had this nervous energy, wanting to put words down on paper before he forgot them or before something else came along.

Near the typewriter was a shortwave radio, smaller than the one out in the living room. Now it was a little past three o'clock on Wednesday morning. He switched on the receiver, let it warm up for a few minutes, and then scanned the dial, searching for a frequency that he knew by heart. There was a burst of static, and then a man's voice, with a Massachusetts Harvard accent, that faded in and out.

'. . . my fellow citizens, the time is upon us in November to make a decision . . .' the voice said, and Carl felt the hair on the back of his arms rise.

'. . . whether to return to the promise of my administration, tragically shortened in its lifetime . . .' More static and pops and crackles. He held his breath and gingerly moved the frequency dial, and the familiar voice, the one he heard back in 1961 on that cold day at the Capitol, went on.

'. . . or we go forward into the darkness, unnoted and unwanted by the world, our bright promise dimmed forever . . .'

More static. He moved the dial around for a few more minutes, and there was nothing but static and the whines and hisses of radio jamming. He reached over to switch off the radio and then stopped. No, he decided. Leave it on. As he had said to Sandy, days before in the ruins of the Hyannisport compound, being in a minority meant being uncrowded, and he liked that.

Then he rolled a sheet of blank paper into the typewriter and began to write.

It was later on Wednesday morning, the day overcast and threatening rain. He was a couple of blocks away from his apartment building, holding a cup of coffee, woozy from not enough sleep, knowing there was a lot to do today. He stood at a pay phone near a used bookstore, dialed the Park Plaza, and asked for Sandy's room.

'I'm sorry, sir,' the operator said. 'Miss Price has checked out.'

Damn, he thought. 'Did she leave any forwarding address or telephone number?'

'No, sir.'

'Anything at all?'

'No, I'm afraid not.'

He hung up the phone and sipped at the coffee. He guessed he could have made the call from his apartment, but he had wanted to get out and he didn't want to use the phone back home. He had been visited twice by unseen strangers, and who knew what kind of listening devices they had left behind. He had no idea who they worked for: the English, French, German, Japanese, Nelson Rockefeller, General Curtis, or even George McGovern. They might be in his apartment right now, maybe looking to see what he had been writing so early in the morning.

Carl patted the inside of his coat pocket, where the freshly typed pages were folded in an envelope. Sorry, spooks. The evidence ain't there.

It's here.

He went back to his apartment building and got the Coronet started after a few grinding tries, then he drove over to State Street, where he lucked out finding a parking space. The clouds that had been threatening earlier in the morning had opened up, and he knew that without a hat or an umbrella he would look like a drowned dog in a few moments.

So what? he thought. I've got things to do and not much time to do them in.

At number 10 State Street, he came to a familiar building, one he had visited less than two weeks ago, and that had eventually propelled him into some very strange places indeed. The British consulate still looked clean and immaculate in its four-story brick splendor, and he went through the black wrought-iron gate and up the flagstone path.

The main door was open and he went into the tiny lobby area, where a young man sat behind a glass window, reading a copy of *The Economist*. There was a speaker grill in the center of the glass and he suddenly remembered, with a wry smile, the pawnshop in Manhattan, run by that strange couple. Jesus, he thought, what were their names?

'Yes?' said the attendant, his tone cultured and showing maybe a hint of irritation at being interrupted. He was wearing a white dress shirt and what looked like an old school tie. 'May I help you?'

'I'd like to see Douglas Harris, please. The press attaché.'

The man smiled as he looked through a ledger. 'I'm afraid that's impossible without an appointment.'

Carl reached into his wallet, pulled out a business card, and slid it through a thin opening at the bottom of the glass barrier. 'I'm Carl Landry, of the *Boston Globe*. I really need to talk to Mr. Harris.'

The desk clerk picked up the creased card and looked at both sides, as if checking for dirt stains, and said, 'I'm terribly sorry, but this is highly irregular. You really need to make an appointment.'

He leaned forward so he was closer to the speaker grill. 'Tell you what, sport. Here's the deal. I'm a reporter for the *Boston Globe,* and I want to talk to your press attaché. You see, I'm running a story tomorrow in the paper, on the front page, saying that your consul general is skimming funds from the Bundles to Boston campaign. I sure would like to get a response from the British consul before it goes to print.'

The man's face paled. 'I see.'

Carl smiled. 'So I know it's fucking irregular and all that, but I need to see Douglas Harris. Now.' He looked around for a chair and seeing none, said, 'I'll just stand here and wait. Or maybe I'll sit on the floor, if you don't mind.'

But the man didn't answer. He was on the phone.

It took a half hour and sure enough, he had been sitting on the floor. But when he heard the click of the door being unlatched he stood up and faced an unsmiling and unhappy Douglas Harris. He wore jeans and a brown turtleneck sweater, and his face was puffy and red as if he had been running up and down a lot of stairs.

'Come in, won't you,' he said, his tone clipped and proper. Carl followed him into the open lobby, and instead of taking the route he had gone last time, they made a sharp right and ended up in a tiny plain office with a dented metal desk, two chairs, and an ugly portrait of the Queen on the far wall. Carl imagined this was the sort of office in which they took care of troublemakers, people who didn't deserve much time and attention. Like those getting turned down for visas to the UK for hospital visits. Like those being turned down for citizenship applications. Or like irritating reporters.

'Mind telling me what all this rubbish is about?' Douglas started as soon as he sat down. 'I don't appreciate having to juggle my schedule to deal with the likes of you.'

'And you're going to like me even less,' Carl said, pulling out the envelope that contained the sheets he had written only a few hours ago. 'There is no story about your consul running in tomorrow's *Globe*. I made it all up.'

Douglas put a finger to his chin. 'Then why in the world did you tell that cock-and-bull story?'

'Because I needed to see you.'

'Need or not, I could call your editor and make things very difficult for you.'

'I doubt it,' Carl said, taking out a pen and writing something on the outside of the envelope, 'since I've already managed to piss off everyone in authority over there. Look, Douglas, I need for you to pass this along to Sandy Price.'

Douglas refused to take the envelope, and Carl let it drop to the desktop. 'What makes you think I can do that?'

'She's checked out of her hotel. I know that she's being deported in a few days. I know that the two of you are friends. At the least. And it's important for her to receive this.'

They sat still for a moment or two, and Douglas abruptly leaned forward and picked up the envelope. '"Sandy,"' he read aloud. '"Thanks for saving my butt in New Jersey. Here's the chapter you suggested. If you want to start telling me the truth, give me a call. If not, have a nice flight back home."'

The press attaché looked up. 'And what does that mean?'

'It means exactly what I wrote.'

'I see,' Douglas said, tapping the envelope on the table. 'You know, I can't promise that I can deliver this.'

'Oh, I'm sure you'll make the effort,' Carl said, standing up. 'Hell, she's probably staying here in the compound, right? Ensuring that her last days are spent in peace, without the problems of being harassed or arrested by the local authorities. Hate to have something like that stir the pot of our fine relations with our cousins across the sea.'

Douglas just looked at the envelope, still in his hand, and then something about his demeanor changed and hardened. 'Do be careful, Mr. Landry. I'm not sure what you're doing, but I believe it could be dangerous. Very dangerous indeed for a simple reporter.'

'Yeah, dangerous. Look, you've been here for a while, right? Ever been to Concord or Lexington?'

His voice was flat. 'I have.'

'Then you know what happened when some simple people like me ran up against folks like you. So thanks for the warning.'

Douglas said nothing and Carl stood up. He wondered if Douglas would have a new job, if the anschluss went through. Maybe a spokesman for the head Brit in Philadelphia?

'Look, can you get me out of here? Or do you trust me enough to find my way out.'

Douglas gave a chilly smile as he stood up. 'Oh, I trust you all right.'

But he still escorted Carl outside.

He spent a lousy afternoon back in East Boston, doing a canvass of Merl Sawson's neighborhood in the rain. Most of the people on the street knew nothing about Merl or his habits, what bars or stores or parks he might have frequented. Carl was hoping to find an acquaintance – maybe a fellow vet, a fellow sports enthusiast, somebody! – but all he got were quizzical looks, some nervous shakes of the head, and many slammed doors.

A couple of elderly people gave him impassioned complaints about their newspaper subscriptions, about missing *Globes* past and newspapers that arrived with torn sections, and as he listened to their gripes he felt time slipping away. Out there, troops from Great Britain were getting ready for action, as were Jim Rowley and his allies. And Jim was depending on him, depending on him to find answers, when all he was getting this afternoon was a whole lot of nothing. He even spent a half hour in the tiny backyard of Merl's apartment building on Winthrop Street, picking up large rocks, looking under the shrubbery, checking for signs of freshly dug dirt, a hollowed-out section of the house foundation, anyplace where the documents could be hidden.

And he found nothing, except an old collection of dog droppings on the scraggly brown lawn, probably from Merl's dead dog.

He sat on the back stoop and looked out across the lawn to the shoulder-high fence with gray, peeling paint that surrounded the yard. Carl folded his hands together tightly and hunched himself forward, feeling the rain mat his hair and the quiet gnawing of desperation in his guts. The rain was cold against his skin. He was afraid that things were slipping away, just out of his grasp.

Think, he thought. Just take a deep breath and think. If the old man had papers, papers that were important, then that means something of bulk. Not much of a bulk, but something. At least a thick envelope. So. If the Army and the police and everyone else had been looking in this building, they hadn't found it, not yet. And now they were depending on a *Globe* reporter, who didn't have the resources or the people to match the Army. Nice that they had such confidence in him pulling a rabbit out of his hat.

So the papers had to have been brought out of Merl's apartment. In a package, sent somewhere? Hand-delivered to a friend that Carl knew nothing about? Or maybe mailed to the local post office in a daze, mailed to President Kennedy at 1600 Pennsylvania Avenue.

Jesus, he thought, looking up. They were here, and now they're gone. So they were taken out.

How?

He looked at the lawn again, feeling a faint trembling of hope. Jesus. Maybe. Just maybe.

When he parked his Coronet in the tiny lot behind his apartment building just before dusk, an older man stood up from behind the dumpster and furtively looked around. He wore an old knee-length wool coat, patched jeans, old sneakers, gray gloves, and his thick black beard was streaked with white. Carl saw the old man approach and reached in his pockets, looking for a quarter or two, but the man shook his head violently and held out his hands.

'No, no, no, man,' he said. 'I'm not lookin' for anything. You're Mr. Landry, am I right?'

'That's right,' Carl said, locking the door to his car. 'I'm sorry, do I know you?'

The man giggled. 'Once upon a time I was a major, but, man, years later, I still want to forget that shit. You can call me Skyman. I'm named that 'cause I used to be a pilot.'

'All right, Skyman. What can I do for you?'

'It's Two-Tone,' the man said. 'He sent me to get you and bring you to his hidey-hole.'

'What for?'

The man stepped closer, almost breathing on him. 'Two-Tone, he's not well. He can't really walk right now, and he asked me to come fetch you.'

He was surprised at the tremor he felt, hearing of Two-Tone. 'What's wrong with him?'

'He got himself beat up, that's what. Come on, he told me

he'd pay me, the minute I spotted you, and I don't want to be wasting any time.'

Carl walked with Skyman across Comm Ave, through the gardens of the narrow park, and then down another block on the cracked sidewalk, past apartment buildings that were twins of his own. Before them was the muted roar of Storrow Drive, with traffic heading out of Boston. Off on the other side of Storrow Drive was the Charles River, and beyond that, Cambridge and the buildings of MIT. Where Troy Clemmons, the draft resister and upstairs neighbor of Merl Sawson, went to school. Now, maybe we could—

'Here we be,' Skyman said, stepping over a low guardrail and going a half dozen yards down the side of a grassy embankment, stopping near a utility pole.

Carl followed him, confused. They were behind a row of brownstones and apartment buildings with tiny parking areas and decks, and a narrow access road. The embankment, filled with waist-high brush and saplings, went down in a small ravine, and then back up to the boundary of Storrow Drive. Skyman looked around and said, 'Yeah, we're right here. C'mon.'

He got on his hands and knees and Carl dropped, too, feeling the wet grass and soil. His guide brushed away some dead grass, until a square piece of metal, about the size of a car door, was revealed. After carefully scanning the area, Skyman huffed and puffed and dragged the piece of metal free. There was a dark tunnel inside, and Carl could make out a faint glow of light, at the far end. Skyman motioned him inside and pulled the metal plate shut behind them. 'There it is. Two-Tone's hidey hole. He's waiting for you.'

A voice from the other end, weak but recognizable, said, 'Skyman, that you? You got Carl with you?'

'See?' the man asked. 'What did I say?'

Carl said nothing. He took out his wallet and passed over a five-dollar bill. 'Thanks. You've done okay.'

'Go ahead in there,' Skyman said. 'I'll go back outside.'

He crawled on his hands and knees, over dry pieces of wood, wincing at the pain from his sore legs, and then the dirt tunnel opened up and he was in a large cavern, about eight feet tall and thirty or so feet wide. It was made of concrete and brick, and was lit by candles and a small gas lantern, hissing in the corner. Two-Tone was lying on a mattress, on a bed made from scrap lumber, and he weakly lifted a hand in greeting.

'Carl,' he said, his voice hoarse, like he had a sore throat. 'I'm glad I could get you. We need to talk. Have a seat.'

There was an old school chair by a salvaged kitchen table, and Carl dragged it over to the bed, looking around at Two-Tone's home. It looked like it might have been a cellar of some sort, back in nineteenth-century Boston. There were lines of shelves, and along the shelves were rows of books and canned food. A couple of posters, torn and tattered, hung on the brick walls. One showed the cherry blossoms of Washington, D.C. Another showed an impossibly handsome John F. Kennedy and an impossibly beautiful Jacqueline Kennedy. The place was crowded but clean, and it smelled of fresh air. A smaller tunnel led off to the left, next to a tiny stove that had a pipe that went up through the brick ceiling.

He looked over at Two-Tone. His face was bruised, his left eye was swollen shut, and he didn't have his hat on, making the bald and scar-tissued half of his head look stark in the candlelight. Carl leaned over and said, 'Who did this to you? Some kids in the neighborhood? Is that it?'

Two-Tone coughed and shook his head. 'No, no, it was nothing like that. It's because of some poker game I won, back in 1961.'

'William, I'm sorry, I don't—'

A wave of the hand interrupted him. 'Carl, m'boy, you've always been polite to me. Always. Very formal and I appreciate that. Always have. But I ain't William no more. That was a long time ago. I'm Two-Tone, all right? That's who I am. So why don't you call me that.'

He nodded, feeling something awful start to tickle at the back of his throat. 'Two-Tone, what did you mean, this happened because of some poker game?'

The older man giggled and burrowed underneath his blankets. 'Sorry. A little fun on my part, nothing serious. You probably think Two-Tone has gone really crazy, right? Off the deep end and into Boston Harbor?'

'No, I didn't think of that at all.'

Another series of coughs. 'Of course you do. But you're too polite to say anything. You see, the thing was, back in '61, I was playing a late-night poker game outside of Fort Bragg. I was doing all right and by the night's end, I was ahead a couple of hundred bucks, and I went to cash out and get some rest. But some cranky young guy, full of piss and vinegar, he didn't want me to leave. Said he wanted a chance to win back his earnings. Being pretty young myself, I told him where to get off and . . . well, I cleaned his clock all right.'

Two-Tone smiled at the memory. 'Them was some good days, feeling young and strong. Nice feelings. Anyway, this guy says, one of these days, I'll get you back. Always remembered his face. Forgot his name, but always remembered the face. Squat head, beady eyes, no neck.'

Carl rubbed at his knees. 'That was over ten years ago. What happened now?'

'Now? What happened now? What happened now is that I'm out there, workin', earning my keep for what you and your neighbors pay me, keeping an eye on things, and I see some guys going into your place. Again. Well, I decided I wasn't going to just stand around and watch 'em do their dirty work, you know?'

He felt tired and angry and worn out, all at once. 'Two-Tone, you didn't have to do a damn thing.'

'The hell I didn't!' Two-Tone raised his head, eyes blazing. 'This is still America, ain't it? People shouldn't be pokin' around in other people's houses without their say-so. Anyway. So I saw these three guys go up and I waited outside on the sidewalk, to see what would happen. Then they come out, looking all smug and arrogant-like, and that's when I lose it. I decide enough's enough and I go over to them and tell 'em to get the hell out of the neighborhood, and they start beatin' on me. I put up a fight, best as I could, and I notice one guy, bigger than the others, and I think "full house." And I thought, why in hell am I thinking full house? Then it came back to me, poker, and there he is, that snot Army lieutenant who got pissed at me back then. Now I get concerned, 'cause he's looking at me and I figure, I gotta end this.'

Carl said, 'So what did you do?'

Two-Tone licked at his lips. 'I gave up and fell and rolled up, and I let 'em do their worst. I was on the ground and then they all punched me a few more times, and then they gave me a couple of good kicks, and then they went off, laughing about the dirty bums in this city.' Two-Tone blinked. 'That wasn't nice, you know. I try to stay as clean as I can. It's not my fault I don't got hot water in this place.'

Carl realized his fists were clenched. 'What else happened?'

'Oh, that was enough for one day, don't you think,' and he laughed and then coughed some more. 'I sat there for a while, bleeding and stuff, and then Skyman came by and drug me back into my hidey-hole, and here I've been sittin'. I asked Skyman to wait around your place and to come fetch you when he could, and here you be.'

'I . . . I appreciate everything you've done, Two-Tone. Everything. I don't know how to repay you.'

The older man moved around in his bed. 'Don't worry none, don't worry none about that. After all, we're both a couple of vets, and us vets gotta look out for one another. Just a few more quarters and maybe some canned hams. I like canned hams, but can't rightly afford them that much. Oh, but two more things, if you don't mind, Carl . . .'

'Name them.'

Two-Tone looked around his place. 'This is my hidey-hole . . . Only a couple of people know where it is. You won't be telling anybody, will you?'

Carl reached over and patted his blanket-covered feet. 'Not a soul, Two-Tone. I won't tell anybody a thing. And look at it this way. If the sirens ever sound, the next time the missiles start to fly, you can stay here and I'll come over. You won't have to come looking for me.'

Two-Tone grinned. 'That's a hell of an idea. And the other thing . . . Carl, there was something about these three guys I didn't tell you.'

'Go on.'

'They said something else, 'fore they left. I thought they was talking about me, but now, I think maybe they was talkin' about you.'

Carl folded his hands. It felt like the walls of Two-Tone's place were closing in about his shoulders. 'Go ahead.'

'One guy said, "What if it don't work with him?" And the other guy laughed, the one from Fort Bragg . . . and he said, "So what. Another dead vet. It gets to be easy once you've killed your first." And then they laughed some more.'

TWENTY-SIX

THE NEXT DAY HE WENT BACK to the *Globe*. It was Thursday and he sat at his desk and looked around. The noise from the typewriters and the telephones seemed to blast at his ears, and everything seemed too bright and too noisy. His desk was clean, which was strange, and the next surprising thing was seeing the bulk of the city editor, George Dooley, as he ambled his way through the jumble of desks and chairs, heading over to Carl's desk. George had once said, 'The only place a reporter should talk to an editor is in front of an editor's desk,' yet here George was, in front of Carl's desk, for the second time in just over a week.

George nodded. He had on his usual black tie, black pants, and white dress shirt, and he said, 'Glad to see you're back.'

'Thanks, George.'

'Learn anything while you were away?'

Carl almost laughed at the absurdity of the question, and managed to say, 'Oh, yeah, but nothing I think I can use here.'

George smiled. 'All right, then, why don't you take it easy for a bit, and here,' he said, handing him a folded piece of paper, 'the mayor's having a press conference at two. Something about the city's participation in the American Cancer Society's fall appeal.'

'Sure,' he said, putting the note down on his desk. George started walking back to his office and turned. 'Oh, and another thing, Carl.'

'Yes?'

'Don't blow this one off, all right?'

Carl felt like the newsroom had tilted up and down again. George being gracious? George being polite?

'You'll have the story on your desk, the end of the day.'

And there were now four days left.

When he came back from getting a cup of coffee, there was a note on his chair.

> *Landry—*
> *Please see me soonest.*
> *—Devane*

He crumpled the note and tossed it in a trash can, then walked over to the oversight editor's office with his cup of coffee. Major Devane, still looking like a well-fed weasel in civilian clothes, stood up behind his desk, eyes glaring.

'Do shut the door behind you, Landry, won't you?'

Carl eased the door closed but didn't shut it completely. There. Hope that upsets you. He didn't wait for an invitation but sat down. Devane still glared at him and said, 'I understand that you're now in the active reserve, Sergeant. I also understand that you now have the confidence of General Curtis and are working on an assignment from him. Be that as it may, if you ever again take a seat in my presence without asking permission, I'll have you brought up on charges.'

Carl took a sip from his coffee. 'Bully for you. What do you want?'

Devane sat down, face reddening. He started to go through a set of papers. 'What I want is to see you serving a sentence in a decon camp outside of Miami for the next ten years. I am told that even now, in the heat, the stench from that place can make a man choke to death.'

The major looked up. 'Failing that, I have been advised to pass along the following information. As you know, Colonel Sawson was in possession of certain papers vital to the national security of this nation. They have not been recovered. Elements of Army intelligence, the Boston police, and the local FBI office have thoroughly searched all apartments in that building. Neighboring apartments have also been searched, the neighbors have been interrogated, and the postman has also been debriefed. Nothing was mailed from that building. Every package and courier delivery business in the Boston area has also been contacted. Nothing.'

'Didn't he have a sister?' Carl asked, remembering the conversation with the landlord.

'He did,' Devane replied. 'She's been dead for more than six years. Her old apartment in Detroit has also been searched.' Devane smiled. 'So there you go, Landry. That is the status of this investigation. Last night I received a personal phone call from General Curtis himself, on a scrambler phone, telling me to give you all of this information and whatever assistance I can provide.'

'And what kind of assistance do you have?'

The smile got wider. 'Hardly any at all. You see, Landry, I don't like you. I've never liked you. And I want to do everything in my power to ensure that you fail in this assignment, so that you fall from the general's good graces, and into my lap.'

'Major, hearing that you didn't like me is the nicest thing I've heard today,' Carl said, feeling an urge to toss his coffee into the man's face. 'The only thing that would have made me happier is to hear that you ran into a pack of dogs while you were in Manhattan. Did you enjoy your little trip there?'

A sharp smile. 'More than you did, I imagine.'

'And what would you have done if you had found me? Shoot me, or interrogate me?'

'One or the other, Landry,' Devane said. 'One or the other. Before you leave, there's one more thing. In the unlikely event you do come up with anything, someone has been assigned to be your liaison to the general.' Devane picked up the phone. 'Clair, send Captain Rowland in, please.'

After hanging up, Devane said, 'In fact, you might know him. He spent part of his career, same as you, with the Special Forces.'

A bulky man in an ill-fitting brown suit appeared, and Carl nearly dropped his coffee. The man was built like a football linebacker, with close-cropped black hair. As he entered the office, Carl recalled a description he had heard yesterday: squat head, beady eyes, no neck.

Carl stood up and Devane said, 'Captain Rowland, this is Sergeant Landry. Have you met before?'

The captain offered a bone-crushing handshake, which Carl did his best to return. Looking down at the thick hand, he saw marks across the knuckles, as if he had punched someone yesterday. The major cocked his head and Carl lied the best he could.

'Sorry, Major Devane, I've never had the pleasure of meeting Captain Rowland.'

Later, back at his work area, he felt a bit out of breath, like he had been in a long and arduous race. In his hand was a plain white business card with Captain Rowland's name and a handwritten phone number. 'Any time of the day or night, Sergeant,' Rowland had said, staring at him. 'You locate what you've been assigned to find, and you call me. Then we'll take it from there.'

Carl had nodded in all of the right places. Sure. We'll take it right from there. Just like you did with Merl Sawson. A couple of bullets to the back of the head and you've got another dead vet.

He slid the business card into his shirt pocket and picked up a reporter's notebook that he had left behind. He flipped through the pages and saw the half-scrambled notes that he had taken while talking to people the first couple days after Merl Sawson's murder. Detective Paul Malone, now called up into the U.S. Navy reserve, and on a patrol boat in the Pacific Northwest. Andrew Townes, run down outside of his apartment building. And Troy Clemmons, MIT student and anti-draft activist, either arrested or on the run after his own apartment was raided.

People who were in the unfortunate position of being connected to the Merl Sawson murder, and now they were either gone or dead. Combined with yesterday's canvass of the neighborhood, not many leads left. About the only thing he'd found yesterday were the droppings of Merl's dog, in that tiny backyard. So, what was next?

Four days. Jim Rowley. Anschluss.

He looked around the newsroom, noticed how people were ignoring him. So what else was new. In another week he might be gone for good, and to hell with them. Then he remembered an old sergeant telling him something, years and years ago: 'Soldier, when things get tough, just shut up and soldier.'

Good advice, then and now.

He flipped through the notebook some more, but then saw Jack Burns stroll by, and something came to him. He put the notebook down and walked to Jack's desk, over by the far wall. Jack was wearing pressed blue jeans and a black pullover sweater. He looked up at Carl and managed a weak smile.

'Hi, Carl. How was your exile?'

'Not bad, as exiles go,' he said, sitting down. 'Look. Can I buy you lunch?'

Jack's eyes wandered for a moment. 'Well, I am sort of backed up on some work and—'

'Look, I'm not going to embarrass you. If you want me to meet you somewhere, fine. But it'll only take a few minutes, and I really need your help, Jack. I really do.'

Jack wrote something on a scrap of paper. 'Sorry, Carl. I can't help you.'

He passed the paper over. On it was written, Old Ale House, noon.

Carl nodded, tore the piece of paper up, and went back to his own desk.

The Ale House was a hole-in-the-wall lunch place a few blocks away, and Jack met him at the rear booth. They both ordered cheeseburgers and when the food arrived, Jack said, 'Don't take this personally, Carl, but right now you're about as hot as downtown Omaha.'

'I can imagine,' he said. 'What happened while I was away?'

Jack took a bite of his burger and spoke around it. 'Lots of grim-faced suits, walking in and out, talking to George and Major Devane. Very hush-hush. Your desk got searched at least twice, which shows you how important you became.'

'Because my desk got searched?'

He shook his head. 'Nope. 'Cause they did it in the middle of the day, with a full newsroom. They didn't care that everybody knew what was going on. So. How's things in spookland?'

Carl started eating. The burger was hot and good, real meat. Damn, maybe the general was telling the truth about something. Recovery was making progress.

'Lonely,' he said. 'Dark. For your own sake, I don't think you need to know any more.'

Jack's smile widened. 'That's the best thing I've heard from you since you got back.'

'But I do need your help.'

The smile wasn't as wide anymore. 'What kind of help?'

'I need help finding someone,' Carl said, and he took out his notebook, scribbled two words in it, and then passed it over. Jack held the paper up in the dim light of the lunch house and said, 'Troy Clemmons? Who the hell is Troy Clemmons?'

'Troy was the upstairs neighbor of that dead vet, the—'

'Jesus, Carl, you'd think that guy was your own uncle or something, the way you go on. Aren't you tired of getting in trouble and seeing your career go into the shits?'

Carl took another bite of his cheeseburger. 'Yep. And I'm tired of being kept in the dark, being lied to, having my apartment broken into, and being treated like a three-year-old.

Damn it, none of us are three years old anymore. I didn't like being told what to do when I was a kid, and I like it even less now.'

'And what's so important about this Troy character?'

'I need to talk to him, and he hasn't been home in over a week.'

'What makes you think I can find him?'

Carl took a cautious sip of water. 'Because he's an MIT student active in the Boston antidraft movement, whatever that's worth, and I need to see him.'

Jack folded the piece of paper in half and placed it on the table between their two plates. 'At the risk of repeating myself, I'll ask again. What makes you think I can find him?'

Carl looked around the restaurant, saw a couple of mailmen leaning against the bar, having a stand-up lunch, and an elderly woman at the other end of the line of booths, slowly spooning chowder into her mouth while reading a folded-over copy of the *Boston Herald*.

'Because you're the only guy I know that could have contacts there, that's why.'

'I'm a music critic, damn you, and nothing else!'

'No, you're a rock critic. Jack, how many times have you told me that rock music is about the only form of rebellion this country has anymore? How many times have you quoted me rock lyrics, showing me the hidden meaning of what was being sung? Is that just talk, or are you really the counter-culture type you say you are?'

Jack picked up his cheeseburger and then put it back on the plate. 'Don't lecture me, Carl. You might not like being told what to do, and that's fine, but I hate being lectured to.'

'Point noted.'

'The thing is,' Jack said, 'I know I have it soft. I get paid fairly well and I write about music and I go to concerts and hobnob with fun people. Parties, free booze, food, tickets, and groupies who don't care if you're with the band or not. They see you as part of the scene, and when that happens, they are terribly eager to crawl into your bed at night and crawl out in the morning with no tears and no strings attached. I like that, I like that very much.'

Jack looked down at the table, spotted with water rings and grease. 'Still, I get tired of it all, just like everybody else. I don't like being told I'm just a kid, either.'

Carl felt like he was holding his breath, waiting to see what would happen next. Then Jack picked up the piece of paper with Troy's name on it and slipped it into his shirt pocket. 'No promises. None whatsoever. And that's it, Carl. All right? No more favors.'

'All right if I pay for lunch?'

'That's fine.'

When he came back from the 2 P.M. press conference that George had assigned him to, there was a thin manila envelope shoved under his typewriter. No name, no return address, just a plain tan envelope. He opened it up and there was a single glossy page inside, torn from a Boston Chamber of Commerce brochure. It showed a statue he recognized: the famed Massachusetts 54th Regiment of the Civil War, one of the first all black regiments during those bloody days. The statue was a raised mural of sorts, showing the marching soldiers and their commanding officer, Major Shaw, leading them off to battle and to the history books.

The statue was at the Boston Common, the large public park across from the State House, within easy walking distance of his apartment. He also remembered that the regiment was decimated during a battle in South Carolina. 'Sorry 'bout that,' he murmured to himself, as he turned the page over. Inked in was 'Noon, Friday, TC.'

Over at his desk, Jack looked up, and then went back to work. Carl remembered to start breathing again.

Then he remembered something else, and went through the papers on his desk. There it was. Tomorrow there was going to be a rally at the Boston Common, with a protest against the draft and a rally for presidential candidate George McGovern. It was a poorly mimeographed flyer, showing stylized drawings of students, teachers, construction workers, and coat-and-tie types, marching under a banner that said, '1972 BOSTON COALITION FOR SURVIVAL.'

Made sense. What better place was there for a draft resister and fugitive hideout, than the middle of a protest march?

When he got home that night she was waiting for him in the shadows by the front door of his apartment building. She stepped away from the empty trash cans. Her voice was tentative. 'Carl? Do you have a moment?'

Carl stopped and looked at her, his hands suddenly prickly with warmth and nervousness. 'Sandy. I take it you got my message from Doug Harris?'

'Yes, yes, I did,' she said, stepping closer.

He looked at her, at the shadows behind her. She seemed pale and haggard, and her hands were hidden in the pockets of her long coat. Carl said, 'I wrote you a note, about what you could do. Seeing me meant that you were going to tell the truth. Is that why you're here?'

Sandy looked down. 'I'm sure you were told some heavy things about me, correct?'

'Very correct. After I was rescued, I eventually ended up having a meeting with General Ramsey Curtis. We talked over a number of subjects, and he had some not-so-nice things to say about you.'

'The general? You actually met with the general?'

'Yeah, and it wasn't much fun, Sandy. I wasn't there as a reporter. I was there as an Army sergeant who had to listen to a superior officer rave on about politics and secrets. And one of these secrets involved you.'

She shuddered. 'I was going to tell you, honestly I was, but there never . . . it never seemed to be quite the right moment.'

Thoughts were clicking through his brain, like a speeded-up slide show. Sandy, the first time he saw her at the consulate. Their conversation out on the balcony. Walking through the rubble of the Kennedy compound. That first night together. The flight into Manhattan, being ambushed, discovering the secrets of PS 19 and Manhattan, and then—

Black-and-white surveillance photographs, scattered across a general's desk.

'Well, take a moment or two right now,' he said. 'Who do you work for, Sandy? And is that your right name?'

'Oh, Christ, of course it's my right name. And I work for the *Times*. That's all truth.'

'And MI6?'

She took a deep breath. 'It's pretty simple, really. I was spending a few weeks over here, covering the tenth anniversary, and I had some interesting contacts lined up. My father . . . well, Papa works in Whitehall and I'm sure he's got intelligence connections, though he's never come right out and said it. So before I came to the States, I was approached and asked to do a few favors. They taught me a little spycraft, real cloak-and-dagger stuff, and sent me on my way. All overseas journalists are asked to do favors. I'm not the first and I won't be the last.'

'What kind of favors?'

She shivered. 'I'm sorry, I'm getting cold and I must get going.'

'Come on up, stay for a while,' he said, surprised at how much he wanted to talk to her.

A quick shake of the head. 'I can't.' She motioned with an arm over to the park. 'I've got my own watchers, making sure I don't get into any more trouble. They made a hell of a fuss over my coming here, but I had to see you, even if it was just for a moment. You . . . you got me out of Manhattan, just like you promised, and I'll never forget that. Ever.'

'You've got to tell me more,' Carl said. 'Damn it, back in Manhattan you said you wanted to help Jim Rowley and his people. Is that still true, or are the people you're doing favors for, are they helping the paras? Were you there to gather intelligence for them, find out about the secret Manhattan?'

She looked down again. 'Carl, I've got to go.'

'Tomorrow,' he said. 'Tomorrow there's an antidraft rally on the Boston Common. Surely you can sneak away to go there, tell your folks you have to cover one more story before you leave.'

He stared at her, this woman from a foreign land who had taken him places he never thought he'd go, had reminded him of things he thought he had forgotten.

Sandy looked over at the park, at her hidden watchers. 'I suppose . . .'

'Then I'll see you tomorrow, at twelve-thirty. There's a

famous Civil War statue on the Beacon Street side of the Common, showing a group of black soldiers marching. Meet me there.'

She smiled nervously for a moment and said, 'All right. I'll try. Now, I have—'

He stepped forward and kissed her. She was reluctant at first, but then kissed him right back and his arms were around her and she whispered in his ear, 'I'm sorry I can't stay. I have so much to tell you. But those people watching . . .'

He squeezed her gently. 'I understand. Thanks for saving my butt, back in New Jersey. And Sandy . . . it was good to see you.'

She squeezed him back. 'The same here, Carl. The same.'

Sandy broke away and they touched hands, and he watched as she jogged across the street, and into the park. She disappeared behind a tree, and when he was sure he couldn't see her anymore, he went upstairs to his empty apartment, remembering the photos he had seen, showing that she was a spy, a foreign spy in his land, and he found himself thinking of her touch, her taste.

Four days left.

EMPIRE: FIVE

A MATTER OF EMPIRE: FIVE

IT WAS COLD and Major Kenneth Hunt stood on a makeshift stage in the aircraft hangar. Before him were the nearly two hundred men who made up his company, the men whom he would lead into battle against an old ally. Beside them were a unit of Royal Engineers, who were coming along for the ride, as they so flippantly put it. They all sat in wooden chairs, lined up in rows. The first part of the briefing was over, and he could see by the shocked expressions on their faces that it would take one hell of a speech to make up for what they had just heard, no matter if most of them had earlier guessed the true nature of their mission.

He didn't know if he had it in him.

Major Kenneth Hunt managed a small smile as he stepped to the edge of the stage, one hand in his pocket, curved protectively around his pipe. Behind him, the briefing boards that had said ABOVE TOP SECRET had been re-covered, just in case someone not cleared for the mission managed to blunder his way into the hangar. He looked over at them, taking his time, and said, 'Right now, you know, is the time when I'm supposed to launch into my Henry the Fifth speech. All that nonsense about "we few, we happy few, we band of brothers."'

There. A few smiles from among the lads. A small victory. He pressed on.

'But I don't have to say it. You already know who you are. You're the Paras. The best among the best. And we've been called upon to prove it yet again.'

He gestured to the far door. 'Out there, in the other hangars, are your comrades of B and C Companies. They have a difficult job ahead of them, just like we do. But they are going into New Jersey and Manhattan. They are moving against civilians. But not us. You know our mission. We are going against America's Air Force, at their Plattsburgh base in New York. It will be difficult, quite challenging. Which is why it was assigned to us, to A Company. You know, the Duke of Wellington's Regiment were in Plattsburgh before us, in 1812, and they took on the Yanks and won. So we have a tough act to follow, a reputation to uphold.'

The lads were silent. He walked a few paces, wishing he could wrap this up, wishing this could all be done so he could be alone in his quarters with a nice bottle of single malt, gazing at his picture of Rachel. Ah, that would be nice.

'This job has been planned, practiced, and planned again,' he said. 'Our flight will go over the border, with the other flights. The radar along the Canadian border will only see air traffic that they'll be expecting. Then, we'll divert to Plattsburgh, saying we have engine trouble. And that's when we'll start dropping in.'

There was some whispering among the troops. He raised his voice, just a little. 'We should have the element of surprise. Their Air Force units won't know what to do at first. Remember, they're not as sharp as they used to be. Years of poor food, minimal training, and resistance to their draft means units that shouldn't put up much of a fight.'

Major Hunt nodded to the engineers. 'We'll help get the Royal Engineers into the weapons bunkers quick enough, get what we need, and then load the warheads and be off. By the time the sun comes up, we'll be back at RCAF Trenton. Just a few hours and it will be over.'

There. One more thing and he'll bloody well be done. 'Any last minute questions, lads?'

Silence. Good.

He started to speak, to say, very well, off to your quarters you go, when a voice spoke up.

'Beggin' the major's pardon . . .' A sergeant stood up, arms clasped behind him.

He tried not to show his irritation. 'Yes, Sergeant? What is it?'

'What about retaliation, sir,' the sergeant asked, anger in his voice. 'What happens when we're done? Won't the Yanks retaliate? What happens if other units miss a couple of bombs. A small country like ours . . . A couple of bombs could destroy us!'

Some murmuring, some catcalls of 'hear, hear.'

'Good question, Sergeant,' Major Hunt said. 'It's been thought through and planned, all the way to the top. We know where every bomb, every warhead is located, whether it's a bomber or a missile or a submarine. I don't know the details but other units will be on the move while we're dropping in. Royal Navy, SAS, Special Boat Squadron. We won't be there for a long fight. Just to take the bombs and go. And even if there are one or two left, we'll still have most of them in our possession. They won't dare retaliate.'

'And what then?' came another question. 'What happens

once we get those fuckin' evil things? We'll just say "here ye go" and give 'em to the UN?'

He kept his voice even. 'I'm confident that will happen. We have no need for them. Our mission is to make this world safer, to disarm a nation that shouldn't have these weapons.'

A loud whisper, again, from someone who wouldn't stand up. 'Oh, right. Overnight we become the most powerful nation in the world again, and we're gonna give 'em up. Pull me the other one, why don't you.'

Some mutters and other whispers, and Major Hunt went out to the edge of the stage. 'Lads, we have something awful to do. I know it and you know it. But we've been asked to take action, and we'll do it honorably and with courage. Not for the bloody PM and his ministers, or the Ministry of Defence, or those high-and-mighty twits in Whitehall.'

They were silent, now, staring up at him. He went on. 'We'll do it because it's our job. And we'll do it for the Regiment. That's all. Dismissed.'

He stepped off the stage, his legs trembling like the first time he had been in an aircraft, years ago, preparing for his first jump.

He had strode a handful of yards out into the compound when the shooting started. He turned, hearing the shots, the stuttering sound of automatic fire. Shouts. Horns blaring. A siren. He started running toward the noise, his hands itching, wanting the comforting feel of a weapon in his hands. Others were running out of the hangars, carrying weapons or torches.

Saboteurs, he thought, as he ran. The Yanks, they found out about Operation Turnabout. They know what we're really doing next week and they've gone pre-emptive. Damn

Whitehall and the PM and every other bloody idiot. Never underestimate the Americans. Never.

And he was embarrassed at feeling hopeful, hopeful that the Americans were shooting first, that this disaster in the making could be canceled. Oh, Rachel, please let it be true.

He kept on running, to where the rows of transport aircraft were lined up, the big four-engined C-130s. He saw knots of men standing around. The shooting had stopped. Someone was yelling. He started to push through the crowds of men, engineers, paras, aircraft personnel, RCAF officers, and he heard someone say, 'Medic! Get a medic in here!'

He stopped inside the ring of men and saw, lying on the tarmac, an RAF ground crewman in a jumpsuit. He was writhing in pain, blood seeping through fingers that were clenched around his left thigh. Armed Canadian soldiers had their weapons trained on him, as two others examined his satchel. The whole scene was lit by torchlight and the head-lights from lorries that had driven up.

'Poor fellow went nuts,' an RCAF officer said. 'Was going to the transports with a bag full of hand grenades, he was. Wouldn't halt, wouldn't stop. So they shot him.'

The RAF crewman started screaming. 'It's not too late! You can all stop it! Don't you see what's happening? If we go through with this, we've lit the fuse for the next world war! Is that what you want? Is it? When we get these bombs, do you think Germany and France and Japan will sit on their back-sides and watch us?'

The assembled men watched him in silence. 'Hell, no! They'll start buildin' their own bombs, start another arms race! And we'll have another war, another world war, and millions more of us will die! Millions! In Japan and France and Germany and England, we'll all die! It'll be our turn! Your

mothers and wives and sweethearts and children and grand-
parents, all of them dead, all of them to ashes, because of us!
Because of what we're going to do!'

Two medics forced their way through the crowd and knelt
beside the wounded man. They pried his fingers loose and
tried to work on his wounds, but he flailed at them with his
fists. 'They'll all die, just like my daddy did,' and then he
started crying, great gasping sobs. 'Just like my daddy . . . He
was in the RAF and he died in Omaha, at the American
base . . . And for what? Is that what you want? Is it?'

By ones and twos and threes, the uniformed men, all representatives in one way or another of the resurgent British
empire, all of them started walking away, including Major
Hunt. Good Lord, he needed that drink, and bad.

He walked slowly to his barracks, ashamed at what he had
just seen, and ashamed at that brief joy of hope he had felt,
that the Americans were going to put a stop to this idiotic
mission.

TWENTY-SEVEN

IT WAS THE WHISTLES AND DRUMS that began to irritate Carl, standing on Beacon Street near the famous statue of Major Shaw and his doomed regiment. It was a sunny day and he was hungry and tired. He hadn't eaten anything for breakfast – save two cups of coffee – because he was nervous about the day's events. If things went well with Troy – and he had no idea how that would play out – then the next several hours would be interesting indeed. And if Troy didn't show up, or if he didn't talk, or if any one of a dozen other things happened, well . . .

Damn it, he wasn't sure. Jim Rowley was hundreds of miles away, trusting in Carl Landry, and Carl had one shot, just one shot, to make it right. For Jim and the country. And he also had Captain Rowland back there in the shadows, ready to grab whatever Carl might find, and to reward Carl with a couple of rounds to the back of his skull.

And then there was Sandy.

He shook his head and resumed watching the crowd. One problem at a time, soldier. One problem at a time. His reporter's notebook was in his hands and at his feet was a small knapsack, with water and a few other things. Ever since coming back from Manhattan, he had felt the need to have supplies with him, readily at hand. In some ways he was probably getting closer and closer to Two-Tone's world, and instead of scaring him, the thought was almost comforting.

Along with the drums and whistles came other sounds. Shouts and yells. Some chants. Amplified music, from a stage set up at the State House end of the Common, up by Park Street. All kinds of people walked by – young and old, dungarees and peasant blouses mixed in with suits and ties. He knew what would be written tomorrow in the *Globe* and *Herald*. There would be solemn opinions about the ill-dressed and unbathed crowds of ruffians who crowded in among the haze of pot and booze in the Common, though so far Carl hadn't seen or smelled any dope. Along with the youngsters he saw a middle-aged couple, walking slowly and with quiet dignity. The mother held a framed photo of a young man in an Army dress uniform. The father held a handmade sign to his chest: MY SON ROY, DEAD OF CANCER AT 21. STOP THE DRAFT. STOP THE KILLING. As they passed by Carl saw how the man's hands were quietly shaking, holding the sign.

There were other signs as well, most of them handmade, most hoisted up by sticks:

FALLOUT ISN'T GOOD FOR PEOPLE AND OTHER LIVING THINGS.

TEN YEARS IS ENOUGH – DECLARE VICTORY AND END THE DRAFT.

WAR CRIMINAL GENERAL CURTIS: ROOM FOR YOU AT LEAVENWORTH

END THE NATIONAL SECURITY STATE.

And many professionally made MCGOVERN FOR PRESIDENT signs, scattered like bright pieces of confetti among the crowd.

Carl noticed other things as well. Like the hard-eyed young men with short hair who tried unsuccessfully to blend in with the crowd. He wondered who their target was. The ranks of the protesters, or Carl Landry? Jesus, he thought. Don't let your paranoia get the best of you.

He checked his watch. Five past noon. Where was he? He looked around the statue, past the shrubbery and the trees. More and more people were crowding up Beacon Street, cutting in front of cars and taxicabs. Horns blew and there were some shouts. A young man with blond hair cut short, wearing an Army fatigue jacket a couple of sizes too large, bumped into him as he went by. Carl paid him no heed. Where in hell was Troy?

Three days left. Jesus.

'Hey,' a voice said, close to his ear and a hand tugged at his elbow. 'What's the matter, vet, your eyesight gone?'

He turned and there was the young man again, the one with the blond hair and too-large Army coat. He stared and everything clicked into focus. 'I see you've gone deep, Troy,' he said.

'Well, yeah, that has to be done sometimes,' he said, eyes casting about, scanning the crowd. 'Getting the hair dyed wasn't much of a problem, but I hate not having the beard. Face feels naked and cold.'

'We've all got our troubles.'

'Yeah, and I don't want any more. What do you need, and make it quick.'

'I need more information about your downstairs neighbor. Merl Sawson.'

The rock music from the stage got louder and Troy shook his head and rolled his eyes. 'That happy crap again? Look, the only reason I came out here is 'cause I owe you one, from back when you warned me about that raid going down. One of the places they hit was my apartment. So, thanks. Instead of being in boot camp, I'm here and I'm grateful.'

'I can tell.'

'Look, you want to talk or what? Time's wasting.'

Carl paused, wondering how he could ask the question without sounding like a fool, and then decided there was no other way. 'His dog. What happened to it?'

Troy put his hands in his coat pockets. 'His what?'

'Merl's dog,' Carl said. 'What happened? Where is he?'

Troy shook his head. 'Jesus Christ on ground zero, I can't believe you got my ass out here to ask me about that old guy's fucking dog. Man, have you been out in the sun too much?'

'Troy, just answer the question, all right? The dog?'

He coughed and looked around again, licking his lips nervously. 'The dog's dead, man. Gone for over a month.'

'And what did he do with it?'

Troy cocked his head at him, and then started laughing. 'Man, that's a good one, like you knew there was an answer there. All right. You know what he did after the dog died? The landlord, old Mr. Townes, he told me what happened, one day while I was taking out the trash. Seems old man Sawson, living on retirement income and whatever shitty pension the Army gives out, he actually spent the money for a funeral. Can you believe that? Homeless and orfie gangs in the street, and this old guy spends his money to bury his dog in a goddam pet cemetery.'

Troy looked around at the throngs of people, and he shook his head again. 'Man, if that isn't just another sign that this is one fucked-up country, than I don't know what is.'

'Where did he bury the dog?'

He shrugged. 'Don't know. Some place up north, in New Hampshire. That's all I know, and that's all I'm saying. All right? We're even, man, except for one thing.'

'And what's that?'

Another glance around at the people, some now elbowing past them. 'There's going to be a bust-up later today. Keep your head together and don't get in the middle of the crowd.'

Carl stared at him. 'Then why are you folks still going ahead with the rally?'

Troy winked. 'Politics, baby, politics. The more heads get busted, especially the ones with the coats and ties, the better the chances of getting the draft ended and getting this country back in shape.'

And with that Troy melted into the crowd and was gone. Carl checked his notebook and his knapsack, and then looked at the crowd, saw in his mind's eye similar crowds a few days hence, marching out from the outskirts of San Diego, Omaha, Miami, DC, counties in Alabama and Georgia, and Manhattan, of course, old New York City. Crowds of people, just as determined, just as angry, marching out for recognition, for their rights. Facing lines and lines of armed soldiers, and foreign troops who had no allegiance to them and who were here as the vanguard of a revitalized empire.

His shoulders felt heavy, like the lining of his coat had suddenly turned into lead.

Then he spotted her, crossing over from the direction of Winter Place, down whose narrow alleyway lay one of

Boston's famous restaurants, Locke-Ober. She wore her long black coat, the tails flapping around her legs, and her head was down. She looked up at him as she walked up the crowded sidewalk.

'You came,' he said simply.

'Yes.'

'And where are your watchers?'

She motioned with her head. 'They said they would leave me alone.'

'Do you believe them?'

'No.'

'Good,' Carl said. 'Neither do I. Let's go someplace quiet, just for a moment.'

He picked up his knapsack and walked with her, trying not to bump into the people as they streamed up to the sound-stage, and he stood with Sandy under a large pine tree. He leaned against the rough trunk and said, 'All right. Let's talk. You said you came here to do your story and to also do some favors for MI6. True?'

'Carl, I really don't know if I can—'

'Look,' he said sharply, moving away from the tree. 'I don't have time for any more games, any more secrets within secrets. What the hell is going on? Was this . . . damn it, was our relationship, was that part of the design? Was it?'

Her eyes started to fill up. 'Damn you, Carl, if that's what you believe—'

He threw up his hands. 'What can I believe, if you're not going to say anything?'

She looked around. 'All right, but make it quick. Please. I shouldn't be saying anything.'

'Favors,' he said. 'Let's talk about favors. One of your favors was to meet up with Merl Sawson. Right?'

There. Surprise in her eyes. 'Carl, I . . .' and the words trailed off.

'Sandy, in Manhattan you asked me about the murdered vet. I never told you that Merl Sawson was a vet. I said he was just an old man. You knew who he was. So, one last time and then I'm walking, Sandy. Were you supposed to meet Merl Sawson?' He could have told her about the surveillance photo, but he ached at confronting her with it. He wanted to give her a chance, at least a chance, to come clean.

Even with the noise and the drums and the music, he could sense the struggle within her. Then she stepped closer to him and said, 'Yes, I was.'

'What for?'

'To pick up some documents, documents of great importance.'

'Why you?'

'It was thought that he was under surveillance,' she said, stammering slightly. 'But I could interview him for my piece on the anniversary of the war, and that would give me enough cover to retrieve the documents and get them to the consulate.'

'And what happened?'

'I got to Boston and before I could set up an interview, he was dead.'

'And then you were told to attach yourself to me?'

Her eyes were watery. 'Yes.'

'And what for?'

'Somebody knew that you had talked to Merl, and were following up on his death,' she said. 'It was thought that you might find the package, or that you might have it already.'

'And what were these documents?' Damn you again, Merl,

he thought. If you had just given me the goddam thing the first time we met . . .

She shook her head and looked away. 'I don't know. All I know is that they were very important and that they had to be got out of the country. And that Merl was meant to come out as well.'

'That was the deal, to get him out in exchange for these papers?'

A sad nod. 'That's right.'

'And what about the dead British general, the one who died just before you got here? Coincidence?'

A pause. 'No, I don't think it was a coincidence. I think he was sent here to see Merl before me. I was second choice.'

'Manhattan,' he said, thinking over their trip. 'Was that for real, or a cover?'

'Oh, that was for bloody real,' she said, kicking at a clump of leaves on the ground. 'I was tired of playing at spooks, and I told them I had to get some real work done. And the Manhattan tour was an opportunity to do just that.'

'And why the invite to me?'

She looked back at him. 'What?'

'Sandy, why did you invite me along to New York City?' he asked, looking intently at those eyes, at that smooth skin, wondering if he could ever understand what was going on behind that cool British exterior. 'If the goal was to see what I knew about Merl Sawson, then why invite me to leave Boston and spend a few days with you in Manhattan? What's the point? Or were you trying to find out more about Jim Rowley and his people?'

She looked pained. 'The point, you oaf, is that I was falling in love with you, and I wanted you to be with me. That was the point. And my watchers were none too pleased to find out about my invitation. They'd have far rather you stayed in Boston, poking your nose into things. And I knew nothing about PS 19 until we met them. That's the truth.'

'And what about PS 19?' he asked, not wanting to tell her about Jim Rowley's plans to come out before the election. 'You know what's planned, with your paras getting ready to go in. You said something before, about wanting to help them. Another story, or the truth?'

She rubbed at the side of her head with her hands. 'The truth. But . . . I'm not allowed to make any overseas phone calls, Carl, and I've been warned that anything I write will be heavily vetted. I . . . I don't think I can do anything, as much as I hate to admit it. I think the consulate might be involved in all of this. And I hate what's going on.'

He thought again about Manhattan. 'That first day, right after the ambush, when you left the apartment and came back with candles. You made a radio call, right? Using that radio you had dummied up to look like a tape recorder.'

For a moment her mouth dropped open and she said, 'How did you know about that?'

'Oh, come now, you know a good reporter never reveals his sources,' he said, feeling a shamed sense of pleasure at the shock in her face. 'What were you doing? Arranging a pickup?'

She still look flustered. 'Yes. I managed to get a quick message out and I got an acknowledgment, but we were moving around too much for them to find us. I knew MI6 would get to us eventually.'

'And these documents, they were going to do what?'

'They were going to make a difference, that's all. A very important difference in our nations' relationship.'

He looked at those bright and intelligent eyes, and he still could not tell what was going on there. Carl paused, remembering the smoothness of her skin, the taste of her mouth, the scent of her hair, and the old feelings she had rekindled. Hope. A hell of a thing to depend on. Hope. He thought for a quick moment, about what had happened and what could happen, and he said, 'You still want those papers?'

'Of course I do,' she said, her voice suddenly eager. 'Do you know where they are?'

'It might mean going away for a day or so. Do you mind ditching your watchers?'

'Not at all,' she said. 'It would be a pleasure, and—'

The music up front stopped and then a chanting started, a chorus that grew and grew, until it almost hurt his ears.

'Hell no, we won't glow, hell no, we won't glow, HELL NO, WE WON'T GLOW!'

Carl leaned forward until his lips touched her ear. 'I think the demonstration is about ready to kick off. Want to get a better look? It will help us slip the guys who are following you.'

'Sure,' she said, and slipped her hand into his and squeezed. After just a moment, he squeezed back. He knew what he was doing. Maybe. 'Stick close,' he said, bending down to grab his knapsack and tossing it over his shoulder.

They stepped away from the tree and then they were swept up by the crowd across the Common's lawn, moving and chanting and waving signs and placards, jutting clenched fists in time to the chorus:

'HELL NO, WE WON'T GLOW!'
'HELL NO, WE WON'T GLOW!'
'HELL NO, WE WON'T GLOW!'

Sandy tugged at his hand and leaned in again. 'Can we get closer to the stage?'

It was hard to talk in all the noise, so he just nodded. He took hold of her hand again and started moving toward Tremont Street. She looked at him with surprise, and then he headed up to the intersection of Park Street. He didn't want to be stuck in the middle of the crowd. As they moved they were jostled and bumped, and he winced a couple of times as his feet were trampled on. He never gave up the hand lock on Sandy, and he looked back occasionally, just to make sure she was all right.

The chanting died down and then someone up on the stage began talking, and the voice was so amplified and distorted that he had a hard time making out complete sentences. The speech came out in a series of clipped phrases that echoed along the buildings on Tremont Street.

'. . . we need a new beginning, a beginning that recognizes our sins of the past and the promise of our future . . .'

Boston police barricades were now up along the street, and he felt something in the air, a tension and a sense of some indescribable forces coming together, like the still air before a late-summer thunderstorm. A helicopter roared overhead, surveying the crowd, and some people shook their fists up at the green machine. He stopped against a lamppost and pulled Sandy in close to him.

'. . . a dictatorship, no matter how helpful and high-sounding, is still a dictatorship . . .'

Sandy leaned in against him, raising her voice to make herself heard. 'Why are we stopping?'

'Needed a break,' he said, his eyes roving over the crowd, picking out the individual faces, the thousands upon thousands of people who streamed around them. They were close enough to the stage to see the makeshift platform that had been set up. Banners flapped in the breeze, with garish colors and letters. Tall amplifiers flanked both ends of the stage, and a figure in jeans and a U.S. flag shirt was in front of a microphone, raising his arms as he talked.

'. . . and a draft that sends our brothers and sons to a wasteland is still slavery . . .'

Beyond the stage was the gold dome of the State House, and Carl saw movement back there, green uniforms coming down the steps and across the sidewalks, up there on the hill. He felt cold. He remembered what Troy had told him a few minutes ago. Sandy said, 'Why can't we get closer? I want to get closer.'

He said, 'No, we don't want to do that. This is good enough.'

She looked at him and then over at the crowd. There were shouts and a scream, as a phalanx of hard-hatted construction workers waded into the crowd by the corner of Tremont and Park, battling a group of bearded youths who were flying an American flag upside down. The voice on the stage got louder.

'. . . and we're not going to take it anymore. We're going to take this country back, one street at a time, one city at a time, one State House at a time!'

The shouting grew and grew and grew, and he leaned against the pole, seeing other scuffles break out in the crowd. A woman went by, sobbing, holding a bloody handkerchief to the head of a male friend. Three or four men stood in a circle, holding their draft cards up and burning them, as people around them applauded. Siren whoops started, off in the distance, and he looked over at the alleyways between the office buildings on the other side of Tremont Street. They were lined with soldiers in riot helmets, carrying clear plastic shields and long wooden batons. Just like the supplies stored back in Manhattan. Beside the soldiers were Boston police officers on horses, and Carl was horrified to see that both the cops and horses were wearing gas masks.

'. . . let's go, let's seize this place and show them what free people can do!'

Sandy reached up and hugged him and said, 'Something bad is going to happen.'

'Yes.'

'Should we get out of here?'

'Let's see if we can.'

Carl looked at the people moving about them, some running and stumbling, and saw the grim face of Captain Rowland, who was heading right for them, a hand under his coat, reaching for something.

Then it was too late.

The popping sounds started, one or two, and then a chorus. Up on the hill behind the stage white and yellow streams of smoke arced into the air and fell into the crowd. The white clouds blossomed and blew in the wind. More screams and shouts and Sandy yelled in his ear, 'Oh, Christ, are they shooting at us?'

'No, it's just tear gas,' he said, grabbing her hand again and heading down the sidewalk. 'Look, we've got to get out of here. It's going to get hairy here, real quick.'

He held her hand tight and spared a glance back. Captain Rowland was stuck in the crowd, but he was one angry soldier and he was coming toward them, and Carl had a pretty good idea why. Consorting with the enemy was still officially frowned upon, even when there wasn't a war on, and Carl also wasn't following orders. A bad combination.

'Carl—'

He moved quickly, not wanting to run. When you run it's easy to lose your footing, to tumble, and with all the people bumping and surging around them, it would be easy to get trampled. The crowd wasn't in a panic, not yet, but there were many anxious looks and fearful glances at the chaos erupting around the stage.

'There's going to be a lot of people hurt here in the next minute or two, and I don't want us to be part of them!' he yelled back at her. Something whistled and there was a loud POP! behind them, and they both turned. Sandy screamed, seeing the huge cloud of teargas sweep upon them. Now the people shouted and broke and ran, and Sandy made to go with them but Carl pulled her to him.

'No,' he said. 'Run this way, close your eyes and hold your breath!'

He fought against the crowd and ran toward the cloud of gas coming at them. Sandy struggled but he refused to let go, and then he held her in his arms and hugged her tight, and shut his eyes and said, 'Now, now, hold your breath!'

The acrid, choking smell swept over them and he heard a chorus of screams and gasping sounds. He buried his face in her coat and held her head tight against his shoulder, and then the cloud passed them by. He opened his eyes and blinked hard at the burning sensation. People were on the ground all around them, gasping for breath, and some were vomiting. Sirens were howling as police cruisers came up the street, followed by Army trucks filled with troops, all wearing gas masks and carrying M-1 rifles with fixed bayonets.

'You okay?' he said, coughing a few times.

She coughed hard and choked and wiped her hand across

her runny eyes. 'You bastard! Why did we run right into it?'

'Because you can't outrun it,' he said. 'Best thing is to run right at it, because then it'll go over you. You try to run away and it catches up to you and knocks you down, and you're still in the cloud. You've got a handkerchief with you?'

She coughed, nodded. 'Yes.'

'Take it out and hold it against your nose and face. We've got to get moving.'

Sandy fumbled in her purse, looked around at the people on the grass and sidewalk. 'What about them?'

'I'm concerned about you, Sandy. That's all. Let's go.'

They moved along Tremont Street at a slow jog, and there was a loud banging noise behind them. Carl turned and saw a row of soldiers in riot gear and gas masks, marching in a ragged line, pounding their batons on their plastic shields. An ear-piercing squeal of amplified feedback echoed across the Common, and then a loud voice, more clear and measured than the previous voice, began to speak:

'Attention, attention, attention. You are ordered to disperse. Under the National Martial Law Act of 1962, this is an illegal gathering. Attention, attention, attention. You are ordered to disperse . . .'

And as the voice repeated itself, he held on to Sandy and moved to the west, heading away from the Common. He held her tight and listened to the man's voice over the loudspeakers, the popping sounds of tear gas canisters, police sirens, screams and shouts, and the ever present rapping sound of batons against riot shields.

They rested for a few minutes, along with hundreds of others, at the pond in the Public Garden, wiping their hands

and faces clear of the tear gas smell. He still had his knapsack with him and pulled out two towels, one of which Sandy
gratefully accepted. They dipped the towels in the cold water
and washed their faces. All around them other protest
marchers did the same, kneeling at the water's edge, splash-
ing their faces. Some huddled with their arms around each
other, and Carl looked on as an old woman, maybe the age of
his mother if she had lived, gingerly wiped the face of a man
about her age wearing a World War II Army Air Corps
uniform.

He looked around with that same nervous sharpness that
he had had while in active duty. There were enemies out
there, enemies in his own nation's uniform, and he had to get
moving. Captain Rowland and his boys were dedicated
members of the Zed Force, and if he and Sandy didn't get a
move on, and quick . . . Well, it wouldn't be pretty. Sirens still
sounded in the distance and there was a gray haze of tear gas
that eddied and moved with the breeze up on the Common.
Some of the mounted police rode at a stately pace through
the gas, their horses looking like some medieval horror in gas
masks and cloaks.

Sandy said, 'Are you all right?'

'Sure,' he said, looking around at the crying and sobbing
people, some on their backs, still gasping for breath. 'Great
day to be an American.'

She looked puzzled. 'Sorry?'

Carl sighed and stood up. 'No, it's me who should be sorry.
A poor attempt at a joke.' He looked back up at the Common
as a line of soldiers and mounted Boston cops advanced,
moving amid the stragglers and lone protesters. A couple of
them tried to make a stand, throwing rocks at the advancing
line of troops and police, but they were quickly overpowered

up by two cops on horseback who rode them down. At least there were no shots fired. Carl doubted the foreign soldiers in a few days would be so generous.

'Look, we can't stay here,' Carl said. 'Chances are, everybody on this Common, press badge or not, is going to get arrested.'

'Your apartment,' she said. 'It's within walking distance, isn't it?'

'It is, but we shouldn't go there,' he said, 'and we need to get moving, now.'

She stood up and they headed away from the pond, toward Commonwealth Avenue. People from inside the apartment buildings and brownstones were standing outside in quiet little knots, watching the drama on the Common, some holding hands up to their faces.

'What's the matter,' Sandy said.

'I was being watched back there, by someone in the U.S. Army Special Forces,' he said, walking quickly and holding her hand. 'Someone who wants to see that I do a certain task.'

'What task?'

He squeezed her hand. 'Something similar to your job, Miss Price, except I'm in the service of this country's intelligence services. You see, they also want those secret documents.'

'And you know where they are, don't you? Can we get them?'

He turned and looked at her. 'Not so fast, Sandy. First, they have to be found. And second, we have to get off the streets or we're going to be arrested.'

'But where can we go? The consulate?'

'Nope, we'll be picked up before we get to the front gate.

And getting a hotel room means using a credit card, which means an arrest within the hour. No, we have to go some-where else.'

'Where?' she asked.

He answered, enjoying the confused look on her face.

'Sandy, how would you like to meet an honest-to-God veteran of the Cuban invasion?'

TWENTY-EIGHT

ALL THROUGH THAT AFTERNOON, Two-Tone was a gracious gentleman and perfect host. Carl had taken Sandy to the hidey-hole entrance, and after hauling off the steel plate and shouting up the tunnel and getting a happy greeting back, he and Sandy had gotten on their hands and knees and started crawling. Two-Tone looked better and was able to move around his home, using a cane. He offered them both water in clean jelly glasses and Carl sat down on a salvaged couch, with Sandy next to him, her eyes wide in amazement, taking everything in.

Carl said, 'I know I promised that I wouldn't tell anybody about your hidey-hole, Two-Tone, but this was an emergency.'

'Well, well, that's all right, Carl, that's all right. Emergencies do pop up every now and then,' Two-Tone said. 'And what is your name again, miss? I'm afraid I was so pleased at seeing a woman in my home that I didn't catch it.'

'Sandra Price,' she said, and Carl was pleased when she held her hand out. Two-Tone quickly shook it and he said, 'England, right?'

'Yes, London,' she said. 'I'm a reporter for the *Times*. And you can call me Sandy.'

Two-Tone giggled and glanced over at Carl. 'Can't believe a woman of this class, a woman like this, is hanging with you, Carl.'

'Me neither.'

She gently poked Carl in the side and said, 'Carl tells me that you were in the Cuban invasion. Is that right?'

He scratched at his face. A Red Sox baseball cap covered his head. 'True, true, but I really don't want to talk about it right now, if you don't mind, Sandy.'

'No, I don't mind,' she said. 'I can understand why you might be reluctant.'

'Oh, hell, I ain't reluctant,' he said. 'It's just that Carl said something was an emergency, and I don't want to dick around talkin'. Carl, what's the emergency?'

He looked over at Sandy and said, 'There was a demonstration up at the Common a little while ago. Things get out of hand and I don't think Sandy and I can go back to our homes. We'd probably be arrested before the night is out. And I saw someone at the demonstration, a Captain Rowland, who didn't look very happy to see me there. Does that name sound familiar?'

Two-Tone nodded, rubbing a hand across his chin. 'Full house. The bastard.'

Sandy was confused. 'What house?'

'The Special Forces officer back at the Common,' Carl said. 'Two-Tone knew him a long time ago, and they had a run-in recently.'

'If that bastard's after you, then you do have troubles,' Two-Tone said. 'Why's he chasin' you, Carl?'

'I'm not sure if he'd call it chasing,' Carl said. 'I think he just wants to know where I am and what I'm doing, and I don't want that, not at all.' He looked over at Sandy, at that face that still caused him to ache with affection and despair, and said, 'We have things to do. Important things. And we want to be left alone.'

Two-Tone clapped his hands together. 'Well, I can sure as hell understand that. I've been trying to be left alone for about ten years now, and look where it's gotten me. D'you want to stay here for a spell? It'd be tight quarters but I'm sure we could work something out.'

Carl said, 'I appreciate the offer, but we need to get moving. I was thinking maybe you could contact Skyman, perhaps he could take my car keys and—'

The old vet shook his head briskly. 'Won't work, son. If you're in this deep, they'll have everything wired, from your apartment to your car. Poor old Skyman would be arrested, maybe even shot while trying to escape. No, I've got a better idea.'

'What's that?' Sandy asked, balancing the water glass on her knee.

'I can get a car,' Two-Tone said. 'Would that work?'

Carl knew there was a shocked expression on his face. 'You? You can get a car?'

Two-Tone laughed again. 'Carl, m'boy, haven't you ever wondered why you don't see that much of me during the winter?'

'Occasionally . . . upstate Florida?'

'Nah, too far south. Too many zoomies still down there. Nope. North Carolina. Nice climate, people friendly to a veteran like me, and warm enough so that my bones don't ache. You see, there's a few of us – including Skyman – who chipped in years ago and got ourselves a car. For survival sake, you know. We figure if things get tense again, like back in '62, we could drive up to Maine and survive. Here—' Two-Tone poked a hand into his trousers and pulled out a thick clump of keys that jangled in his fist. He prodded one free and handed it over. 'There ya go. I'll tell you where it is in a couple of minutes, after I freshen up your drink. But one more thing.'

Carl examined the key, saw that it belonged to a Volkswagen. 'And what's that?'

'The car.'

'What about it?'

Two-Tone grinned. 'Make sure you top off the tank before you bring it back. Don't want to piss off Skyman and the others.'

Two hours later they were in New Hampshire, parked in a state liquor store lot, just over the border into Nashua. The drive usually took just an hour, but this wasn't a usual time. He had taken side streets to get out of Boston, and had stuck to secondary roads all the way north. There was too much depending on this little ride for them to be stopped at a checkpoint. Along the way they had caught the news on WBZ, one of the state's largest AM stations. The fourth story, after a traffic update, mentioned a brief disturbance at the Boston Common. And that was it.

Sandy had said, 'Even though I've been here for almost a month, I still can't get used to the censorship. How could they bury a story like that? Do they really think they're fooling anyone?'

'Probably not, but appearances must be kept,' he had replied.

Now he strode back to the fire engine red Volkswagen Beetle, after having spent the previous half hour on a pay phone outside of the liquor store. Sandy sat in the passenger's seat, arms folded, looking grim. He opened the door and got in. 'We got some luck, for a change. I started going through the Yellow Pages and found a couple of pet cemeteries, and got the right one on the third call. Merl Sawson purchased a plot some weeks ago at a place called Happy Farms. It's in Hudson, next town over. I also got us a place to spend the night, right near there.'

Three days. He just might make it.

He turned the key to the Volkswagen a few times before the engine caught, and then drove out onto the highway, looking for the first exit. Sandy said, 'I cannot believe that you brought us up here on this . . . this ridiculous idea that these documents might be buried with a dead dog. You still can't be serious!'

Carl tried to keep his voice level. 'I know it sounds silly, but it's the only idea I have. That house has been searched, time and time again. Everything about Merl Sawson's life from that apartment has been sifted, studied, and collected. His landlord is dead and his upstairs neighbor is on the run. The Army and the Boston cops have been more thorough than anything I can do. The documents were once in his possession. Now they're not. And that leaves me with a dog that's not there and documents that aren't there. It's a long shot but it's the only one I can think of.'

'Hah,' she said, arms still folded. 'The idea that these top-secret documents, papers that men have died over, are hidden in a pet cemetery . . .' She turned, eyes sharp. 'You're not going to dump me, are you? That's not your plan, is it? Abandon me, and then find these papers by yourself?'

He turned to her. 'Pretty bold talk for someone working in this country as a spy.'

The inside of the car was quiet, the only sound the incessant chugging noise of the engine. He took an exit and was soon on Route 111, heading east, passing farms and houses and a couple of stores. He had never particularly liked New Hampshire. It seemed a mean-spirited, money-grubbing Yankee state, in the truest sense of the word. They had no sales or income tax and made their money selling cheap booze and cigarettes, and the state was solidly Republican. They also continued to gloat over the fact that in 1960, even with a son of Massachusetts running for the presidency, the state had still gone for Nixon.

'I'm sorry,' she said. 'I shouldn't have said that. You've been . . . Carl, you've been wonderful. Though I do wonder why you've brought me along, considering everything.'

He reached over and touched her hand. 'I didn't want to do this alone, and . . .'

'And what?'

He stared ahead. 'I guess when you're in love, you do crazy things.'

She said nothing, but leaned over and kissed his cheek.

Most of the motels in the area were booked full with leaf-peepers heading out into the woods to see the fall foliage, and he was embarrassed at their lodgings. The place was called The Matador Inn and looked like a honeymoon motel for those honeymooners in the nearby mill towns of Lawrence and Lowell who couldn't afford to go very far north. They were in a quaintly named cabin that was actually a poorly built shack. The walls were fake wood paneling that was pulling away from the mounting studs, and the bed was a lumpy mattress on a sagging spring set. There was a kitchenette in one corner and a bathroom in the other, and the only concession to luxury was an open brick fireplace set in the center of the one-room cabin. A black stovepipe came through the roof and was suspended over the circular pile of stones and rocks.

Carl saw a small metal lever and pulled it toward himself. There was a popping sound and then a *poof* as the gas lit from a small pilot light. The blue-yellow flames leapt up and he looked over at Sandy, who was standing by the door, rubbing her hands together.

'Cozy, ain't it,' Carl said.

'You know, I keep promising to take you to the Savoy, and all you do is bring me to these dreadful places,' she said, walking over to the gas fire. 'I'm beginning to wonder whether I should retract my offer, after all you've put me through.'

'Well, the day's not over yet,' he said, picking up his knapsack. 'If you have to go to the loo, here's your chance. I want to get out there soonest.'

She grabbed her coat. 'I'm ready. Let's go.'

He had one scary moment, in a hardware store on Route 3 in Hudson, buying a shovel. There were only two singles left in his wallet after he had paid for a night at the motel and here he was, with a shovel costing $4.99. He had a humiliating thought of having to borrow money from Sandy, but reached into his other pocket and found a crumpled ten-dollar bill.

When he got outside and put the shovel in the rear of the Volkswagen, he said, 'Amazing, when you think of it.'

'What's amazing?'

'That finding the answer to what in hell's been going on with Merl Sawson's death, that it would depend upon me having enough money for a shovel.'

'I don't understand.'

'I'll tell you later.' Unbelievable. The fate of two nations dependent on a $4.99 shovel.

The drive to the Happy Farms pet cemetery took another ten minutes. The place was run by a stout, elderly woman in tan slacks and a dungaree workshirt who didn't seem eager to assist, until Carl slid his last five-dollar bill across the wooden counter. Her face brightened, the money disappeared, and she said, 'You know, now that you mention it, I do remember a man from Massachusetts coming up here some few weeks ago, bringing his dog.'

Carl clenched the car keys so tight in his palm he thought the skin would break. 'And that's what the other woman told me over the phone, just an hour ago.'

'Oh, that's my daughter,' she said, making a dismissive wave in the air. 'She's so scatter-brained, I wouldn't trust her to tell me if it was snowing in the middle of a blizzard.'

She reached under the counter and brought out a leather-bound ledger book. She licked her fingers, opened the book, and ran her fingers down the columns and said, 'Here it is. Lot one seventeen. Bought by a Mr. Sawson. There should be a metal post with a number on it. Would you like me to walk you out there?'

'No, that's all right,' Carl said. 'Mr. Sawson was a friend of ours, and we bought a little headstone for his dog, just to show him we care. We'll go out there by ourselves.'

The woman shut the ledger with a confident slap of her hand. 'Funny thing, that.'

'Excuse me?'

She took a rag and started wiping down the counter. 'That's what he asked to do, when he brought his dog in. He didn't want any help, didn't want any supervision. He just wanted to go out there by himself and do the job alone.'

He took the shovel out of the car and concealed it close to his leg, in case they were being watched through the windows of the one-story building. He started walking across the cemetery with Sandy at his side and his knapsack over one shoulder. She said, 'You know, I'm beginning to get a little excited. Just a little, mind you.'

'Excited?'

She looped an arm through his. 'What that woman said, about him coming out here alone. My God, maybe you are right after all.'

'Don't start thanking me yet.' Three days. Maybe, just maybe . . .

They walked among the headstones, some decorated by flowers, either fresh or plastic. The stones were simple, honoring dogs and cats and other pets, though Carl noticed the cats outnumbered the dogs. Sandy shivered and pressed his arm close. 'I don't know why, but I find this place depressing, even more so than a cemetery for people. Why is that?'

Carl looked at the small stones, each marking a loved pet. 'Because they're all so innocent. They don't think up exotic ways of killing or cheating or lying to each other. Maybe that's why.'

'Maybe.'

At the far corner of the cemetery was a metal pole, about six inches tall, and on top of the pole was a round metal plate. The numerals 117 were engraved on it. He dropped his knapsack and leaned on the shovel. The cemetery was a square lot of land, bordered on three sides by woods. It was dusk and the sky was clear. Lights were already on in the tiny building on the far side of the lot, where the only vehicles were the woman's station wagon and their Volkswagen. A truck rumbled by on the far road. Sandy said, 'Are you all right?'

'Just catching my breath,' he said, picking up the shovel. 'Just catching my breath.'

He dug slowly at first, freeing up the metal pole, which was anchored about a foot in the ground. He tugged the pole free, tossed it aside, and resumed digging. Sandy stood next to him, eyes downcast, hands trembling, and he wondered what was going through her mind.

'Secrets,' he said.

'I'm sorry, what did you say?'

'Secrets, Sandy,' he said, tossing aside another shovelful of dirt. 'It's time for us to tell each other some secrets. Like what might be down this hole. You said you were supposed to get some documents from Merl Sawson and deliver them to your superiors. What's in the documents?'

'Carl, I told you before—'

'I know, I know. You told me the documents were something of great importance, something that had to be gotten out of the country. And I want to know what your people think they are. Sandy?'

He stopped shoveling, letting the blade sink into the wet soil. Sandy had her fists clenched to her side and looked downward. Then she cleared her voice and said, 'Codes.'

'What kind of codes?'

'Dispersal codes,' she said resignedly. 'You don't know how scared we are of you . . . You're the only nation left with its own nuclear force, and that frightens everyone, whether they live in Tokyo, Paris, Berlin, or London. Somehow . . . from what I was told, Colonel Sawson had dispersal codes for your remaining strategic forces. The bombers and the submarines.'

'And a few missiles,' he said.

'Oh, yes, but just a few. It's the bombers and the submarines that concern us, and Colonel Sawson supposedly had the codes that would send them to other countries.'

He rubbed his hands across the shovel handle. 'Dispersal codes . . . If there was a threat, you'd want your bombers and submarines out of their bases. And the right code might send them to another country. Like air bases in Canada for one's bombers, and naval bases in Great Britain and Hong Kong for your submarine force. So let's say these codes get overseas to your friends and are transmitted on the right frequencies. Then this country disarms itself, sending its nuclear forces to our British and Canadian friends. And when they arrive . . . interned, right?'

'Right,' she said, nodding quickly. 'And disarmed. And then maybe General Curtis and the other lunatics here would start talking sense, start cooperating with us and the UN.'

'Some people might call that meddling in another nation's affairs.'

'And others might call it meddling in the survival of this planet,' she said sharply.

He resumed his digging. 'Now, that's funny.'

'Why? What's so amusing?'

'That story,' he said. 'That's the fourth story I've heard about what Merl Sawson was hiding. Another is that he was hiding the original Declaration of Independence and our Constitution, smuggled out of Washington before the bombing ten years ago. Another is that he had important documents that can impact the upcoming election.'

And Resurrection Day, but he still didn't want to tell Sandy that part of the story. Not yet.

'And yet another story . . . well, that's one so crazy, I can't even believe it. It involves what might be the hiding place of President John F. Kennedy. Confirming that he is alive after all.'

'That's insane,' she said.

'Ain't that the truth,' he said, picking up the shovel. 'Let's find out.'

He widened the hole and kept digging, and Sandy moved around, trying to look closer and closer. Back at the parking lot the Volkswagen was now the only vehicle there. It was getting dark and a wind was picking up, and Carl was contemplating resting for just a few minutes when the shovel struck something that made a scratching noise.

'What is it?' Sandy asked, leaning into him and looking into the hole.

'Not sure,' he said. 'In the top flap of the knapsack, there's a flashlight. Get it out, will you?'

Sandy got to her knees and opened up the knapsack and clicked on the flashlight, holding it with both of her hands. She aimed it down the open hole and he scraped the shovel back and forth. There was a piece of blue cloth down there, and he moved the cloth away with the shovel blade, exposing something white and firm. He pushed aside some more dirt, and then Sandy said, 'Oh!' and he felt something go sour in his mouth.

The fur-covered skull of a dog grinned up at them.

Sandy sat on the ground, still holding the flashlight, and Carl felt his hands burn with the pain of shoveling. His legs were aching, too. Then he muttered something and resumed digging, and Sandy said, 'What are you doing?'

'Just closing the circle,' he said. 'Finishing the job.'

He gingerly removed the remains as best he could, wrapped up as they were in a thready blue towel. Then he dug for another five or ten minutes, and when the shovel blade scraped against something else, Sandy stood up, flashlight again pointing down to the hole.

'What was that?' she said, her voice once more eager.

'Don't get excited,' he said. 'Might just be a rock. Or another bone.'

But he felt his own arms tremble with excitement as he scraped more dirt away, widening the hole even more. The sound of this scraping was different than before: metal upon metal, and in the wavering light of the flashlight, he saw something dark green in the hole. A few shovelfuls of dirt later and he saw the top of a green metal lid, narrow and long. Two more shovels of dirt and he recognized it for what it was, and he laid the shovel down and got on his hands and knees.

On top of the metal lid was a handle, and he grabbed on to it and pulled.

It wouldn't budge.

'Damn it,' he whispered, though he knew no one was around to hear them.

'What's wrong?'

'It's stuck in there, like a cork in a bottle.' He stood up and worked the shovel in and around the metal box, scraping and prying, and then Sandy said, 'Carl. Look over there.'

He looked up. Two cars were pulling into the small parking lot next to Two-Tone's Volkswagen.

'The light,' he said. 'Kill the damn light and hit the dirt!'

She clicked off the flashlight and lay flat on the ground, and he joined her, pushing his hand into the hole. He grabbed at the box again, feeling the sharp metal cut into his skin. He tugged. Nothing moved.

'I don't know if they spotted us,' Sandy whispered. 'They're going toward the building, but I think it's closed now. Most of the lights are off.'

Another tug. Nothing. He swore and put both arms down into the hole, scraping a fingernail in the process, and he grabbed the handle again.

'It looks like three or four men,' Sandy said. 'They're knocking at the door and looking through the windows.'

Carl gritted his teeth, pulled up, and finally, something gave. Dirt trickled back into the hole, tinkling off the cover of the metal box.

'Carl,' she whispered again, her voice strained. 'I think they're looking over here.'

'Too bad,' he whispered back, and he gave another tug, and another, and the box slowly came out, revealing itself to be a metal ammo box, clamped and clipped shut. Carl took a breath and said, 'Can you crawl?'

'Of course.'

'Then let's start crawling, to that woods line, and let's get a move on.'

As he crawled the short distance into the woods, he felt something cold on his spine, like someone was lining up a rifle's target scope on the middle of his back.

TWENTY-NINE

THE TRIP THROUGH THE WOODS and through the streets of Hudson seemed to take all night, although the cabin clock said they had only been gone two hours. They had traveled among trees and across fields, and then had walked quietly and quickly along the side streets of the small town, heading toward the sound of traffic. That had led them to Route 3 and back to the Matador Inn.

Carl had forced Sandy to hold back and they had hidden in a thicket of bushes and brambles across the street, looking for anything out of the ordinary, anything that didn't belong. Like an unmarked Chevy van or Ford LTD in the motel's parking lot. Or a couple of husky young men, lounging about the motel's check-in area.

When he was satisfied that all was clear, he led her across the street, shouldering his knapsack and carrying the ammo box in his free hand. He unlocked the door to the cabin and kept all of the lights off while he drew the curtains, then closed and locked the door. Then he switched on a small table lamp and walked over to the fireplace in the center of the room.

'No need to bring any attention to ourselves,' he said. 'We'll stay for a bit, see what we've got in the box, then wash up and get the hell out of here.'

'Where to?'

'First things first,' he said. He dropped the knapsack and the box to the floor, and then lit the fireplace, keeping the flame low. His hands were scratched and scraped, and he had a sharp cut over his left cheek. Sandy looked just a little better, her fine hair tangled with bits of leaves and twigs.

'I'm sorry, I just can't wait anymore,' she said. 'Open it, please open it.'

He perched the ammo box on the brick edge of the fireplace, wiping it clear of dirt. Faded yellow paint on the side of the box announced that it contained five hundred rounds of .30 caliber ammunition. He almost giggled with despair. The yellow letters might just be right. That's all. All this work and skullduggery and traipsing through the woods on a cold fall night, all for a few hundred rounds of ammunition. Sorry, Jim. Sorry, PS 19. Sorry, United States.

The lid was held down by a spring clamp, which easily popped open. Sandy was looking at the box with eagerness, her eyes wide with anticipation. He felt his own shaking hands grow cold as he lifted up the lid. In the faint firelight he saw something inside, wrapped in plastic. He picked it up and started unwrapping it. The package shifted in his hands.

'Papers,' he said softly. 'That's what's in here. Papers. And it's definitely not the Declaration of Independence or the Constitution.'

Sandy hugged herself. 'The codes,' she said. 'They were right. The codes. Carl, do you realize what this means?'

The plastic came off and fell to the floor. He looked down

at what he held, at the top document, and he wordlessly handed it to Sandy. She read it with a low moan and said, 'That's it? We've gone through all of this, and all we've got are memos? Bloody memos? No codes?'

'I'm afraid so,' he said, holding another document up to the trembling firelight, and read the first few paragraphs:

SECRET

SPECIAL
NATIONAL INTELLIGENCE
ESTIMATE
NUMBER 85-3-62

The Military Buildup In Cuba

19 September 1962

THE PROBLEM

To assess the strategic and political significance of the recent military buildup in Cuba and of the possible future development of additional military capabilities there.

He flipped through the pages, revealing other documents from that long-dead building known as the White House:

TOP SECRET
_____

SUPPLEMENT 7

TO

JOINT EVALUATION OF

SOVIET MISSILE THREAT IN CUBA

PREPARED BY

Guided Missile and Astronautics Intelligence Committee
Joint Atomic Energy Intelligence Committee
National Photographic Interpretation Center

0200 Hours
27 October 1962
SUMMARY

1. Detailed analysis confirms the rapid pace of construction reported in our last supplement. As of 25 October there is no evidence indicating any intention to halt construction, dismantle or move these sites.

2. There are no changes in the dates of estimated operational capability for the MRBM and IRBM sites. Five of the six MRBM sites are now believed to have a full operational capability and the sixth is estimated to achieve this status tomorrow – 28 October (See Figure 2). This means a capability to launch up to 24 MRBM (1020 nm) missiles within 6

to 8 hours of a decision to do so, and a refire capability of up to 24 additional MRBMs within 4 to 6 hours (see Table 1).

There were easily a hundred pages of memos and reports. A name caught his eye on one document, a hastily typewritten memorandum that had several typeovers and cross-outs:

THE WHITE HOUSE
Washington

October 27, 1962

MEMORANDUM FOR THE PRESIDENT

The Joint Chiefs of Staff Operational Plan No. 312 specifically called for the destruction of any Cuban or Soviet SA-2 missile sites within two hours of their having shot down a U-2 surveillance craft. To support this directive, 16 F-100 fighters have been on station at Homestead Air Force Base in Florida on 30-minute alert since the start of the crisis.

At about 10 a.m. EST today, a U-2 flight near the Cuban northern coast was shot down. Shortly after 2 p.m., per the direct order of the President, this office contacted Air Force General Ramsey Curtis to ensure that the retaliatory strike against the SA-2 site that shot down this U-2 would not occur except upon the direct order of the President.

General Curtis replied, quote, 'The Russian bear has always been eager to stick his paw in Latin

American waters. Now that we've got him in a trap, let's take his leg off right up to his balls. On second thought, let's take off his balls, too.'

He looked up from the memo, the page shaking in his hand. Could this be . . . Sandy was sitting by the fireplace, leaning against the brick supports, shaking her head. 'All of this . . . all of this work and blood and tears and sweat, all for a bunch of bloody ten-year-old memos.'

'Sandy, don't start panicking,' he started, scanning the memo again, wondering how in God's name it had gotten out of the White House in time. 'It could work out to be—'

The bathroom door inside the cabin slammed open and Sandy sat up with a shriek as a male voice said, 'Right, Landry, because *you* should start panicking, you traitorous asshole.'

Standing by the open bathroom door, in jeans and turtleneck and holding a revolver, was Captain Rowland.

'Idiot,' he said, pointing the revolver at Carl. 'You out of the service so long you forget your tradecraft? We had you under the gun all day, right up to the riot in the Common. You didn't even look through the goddam place when you got here. Amateur. You, honey, get your Limey ass over there, next to your stupid boyfriend.'

Sandy's face was ashen but she picked up her purse and joined Carl. He looked at the smug, beady eyes and thought about that beefy, well-fed man, beating up on Two-Tone. To come this far, after Manhattan and the Boston Common and everything else . . .

Carl said sharply, 'And what about you, Captain? Did you forget the motto of the Special Forces? *De Oppresso Liber* – To Free the Oppressed. Is that what you're doing here, or are you just busy helping the oppressors?'

Rowland grinned, not a pretty sight. 'Sorry, pal, I haven't been with the Special Forces for a long while, a very long while. I didn't fit in with those Boy Scouts and I ended up where I am, in Zed Force, doing the naughty deeds that need to be taken care of.'

Sandy spoke up, her voice quavering. 'Like killing Merl Sawson? And trying to kill us in Manhattan?'

If anything, the grin got wider. 'Whatever it takes, baby. Whatever it takes. Old Merl, he thought he could go to the Brits without anyone noticing, and he was wrong. We screwed up in New York, that I admit, but we had you guys wired tight back at the Common. That draft-dodger friend of yours, he gave you up in about five minutes, and we were right behind you, all the way to the liquor store and the pet cemetery and back here. Now,' he said, waving the fingers of his free hand. 'Hand 'em over.'

Carl felt a dark despair starting to grow within him. All these years, these documents had been saved – from the nuclear fire of Washington and through the turbulent years of the early recovery, and now, only by chance, had they been found. Now they meant something important again. A way to stop a new madness, a way to change direction after ten years, a way to finally put things right. But they were about to be turned over to a new barbarian.

'No,' he said. 'I can't do that.'

Now the smile was gone. Rowland gestured with his revolver. 'Look, pal, I don't have time to debate. Hand over the documents right now or your Limey girl gets one in the shoulder. And if that doesn't do it, I'll do her knee, and maybe some other pretty parts.'

A gunshot, outside, and then two more. They all looked to the front door and Carl couldn't believe what he saw:

Rowland looked puzzled. Another gunshot, and the far-off drone of a helicopter.

'What's the matter, Captain?' Sandy asked, a sly smile on her face. 'Is somebody coming along without an invitation?'

'Shut your mouth,' Rowland said, his eyes moving back and forth, from Carl and Sandy to the front door and then back again. 'You hand over those papers, or I'm going to—'

There was the harsh crash of automatic weapons fire from outside and Carl fell to the floor, pulling at Sandy, who struggled against him. Rowland yelled, 'Jesus Christ,' and went to look out the near window, revolver at his side. Sandy pulled herself loose from Carl's grasp and he was going to yell at her to get her foolish head down, when she popped open her purse and pulled out a small, black automatic pistol. She tossed the pistol to Carl and he grabbed it with one hand, and worked the action back with his other.

The captain turned at the noise, face angry, revolver in their direction. He fired and Sandy screamed, and Carl raised the pistol and shot the captain twice in the chest.

Rowland lurched backward to the ground and Carl grabbed Sandy and pulled her down and yelled, 'Where in hell did you get the gun?'

'Where do you think?' she said, face bright red. 'When MI6 prepared me for this trip, they didn't just give me a radio.'

The sound of the helicopter grew louder. Sandy said, 'That horrible man. Is he dead?'

He crawled over to where Rowland was lying, facedown. Carl retrieved the revolver and checked Rowland's breathing, then went back to the fireplace and said, 'He's not doing well, but he's still alive. Jesus, Sandy, are these your folks showing up?'

Her face was smug, a sight that made him angry and sad, all at once.

'Of course,' Sandy said. 'They're the very best, and they're here to finish the job.'

Carl sat up against the fireplace, holding the precious documents in his lap. He looked back down at the memo he was reading, and finished the last few paragraphs:

> . . . Shortly before noon, per the direct order of the President, this office contacted Air Force General Ramsey Curtis to ensure that the retaliatory strike against the SA-2 site that shot down this U-2 would not occur except upon the direct order of the President.
>
> General Curtis replied, quote, 'The Russian bear has always been eager to stick his paw in Latin American waters. Now that we've got him in a trap, let's take his leg off right up to his balls. On second thought, let's take off his balls, too.'
>
> The message to General Curtis was repeated, that he was not, repeat, not, to launch the retaliatory strike at all costs. The General replied with a vulgarity and said, quote, 'That Ivy League boy screwed the pooch at the Bay of Pigs, and we ain't gonna be left holding the bag this time.' The General then hung up.
>
> Subsequent attempts to contact General Curtis were unsuccessful. Contact through the White House Switchboard to the Operations Officer at Homestead AFB determined that the retaliatory strike had been launched. The Operations Officer refused to issue a recall order without the proper

authority or coding.

Attempts to secure the recall order or codes by this office proved unsuccessful. Initial reports are that the SA-2 sites have been bombed and that follow-up raids are being conducted on other SA sites in the area.

Attached to the memo was a handwritten note, on a piece of White House stationery, dated October 28, the day after the raid:

Damn it, Merl, that fool Curtis has gotten us into a full-out war. Word is the Marines and Airborne are going in shortly. What a hell of a fucking mess.

The note was unsigned.

Something smashed through the windows and the front door, and he rolled over, pulling Sandy close to him.

'Clear!' someone shouted, and another voice echoed, 'Clear!' Carl looked up and saw four men, dressed in black jumpsuits, helmets, and body armor, carrying short stubby Sten machine guns. British-made. They had come through the front door and windows, and one of them bent over Rowland and shouted, 'Medic! We need a medic in here!'

There was a quick shuffle of people around the fallen form of Rowland and then a young man strode through the broken front door, wearing a business suit and necktie and dress shoes.

'Hullo, Sandy,' he said. 'Sorry about all the noise. Are you all right?'

'I'm fine,' she said, standing up and smiling widely. 'Just fine.'

Douglas Harris, press attaché to the British consulate in Boston, nodded in Carl's direction. 'And how is Mr. Landry of the *Globe?*'

Carl got to his feet as two of the soldiers came over and took away his knapsack and both of the weapons. The papers were still in his hands. 'Mr. Landry is one confused person,' he said. 'And his ears hurt. And he wants to know what the hell is going on.'

Harris smiled. 'Of course you do. But first things first, Mr. Landry.' He held out a hand. 'The papers, please.'

They felt as light as feathers in his hands. 'I'm sorry, could you say that again?'

A small nod, and he saw that Sandy was looking at him, a touch of fear in her eyes. 'Those papers you have, Mr. Landry. They were promised to us and we want them.'

Rowland was hustled out of the room and it was quiet, except for the thrumming sound of the helicopter engine outside. They must have landed the damn thing in the motel's parking lot.

'I'm sorry, but you can't have them.'

Harris was obviously trying to hold his temper in check. 'Damn it, man, we don't have time for this,' he said, stepping forward. 'We've just shot up this piece of property and the local constabulary are probably on the way. We've got a fucking chopper in the front yard of this place, and I want those papers. Now!'

'If you're in such a hurry,' Carl shot back, 'then why don't you get in your fucking chopper and fly out of here?'

Sandy spoke up. 'Carl, it really—'

'Shut up, Sandy,' Harris said, interrupting. He turned to

two of the soldiers and said, 'You and you. Get those papers, and you don't have to be gentle.'

Carl threw the whole load of documents into the fireplace.

Both Sandy and Harris shouted and sprang forward, but Carl yelled, 'Shut up and freeze!' in his best Army sergeant voice, and moved his hand down to the gas supply lever.

'Now,' he said, speaking slowly and loudly, a part of him not believing what he was doing. 'Listen closely. Those papers belong here, to the American people. They don't belong to you. Every second that passes, they're getting burned. Not so badly since the fire is on low, but see where my hand is? I'm controlling the flow of gas into the fireplace. Anyone moves closer, anyone at all, and I'll flip this lever up and you'll have nothing but ashes.'

The pile of documents had landed right in the center of the fireplace, and first one, and then another sheet of paper curled itself over and started smoldering.

Harris said, 'You're bluffing.'

'Try me, Dougie,' he said. 'My guess is, there's important things here, important things that you might want to see publicized. Or not publicized. Fine. Either way, you want them. What I'm saying is it's not your responsibility. The papers belong here.'

Sandy said, 'Carl, look, I know how you feel, but if they are to be publicized, it has to happen outside the country, away from your censors.'

'You let me worry about the censors,' Carl said. 'And we don't know if Dougie here will allow them to be published anyway, do we?'

Harris looked horrified. 'My God, man, don't you realize

the treasure trove you have there? You have documents from the White House, explaining how the war started, secrets that will affect your election. And you're letting them burn!'

'No, you're the one letting them burn, and there goes another sheet,' Carl said, trying to speak clearly and quickly, all at once. 'Here's the deal. You give me transportation back to Boston, leave me and these papers alone, and I'll get them publicized. If I fail, I'll make sure that the next day they end up at your consulate. But that's the deal. Make up your mind or there's nothing left. Something tells me, Dougie old boy, that your superiors won't be so happy if everything goes up in flames. But you better hurry, I think I hear sirens coming. You want to explain to the New Hampshire State Police why there's armed British nationals on the ground in American territory?'

Harris's face was quite red. 'Damn you, how can I trust you?'

'Ask Sandy. She'll vouch for me.'

A brief look passed between them. 'All right, and how do you know that you can trust me?' Harris asked.

'Just give me your word as an Englishman and a gentleman and a member of the British diplomatic corps, and that will do,' Carl said.

'That's it?'

'That's it.'

Harris sighed. 'You bastard. I give you my word as an Englishman, a gentleman, and a member of the British diplomatic corps, that you will be taken back to Boston unharmed.'

'And with all of the papers in my possession.'

'Yes, yes, yes, the papers still in your possession. Damn it, turn the gas off!'

Which is what he did. He picked up the thick stack of papers and brushed away the burnt remnants of two or three sheets.

'I suppose it's time to go, right?' Carl asked.

'Right,' Harris said. 'Let's get out of here.'

Some people had pulled their cars over to the side of the highway to look at the helicopter in the parking lot, blades still turning. The soldiers were carrying Carl's and Sandy's belongings, and as they made their way to the helicopter, Sandy put her mouth next to his ear and said, 'That was pretty tough.'

'Had to do it,' he answered, the precious cargo firmly clamped under his arm.

'Weren't you afraid of damaging the papers?'

Carl looked at her and raised his voice against the engine's noise. 'Sandy, I was scared shitless.'

They got closer to the helicopter and Dougie jumped ahead of them, with a smile on his face, a triumphant smile that was wrong. Quite wrong. Two of the soldiers in the helicopter were staring right at them, and Sandy went ahead and there was a movement as a man leaned forward from inside the cabin to see what was going on. Tall, angry looking, with a large mane of white hair . . . Damn it, why was that familiar?

He took a couple more steps to the helicopter.

Stewart. Stewart Thompson. The head of MI6 in Boston and the name on the card that Merl Sawson had had hidden among his papers, back in his freezer.

Another step to the helicopter. The noise of the blades was deafening. Something was wrong, something was wrong. Stewart Thompson was leaning further out, face twisted in anger, and there was Dougie, smiling, smiling because—

Carl had made an agreement with Dougie, not with Stewart Thompson.

He took a deep breath, hunched down, and then threw himself under the helicopter, rolling on the cracked pavement, the noise in his ears and the grit against his face overwhelming, and he rolled, rolled, until he was free.

And then he ran to the woods, as police cars howled their way into the parking lot and the helicopter lifted off.

THIRTY

HE KNEW HE WAS BEING CHASED, and in the end, there was only one place to go.

Carl walked gingerly through the empty rooms of the small house, a candle flickering in his hand. He was exhausted. After spending some long minutes thrashing through the woods near the Matador Inn, he had managed to get back to the pet cemetery, and to the borrowed Volkswagen. Driving back to Boston at that time of night would have been foolish. Any kind of random checkpoint would have ended everything. Not to mention the Zed Force, furious that one of their own had been shot. And not to mention the equally furious British.

So he had come home. To Newburyport, for the first time in more than ten years. He had hidden the car in some woods down the street, and had made his way here, walking along the familiar road. It was getting colder but he sat for a while in the tiny backyard, looking at the unlit and shuttered Cape Cod house with peeling paint, the place he and Mom and Dad and his sister, Sarah, had once called home. The landscape had reverted back to the wild, with tall grass and saplings growing on the lawn. Plants had also grown around the rusted remains of a swing set in the rear yard. Faded plywood covered the lower windows of the house. Some time ago – '64, maybe? – he had gotten a letter about the house. A company calling itself Real Estate Salvagers had offered to go in, clean out the belongings, disconnect the utilities, and then put it on the market. With millions dead in '62 and '63, it was another growth industry from the Cuban War. He had paid the company, they had done their job, and each year he paid the minuscule real estate taxes from the city. It had never been sold.

Tonight, he had gone to the back of the house and loosened a brick in the rear walk, where he had found the rusted but still serviceable spare key that had let him in. A search of the kitchen had found a candle stub and an old packet of matches, and on the fifth try a match sputtered into life. He looked around, at the dusty floor and shelves. Mom had made countless breakfasts here, lunches and dinners, too. He remembered as a child coming downstairs in the morning in winter, chilly from the low temperatures, and eating cereal on the floor with Sarah, huddled up against the hot-air register, trying to warm up their feet.

He went down a short hallway, the candle making long shadows on the walls. The family room was empty, the carpets having been rolled up. Here they had watched television on a black-and-white Philco, and he had a sweet pang of memory, recalling Howdy Doody and Sky King and Tom Corbett, Space Cadet. He remembered Mom ironing clothes here during the televised McCarthy hearings, back in '56, and Dad watching the Friday evening boxing matches. At the end of the hallway he paused, letting the candlelight illuminate the empty room. There. His parents' bedroom. When he or Sarah had been sick and had to stay home from school, Mom would let them stay in this room, convinced that they would recover quicker if she was nearby. Carl's eyes teared up. He wondered what had gone though his mother's head those last few days, huddled in bed here with her husband, probably wearing every piece of clothing they owned, with no power and no heat, while snowstorms raged outside and there was no food inside.

He wiped his eyes and went upstairs. To the left, Sarah's room, the walls empty. He remembered what had been there. Photos of horses and a couple of folk singers, including a guy named Dylan, who now played in exile in Canada. He remembered late nights with Sarah reading thick books from the library, halting sounds on the guitar, and the smell of tobacco coming from under the door.

Then he went to his old room. His bed had been there, and a couple of bookshelves and a dresser over by the window. He held up the candle and saw tiny holes in the ceiling, holes made by thumbtacks that had once held black thread from which he had dangled carefully made models of aircraft from wars past: Sopwith Camels and Fokker triplanes and B-17 bombers and P-51 fighters and F-86 jets.

Home again. He had never thought he would return, but tonight, it seemed right, so very right. Rummaging around in the attic, he found an old bedspread. He wrapped himself up in it and lay down on the threadbare carpet in his old bedroom, blinking again as tears started trickling down his cheeks, the recovered papers still by his side.

Only a couple of days left. He thought about what he had to do tomorrow, to fulfill the promise he had made last week. He tried to think of Jim Rowley and PS 19, the hidden communities across the country, and the British soldiers and the upcoming anschluss, but he couldn't focus. All he could think about was the small-town family that had lived in this house at the start of a new and hopeful decade, headed by a young president filled with vigor and promises. He thought of his family, shattered and destroyed by a war that should have never happened, and how, finally, he was now able to do something to make it right. He checked the time. It was just after midnight.

Just two days left.

He had gotten up early this Saturday and was now back in Boston. After leaving the house in Newburyport and locking the door behind him, Carl had walked to a Greyhound station and caught a bus to Boston, just at morning rush hour, knowing that checkpoints at that hour were few and far between. Back in the city another hour of walking had brought him to Morrissey Boulevard. He was tired but alert, knowing that in the next few minutes or so, he'd be doing something he never thought he'd ever do: sneak into work.

Joining some of the print workers coming into the facility, he got into the *Globe*'s building through the loading dock area, where large rolls of newsprint were shoved into the printing plant section of the newspaper. He took a service elevator upstairs and moved quickly, avoiding people and their stares, until he found his refuge, inside George Dooley's office.

The small office was still clean and he moved the typewriter over to the desk. It was not yet 8 A.M. He had a couple of hours to get some work done before George showed up. It was a gamble, a gamble with impossibly high stakes, but he knew he had no other choice. This was the only place that made sense. Where else could he have gone? What else could he have done?

He started reading the papers he had brought down from New Hampshire, and quickly sorted them into two piles. One pile was a collection of special reports and briefing papers on what was going on in Cuba in 1962, and he put that on one side of the desk. The other pile, which was much smaller, was beginning to lead him to the story that he was going to write this morning, and he took his time, reading and rereading.

There were two or three sheets clipped together, all with the same heading, 'THE WHITE HOUSE WASHINGTON,' and the sheets were filled with scribbling:

ExComm met at 2300 hours 27 Oct. Saturday. President furious re: Curtis decision to go ahead with air strike. AG demands his firing. McNamara reminds of current facts, we are now in a shooting war, killing Cubans and Russian techs. Hard to back away. Sacking Curtis would show sign of weakness. Curtis now airborne in command post.

AG adamant. Curtis is to go. Disobeyed direct orders. JCS Chief Taylor points out events are moving quickly. Must look to what is to be done now. AF is bombing SA-2 sites and MRBMs can be brought up to launch capability within hours. Must start bombing missile sites now, before nuclear-armed MRBMs and IRBMs are launch-capable.

SecState Rusk said whole mess has destroyed last diplomatic chance to solve crisis. UN, world opinion now firmly against us. McNamara points out that real events now rule, diplomacy is over. War in Cuba has started.

President brings discussion to close. Cannot

allow missiles to become operational. They must be
bombed. JCS Taylor points out that op plans do not
rely on bombing of missile sites solely – ground
forces must be inserted to ensure full destruction of
offensive capability. President agrees. Marines and
Airborne to enter Cuba Monday, October 29, at the
latest.

Question to McNamara. What will be response
of Soviet Union to invasion? McNamara answer: we
must be prepared for a response elsewhere, most
likely Berlin.

Question to McNamara. What about Soviet
force response in Cuba? Answer: There may be some
Soviet forces in Cuba with light armor and other
weapons. Do not expect much of an impact.

President ends meeting with comment that if we
live through this and achieve our goals, that SOB
Curtis will get the Medal of Honor. And then I'll
have the bastard shot.

Carl found it hard to focus on the sheets of paper that were
telling him a story that had been kept secret for years and
years. It had been secret for a very good reason. It told the
truth.

MEMORANDUM FOR FILE

State Dept. source contacted me today, almost crying in frustration and fear. Said that back channels
with Soviet Embassy in DC had arranged a deal to
resolve the crisis this past Saturday. Sovs would take

missiles out of Cuba, JFK would agree to respect Cuban government and territory, and in a few months, we'd haul out obsolete Jupiter missiles in Turkey.

State Dept. guy says deal was killed when AF started bombing SA-2 sites after the U-2 shootdown. Back channels closed down, Soviet Embassy burning its papers, and he's quitting State and taking his family to West Virginia.

And another single sheet, right after that one, on a plain piece of paper:

ExComm meeting today chaotic. A third of ExComm members have left DC with families. Only scattered communications left with Marine/Airborne units in Cuba. Soviet tactical nukes used with Frog ground-to-ground missiles. Horrific casualties. SAC has begun full retaliatory response. Our forces in West Berlin overrun. President is urged to leave DC immediately with his family. McNamara still thinks armistice can be reached. AG almost engages in fistfight with McNamara. Word comes in that Deputy Director CIA in charge of intelligence gathering re: Soviet forces in Cuba has committed suicide. AG says other CIA SOBs should join him. President says he will try for armistice, will stay in DC to the end to try to stop the war.

Then, near the end bottom of the papers, was a typewritten document of a more recent vintage:

The following is the sworn affidavit of Merl Sawson, of Boston, Massachusetts:

1. My name is Merl Sawson. At the time of the Cuban War, I was a colonel in the U.S. Army, assigned to the White House for certain liaison duties. As part of my duties, I attended meetings of Cabinet members, military officials and other government representatives in response to the Cuban missile crisis. This group was called the Executive Committee, or ExComm.

2. On Saturday, 27 October 1962, an Air Force U-2 surveillance aircraft was shot down over Cuba. I was directed by the President to contact Air Force Chief of Staff General Ramsey Curtis, to ensure that the planned retaliation against the SA-2 site that destroyed the U-2 would not take place. This retaliation had already been planned for under Joint Chiefs of Staff Operational Plan No. 312.

3. General Ramsey Curtis disobeyed the direct orders of the President and allowed the retaliatory mission against the missile sites to occur. General Curtis, upon his own initiative and without any orders from the President or any other National Command Authority, authorized follow-up bombing raids upon other Cuban targets.

4. It was the opinion of the President and the members of the ExComm that bombing raids upon the MRBM and IRBM missile sites and the subsequent invasion of Cuba were inevitable following

the decision by General Curtis to allow the retaliatory mission to take place.

5. To the best of my knowledge, I was one of the last individuals to leave the White House on the day of the attack on Washington. Although he had ample opportunity to leave the White House for safety, President John F. Kennedy remained there, convinced he could reach a cease-fire with surviving Soviet authorities.

6. Since the conclusion of the Cuban War, I have spent several years attempting to locate surviving members of the ExComm and their associates who may have direct knowledge of General Curtis' actions just prior to the onset of hostilities in Cuba. My research has shown that since the war, those ExComm members and associates who were not in Washington, D.C., at the time of its bombing, are either dead, in prison, or missing.

7. Several of the deaths of the surviving ExComm members, in my opinion, are suspicious in nature.

8. Since the conclusion of the Cuban War, I have technically been a deserter, since I did not contact any military authority to report for duty. I once regretted not having done this. Having seen what has happened to members of the ExComm, I regret this no longer.

This affidavit was sworn before me in Boston, Massachusetts, on May 30, 1971.

Carl looked at the two signatures on the affidavit. One was Merl Sawson's. The other belonged to a notary public, and his name was Andrew Townes, Merl's neighbor and landlord.

'Oh, you poor bastards,' Carl said. 'When you signed this, you were signing your own death warrants.'

His head was pounding, he was hungry, and his feet throbbed with pain from all the walking he had done, but he knew he didn't have much time. He rolled a sheet of paper into the typewriter and after typing in his name and slug 'CUBA STORY,' the door opened up and George Dooley came in, carrying a cup of coffee and a small brown paper bag.

'Carl, what the hell are you doing here?' he asked, his eyes blinking in surprise behind his black-rimmed glasses.

'I'm writing a story for Sunday's newspaper,' he said.

'Good,' George said, sipping at his coffee. 'That's what we pay you for. But in here?'

'Privacy,' Carl said, typing out the lead, which practically wrote itself. 'And you'll see why in just a moment.'

Carl typed up a half sheet of paper and passed it over to George, and he sat there, his heart pounding so hard he thought the pressroom boys next door might hear it. This was it. This was the moment to see if his gamble would pay off, for if George said anything disparaging or cautionary or remotely challenging, anything at all, he was going to grab the papers and get the hell out of Dodge, and make his way to the British consulate.

George read the sheet, grunted, and passed it over. 'Okay, privacy it is. Coffee?'

'Yeah, and something to eat, too.'

'You got it.'

———

A copy boy brought him coffee and a handful of doughnuts, and he kept on writing. George ambled back in after a while and started reading the typewritten sheets, and out of the corner of his eye, Carl could see him making some minor edits. George asked to see the source materials and he passed them over, and George read and grunted and raised an eyebrow, and then handed them back. That was about as excited as George could get over a story. George said, 'Need anything else?'

'Yeah,' he said. 'Bound back issues of the *Globe*. And the *Times*. From October 1962. I want to get the history down right.'

'Don't we all,' George said. 'Anything else?'

Carl yawned and stretched in the chair. 'Lunch, I'd guess. And this great privacy.'

George leaned forward, his eyes direct. 'You've got lunch, and you've got your privacy, but not for long. I can't do anything with this story just on my say-so, and you know it, Carl. I need to bring in other editors and probably the goddam newspaper owners as well.'

Something cold crawled up his throat. Still only two days left. 'Including Major Devane?'

George snorted in contempt. 'That man's a lot of things, but he sure as hell ain't no editor. Look, you got enough time to make deadline this afternoon?'

'I do. I have to.'

'Then keep on working.'

The bound copies of the old newspapers came in, and he delved back in history, matching the names and faces mentioned in the documents with the stories from ten years ago. The dead Kennedy Administration. John F. Kennedy and his family. Bobby Kennedy and his family. Vice President Johnson. Secretary of Defense McNamara. Secretary of State Rusk. Spokesman Pierre Salinger. All of them were dead now, yet magically still alive in the scribbled notes and faded memorandums and crisply written reports.

Across from George's office was a small conference room, and Carl looked up to see several of the editors assembling in there. There were some shouts and raised voices, and once, a slammed door. He recognized the managing editor, the executive editor, the editorial page editor, and even the publisher himself, head of the family that had owned the *Globe* for years. George was in the middle of it all, cajoling and talking and waving his hands. Eventually, lunch came, and he ate half the sandwich before realizing it was roast beef and cheese, and remembering Manhattan, he tossed it in the trash can, just above crumpled sheets of his copy.

George came back into his office, the group of editors in tow, and Carl looked at their faces. They were men who had been at the *Globe* for years and had built their careers here, as best as they could with the censorship, and now they were looking at him in an odd way. Carl knew what they were thinking. Who in hell was this character before them, and what kind of story was he spinning that could destroy the newspaper and give them all prison terms?

The executive editor said, 'I'd like to look at your source documents, please.'

Carl wordlessly passed them over, and the executive editor started reading them with the other senior editors grouped around him, like a young man with his friends, reading a letter from a suitor. One of the editors whispered, 'Jesus Christ' and another said, 'I knew it, I always knew it,' and the executive editor held up his hand. 'Quiet, please. We don't have much time.'

Papers were passed from hand to hand. George passed around the first four or five pages of Carl's story, and that was also read, and one editor looked up and said, 'Good job, Carl.'

'Thanks,' he said, feeling comfortable for the first time that day.

The executive editor took a chair, stretched out his long legs, looked around the small office at the other editors, and smiled and said, 'Do you realize what we have here?'

'Yeah, a goddam Pulitzer Prize-winning story, if the judges have any balls,' one editor said. Another laughed and said, 'No, I think what we got here is five years in a decon camp.'

The executive editor held up Carl's story. 'Close. No, what we have here is the *Globe* with a story that says General Ramsey Curtis, the most powerful and respected man in this country, started the Cuban War. That up to the last minute, the war could have been avoided. That General Curtis was ultimately responsible for a war that destroyed the Soviet Union and its people, killed several million of our country-men, and tossed this world upside down.'

A voice from the back said, 'Hardly, John. The man had some help.'

The executive editor shook his head. 'No, there's more here. We're destroying two myths, don't you see? The myth of a noble Air Force general, saving this nation from further destruction during our most horrible days, and the myth of a weak and cowardly president, throwing this land into nuclear war because his ego was hurt when the Bay of Pigs invasion went sour. Believe me, gentlemen, people don't like losing their myths. With Rockefeller so closely tied to Curtis . . . well, the election next week just got more interesting.'

The editorial page editor said, 'I'm nervous about the provenance of those documents, John. Might be a setup. Either foreign intelligence or black ops. Something to hurt us.'

There was some murmuring and a raised voice or two, and Carl tried to remember to breathe. George spoke up. 'That's a slight possibility, I'll grant you that. But look at 'em. Haven't all of you – every one of us – known that we never knew the real story of what happened back in 1962? That General Curtis was just too brave and too perfect? That JFK was too easy a villain?'

A few voices spoke up and then the managing editor, the oldest man in the room, raised a hand. 'I knew Kennedy, you know.'

The room fell silent as the managing editor began to speak. 'I knew Jack when he was a congressman, and then a senator. He wasn't perfect. None of us are. He had an eye for pretty girls and he also knew how to work the press. But he was a damn good man. He might have screwed up in the Pacific with his PT boat, but he got his boys out. And he was hurt at the Bay of Pigs, everyone knew that, but he learned from his mistakes. He had great plans for this country, for its people. I knew Jack, and the stories of him that came out after the war, that he was overwhelmed, that he was cowardly, and that the last anyone saw of him, he was weeping in the Oval Office, too frightened to leave on an escape helicopter . . . that wasn't the Jack I knew.'

He pointed to the source documents still in the executive editor's hands. 'That's the Jack I knew. The man in those memorandums, the man who had to deal not only with Russian missiles in Cuba, but a crazed general who wanted war. And the man who stuck it out in the White House, to the end, trying to reach an armistice. That's the Jack I knew.'

The managing editor turned away, as if ashamed of the tears that were now streaming down his face. 'You want to know what I think? I think I've been waiting for this day for ten years now. We have a responsibility to print the news. That's what we're here for.'

More voices, and someone said, 'Look, we've got to wait on this. We can't rush this into press,' and another voice, 'Paul's right, we need additional confirmation.'

George said, 'The hell we do! Look, either we go with this in the next edition, or it'll never run. You know that. People will start talking and whispering and spreading rumors of what we've got here, and by the end of the day, Army Intelligence will have these papers and most of us will be in a detention camp. You know that. We can't wait.'

The executive editor was now looking directly at him. 'Carl, this is your story. What do you say?'

He looked around at the editors and George and all those faces, all now looking at him for advice, looking at him for counsel. A high school graduate from a little port town who didn't do much except wear the Army green for a few years, and who eventually learned how to write for a newspaper. Now all of these eyes were staring at him, waiting for him to say something, anything, about this story. A story that was going to change the world.

He cleared his throat. 'I've been at the *Globe* nearly four years. I've always wondered what kind of newspaper we would be, and what kind of nation we could have, if it weren't for the censorship.'

Another moment of silence, and then the executive editor slowly nodded, got up from his chair, and handed the papers back to him. 'We haven't been a real newspaper for a decade,

Carl. I guess it's time we learn what it's like again.' He turned
to the other editors and smiled wearily. 'Anyone pack an extra
toothbrush today? I have a feeling there's a good chance we
might not be at the newspaper tomorrow.'

The managing editor wiped his face with a handkerchief.
'Remember what Ben Franklin said. If we are to hang, it's best
we all hang together.'

Carl thought the laughter was forced and not so hearty,
but it was good enough. The executive editor looked to
George and said, 'We still have a problem. Major Devane.'

George had a satisfied look on his face. 'Don't worry about
Major Devane. I'll take care of it.'

The executive editor nodded and said to the room,
'Gentlemen, let's leave Carl and George to their work.'

About a half hour before deadline, after a long hour of edits
and rewrites and retyping, the story was done. Carl's head was
throbbing with a headache, his back ached, and his fingers
were cramped, but it was done. He wasn't sure how, or where,
he would sleep tonight but at least the damn story was
finished.

Jim, he thought. I kept my promise to you and PS 19 and
the others. Let's see if that was good enough.

George called to the newsroom and a copy boy came over,
and he handed the story to him in a plain brown envelope.
'Send this to Phil in typesetting. Tell him it's from me and it's
"eyes only." He'll know what that'll mean.' Then he made a
phone call to the print shop. 'Mark? George over in the newsroom. You remember I told you a while ago I might need some
help? Yeah, yeah, I still owe you fifty bucks from last week's
game. You'll get it soon enough, maybe from my estate. Look,

I need your help, in about fifteen minutes. All right? Great.'

George hung up the phone, reached into a filing cabinet, and pulled out a small flask. He poured them each a drink. 'No tea this time,' he said, grinning. 'Just real sippin' whiskey.'

Carl took a tiny mouthful, to be polite, and said, 'You were in on this right from the beginning, right?'

George's eyes narrowed a bit as he took a drink from the small glass. 'I'm not sure I'm following you, Carl.'

'Right from the beginning,' Carl said. 'I was assigned to the Merl Sawson murder story. And you sent me to the British consulate, to meet up with the British reporter, Sandy Price. And this morning, when you saw what I was writing, it was like . . . it was like you expected that I would come up with something. There was something going on with the Merl Sawson case and you thought I'd get to the bottom of it.'

Carl gestured to the framed photo of the young girl on George's desk. 'Your niece. She received medical treatment in London. That was a deal, wasn't it? Your future cooperation with British authorities in exchange for the medical treatment. Am I wrong?'

George put the glass down on the desk. 'Nope.'

Even as tired as he was, he felt a flash of anger. 'You might have told me.'

'Wouldn't have worked,' George said, picking up the flask again and then, apparently thinking better of it, putting it back on the desk. 'When you started here, Carl, I checked out your service record. I had a good idea of what you were capable of. I saw you working here in the newsroom, putting up with a lot of crap, not losing your cool, getting the job done. You're no quota baby, Carl. You're a damn fine man and an even better reporter. Well, this was one job I wanted to see get finished. You were my first, last, and only choice to do it.'

Carl stared at the overweight man with the ridiculous retro black-and-white clothing. 'Who the hell are you working for? British intelligence? The McGovern campaign?'

George sighed, like an old prizefighter trying to gear himself up for one more match. 'No, to both of those questions. In fact, I don't much like McGovern. Too soft in the middle, don't think he could make the tough decisions. No, Carl, you know what I am? I'm a newspaperman, that's all. Just a newspaperman trying to get something back. Trying to loosen things up so we can have real newspapers again, report real news, have real elections, and maybe have a real government to call our own. That's all. There are other people out there who think the same way. Some are organized, others aren't. All I know is that I got a couple of phone calls from people I trusted, asking me for help. Some of these people were Americans, some were British. And I provided it.' He patted a hand on Carl's notes and the ten-year-old documents. 'Gladly.'

Carl took another polite sip and then said, 'You know, here's the truth for you, George. I hate whiskey. I hate being told what to do. I hate being used for other people's purposes. And right about now, I think I hate being a newspaperman.'

'Good for you, it's a hell of a business,' George said, finishing off his whiskey. 'What are you going to do instead, write a book?'

He started gathering up some of his notes and papers. 'Truth be told, George, I just finished one, not a few days ago.' He shook his head. 'The last chapter might need a bit of a rewrite. I wrote it before this stuff all showed up.'

George stood up, clapped him on the shoulder. 'Well, before you start rewriting, let's go to the newsroom. I think you'll enjoy what's going to happen next.'

He opened the door to the usual bustle and noise as the deadline for the next day's newspaper approached. Carl made to go to his own desk but George smiled widely and said, 'Here, have a seat next to me. A ringside seat, you could call it.'

Carl sat down and looked out at the reporters, seeing with satisfaction the puzzled look from Jeremiah King. He wondered how his guided tour of Manhattan had gone. And then he noted with surprise a furtive wink from Jack Burns, the music critic. What kind of place was this? Secrets within secrets? A newspaper that was doing more than just reporting the news? There was a flash of blue and he looked over to the vending machines and coffeepots, where a group of five or six pressmen in their blue, ink-stained jumpsuits were talking among themselves.

Then, more noise, more disruption. He looked up and Major Devane was striding through the newsroom, his shirt-sleeves rolled up, his tie askew, a fist clenched around some yellow copy paper. 'Dooley!' he yelled. 'You stupid clown. How in God's name . . .' Then he spotted Carl and said, his lips firm with fury, 'You! Sergeant Landry, you better hope you got your lead-lined underwear packed, because before this night is out, you're on your way to Omaha.'

George smiled sweetly up at the major. 'Something I can help you with?'

'This!' Devane snarled, shoving the papers under his nose. 'Do you realize . . . this is outrageous! Slanderous! Not to mention violating at least six sections of the National Security Act, which you and everyone in this newsroom has signed! This cannot and will not go to press!'

George rested his hands behind his head. 'And what do you plan to do about it?'

'You . . . So that's why my phones are out!' Devane looked around the newsroom, his eyes wide. 'You've planned this. All of you! All of you are conspirators! All of you will be facing serious jail time for even attempting to print something like this! And I'm not going to allow this to go to press!'

Devane reached for a phone on the desk and George snapped forward and grabbed his wrist. 'I don't think so.' Devane struggled and said, 'You fool, that's assaulting an Army officer,' and then Carl sat up as the group of pressmen were suddenly at George's desk. The largest of the group, whose beefy hands were stained with ink, said, 'Mark said you might need some help, Mr. Dooley.'

George was now grinning widely and let go of Devane's wrist. 'That's right. Take the good major here and take him back to the rear conference room. Be nice and polite but don't let him leave, don't let him get near a phone. And don't worry about anything he says. It's all been taken care of.'

Devane looked around again. His face was flushed, and Carl knew what he was thinking. Besides everything else, Devane was now seeing his career fade away. 'You . . . you . . .'

The city editor's smile was now gone. 'Would love to chat with you, Major, but you know what? We've got a newspaper to put out. A real newspaper, for the first time in ten years. And you know what else? You're fired. You're a lousy person and an even lousier editor. Guys, get him out of here.'

Devane started yelling again but the pressmen – a couple of whom got into their task with some enthusiasm – started pulling him down the corridor. Some people in the newsroom stood up to get a better view, and a handful of others started clapping.

'And another thing,' George called out, standing up. 'You couldn't edit worth shit. I don't even think you could spell "cat" if I spotted you two of the letters.'

Carl looked on. 'It's not going to be that easy. There might be some people here working for him.'

George settled back down in his chair. 'Tough. The thing is, this place has been stuck in a rut. We've just smashed the routine. Without hearing from Devane, the Boston C.O., he's not going to do anything on his own. He'll buck it up the ladder and by the time a decision is made, the paper will be on the streets. We'll send it over the wire. And we're going to courier it out tonight, to other newspapers, just in case the news wires get cut.'

Carl laughed and George looked at him strangely. 'What was that about?'

'Oh, just a historical note, I guess. That just seems appropriate, considering what Paul Revere started from this city, almost two hundred years ago.'

'Don't get silly on me, Carl. Besides, I'm allergic to horses.'

He thought about Jim Rowley, about the anschluss, about a lot of things. 'This story is going to have an impact on the election, you know.'

'Good.'

Carl said, 'And another thing, George. There's going to be a big story coming out of Manhattan in the next day or two.'

George turned to him. 'Really? What kind of story?'

'One that will be on the front pages of every newspaper in the country. But the *Globe* can get to it first.'

He was grinning again. 'Tell me more, later. Do you want to do it?'

'No,' he said. 'I've had my fill of Manhattan. Send somebody else.'

'Jeremiah King?'

A dead island, he thought. Maybe it was time for someone

to visit a living island. 'No. Send Bobby Munson.'

Then the executive editor came in, holding layout sheets for the next day's paper. 'Heard some commotion out there. Everything all set?'

'Things are just fine,' George said.

The executive editor put a layout sheet on George's desk. 'I was just going over the final layout·for tonight. There's an item I want cut from page two. Put in a house ad or a news brief or something. But I want this goddam item cut out. Care to do the honors?'

George picked up the layout sheet, eyes glistening with emotion, and then he passed it over to Carl. 'John, I think Carl should take care of this little business.'

Carl looked down at the layout sheet, seeing the locations of the ads and the placement of the page two stories and headlines. And stuck down by the corner, in all its glory, was a small little piece:

> To our readers: The stories appearing in today's *Boston Globe* have been cleared by the U.S. Army under the provisions of the Martial Law Declaration of 1962 and the National Emergency Declaration of 1963.

He picked up a pencil and with a fury that even surprised him, he drew a large X across the copy with such force that the point of the pencil broke.

EMPIRE: SIX

A MATTER OF EMPIRE: SIX

AND SO IT BEGAN.

Major Kenneth Hunt was in the loud and cramped hull of an RAF C-130 Hercules transport, heading south to their target, heading south for what he knew in his bones was a mission that would eventually lead to the deaths of millions. He found himself thinking of that poor RAF crewman, the one who had so desperately tried to sabotage the mission. He hated himself for thinking so, but he wished the poor bloody bugger had succeeded.

He was forward, near the cockpit, and he glanced back at the helmeted paras, sitting stiffly in the webbed seating, their 7.62 mm SLRs at the ready. Each had a main chute on his back, a smaller, emergency parachute on his chest, and a small pack attached to a leg, which would be released just before landing. The sound of the four engines made normal conversation impossible, and most of the men simply stared straight ahead. In less than an hour his lads would be forming two lines and exiting through the doors on either side of the aircraft, behind the landing gear fairings, jumping into

America, ready to kill men who thought they were allies.

He thought about his brother Clive, and the talk they had had, some weeks ago, about empires gone and empires reborn. He was sure Clive would see some sort of black amusement in the fact that the troops of the new British empire were out to do their dark deeds in America tonight, in transport planes manufactured in these same United States.

Well, in just a few hours it would be over. He checked his watch. Hell, in less than twenty minutes they'd be on final approach to Plattsburgh Air Force Base, and a number of young American Air Force men down there, working or maybe dreaming in their sleep, well, they would be dead very soon. He and the lads were going to do their job, and do it right, for the Queen and the Regiment, and after it was over, maybe it was time to muster out, go overseas. Australia, he thought. When the next nuclear wars started, maybe Australia would make it through. Now, if only he could convince his sister and Clive to join him, that would be wonderful.

But the guilt, he thought. Could you live with it, after what happened?

He closed his eyes, thinking of Rachel, her laugh, her touch. Poor Rachel, dead all these years, probably buried in some mass grave in India. He sighed, felt something begin to ache in his chest. Maybe we wouldn't get to Australia, he thought. There would no doubt be shooting on the ground when they landed, when the Americans realized what was going on. A little aggressiveness on his part, and he could end it all tonight, on the ground, and be with Rachel again.

Yes, he thought, that might work. It just might—

Somebody tugged at his elbow and he turned. A radioman,

sitting behind the copilot, passed over a message flimsy and leaned forward, yelling in his ear. 'A message for you, Major! '

The airplane struck some turbulence, and his head bumped against the bulkhead. He held up the message and in the dim red light saw three words that made everything right, that made him smile for the first time in months.

ABORT ABORT ABORT

Then the aircraft made a steep, banking turn, and headed back to Canada. A couple of the paras looked up and saw the smiling face of their commanding officer. One, and then another, started hooting, and soon the entire plane was cheering and clapping. Major Hunt just nodded, grinning at his lads.

THIRTY-ONE

THE DEPARTURE LOBBY for international flights from Logan Airport was crowded, but he found her, sitting in a hard red plastic chair, looking through a day-old copy of the *Times*. She had on her long leather coat and when she looked up and saw him approaching she smiled. Despite himself, despite knowing who she was and what she had done, he smiled back.

'Well, I'll be damned, it's the famous Carl Landry of the *Boston Globe*, rescuer of lost ladies from Manhattan,' she said, folding her newspaper in half and standing up.

He grasped a hand and kissed her and said, 'Not that famous, and not sure if I'm still with the *Globe*.'

'Really? I though they'd be giving you a raise or even a promotion.'

He sat down and she sat next to him. He looked around the terminal and saw one and then another well-dressed man pretending not to look in their direction. She saw what he was doing and laughed for a second. 'I see you've noticed my watchers.'

'Who do they belong to?' Carl asked.

'Well, it looks like there's four of them,' she said, craning her neck to look around. 'I believe half of them belong to my people, ensuring nothing untoward happens to me, and I believe the other half belong to your lot, ensuring I get deported on time.' She squeezed his hand. 'It's hard to believe things here are changing so much, but the old bureaucracy grinds on. The presidential election is in chaos, people are marching in the streets, and McGovern may win after all, but one lowly newspaper reporter must be sent home to England.'

'You're a lot of wonderful things, Sandy, but you're not just a lowly reporter.'

Her face flushed. 'I know what you're saying, me doing things that weren't exactly reporter-like when I was here. But I was asked by my country to do something, and I did it.'

'I'm sure,' he said. 'In a way, you remind me of your home country. Or maybe even your grandmama, from what you've said. Polite and reasonable and when push comes to shove, utterly ruthless.'

She looked at him with no expression for a moment or two, and then she smiled. 'Father would say you're absolutely right. He says that in some ways, I'm like the son he's never had. I can be utterly focused on accomplishing something, whether it's a story, or a favor for one of father's friends. But not anymore. When . . . when I saw you run out into the woods after scrambling under the helicopter, I was proud of you, and I realized that not everything I had done before was right. Remember when we first met?'

'Of course.'

'You said something about the relationship of our two countries, that it had to be based on our regarding each other as equals, not as master and servant. I'm afraid for a while I was unthinkingly working for those who wanted to maintain the master-servant relationship, those who were behind the paras being readied to go into Manhattan. I'm glad I failed.'

'Don't take offense, but I'm glad, too.'

She changed her voice, tried to be more cheerful. 'And where do you go from here?'

He could feel the eyes of the watchers upon him. 'I now have what snipers delicately call a high profile. Once the *Globe* came out, other newspapers picked up the story. Even the *New York Times* did a follow-up, talking to someone who had been at the ExComm meetings back in '62, and who confirmed my story. Then other stories appeared, about the people in the RZs, marching out and demanding their rights. One of them was a civil rights leader, back from the early sixties, a preacher named King. It's . . . it's like a flood, now, as the censorship and the national security codes just collapse. It's an amazing thing, and . . . well, after something like that, it's hard to go back to doing a story about a three-car fatal on Storrow Drive.'

'There's always your book,' she said. 'I read the last chapter at the consulate and thought it was a pretty good conclusion to the whole thing. Especially the piece you wrote on General Curtis. Did you really see him in South Vietnam?'

He remembered that hot evening in Saigon, he and other advisers meeting the assembled generals during a cocktail party after a long briefing. A lot of drinking had gone on, and the cocky general had been in the middle of it, boasting that he could save time, money, and trouble by dropping a special weapon on Hanoi and taking care of the Vietnam problem in one day. That had been the last chapter of his book, the one he had passed on to Sandy. A chapter that exposed a lie, a lie he knew personally, because when he had seen the general last in Pennsylvania, he had said that Vietnam hadn't been worth a thing. A lie that represented everything wrong that had happened.

Lies, one after another, and he had finally got tired of them.

'That I did, and that last chapter is still going to need a rewrite. Maybe when that's done, there'll be a publisher in this country who'll have the newly found guts to publish it.'

'What about the good general?'

He shrugged. 'He's still among the missing. His farm is empty, and about twenty or thirty of his friends and fellow officers are missing as well. Latest rumor has it that he's headed south, maybe to Brazil. Who knows. Maybe he can write his own book about what happened.'

She shook her head in distaste. 'Cold-blooded bastard . . .'

'No,' he said sharply. 'No, I can't say that. He made mistakes and he hung on too long and too many bad things happened in his name, but still . . . Sandy, he did stop the war. He had a hand in starting it but he also stopped it before it got out of control, before it spread to Europe and elsewhere. If he had come clean with all of us about what had really taken place, well, who knows what might have happened. We might have avoided a decade of a national security state. We might have avoided turning almost everyone in this country into a nation of cynics who don't believe the government or the press or even their neighbors. Who knows.'

'Well, I know one thing,' she said, rearranging her coat. 'We certainly were snookered when it came to those papers. I thought I was getting top-secret codes, and you thought that you might be getting the Declaration of Independence and the Constitution. And some crazy man thought you were getting the real secret behind the still-living John F. Kennedy. We were all wrong.'

He remembered the shaky, scared face he'd seen in an abandoned New York City subway station. He knew that when he had a chance, he would do his best to reunite two old and bitter brothers. 'No, the crazy man was right. He was the only one who was right.'

She was puzzled. 'I don't understand.'

'He said that the documents were the key to "He Lives." I thought he meant that in a real, physical sense.' He smiled at the memory of Caz. 'But he didn't. He just meant we were getting JFK to live again in our memories as a man and a leader, as someone who inspired us, even for a short while. That real part of him lives, not the fake story of his cowardice and the bumbling that led us into war. That's what he meant, and he was right. The old myths are gone. The truth is starting to come out, in fits and starts, but it's here.'

'Thanks to you,' she said, reaching over to squeeze his hand. 'Thanks to you. And that reminds me that you need a reward, so my offer still stands.'

'The offer from Manhattan?'

'The same. Afternoon tea at Harrods. A walk in the park. A room at the Savoy. What do you say? Why don't you fly across the pond and I'll show you all of London. My treat, and my father's, if I have anything to say about it.'

She pulled an envelope from within her coat. 'All prepared, just in case you did as I asked and showed up to say au revoir. Tickets to London, in your name. A seat right next to mine. Say yes and by this time tomorrow, I'll be showing you my country.'

He struggled at what to say. 'I don't have a passport.'

'Oh, nonsense,' she said, motioning with her head to the crowd at the far wall. 'I'm sure one of my watchers is from the Foreign Office. I'm sure we could work something out, if I raised a stink, and you know how I can raise a stink. Come along, Carl. Say yes.'

He looked into those lovely but deadly eyes and said, 'Maybe.'

She didn't hide her disappointment. 'Oh, Carl . . . Well, look, here's something I want to leave with you.' She reached into her bag and passed him a book, the one that he had seen back in her hotel room, the one with the cover of a White House and a tired knight. *An American Camelot*, by Jack Hagopian.

'Did you finish it?' he asked.

'I did, and I enjoyed it tremendously. I'm sure you will, too.'

'And how does it end?' he said, looking at the cover. 'How is the world in this author's universe, where there wasn't a Cuban War?'

She touched his knee. 'You'll have to read it for yourself, won't you?'

'I guess I will,' he said. 'Look, your flight should be leaving shortly, right?'

She looked at her watch. 'Yes, why?'

'Just a question. Where did you keep the homing device. In your purse, or on your clothing?'

She hesitated, just for a moment. 'What do you mean?'

'You must have had a homing device with you. In Boston and in Manhattan and even in a little motel up in New Hampshire. That's why you were confident that we would get rescued back in Manhattan. And that's how your well-armed friends from the consulate managed to find us so well. You and your folks always knew where we were. Just one more secret, right?'

He could see a conflict of emotions playing in her face, and then she managed a short laugh. 'It was in the purse, in the bottom lining. Oh, you're good. No one can fool Carl Landry, can they?'

An announcement came over the speaker about boarding beginning for the next BOAC flight, headed for London, and all around them, people started to get up and gather their coats and carry-on bags. He stood up, too, and he held her hand and said, 'No, you're wrong. It seems like everyone's been able to put one over on Carl Landry, and I'm tired of it all. Eventually I find out, but it's always too late.'

She reached for him and hugged him tight, burying her face into his chest. She whispered, 'Just say the word, and come along. I owe you so much for getting me out of Manhattan, for helping me so much. I want to show you London, just the two of us, without your censors and MI6. So we can get to know each other without all this baggage.'

'Maybe someday, Sandy,' he said. 'Not today. I have a promise to keep. I have to retrieve the car we borrowed. And fill it with gas.'

Her kiss was soft but quick, and he thought he could see her eyes beginning to fill. 'All right. You know the invitation is there. Always will be. You can reach me through the *Times*.'

'I know.'

'Now, go before I start bawling.'

He kissed her again, and the last he saw of her, she was standing in line, waiting to go out through the gate.

Carl found an observation deck and he stood by the railing, book under his arm, hands in his coat, being battered by a cold wind off the ocean. He made out her plane as it taxied away and he imagined that he could see her in one of the windows, but he wasn't sure. He looked around at East Boston and realized with a start that everything had started here, everything from beginning to finish, just a short distance away on Winthrop Street, where he'd stood in that tiny apartment and saw a dead body that held the secrets that would change everything. Merl Sawson, with one more mission to go. Well, Merl, mission completed. Well done.

He looked at the book again. What might have been, he thought. What might have been had now changed. It was now, what might be possible. And the answer was, of course, anything. Anything at all. All you needed was a little hope.

The jet started its way down the runway and he huddled his body against the wind, thinking of her going back home, where there was always fresh food and plenty of electricity. Where there were no such things as orfie gangs, Restricted Zones, or martial law. Back to a place where rules were rules and things worked. The BOAC jet accelerated and took off and he watched for a long while as it winged its way over the cold and dark Atlantic Ocean, heading back to a quiet and peaceful place, and for just a moment, a sense of regret burned inside him.

But just for a moment.

When the jet was gone, Carl Landry turned around, looked about him, and started walking to the stairs.

EPILOGUE

THE DAY BEFORE THE ELECTION, he was watching
the news on television when there was a knock at his door.
Carl looked up from the screen where Walter Cronkite –
looking thin but in good shape after spending the last several
years in Leavenworth – was broadcasting a special report
about the tens of thousands of marchers that had appeared
the previous days from hidden areas around San Diego and
Miami and Omaha and Manhattan, especially Manhattan.

The knock repeated itself. He felt like ignoring it. He had
spent the past few days in his apartment, brooding, looking at
the breathless news being reported from the television, long
hours of broadcasts and special reports. General Curtis had
been spotted in Uruguay. Polls now showed a tight race for
the upcoming election. Rockefeller was trying to put distance
between himself and General Curtis, and there were strange
reports of British aircraft on training missions that had, the
other night, temporarily crossed over into American airspace.

The slush, he thought. The slush never came after all.

He knew he should have felt some sort of closure, some
sort of satisfaction that all this was happening because of

what he had done and the article he had written, but there was still a bitter taste in his mouth that he thought would never go away. History was being changed, in ways he never thought possible, and he knew he should be excited. He tried to focus on what was going on, what could go on, but all he could think about was that empty and dead house up in Newburyport.

The knock, more forceful.

Carl got up from the couch and went to the door, thinking that maybe he should pick up his pistol before answering. It could be almost anybody out there, from an angry Rockefeller supporter to a member of the Zed Force to British intelligence, wanting to even out the score.

To hell with them all, he thought, and opened the door.

A slim man stood there, wearing a corduroy jacket and a New York Yankees baseball cap, and in the dim light of the outside hallway, there were a mass of scars along his face, very familiar, and—

'Mother of . . . Jim Rowley, what the hell are you doing here?' Carl asked, holding onto the doorknob for support.

The young man grinned, probably happy at the shock he had just produced. 'Hell, Carl, I was in the neighborhood and thought I'd stop by to say hi, and thanks.'

Carl grinned. It was good to see him. 'Seriously?'

Jim shrugged. 'Half seriously. I did want to say thanks, for me and everybody at PS 19. You did pull through, and if you ever get back to Manhattan, the city's yours. Honest. We owe you so much—'

'Knock it off,' Carl said, interrupting him. 'I was just glad to help. Look, you want to come in?'

Jim shook his head. 'Nope, sorry. I got someplace else to be tonight. But there is one more thing.'

'Which is?'

Jim motioned to the shadows by the stairway. 'I brought someone up here from Manhattan. Took some work on my part to track 'em down, contacting the other RZs, but I think it was worth it.'

Carl looked into the shadows, into the darkness, and then someone stepped up from the stairwell, and he felt like a bright light was now shining, a bright light that was comforting and cleansing and just so damn warm and right. It seemed like everything had faded away and that nothing else existed, save for that smiling person, a person who came to him and stood there, just a foot or so away, hair cut short but face oh so familiar, and then gently grasped both of his trembling hands.

'Hello, Carl,' his sister, Sarah, said.

GIDEON

Russell Andrews

When they asked him to be a ghost writer, he didn't realise
they wanted him dead.

Struggling writer Carl Granville is hired to turn an old diary,
articles and letters – in which all names and locations have
been blanked out – into compelling fiction. But Carl soon
realises that the book is more than just a potential bestseller.
It is a revelation of chilling evil and a decades-long cover-up
by someone with far-reaching power. He begins to wonder
how his book will be used, and just who is the true
storyteller.

Then – suddenly, brutally – two people close to Carl are
murdered, his apartment is ransacked, his computer stolen,
and he himself is the chief suspect. With no alibi and no
proof of his shadowy assignment, Carl becomes a man on
the run. He knows too much – but not enough to save
himself . . .

'A fast-moving thriller in the Grisham genre'
Sunday Telegraph

ISBN 0 7515 2890 0

STATE OF MIND

John Katzenbach

A pulse-pounding ride of non-stop action and psychological suspense . . .

A professor of abnormal psychology, Jeffrey Clayton struggles with a dark past. Twenty-five years before, Jeffrey and his mother and sister fled his tyrannical father – a man who was later suspected in the heinous murder of a young student. Though never charged, he committed suicide. Or so it seemed. Jeffrey's mother and his sister, Susan, have since concealed themselves in the remote tangled swamps of Florida's Upper Keys. But someone has sent Susan a cryptic note that carries a terrifying message: I have found you.

'Katzenbach has a sure way with suspense and there are moments of genuine horror'
Crime Time

'Smart, American serial killer thriller, dedicated to the atmosphere of pursuit and fear . . . This is Thomas Harris land, Stephen King country'
New Law Journal

'Very clever with real characters and an excellent plot'
Publishing News

ISBN 0 7515 2319 4